· T H E ·
Twentieth
Wife

· THE ·
Twentieth
Wife

Indu Sundaresan

POCKET BOOKS

NEW YORK LONDON TORONTO SYDNEY SINGAPORE

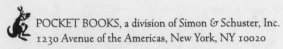 POCKET BOOKS, a division of Simon & Schuster, Inc.
1230 Avenue of the Americas, New York, NY 10020

Library of Congress Cataloging-in-Publication Data

Sundaresan, Indu.
   The twentieth wife / Indu Sundaresan.
     p. cm.
   ISBN 0-7434-2714-9
     1. Når Jahån, Empress, consort of Jahangir, Emperor of Hindustan, d. 1645—Fiction.
2. Jahangir, Emperor of Hindustan, 1569–1627—Fiction. 3. India—History—1526–1765—
Fiction. 4. Taj Mahal (Agra, India)—Fiction. 5. Empresses—Fiction. I. Title.

   PS3619.U53 T88 2002
   813'.6—dc21

                                     2001056123

First Pocket Books hardcover printing February 2002

10 9 8 7 6 5 4 3 2 1

For information regarding special discounts for bulk purchases,
please contact Simon & Schuster Special Sales at 1-800-456-6798
or business@simonandschuster.com

Designed by Joseph Rutt

Printed in the U.S.A.

For my parents,
Group Captain R. Sundaresan and Madhuram Sundaresan
For all of who I am

ACKNOWLEDGMENTS

My deepest thanks:

To my "writing buddies," for kind praise and unstinted critique, and because they love to write as much as I do: Janet Lee Carey, Julie Jindal, Vicki D'Annunzio, Nancy Maltby Henkel, Angie Yusuf, Joyce O'Keefe, Beverly Cope, Louise Christensen Zak, Gabriel Herner, Sheri Maynard, Michael Hawkins, and Laura Hartman.

To my agent, Sandra Dijkstra (who is an unexpected gift and blessing), and others in her agency, for their knowledge and experience and for their passionate belief in my writing.

To my editor at Pocket Books, Tracy Sherrod, for her vision and for astute and generous insights on the manuscript.

To my publisher at Pocket Books, Judith Curr, for her confidence and trust in me and my work.

To my husband, Uday, who has always supported my writing habit and who read the novel in its very first avatar and liked it beyond the call of duty.

To my sister Anu, who stayed up nights reading the story while taking care of my two-week-old niece (and despite the excitement of a new baby was still thrilled by it).

To my sister Jaya, whose unbounded love and vivacity spills into every aspect of my life, and who is fired with the utmost faith in her little sister.

To the excellent libraries of the King County Library System and the University of Washington Suzzallo and Allen Libraries, for giving me a place to rest my thoughts, and because my research would have been hugely incomplete without their collections.

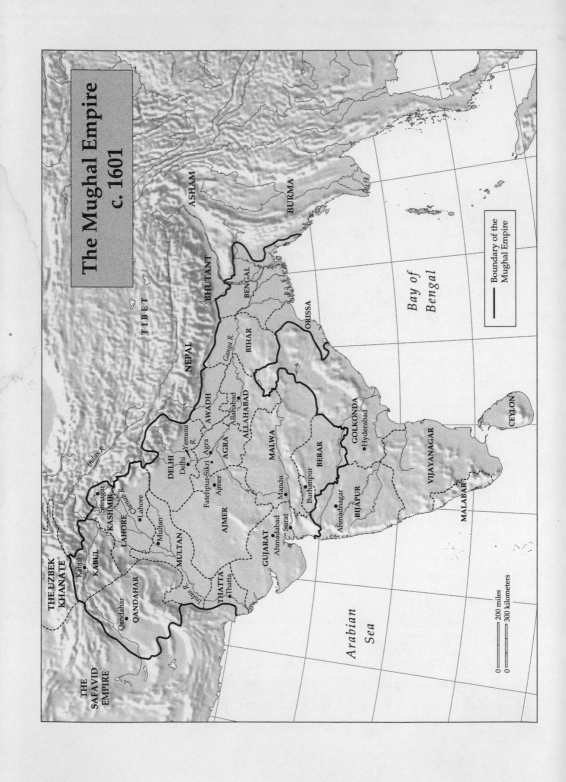

The Mughal Empire
c. 1601

Boundary of the Mughal Empire

THE UZBEK KHANATE

THE SAFAVID EMPIRE

TIBET

ASHAM

BURMA

BHUTANT

NEPAL

BENGAL

Ganga R.

BIHAR

ORISSA

Bay of Bengal

AWADH

Allahabad

ALLAHABAD

Yamuna R.

Agra

AGRA

MALWA

BERAR

GOLKONDA

Hyderabad

DELHI

Delhi

Fatehpur-Sikri

Ajmer

Mandu

Burhanpur

VIJAYANAGAR

CEYLON

Kabul

KABUL

Srinagar

KASHMIR

Chenab R.

LAHORE

Lahore

Multan

MULTAN

Indus R.

Qandahar

QANDAHAR

AJMER

Ahmadabad

GUJARAT

Surat

Ahmadnagar

BIJAPUR

MALABAR

THATTA

Thatta

Indus R.

Arabian Sea

0   200 miles
0   300 kilometers

Selected Members of Mehrunnisa's Family

Selected Members of the Mughal Imperial Family

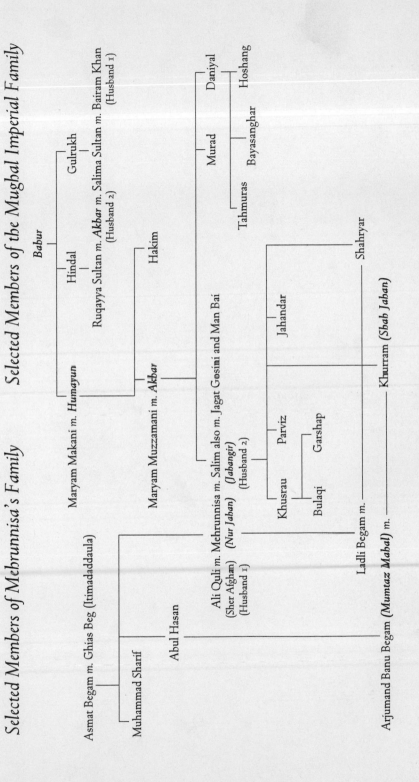

PRINCIPAL CHARACTERS
(In Alphabetical Order)

Abdur Rahim	The Khan-i-khanan, Commander-in-chief of the imperial army
Abul Hasan	Mehrunnisa's brother
Akbar	Third Emperor of Mughal India
Ali Quli Khan Istajlu	Mehrunnisa's first husband
Asmat	Mehrunnisa's mother, Ghias Beg's wife
Ghias Beg	Mehrunnisa's father
Hoshiyar Khan	Chief eunuch of Salim's harem
Jagat Gosini	Salim's second wife
Jahangir	Salim's title upon becoming the fourth emperor of Mughal India
Khurram	Salim's third son, born of Jagat Gosini
Khusrau	Salim's first son, born of Man Bai
Ladli	Mehrunnisa's daughter by Ali Quli
Mahabat Khan	Salim's childhood cohort

Mehrunnisa   Ghias's daughter, later titled **Nur Jahan**

Mirza Aziz Koka   Khusrau's father-in-law

Muhammad Sharif   Salim's childhood cohort, later made Grand
                          Vizier of the Empire

Muhammad Sharif   Mehrunnisa's eldest brother (not the same as
                          the Grand Vizier)

Qutubuddin Khan Koka   Salim's childhood cohort, later Governor of
                          Bengal

Raja Man Singh   Khusrau's uncle

Ruqayya Sultan Begam   Akbar's chief queen, or Padshah Begam

Salim   Akbar's first son, later **Emperor Jahangir**

PROLOGUE

THE WIND HOWLED AND SWEPT DOWN, ALMOST RIPPING THE TENT flap from its seams. Frigid air elbowed in, sending arctic fingers down warm napes, devouring the thin blue flames of the fire. The woman lying on the thin cotton mattress in one corner shivered. She clasped her arms around her protruding stomach and moaned, "Ayah . . ."

The midwife rose slowly from her haunches, aged joints creaking, and hobbled to the entrance. She fastened the flap, came back to the woman, lifted the blanket, and peered between her legs. The woman winced as callused dirt-encrusted fingers prodded her.

The ayah's thick face filled with satisfaction. "It will not be long now."

The brazier in the corner flared to life as the midwife fanned the camel-dung embers. The woman lay back, sweat cooling on her forehead, her face worn with pain. In a few minutes, another contraction swept her lower back. She clamped down on her lower lip to keep from crying out, not wanting them to worry outside the tent, unaware that the screeching gale swallowed even the loudest wail.

Outside, an early night closed in on the campsite. Men huddled around a fire that sputtered and crackled as the wind lashed about their ears, kicking sand in their eyes and under their clothes, stinging their faces.

A few tents, tattered and old, crowded in a tight circle at the edge of the desert on the outskirts of Qandahar. Camels, horses, and sheep clustered around the camp, seeking warmth and cover from the storm.

Ghias Beg broke away from the group around the fire and, picking his way past the animals, trudged to the tent where his wife lay. Barely visible in the flying sand, three children crouched against the flapping black canvas, arms around one another, eyes shut against the gale. Ghias Beg touched the shoulder of the elder boy. "Muhammad," he yelled over the sound of the wind. "Is your mother all right?"

The child raised his head and looked tearfully at his father. "I don't know, Bapa." His voice was small, barely audible; Ghias had to lean over to hear him. Muhammad clutched at the hand on his shoulder. "Oh, Bapa, what will happen to us?"

Ghias knelt, drew Muhammad into his arms, and kissed the top of his forehead gently, his beard scratching the sand on Muhammad's hair. This was the first time he had shown any fear in all these days.

He looked over the boy's head at his daughter. "Saliha, go check on your Maji."

The little girl rose in silence and crawled inside the tent.

As she entered the woman looked up. She stretched out a hand to Saliha, who came immediately to her side.

"Bapa wants to know if you are all right, Maji."

Asmat Begam tried to smile. "Yes, *beta*. Go tell Bapa it will not be very long. Tell him not to worry. And you don't worry. All right, *beta*?"

Saliha nodded and rose to leave. On impulse, she bent down again and hugged her mother tightly, burying her head in Asmat's shoulder.

In her corner, the midwife clucked disapproval, rising as she spoke. "No, no, don't touch your mother just before the baby is born. Now it will be a girl child, because you are one. Run along now. Take your evil eye with you."

"Let her be, Ayah," Asmat said weakly as the midwife hustled her daughter out. She said no more, unwilling to argue with the woman.

Ghias raised an eyebrow at Saliha.

"Soon, Bapa."

He nodded and turned away. Adjusting the cloth of the turban over his face, he wrapped his arms around his chest and walked away from the camp, head lowered against the shrieking wind. When he had reached the shelter of a large rock, he sat down heavily and buried his face in his hands. How could he have let matters come to this?

Ghias's father, Muhammad Sharif, had been a courtier to Shah Tahmasp Safavi of Persia, and both Ghias and his older brother, Muhammad Tahir, had been well educated as children. Brought up in an increasingly prosperous household, the children were happy growing up, moving from one posting to another: first to Khurasan, then to Yazd, and finally to Isfahan, where Muhammad Sharif had died the past year, 1576, as *wazir* of Isfahan. If things had remained at an even temper, Ghias would have continued his life as a nobleman with few cares, debts to tailors and wine merchants easily paid off every two or three months, and his hand open to those less fortunate. But this was not to be.

Shah Tahmasp died; Shah Ismail II ascended the throne of Persia; the new regime was not kind to the sons of Muhammad Sharif. And neither were the creditors, Ghias thought, reddening under cover of his hands. Like pariah dogs sniffing at a rubbish heap, the creditors descended upon his father's household, running practiced eyes over the furniture and carpets. Bills came piling onto Ghias's desk, bewildering both him and Asmat. The *vakils*—his father's clerks—had always taken care of them. But the *vakils* were gone. And there was no money to pay the creditors because his father's property—Ghias's inheritance—had reverted to the state upon his death.

One of the Shah's courtiers, a longtime friend of his father's, informed Ghias of his fate: death or imprisonment in the debtors' prison. Ghias knew then that he could no longer live honorably in Persia. His head sank lower into his hands as he remembered their hurried escape at night, before the soldiers came to arrest him. They had bundled Asmat's jewels, her gold and silver vessels, and any other valuables they could carry with them to trade on the way.

At first, Ghias had no idea where he would seek refuge. They joined a caravan of merchants traveling south, and during the trip someone suggested India. And why not, Ghias had thought. India was ruled by the

Mughal Emperor Akbar, who was known to be just, kind, and above all open to men of education and learning. Perhaps he could find a position at court, a new start in life.

Ghias raised his head as the howling wind faltered for a second and the faint scream of a newborn babe pierced through the sudden lull. He immediately turned west toward Mecca, knelt on the hard ground, and raised his hands. Allah, let the child be healthy and the mother safe, he prayed in silence. His hands fell to his side when the prayer was done. Another child now, when his fortunes were at their lowest. He turned to look toward the camp, the black tents barely distinguishable in the dust storm. He should go to Asmat, but his feet would not move toward his darling wife.

Ghias leaned back against the rock and closed his eyes. Who would have thought the daughter-in-law of the *wazir* of Isfahan would give birth to her fourth child in such surroundings? Or that his son would have to flee his homeland, a fugitive from justice? It was bad enough that he had brought dishonor upon his family, but what followed on their journey had been worse.

On the way south to Qandahar, the caravan had passed through the Dasht-e-Lut, the great desert of Persia. The arid country had its own beauty: miles of land barren of vegetation, and spectacular dusky rose cliffs rising, it seemed, out of nowhere. But those cliffs were treacherous, too; they had hidden a group of desert bandits until it was too late for the ill-fated caravan.

Ghias shuddered, drawing the coarse woolen shawl closer around his shoulders. The thieves had swept over them in a confusing cloud of shrill noise and violence. They had left almost nothing; the jewels were gone, the gold and silver vessels gone, the women raped where they lay. Asmat had been left untouched only because she was so heavily pregnant. After the pillage, the caravan dispersed as people fled in search of refuge. And in the aftermath of the carnage, Ghias found two old mules, on which they had taken turns riding toward Qandahar, begging for hospitality from the numerous caravanserais along the way.

Exhausted, dirty, and bedraggled, the family wandered into Qandahar, where a group of Afghan *kuchi*—nomads—had offered them shelter and what little food they could spare. But they had little money, and even the journey to India seemed impossible. Now they had another child.

A few minutes later, Ghias stirred and made his way slowly to the tent.

Asmat glanced up from her bed. With a heavy heart, Ghias noted the dark shadows under her eyes as she smiled at him. Her face was almost impossibly thin, the skin stretched to breaking over her cheekbones. He reached out and smoothed the still sweaty hair from her forehead. Cradled in Asmat's arms and swathed in some old cloth lay a perfect little child.

"Our daughter." Asmat handed the baby to Ghias.

As he held the child, Ghias felt helplessness overcome him again. She lay in his arms, cleaned and clothed, a tiny infant, dependent on him for her life and sustenance. She was beautiful, with well-formed arms and legs, a thick head of shiny black hair, and long, curling, black eyelashes resting against delicate cheeks.

"Have you thought of a name for her?" he asked his wife.

"Yes . . ." Asmat replied, hesitating a little. "Mehrunnisa."

"Meh-ru-nnisa," Ghias said slowly. "Sun of Women. It is an appropriate name for this beautiful child." He touched the baby's little fist, curled against her chin in sleep. Then he handed Mehrunnisa back to Asmat. It was almost certain Asmat could not feed the baby herself. She would have little milk. Months of near starvation had made sure of that. Where would they find the money to pay a wet nurse?

Someone prodded him in the ribs. Ghias turned to see the ayah with her hand stretched out, palm open. He shook his head.

"Sorry. I have nothing to give you."

She scowled and spat out a stream of brown tobacco juice on the ground. "Nothing." He heard her grumble as she went out of the tent. "Even a girl child should be worth *something*."

Ghias drew back to one corner, rubbing his forehead tiredly, and watched as their children—Muhammad Sharif, Abul Hasan, and Saliha—crowded around their mother and the new baby.

They could not afford to keep the child. They would have to give her up.

THE WIND DIED down during the night as suddenly as it had started, leaving a clear sky jeweled with twinkling stars. Ghias rose early the next morning while it was still dark and sat outside his tent. A hot cup of *chai*, more watery milk than tea leaves, warmed his hands and his chilled body. A few minutes later, the eastern sky was brushed with glorious reds, golds, and amber, the aftermath of the storm lending nature a new wardrobe of colors.

He reached inside his shawl and drew out the four precious gold *mohurs* nestled in his cummerbund. The morning sun touched the *mohurs* with a liquid fire, set off by his grimy hand. This was all they had left in the world. The thieves had overlooked the *mohurs* that Asmat had hidden in her *choli*, and Ghias was determined to buy his passage to India with the money. But this was all the gold would pay for; they needed more to survive.

Ghias turned to look at the turquoise domes and minarets rising in the distance, framed against the red morning sky. Perhaps he could find some work in Qandahar. Ghias had not worked a day in his twenty-three years. But Asmat needed lamb's meat and milk to regain her strength, the children needed more clothing as winter approached, and the baby . . . Ghias would not even think of her, not even by name. What use was it, when someone else would look after her? He rose as the sun broke from the horizon and climbed in the sky, sending golden rays to embrace the camp. His jaw was set, and in his eyes there was the steely glint of new-found determination.

THAT AFTERNOON, GHIAS stood, shoulders hunched, outside a bakery in the narrow street of the local bazaar. The long folds of his *qaba* dragged on the cobbled street. People milled about, jostling him, yelling to their friends, calling out greetings to acquaintances.

Ghias raised his head and stared unseeingly into the distance. At first, he had tried for a job as a tutor to children of the wealthy nobles in the city. But everyone, looking at his torn clothes and grimy face, turned him away from their doorsteps. Then he sought work as a laborer, but his cultured accent and speech gave him away as a nobleman.

Suddenly Ghias was aware of the delicious smell of fresh baked *nan*, the local bread. His stomach growled insistently, reminding him that he had eaten nothing after his morning cup of *chai*. He turned to watch the baker pat out the thick white dough with his hands, scoop it with a wooden paddle, and then carefully slap it against the walls of the flaming-hot underground oven through a hole in the floor. Fifteen minutes later, the baker used a pair of iron tongs to peel the freshly baked bread off the walls of the oven. He stacked the bread, cream and rust-golden, on a pile near the front of the shop.

The aroma wrapped itself tantalizingly around Ghias. He drew out one gold *mohur* and looked at it. Before he could change his mind, he had bought ten pieces of *nan* and, with the change, some skewers of freshly grilled lamb kebabs, glistening with a lime and garlic marinade, from a nearby shop.

He tucked the valuable hoard under his *qaba*, the hot *nan* warming his chest, the smells watering his mouth, and wound his way through the bazaar. Asmat and the children would have something to eat for a few days. The weather was cold, the meat would keep, and perhaps their luck would change . . .

"Hey, peasant! Watch your step."

Ghias felt a jolt, and the packets of meat and bread fell to the ground. He bent down hurriedly, arms spread out, before the crowds could step on the food.

"I beg your pardon, *Sahib*," he said over his shoulder.

There was silence behind him. But Ghias, intent on grabbing his packets of food, did not realize that the merchant had stopped to look at him. He turned to the man and looked into kindly eyes in a sunburnt, lined face. "I am sorry," Ghias said again. "I hope I did you no harm."

"None at all," the merchant replied, his gaze assessing Ghias. "Who are you?"

"Ghias Beg, son of Muhammad Sharif, *wazir* of Isfahan," Ghias replied. Then, seeing the surprise on the man's face, he gestured ruefully at his torn *qaba* and at the dirt-smudged pajamas he wore. "In another time, these were splendid and pristine. But now . . ."

"What has happened, *Sahib?*" The merchant's voice was respectful.

Ghias looked at him and saw his blunt capable hands, the dagger tucked into his cummerbund, his worn heavy leather boots. "We were on our way to Qandahar when we were robbed of our belongings," he replied, hunger slurring his words.

"You are far from home."

Ghias nodded. "A long story. A change in fortunes, so I had to flee. May I know whom I have the pleasure of addressing?"

"Malik Masud," the merchant said. "Tell me your story, *Sahib*. I have the time. Shall we go to the *chai* shop?"

Ghias looked toward the shop across the street, where steam rose from a cauldron of boiling milk and spices. "You are kind, Mirza Masud, but I cannot accept your hospitality. My family waits for me."

Masud put an arm around Ghias and pushed him toward the shop. "Indulge me, *Sahib*. I want to hear your story as a favor, if you will grant me that."

Still hesitating, Ghias allowed himself to be led to the shop. There, his precious package of lamb kebabs and *nans* secure on his lap, sitting shoulder to shoulder with the other patrons, he told Masud of all that had happened, even Mehrunnisa's birth.

"Allah has blessed you, *Sahib*," Masud said, putting down his empty cup.

"Yes," Ghias replied. And blessed he was, even though things were difficult now. Asmat, the children—they were indeed blessings. The baby too . . .

Ghias rose from his bench. "I should go now. The children will be hungry. My thanks to you for the *chai*."

As he was leaving, Masud said, "I am on my way to India. Would you like to accompany my caravan, Mirza Beg? I cannot offer you much, only a tent and a camel to carry your belongings. But it is well guarded, and I can assure you that you will be safe on the journey."

Ghias abruptly turned back and sat down, his face mirroring the shock he felt. "Why?"

Masud waved the question away. "I will be going to pay my respects to Emperor Akbar at Fatehpur Sikri. If you follow me that far, I may be able to present you at court."

Ghias stared at him, unable to believe what he had just heard. After so much trouble, when one problem seemed to come at the heel of the other, here was a gift from Allah. But he could not just accept this offer. He had nothing to offer in return. And as a nobleman's son, and a nobleman himself, he should never be indebted to another for kindness. Why was Masud doing this?

"I . . . ," he stammered, "I do not know what to say. I cannot—"

Masud leaned forward across the rutted wood table of the shop. "Say yes, *Sahib*. Perhaps if I fall to ill times in the future you can assist me."

"That I would, Mirza Masud, without hesitation, even if you did not do this for me. But this is too much. I am grateful for the suggestion, but I cannot accept."

Masud beamed. "For me this is nothing much, Mirza Beg. Please agree. You will give me the pleasure of your company on the journey. It has been lonely since my sons stopped traveling with me."

"Of course I will," Ghias replied. Then he said, smiling at the merchant's insistence, "Any thanks I can give will be inadequate."

Masud gave Ghias the directions to his caravan, and the two men parted in the bazaar. During the next few hours, as Asmat and the children packed their meager belongings, Ghias sat outside the tent, thinking of his meeting with Masud. Once, a long time ago, Ghias's father had told him that a nobleman was as gracious in accepting help as in giving it.

Remembering his father's words—the only memories he had now of Muhammad Sharif—Ghias thought he would accept Masud's help and repay him later.

Ghias and his family took leave of the *kuchi* who had sheltered them. In a fit of reckless generosity, Ghias gave away his last three gold *mohurs* to the kindly but poor nomads. They had sheltered his family when no one else had. To them was his first debt of gratitude, to Masud a lifelong one. He had kept the money to pay for their passage to India; now it was no longer necessary. They made their way to Masud's camp. There, they were provided with a fine tent, and food from the common kitchen until Asmat was well enough to cook for them.

The caravan, winding almost one kilometer from head to tail, started toward Kabul. As the weeks passed Asmat slowly recovered her strength, color blooming in her cheeks again, her hair regaining its shine. The older children were well fed and happy, sometimes walking along the caravan, sometimes climbing up on the camels to rest. But all was not well. Ghias still had no money to pay a wet nurse, and though Mehrunnisa did drink some goat's milk, she was growing more and more feeble each day. He thought with a pang of the three gold *mohurs;* they would have been useful now. But then, the *kuchi,* poor as they were, had been helpful to his family . . . no, it had been the right decision. When Asmat asked after the money, Ghias said so, firmly, not looking at his daughter.

One month after Mehrunnisa's birth, striking eastward from Kabul, the caravan pitched camp near Jamrud, south of the Hindu Kush Mountains in the Khyber hills. The day was just failing, the clean sky ochre-toned. The colors of the land were muted: dull white of snow, smudged blue-black of rocks and boulders, dry brown of dying grass. The slow, biting cold of winter crept in through layers of wool and cotton shawls. Near the camp, lights twinkled from the last village they would come upon for the next few weeks, clinging to the hillside. And farther in the distance lay the first rising path into the mountains through the Khyber Pass.

Ghias helped Asmat collect twigs and dry branches for a fire. Then he sat near her, watching her chop a wilted cabbage and some carrots along with a shank of lamb for the *kurma*. Her hands were raw in the cold, her knuckles white. Mehrunnisa lay wrapped in a bundle just inside their tent. Muhammad, Abul, and Saliha played with the other children in the twilight. From where he sat, Ghias could hear their screams of delight as they threw snowballs at one another.

"They will get cold and wet," Asmat said, looking up from her work. She put a cast-iron skillet on the makeshift *chula:* three flat stones in a triangle, holding the twig fire inside them.

"Let them be," Ghias said softly, watching her. Asmat poured a little oil from an earthenware jar into the skillet, waited for it to heat, and added cardamom pods, a few cloves, and a bay leaf. The lamb meat went in next, and she browned it deftly with a wooden spoon.

"When did you learn to cook?" Ghias asked.

Asmat smiled, tucking in a stray lock of hair behind her ears. She watched the meat on the skillet intently, her face red and glowing in the heat from the fire. "I never learned, Ghias; you know that. Meals were always brought to me. They appeared like magic, out of nowhere. But the woman in the next tent taught me this *kurma*." She turned to him anxiously. "Are you tired of it? I can learn something else."

Ghias shook his head. "No, not tired of it. Even though," he smiled wickedly, "we have eaten this every night for one month."

"Twenty-two days," Asmat said, as she added the vegetables to the meat and poured water into the skillet. A few pinches of rock salt from a gunnysack, a sprinkling of pounded masala of cloves, chili powder, and cardamom, and Asmat covered the skillet and sat back. She looked up at Ghias. "At least I do not burn the *kurma* anymore."

"Asmat, we have to talk."

Asmat turned away from him, pulling out a copper vessel. She dipped her hand into another sack, poured five handfuls of wheat flour into the vessel, and started to knead the flour into dough for *chappatis* with some water and oil. "I have to make dinner, Ghias."

"Asmat . . . ," he said gently, but she would not look at him. Her back was stiff, her movements jerky.

From inside the tent, Mehrunnisa cried. They both turned to the sound and waited. She cried again, feebly, without strength. Then, as though exhausted by the effort, the sound stopped. Asmat bent over the dough again, her fingers kneading it with a vengeance. Her hair fell over her face, sheltering her from her husband. One tear, then another fell into the dough, and she kneaded them in. Ghias rose and came over to her. He took her in his arms and she burrowed into him. They sat there for a few minutes, with Asmat leaning into Ghias, her hands still in the flour.

"Asmat," Ghias said quietly, "we cannot afford to keep Mehrunnisa."

"Ghias, please," Asmat raised her face to his. "I will try to feed her. Or she will take to the goat's milk, or we will try to find her a wet nurse. The woman were talking the other day of a peasant who just had a child. We could ask her."

Ghias looked away from her. "With what would we pay her? I cannot ask Malik for money." He gestured around him. "He has already given us so much. "No," his heart strained as he spoke, "it is better for us to leave her by the roadside for someone else to find her, someone with the means to look after her. We cannot do so anymore."

"You should have kept . . ." Asmat pulled away and started sobbing. But Ghias was right. He was always right. The *kuchi* had needed the money. Now they could not possibly look after the child, and Asmat's tears would not stop.

Ghias rose, leaving his wife near the fire, and went into the tent. He had thought about this for a long time. Asmat could not feed the child because her milk had dried up, and at every cry her heart broke, for her child cried for milk, and she had none. They were feeding Mehrunnisa sugar water, into which they dipped a clean cloth and gave it to her to suck on, but it was not enough. She had lost weight at an alarming rate and was now much smaller than she had been at birth. Ghias was deeply ashamed that he could not take care of his family, that he had brought them to this. And he was terrified about this decision. But in his mind, it had to be done. He could not watch as Mehrunnisa became weaker and weaker each day. If he left her for someone else to find, they would bring her up and look after her. Others had done this, Ghias knew. Others had found children on the wayside and brought them into their homes as their own children. He picked up the baby and an oil lantern. She had fallen asleep again, a fretful sleep of hunger. When he came out of the tent he said to Asmat, "I should do so now, when she is asleep."

Leaving Asmat with silent tears running down her face, he walked away from the camp. When he had reached the outskirts of the village, he wrapped his shawl around the sleeping baby and laid her down at the base of a tree on the main highway. Then he turned the wick of the lantern up high and set it near her. Surely someone would chance upon the baby soon, for it was not dark yet, and this was a well-traveled road. With a prayer on his lips, Ghias turned toward the village, which straggled up the mountainside. A sharp gust of wind brought the aroma of wood smoke from the village chimneys. Perhaps someone from the village, please Allah, someone with a kind heart. He looked down at the baby again. She was so small, so slight; her breathing hardly made a dent in the shawl.

Ghias turned to go. As he did a small whimper came from the bundle on the road. He went back to the baby and smoothed her cheek with his finger. "Sleep, precious one," he murmured in Persian. The baby sighed, soothed by his voice and his touch, and went back to sleep.

Ghias glanced down at Mehrunnisa, then swiftly walked away. Once, just once, shivering now in the cold, at a bend in the road he turned back to look. The light from the lantern flickered in the approaching darkness; the tree loomed over, gnarled arms stretching in winter bareness. Mehrunnisa, wrapped in a bundle, he could barely distinguish.

As DUSK SETTLED, the mountains took on purple hues in anticipation of the coming night. The white of the snow gleamed briefly and then dulled, and silence laid its gentle folds over the camp. Voices were tempered with fatigue. The campfires spit bits of wood and ash in sparkles. A wind from the north picked up tempo, whistling through the barren trees. A musket shot reverberated through the mountains and faltered in soft echoes. Just as the last sound died, a sharp wail filled the air.

The hunting party stopped in surprise, and Malik Masud held up his hand for quiet. They were near the camp, and for a moment the only sound they heard was from the crackling campfires. Then they heard it again.

Masud turned to one of his men. "Go see what that is."

The servant kicked his heels into his horse's flanks and rode toward the cries. In a short while he came back, holding Mehrunnisa in his arms. "I found a baby, *Sahib*."

Masud looked down into the bawling face of the child. He thought he recognized her; then he was sure. The shawl she was wrapped in belonged to Ghias Beg; he had given it as a gift to the young man.

He frowned. How could Ghias abandon such a beautiful child? As the hunting party returned to camp his expression became meditative. He thought back to his first meeting with Ghias. He had judged the young man quickly, as he had other men all his life, but correctly as usual. Looking beyond the young man's torn clothes and grimy face, Masud had seen intelligence and education—two qualities he knew Emperor Akbar would appreciate. And there was something endearing about him, Masud thought. Over the last month, the two men had spent a few hours together almost every night; for Masud it was as though his eldest son, now settled in Kurasan, was with him again. When the hunting party returned to camp, Masud dismounted and commanded a servant to bring Ghias to him.

A few minutes later, Ghias entered Masud's tent.

"Sit down, dear friend." When Ghias was settled, Masud continued, "I have had the good fortune to find a child abandoned nearby. Tell me, hasn't your wife just had a baby?"

"Yes, Masud."

"Then will you request her to nurse this child for me?" Masud brought forward Mehrunnisa. Ghias looked at his daughter in surprise, then at Masud. The older man smiled at him.

"She is now like a daughter to me," Masud said, as he drew out a richly embroidered bag and took out some gold *mohurs*. "Please take these *mohurs* for her upkeep."

"But—" Ghias started, holding his arms out for Mehrunnisa. At his touch, she turned her eyes to him.

Masud waved away his objections. "I insist. I cannot burden your family with another child without providing for her."

Ghias bowed his head. Here was another debt he would find impossible to repay.

Asmat was in the tent when Ghias entered with Mehrunnisa. She stared at the bundle in his arms, knowing it was her daughter, reaching out for her instinctively. "You brought her back?"

"Masud did."

Asmat hugged Mehrunnisa. "Allah wants us to keep this child, Ghias. We are indeed blessed." She smiled fondly at the gurgling baby. "But how—"

Ghias silently pulled out the gold *mohurs*. The coins gleamed dully in the light from the lantern. "Allah does want us to keep this child, Asmat," Ghias said softly.

The next day, Dai Dilaram, who was traveling with the caravan, agreed to nurse the baby along with her own. The caravan traversed the Khyber Pass safely, then went on to Lahore. From Lahore, Malik Masud guided his caravan toward Fatehpur Sikri, where Akbar held court. Almost six months to the day after Mehrunnisa's birth, in the year 1578, the caravan entered Fatehpur Sikri.

A few weeks later, when Masud went to pay his respects to Emperor Akbar during the daily *darbar*, he took Ghias along with him. At Masud's home, while the other children played in the street, Asmat waited for her husband in an inner courtyard, holding six-month-old Mehrunnisa in

her arms. Mehrunnisa babbled at her mother's solemn face, trying hard
to draw a smile. Asmat, deep in thought, did not notice. She wondered
whether they had reached the end of their long, tiresome journey,
whether they could put down roots and survive in this foreign land,
whether India would be home now.

ONE

When my mother came near the time of her delivery, he (Akbar)
sent her to the Shaikh's house that I might be born there. After my
birth they gave me the name of Sultan Salim, but I never heard
my father . . . call me Muhammad Salim or Sultan Salim, but
always Shaikhu Baba.

> —A. Rogers, trans., and H. Beveridge,
> ed., *The Tuzuk-i-Jahangiri*

THE MIDDAY SUN WHITENED THE CITY OF LAHORE TO A BRIGHT HAZE.
Normally, the streets would be deserted at this time of day, but today the
Moti bazaar was packed with a slowly moving throng of humanity. The
crowds deftly maneuvered around a placid cow lounging in the center of
the narrow street, her jaw moving rhythmically as she digested her
morning meal of grass and hay.

Shopkeepers called out to passing shoppers while sitting comfortably
at the edge of jammed, cubical shops that lay flush with the brick-paved
street. A few women veiled in thin muslins leaned over the wood-carved
balconies of their houses above the shops. A man holding the leash of a
pet monkey looked up when they called to him, "Make it dance!" He
bowed and set his music box on the ground. As the music played, the
monkey, clad in a blue waistcoat, a tasseled fez on its head, jumped up
and down. When it had finished, the women clapped and threw silver
coins at the man. After gathering the coins from the street, the man and
his monkey gravely bowed again and went on their way. On the street
corner, musicians played their flutes and *dholaks*; people chatted happily
with friends, shouting to be heard above the din; vendors hawked lime-
green sherbets in frosted brass goblets; and women bargained in good-
natured loud voices.

In the distance, between the two rows of houses and shops that crowded the main street of the bazaar, the red brick walls of the Lahore fort rose to the sky, shutting out the imperial palaces and gardens from the city.

The city was celebrating. Prince Salim, Akbar's eldest son and heir apparent, was to be married in three days, on February 13, 1585. Salim was the first of the three royal princes to wed, and no amount of the unseasonable heat or dust or noise would keep the people of Lahore from the bazaar today.

At Ghias Beg's house, silence prevailed in an inner courtyard, broken only by the faint sounds of the *shenai* from the bazaar. The air was still and heavy with perfume from blooming roses and jasmines in clay pots. A fountain bubbled in one corner, splashing drops of water with a hiss onto the hot stone pathway nearby. In the center of the courtyard a large *peepul* tree spread its dense triangular-leaved branches.

Five children sat cross-legged on jute mats under the cool shade of the *peepul*, heads bent studiously, the chalk in their hands scratching on smooth black slates as they wrote. But every now and then, one or another lifted a head to listen to the music in the distance. Only one child sat still, copying out text from a Persian book spread in front of her.

Mehrunnisa had an intense look of concentration on her face as she traced the curves and lines, the tip of her tongue showing between her teeth. She was determined not to be distracted.

Seated next to her were her brothers, Muhammad and Abul, and her sisters, Saliha and Khadija.

A bell pealed, its tones echoing in the silent courtyard.

The two boys jumped up immediately and ran into the house; soon Saliha and Khadija followed. Only Mehrunnisa remained, intent upon her work. The *mulla* of the mosque, who was their teacher, closed his book, folded his hands in his lap, and sat there looking at the child.

Asmat came out into the courtyard and smiled. This was a good sign, surely. After so many years of complaints and tantrums and "why do I have to study?" and "I am bored, Maji," Mehrunnisa seemed to have finally settled down to her lessons. Before, she had always been the first to rise when the lunch bell summoned.

"Mehrunnisa, it is time for lunch, *beta*," Asmat called.

At the sound of her mother's voice, Mehrunnisa lifted her head. Azure blue eyes looked up at Asmat, and a dimpled smile broke out on her face, showing perfectly even, white teeth with one gap in the front where a permanent tooth was yet to come. She rose from the mat, bowed to the *mulla*, and walked toward her mother, her long skirts swinging gently.

Mehrunnisa looked at her mother as she neared. Maji was always so neat, hair smoothed to a shine by fragrant coconut oil, and curled into a chignon at the nape of her neck.

"Did you enjoy the lessons today, *beta?*" Asmat asked as Mehrunnisa reached her and touched her mother's arm softly.

Mehrunnisa wrinkled her nose. "The *mulla* doesn't teach me anything I don't already know. He doesn't seem to *know* anything." Then, as a frown rose on Asmat's forehead, she asked quickly, "Maji, when are we going to the royal palace?"

"Your Bapa and I must attend the wedding celebrations next week, I suppose. An invitation has come for us. Bapa will be at the court with the men, and I have been called to the imperial *zenana*."

They moved into the house. Mehrunnisa slowed her stride to keep pace with her mother. At eight, she was already up to Asmat's shoulder and growing fast. They passed noiselessly through the verandah, their bare feet skimming the cool stone floor.

"What does the prince look like, Maji?" Mehrunnisa asked, trying to keep the eagerness out of her voice.

Asmat reflected for a moment. "He is handsome, charming." Then, with a hesitant laugh, she added, "And perhaps a little petulant."

"Will I get to see him?"

Asmat raised her eyebrows. "Why this sudden interest in Prince Salim?"

"No reason," Mehrunnisa replied in a hurry. "A royal wedding—and we shall be present at court. Who is he marrying?"

"You will attend the celebrations only if you have finished with your studies for the day. I shall talk to the *mulla* about your progress." Asmat smiled at her daughter. "Perhaps Khadija would like to come too?"

Khadija and Manija had been born after the family's arrival in India. Manija was still in the nursery, too young for classes and not old enough to go out.

"Perhaps." Mehrunnisa waved her hand in a gesture of dismissal, her green glass bangles sliding down her wrist to her elbow with a tinkling sound. "But Khadija has no concept of the decorum and etiquette at court."

Asmat threw her well-groomed head back with a laugh. "And you have?"

"Of course." Mehrunnisa nodded firmly. Khadija was a baby; she could not sit still for twenty minutes at the morning lessons. Everything distracted her—the birds in the trees, the squirrels scrambling for nuts, the sun through the *peepul* leaves. But that was getting off the topic. "Who is Prince Salim marrying, Maji?" she asked again.

"Princess Man Bai, daughter of Raja Bhagwan Das of Amber."

"Do princes always marry princesses?"

"Not necessarily, but most royal marriages are political. In this case, Emperor Akbar wishes to maintain a strong friendship with the Raja, and Bhagwan Das similarly wants closer ties with the empire. After all, he is now a vassal to the Emperor."

"I wonder what it would be like to marry a prince," Mehrunnisa said, her eyes glazing over dreamily, "and to be a princess . . ."

"Or an empress, *beta*. Prince Salim is the rightful heir to the throne, you know, and his wife, or wives, will all be empresses." Asmat smiled at her daughter's ecstatic expression. "But enough about the royal wedding." Her face softened further as she smoothed Mehrunnisa's hair. "In a few years you will leave us and go to your husband's house. Then we shall talk about your wedding."

Mehrunnisa gave her mother a quick look. Empress of Hindustan! Bapa came home with stories about his day, little tidbits about Emperor Akbar's rulings, about the *zenana* women hidden behind a screen as they watched the court proceedings, sometimes in silence and sometimes calling out a joke or a comment in a musical voice. The Emperor always listened to them, always turned his head to the screen to hear what they had to say. What bliss to be in the Emperor's harem, to be at court. How she wished she could have been born a princess. Then she would marry a prince—perhaps even Salim. But then Asmat and Ghias would not be her parents. Her heart skipped a beat at the thought. She slipped a hand into her mother's, and they walked on toward the dining hall.

As they neared, she said again, pulling at Asmat's arm, "Can I go with you for the wedding, Maji? Please?"

"We'll see what your Bapa has to say about it."

When they entered, Abul looked up, patted the divan next to him, and said to Mehrunnisa, "Come sit here."

Giving him a quick smile, Mehrunnisa sat down. Abul had promised to play *gilli-danda* with her under the *peepul* tree later that afternoon. He was much better than she was at the game, managing to hit the *gilli* six or seven times before it fell. But then, he was a boy, and the one time she had tried to teach him to sew a button he had drawn blood on all his fingers with the needle. At least she could hit the *gilli* four times in a row. She clasped her hands together and waited for Bapa to signal that the meal had begun.

The servants had laid out a red satin cloth on the Persian carpets. Now they filed in, carrying steaming dishes of saffron-tinted *pulavs* cooked in chicken broth, goat curry in a rich brown gravy, a leg of lamb roasted with garlic and rosemary, and a salad of cucumber and plump tomatoes, sprinkled with rock salt, pepper, and a squeeze of lemon juice. The head server knelt and ladled out the food on Chinese porcelain plates. For the next few minutes silence prevailed as the family ate, using only their right hands. When they were done, brass bowls filled with hot water and pieces of lime were brought in so they could wash their hands. A hot cup of *chai* spiced with ginger and cinnamon followed.

GHIAS LEANED BACK against the silk cushions of his divan and looked around at his family. They were beautiful, he thought, these people who belonged to him. Two sons and four daughters already, each special in an individual way, each brilliant with life. Muhammad, his eldest, was a little surly and sometimes missed his classes on a whim, true, but that would change as time passed. Abul showed the most promise of becoming like his Dada, Ghias's father. He had his grandfather's even temper and a small streak of mischief that made him tease his beloved sisters. All the more reason he would continue to love them deeply when they were older. Saliha was becoming a young lady now, suddenly shy of even her own Bapa. Khadija and Manija—they were children yet, unformed, inquisitive, curious about everything. But Mehrunnisa . . .

Ghias smiled inwardly, letting his eyes rest on her last. She was his favorite child, a child of good fortune. He was not normally a superstitious man, but somehow he had the feeling that Mehrunnisa's birth had been a good omen for him. Everything good in his life had come from that time after the storm at Qandahar.

Eight years had passed since their hasty escape from Persia. Sitting here in this safe room, Ghias was suddenly transported to that moment before his introduction to Emperor Akbar in the *darbar* hall by Malik Masud. They had entered past the forbidding palace guards into the blinding sunshine of the *Diwan-i-am*, the Hall of Public Audience at Fatehpur Sikri. The courtyard was crowded. The Emperor's war elephants stood at the very back in a row, shifting their weight from one heavy foot to another. Their foreheads were draped with gold and silver livery, and mahouts were seated atop their thick necks, knees dug into their ears. Next came a row of cavalry officers on perfectly matched black Arabian horses. Then came the third, and outermost tier, for commoners. The second tier around the imperial throne was for merchants and lesser noblemen, and this was where Ghias and Masud took their places, behind the nobles of the court.

When the Emperor was announced, they bowed low from the waist. Ghias glanced behind him to see the elephants lumber to their knees, tilting the mahouts to a sharp angle, and the horses and cavalry officers bend their heads. When they rose from the salutation, he gazed with awe at the figure on the faraway throne across a sea of jeweled turbans.

They all stood silent as the Mir Arz, in charge of official petitions, read out the day's business in his singsong voice. Ghias watched and listened to the proceedings in a daze. The cloud of sandalwood incense, the richness of the Emperor's throne with its jasper-studded beaten gold pillars and red velvet cushions, the sleek gray marble floor in front of the throne—all overwhelmed him. Finally, Masud was called forward. Ghias went with him, and in unison they performed the *taslim*, touching their right hands to their foreheads and bending from the waist.

"Welcome back, Mirza Masud," Akbar said.

"Thank you, your Majesty," Masud replied, straightening.

"You had a good journey, we trust?"

"By the grace of Allah and your Majesty," Masud said.

"Is this all you have brought us from your travels, Mirza Masud?" Emperor Akbar asked, gesturing toward the horses, and the plates of piled silks and fruits from the caravan.

"One more gift, your Majesty," Masud nodded to Ghias. "If I may humbly be allowed to introduce Mirza Ghias Beg to your court."

"Come forward, Mirza Beg. Our eyes are not as good as they once were. Come forward so we may see you well."

Ghias finally straightened from his *taslim* and took a few steps forward, raising his eyes to the Emperor. He saw a stout, majestic man with a kind face, a mole on his upper lip. "Where are you from, Mirza Beg? Who is your father?"

Stumbling over his words, Ghias told him. Every sentence he spoke echoed in his ears. His throat was dry, his palms damp with sweat. When he had finished, he looked at the Emperor anxiously. Had he pleased him?

"A good family," Akbar said. Turning to his right, he asked, "What do you think, Shaiku Baba?"

Ghias then saw the child seated next to the emperor, a little boy perhaps eight or nine years old, his hair slicked back, wearing a short *peshwaz* coat and trousers of gold shot silk. Prince Salim, heir to the empire. Salim nodded solemnly, the heron feather in his small turban bobbing. Trying to mirror his father's tone of voice, he said in his clear, childish voice, "We like him, your Majesty."

Akbar smiled. "Yes, we do. Come back to see us sometime, Mirza Beg."

Ghias bowed. "Your Majesty is too kind. It will be a great honor for me."

Akbar inclined his head to the Mir Arz, who read out the name of the next supplicant from his scroll. Malik Masud gestured to Ghias and both men bowed again and backed to their places. They did not talk. When the *darbar* was over, Ghias left the hall in a stupor, the Emperor's kind words singing in his ear. He had gone back to the court the next day, waiting for hours until the Emperor was free to talk with him for five minutes. After a few days of conversation, Akbar had graciously granted Ghias a *mansab* of three hundred horses and appointed him courtier.

The *mansab* system was used by Mughal kings to confer honors and estates. The *mansabs* translated into parcels of land used to support the upkeep of cavalry or infantry for the imperial army, so Ghias's *mansab* could support, from its produce, a cavalry of three hundred horses. All this Ghias had to learn anew. The Mughal courts were different from the counts at Persia.

As the years passed, Ghias made himself indispensable to Akbar, accompanying him on hunting parties and campaigns and entertaining him with stories of the Persian courts. Akbar replied to Ghias's efforts in kind, granting him the land and building materials for two splendid houses: one at Agra, the other at Fatehpur Sikri.

Today, they sat down to their midday meal at a rented house in Lahore. A few months ago, a new threat had reared its head on the northwestern frontier of the empire. The Emperor's spies had brought news that Abdullah Khan, king of Uzbekistan, was planning to invade India. Fatehpur Sikri, though nominally the capital of the empire, was too far southeast for the Emperor's comfort. Akbar wanted to be closer to the campaign mounted against the Uzbeg king, and he gave orders for the move to Lahore. The entire court had traveled with the Emperor, leaving the newly built city of Fatehpur Sikri deserted.

Allah had been kind to his family, Ghias mused as he stroked his bearded chin. Opulence surrounded them, a far cry from the destitute manner in which they had entered India. Thick Persian and Kashmiri rugs were piled on the stone floors. The lime-washed walls were hung with paintings and miniatures framed in brass. Little burnished teak and sandalwood tables held artifacts from around the world: Chinese porcelain statues, silver and gold boxes from Persia, ivory figurines from Africa. The children were clothed in the finest muslin and silks, and Asmat wore enough jewelry to feed a poor family for a year.

He still could not believe the blessings that had come his way and how much they had gained in the past years. The children had flourished here, strong and resilient, taking to the country and its people as though their own. Abul, Muhammad, and Saliha had been diffident at first about learning new languages and customs and playing with the children of the neighboring lords and nobles. Young as they were, they remembered much of the long, traumatic journey from Persia. For Mehrunnisa, everything was new and wonderful. The dialects in Agra had come more easily to her mouth. The blistering dry heat of the Indo-Gangetic plains did not seem to bother her; until she was five she ran about the house in a thin cotton shift, balking at having to dress up for festivals and occasions. She took their position for granted as promotions came to Ghias and they moved from one house to a bigger one until Akbar gave them a home of their own. This was the only life she had known. Ghias had worried most about Asmat, anxious about uprooting her and bringing her here. When her father had entrusted her to his care, he surely would not have expected that Ghias would take her away from her family.

Ghias looked at her, warming with pride and love. Asmat was in the early stages of yet another pregnancy, visible only by a slight rounding of her stomach. The passing years had not diminished Asmat's beauty. Time had painted some gray in her hair and etched a few lines on her face. But it was the same dear face, the same trusting eyes. She had been brave, giving him strength at night when they lay beside each other in silence, darkness closing around them, and during the day when he was home working or reading, and she passed by, her anklets chiming, her *ghagara* murmuring on the floor. Islamic law allowed four wives, but with Asmat, Ghias had found a deep, abiding peace. There was no need to even look at another woman or think of taking another wife. She was everything to him.

. A sudden movement caught his eye. Mehrunnisa was sitting at the edge of her divan, her eyes sparkling with excitement, smoothing the long pleats of her *ghagara* with impatient fingers. He knew she wanted to say something and could not keep still. He looked at her, thinking again of these past eight years, of how they would have been different if she had not been with them. A huge gap would have opened in their lives, never to be filled no matter how many children they had. How he would have missed her musical "Bapa!" when he came home and she flung herself into his arms with a "Kiss me first, before anyone else. Me first. Me first."

Ghias bowed his head. *Thank you, Allah.*

Then he put down his cup and said, "His Majesty was in a good mood at the *darbar* this morning. He is very happy about Prince Salim's forth-coming marriage."

"Bapa—" Both Abul and Mehrunnisa spoke simultaneously, relieved that the enforced silence during lunch had finally been broken. Asmat and Ghias were very strict about not speaking during meals: a sign of good manners. And only when Ghias spoke could the rest of the family join in.

"Yes, Mehrunnisa?" Ghias hushed Abul with a hand.

"I want to go to the royal palace for the wedding," Mehrunnisa said. Then she added hastily, "Please."

Ghias raised an eyebrow at Asmat.

She nodded. "You can take the boys. Mehrunnisa and Saliha will be with me."

MEHRUNNISA TUGGED AT her sister's veil. "Can you see anything?"

"No," Saliha said, her voice almost a wail. Just then, one of the ladies in the *zenana* balcony elbowed them to one side, allowing the crowd to swarm to the marble lattice-worked screen.

Mehrunnisa craned her neck, standing on tiptoe until the arches of her feet hurt. It was of no use. All she could see were the backs of the ladies of Akbar's harem as they stood exclaiming at the scene below in the *Diwan-i-Am*.

She fell back on her heels, her foot tapping impatiently on the stone floor. The day of the wedding had finally arrived, and she had not been able to catch a glimpse of the ceremony or of Prince Salim. It was unfair that her bothers were allowed to be present at the courtyard below while she had to be confined behind the *parda* with the royal harem. And what made it all the more unfair was that she was not even old enough to wear the veil, but for some reason her mother had insisted on keeping her in the *zenana* balcony.

Mehrunnisa jumped up and down, trying to look over the heads of the *zenana* ladies. At that moment, it did not strike her that she was actually in the imperial palace. Everything, every thought, centered on Salim. When the gates had opened and the female guards had eyed them with suspicion before letting them into the *zenana* area, Saliha had bowed to them in awe. Mehrunnisa had ignored them, her eyes running everywhere, not seeing the rainbow silks or the luminous jewels or the flawlessly painted faces. Her only thought had been to find a good spot at the screen to see the prince. And now they had been pushed to the back because they were younger and smaller than all the other women.

"I am going to push them aside and take a look."

"You cannot do that. This is the Emperor's harem; they are the most exalted ladies in the realm," Saliha said in a horrified whisper, holding Mehrunnisa's hand tight in hers.

"With very bad manners," Mehrunnisa replied, her voice pert. "I have been pushed out of the way four times already. How are we supposed to see Prince Salim? They are not made of water that we can see through them."

She pulled her hand out of Saliha's grasp and ran to the front of the balcony. She tapped one of the concubines on the shoulder and, when she turned, slipped through the opening to press her face against the screen, her fingers clutching the marble.

Mehrunnisa blinked rapidly to adjust her eyes to the blinding sunshine in the *Diwan-i-Am* and gazed at the figure seated on the throne at the far end. Akbar was dressed in his magnificent robes of state, the jewels on his turban glittering as he nodded graciously to his ministers. The Emperor's eyes were suspiciously bright when he looked at his son.

Mehrunnisa shifted her gaze to Prince Salim and held her breath. From here she could only see him in profile. He held himself with grace, shoulders squared, feet planted firmly apart, right hand on the jeweled dagger tucked into his cummerbund. Princess Man Bai stood next to him, head covered with a red muslin veil heavily embroidered in gold *zari*. If only the princess would move back a step so she could see Salim a little better, Mehrunnisa thought, her face glued to the screen. Perhaps if she leaned over to the right . . . The Qazi who was performing the cere-mony had just finished asking Prince Salim if he would take the Princess Man Bai to be his wife. He now turned to the princess.

Mehrunnisa, along with the rest of the court, waited in silence for Man Bai to respond. Just then, someone rudely pulled her by the shoul-der. She turned around to see the irate concubine glaring at her.

"How dare you?" the concubine hissed between clenched teeth, her face twisted in anger.

Mehrunnisa opened her mouth to reply, but before she could, the girl lifted her hand and slapped Mehrunnisa's face, her jeweled rings cutting into her cheek.

Mehrunnisa raised a trembling hand to her face and stared at her, eyes huge in a pale face. No one—*no one*—had hit her before, not even her parents.

Tears sprang to her eyes as she glowered at the woman, spilling down her cheeks before she could stop them. Mehrunnisa wiped them away with the back of her hand. The concubine leaned over her, hands on hips. Mehrunnisa did not flinch. Instead, she bit her lip to keep back a retort, the slap still ringing in her ears. Suddenly she was terribly lonely.

Somewhere in the background she saw Saliha, her face drained of color. But where was Maji?

"I beg your pardon." Asmat had come up behind Mehrunnisa. She put an arm around her daughter and pulled her away from the furious concubine. "She is just a child—"

"Let her be!" a rich, imperious voice commanded.

Mother and daughter turned to look at the speaker, Ruqayya Sultan Begam, Akbar's chief Queen, or Padshah Begam. Sensing conflict, the ladies around them turned from the *Diwan-i-am* to the drama in the *zenana* balcony. Their faces were tinged with excitement. So rarely did Ruqayya interfere in squabbles that this child must be special. A path cleared from Mehrunnisa to the Padshah Begam, and all eyes turned to Akbar's main consort.

She was not a beautiful woman; in fact, she was quite plain. Her hair was streaked with gray, which she made no effort to conceal with a henna rinse. Inquisitive black eyes glittered out of a round, plump face.

Ruqayya's importance to Akbar was far more than the brief physical satisfaction his mindless concubines could provide him. He valued her quick mind, sharp wit, and comfortable presence. Her position in the *zenana* secure, Ruqayya made no further attempt to beguile the Emperor—a waste of time in any case, when every day a fresh, new face appeared at the harem. So she left the satisfaction of Akbar's physical needs to the younger girls while she made sure that he came to her for all else. That security lent her a calm demeanor, an arrogance, and a self-assurance. She was the Padshah Begam.

Ruqayya beckoned to Mehrunnisa with a plump jewel-studded hand. "Come here." Turning to the concubine, she said harshly, "You should know better than to hit a child."

The girl subsided mutinously to one corner, her kohl-rimmed eyes flashing.

Her mouth suddenly dry, Mehrunnisa walked up to the Padshah Begam. She wiped clammy hands against her *ghagara*, wishing she were anywhere but here.

The scent of ketaki flowers wafted to Mehrunnisa's nostrils as the Empress put a finger under her chin and tilted her face. "So you like to watch the wedding celebrations, eh?" Ruqayya's voice was surprisingly soft.

"Yes, your Majesty," Mehrunnisa replied in a low voice, head bent to hide the gap in her teeth.

"Do you like Prince Salim?"

"Yes, your Majesty." Mehrunnisa hesitated and looked up with a smile, the gap forgotten. "He is . . . he is more beautiful than my brothers."

All the ladies around them burst out laughing, their laughter carrying down into the courtyard.

Ruqayya held up an imperious hand. "This child thinks Salim to be beautiful," she announced to the ladies. "I wonder how long it will be before she finds him handsome." Laughter swept through the room again.

Mehrunnisa looked around, bemused.

The wedding ceremony had just been completed, and the Qazi was registering the marriage in his book. The ladies shifted their attention to the *Dwian-i-am*, and Mehrunnisa escaped thankfully into her mother's arms. Asmat pushed her daughter toward the door, signaling Saliha to join them.

As they were leaving, Ruqayya said, without looking in their direction, "The child amuses me. Bring her to wait upon me soon."

Mehrunnisa and Asmat Begam bowed low to the Empress and let themselves out.

The wedding parties continued for almost a week, but Mehrunnisa, frightened after her encounter with Ruqayya, refused to go for the festivities. The concubine had merely made her angry; the Empress, with her glittering eyes and her aura of power alarmed Mehrunnisa. Asmat Begam and Ghias Beg went every day to pay their respects to Akbar and his queens and to take part in the rejoicing.

A few days later, Ruqayya sent an imperial summons commanding Mehrunnisa's presence at the royal *zenana*.

TWO

*This Begam conceived a great affection for Mehr-un-Nasa; she
loved her more than others and always kept her in her company.*
—B. Narain, trans., and S. Sharma,
ed., *A Dutch Chronicle of Mughal
India*

A TALL EUNUCH WITH A WILTING MOUSTACHE MET MEHRUNNISA
and Asmat at the entrance to Empress Ruqayya's palace. He put a hand
out to Asmat.

"Only the child," he said. Then, seeing the sudden spurt of apprehen-
sion in Asmat's eyes, he relented a little and added, "She will be sent
home safely, but only the child must enter."

Asmat nodded. It would have been futile to argue in any case. She leaned
over to whisper, "Be good, *beta*. You will be all right, don't worry." Then she
was gone. Mehrunnisa watched her mother leave, wanting to beg her to
stay. How could she leave her alone here with the funny-looking man?

When she turned around, she found the eunuch scrutinizing her.

"So you are the child she likes," he said, his voice a growl. He stepped
back to allow her to enter into a dark antechamber. Beyond in the courtyard a rectangle of sunshine slanted through. The eunuch stopped
Mehrunnisa's progress with a hand. "Turn around."

Mehrunnisa turned slowly, feeling the unnatural weight of her
embroidered *ghagara* swirl around her. The blouse was loose; it hung
about her shoulders even though it was laced tightly at the back. At
home she wore thin muslin *ghagaras* and *salwars*. For the Empress,
Asmat had dressed her in her best outfit, even though it was only a morning visit and not even a day of festival. The eunuch put a finger to her
nape and turned her around until she stood facing him.

He pulled Mehrunnisa's plait over her shoulder, checking its length against her hip, and touched her cheeks. Then he pinched her skin and peered at her teeth. Mehrunnisa pulled back, her face flushing, as his head loomed in front of her. What was she—a horse for sale?

The eunuch laughed, showing *paan*-stained red teeth. "So thin, so scrawny." He poked her in the ribs. "Look at the bones sticking out here. What, don't your parents feed you? Was that woman your mother? Now, *she* is pretty. But you—even your teeth have a hole in them. I wonder what she sees in you. She will tire of you soon. Come," he said, pulling her by the arm, his nails digging into Mehrunnisa's flesh. "Now remember not to repeat what I just said. Perhaps this should be your first lesson, girl. Never talk of what you hear in the *zenana*."

Still laughing, he half-dragged, half-pulled Mehrunnisa down the corridor to the bathhouse. Slave girls bowed to the man as they passed. Her heart thumping, Mehrunnisa saw this and didn't pull away from him. Maji was not here; she was all alone with this strange, pasty-faced, limp-moustached creature. Who was he? And why did he have so much power here, in this harem of women?

The Empress was preparing for her bath when Mehrunnisa entered the *hammam*. By this time a thin film of sweat had coated her forehead and dampened her armpits. If this man was so strange, how would the Empress be? She had been even more frightening the other day. The eunuch let go of Mehrunnisa's arm and bowed deeply to Ruqayya.

"The child is here, your Majesty." Then, not waiting for Ruqayya's reply, he slid backwards out of the room.

Mehrunnisa was alone. She stood still, blinking in the sunlight that pooled around her from an overhead skylight, throwing lattice patterns on the ground. A tinkle of gold bangles made her look to one corner of the room. The Empress sat on a stool as sleekly muscled slave girls, their skins colored with the brown hues of the earth, took off her jewels. A eunuch stood nearby, holding a silver tray on which the jewels were laid. In the center of the room was an octagonal pool carved into the floor. A wooden bench ran along the inside of the pool.

"Come here, child."

At the sound of the Empress's voice, Mehrunnisa moved to the corner of the room where Ruqayya was seated, wearing a peacock-blue silk
robe ablaze in gold *zari*. Her arm still hurt from where the eunuch's fingers had pinched, but she suddenly wanted even his presence. She didn't
want to be alone here in the semidark room lit only by shards of sunlight from above, while slave girls and eunuchs watched her with deep-
eyed curiosity.

"*Al-Salam alekum*, your Majesty."

Mehrunnisa," Ruqayya said, leaning back against a pillar. "It is a
pretty name. Sit."

Mehrunnisa came near her and sat down. Ruqayya reached out a hand
to touch her dense black hair.

"Such lovely eyes. You are Persian?"

"Yes, your Majesty."

Ruqayya's round face creased into a smile. "Who is your father?"

"Mirza Ghias Beg, your Majesty."

"Who is your grandfather?"

And so they talked for five minutes. Mostly, the Empress asked the
questions—about Mehrunnisa, about Asmat, Ghias, her brothers.
What they did, which *mulla* they studied with, what she had read
recently. The Empress was not so frightening after that conversation.
Her voice slipped into low, slumberous tones as the robe was removed
and the slave girls massaged her with jasmine oil. Mehrunnisa watched
as a slave girl's brown fingers, glistening with oil, moved over Ruqayya's
large body. The slave kneaded the muscles in Ruqayya's shoulders, and
the Empress's head fell forward with a sigh. The slave's hands slid over
the slope of her breasts, around her stomach, over her thighs, her movements quick with practice.

Then the Empress rose to descend into the pool slowly. Her hair
swirled around her, loose from its usual bun. Mehrunnisa watched as
the slave girls, still clad in cotton pajamas and *cholis*, went into the water
with the Empress. Ruqayya lay back in the water as they soaped her,

their palms frothing with wet soap nuts, then washed her hair and rinsed it.

At one point, the Empress sat up and said sharply to one of the slaves, "Did you bathe today?"

The girl, very young, and frightened now, stammered, "Yes, your Majesty."

"Let me see," Ruqayya commanded, sniffing at the girl's hands, at her hair, under her armpits. She turned away and said in a menacingly quiet voice, "Get out. Now. And don't ever come into my bath water unless you have bathed first."

The girl scrambled out of the tub, dripping water over the floor and fled from the room, leaving wet footprints in her wake.

Mehrunnisa shuddered at the venom in Ruqayya's voice. Goose-bumps crawled up her back. She cowered into the shadows of the room, hoping the Empress would not notice her. There she sat in silence for the next two hours as Ruqayya finished dressing, throwing back one outfit, then another at the eunuchs until one finally pleased her. When the Empress left the room, she looked back at Mehrunnisa and said, "Go home now. Come again tomorrow."

That was all.

Over the next few months, Mehrunnisa went when Ruqayya called for her, talking when the Empress wanted to talk, sitting in silence next to her when she didn't. She saw that most of Ruqayya's tantrums were just for pretense. The slave girl had insolent eyes, Ruqayya had told Mehrunnisa later in passing. But it had been no such thing. The girl had been too callow and too timorous to raise insolent eyes at the empress. Sometimes, though, Ruqayya was truly roused to anger, but mostly the Empress raised her voice just because she could. The title of Padshah Begam was not lightly bestowed nor lightly taken. Everything that happened within the harem walls, and quite a bit that happened outside, came to Ruqayya's ears through various spies. Nothing was too big or too small for the Empress's notice. Every illness, every preg-nancy, every missed period, court intrigues, squabbles between wives and concubines or slave girls—every bit of information found its way to her palace.

Mehrunnisa began to look forward to these visits with Akbar's favorite wife. She was fascinated by Ruqayya's chameleonic moods, her calm and quiet, her fiery rages. She was fascinated too by how important she was, and thrilled that Ruqayya found *her* interesting.

But it was Salim she wanted to see. One day, as Mehrunnisa ran back to the *zenana* gates after spending time with the Empress, she entered the grounds of an adjoining palace by mistake. It was not until corridor after corridor had led her deeper into the palace that she realized she was lost. It was late in the afternoon, and the palace was silent. Even the omnipresent maids and eunuchs were hidden in the dark shadows of the bedchambers, waiting for the sun to wane. Mehrunnisa looked around and tried to retrace her steps. The gardens she passed were immaculate, the grass green even in the heat, the bougainvillea vines drooping with watermelon-colored flowers. She came to an inner courtyard paved with marble, a rectangle of blue sky above. The four sides of the courtyard were enclosed with deep, many-pillared verandahs. The pillars were also of marble and glowed a cool white in the heat of courtyard. Mehrunnisa slipped her arms around a pillar, reaching only halfway, and laid her sweating forehead against the stone. Perhaps in an hour someone would find her and show her the way out. She was too tired to wander any longer.

Even as she stood there a man came into the courtyard carrying a silver casket. He was dressed simply in white: a loose *kurta* and pajama, his feet in leather sandals. Mehrunnisa straightened from the pillar and started to call out to him. Then she drew back. It was Prince Salim. She slid down behind the pillar and peeped around it. Why was he alone, without attendants?

Salim went to the opposite end of the courtyard and sat down on a stone bench under a *neem* tree, its branches heavy with grapelike yellow fruit. He made a clicking sound with his tongue. Mehrunnisa almost fell into the courtyard in surprise as hundreds of pigeons roosting in the eaves came rustling out and flew to the prince. They swarmed about his feet, their throats moving furiously under a ring of iridescent green feathers. Salim opened the casket, dipped his hand inside, and threw a handful of wheat into the air. The grains caught the golden light of the sun as they showered onto the marble paving stones. The birds immediately began pecking at the wheat, their heads bobbing up and down. Some turned expectant looks at the prince.

He laughed, the sound echoing softly through the silent courtyard. "You are spoilt. If you want some more, come and get it."

He held out the next handful on his palm. Undetected, hidden behind the pillar, Mehrunnisa watched the birds waddle around him as though undecided. Then, with great daring, one pigeon flew up to Salim's shoulder and sat there. He stayed perfectly still. Soon the pigeons swarmed all around him, their gray and black bodies almost covering the prince.

"What are you doing here?" A hand caught Mehrunnisa by the shoulder and spun her around. Mehrunnisa stood up and dusted off her *ghagara*, lifting her face to meet the gaze of the eunuch.

"I'm lost."

"Silly girl," he whispered fiercely, pushing her from the courtyard. "You are in the *mardana*. Don't you know it is forbidden to come into the men's quarters? Go now, before Prince Salim sees you. He does not like anyone around him when he feeds the pigeons."

"What are *you* doing here then?"

The eunuch raised his eyebrows. "I am Hoshiyar Khan."

Mehrunnisa raised her eyebrows in response. "And I am Mehrunnisa. But who *are* you?"

He made a clicking sound with his tongue. "I . . . it does not matter. You have to go now, girl."

Mehrunnisa turned for one last look at Salim before she left. He sat on the bench, crooning softly to the pigeons. When one lit on his hair, he laughed again, trying to look at it without tilting his head.

"Come on, come on," the eunuch said impatiently. "No women are allowed in the *mardana*. You know that. The Emperor will have your head if he finds out."

"He will not!" Mehrunnisa said. "I got lost. I did not come here deliberately."

"*Bap re!*" Hoshiyar sighed, still pushing her in front of him until she almost tripped over the skirts of her *ghagara*. "She argues, too. I find her making moon eyes at Prince Salim, and she tells me she was lost."

He took her out of the palace and pointed to the gates. "Go—and don't let me see you here again, or *I* will have your head."

Mehrunnisa stuck her tongue out at him and ran toward the gates. She looked back over her shoulder. Hoshiyar did not follow. He just stood there, and when she turned, he stuck his tongue out at her.

"GOING TO SEE the Empress?"

Mehrunnisa whirled around, her hairpins tinkling to the floor, some bouncing to camouflage themselves against the pattern of the Persian rug.

"See what you have done!" she exclaimed, bending down to gather the hairpins. But a few were hopelessly lost, lying on the rug to poke bare feet at some later time. She straightened up and looked into the mirror.

Abul was leaning against the doorway, his arms folded across his chest. Abul was fifteen years old now, old enough not to tease her. But she knew he had a free afternoon, and she was his best target. Saliha ignored him. Khadija and Manija cried when he approached because he invariably pulled their hair or wrapped their *ghagaras* around their heads so they could not see, and he had to beat a hasty retreat before Maji or Bapa scolded him. So he came seeking her when his male friends did not take him away hunting or to the public houses—this last without Bapa's knowledge, of course. Mehrunnisa forgot Maji's injunctions about how a lady should behave and scowled at her brother's image in the mirror.

Abul shook his head with a silent tut-tut. "Your face will freeze like that, and no one will marry you. You haven't answered my question yet."

"I am not going to, Abul," Mehrunnisa said, composing her face again. Allah forbid that what Abul said might come true. "It's none of your business. Go away and leave me to do my hair."

"Come out with me, Nisa. We can play polo with mallets in the gar-den—without the horses, of course."

She shook here head. "I cannot. I am going to the palace. Don't bother me now, Abul, or I will tell Bapa you went to the *nashakhana* last night."

"And *I* will tell Bapa that you went with me three nights ago. Dressed as a man, with a khol-painted moustache, and got drunk on three sips of wine. That I had to carry you home early. That my friends still ask after the pale-faced youth who has such a weak stomach that 'he' puts even a baby to shame."

Mehrunnisa ran up to Abul and pulled him into the room. She peered outside the door. No one was passing. She pinched the arm she was still holding. "Are you crazy? No one can ever know that I went to the *nashakhana* with you. You forced me to, Abul."

Abul grinned. "I did not have to force you very much, Nisa. You wanted to come. Be thankful Khadija did not wake up and wonder why you weren't in bed. Bapa would have beaten you for sure if he found out."

Mehrunnisa shuddered. What stupidity that had been. Tempting, but stupid. "You must never tell anyone. Promise me that. Promise." She pinched his arm harder.

Abul pulled away, rubbing his sore arm. "All right, *baba*. I won't. But come with me tonight. We can dress you up again and jump over the wall like last time."

Mehrunnisa shook her head and went back to the mirror. "Once was enough. I just wanted to see what it would be like. Why do you go to that place anyway? All those men getting drunk and lolling over the divans, the serving girls wearing next to nothing sprawling all over them. . . ." She shuddered. "It was horrible. Don't go there again, Abul. It's not right."

Abul wrapped a finger around her hair and pulled it. "That is none of your business, Nisa. You asked to go there; I took you. Now don't tell me what to do. The promise not to tell Bapa only holds so long as you keep your moralizing tongue in your mouth. Is that clear?"

Mehrunnisa glared at him, reaching for a comb. Her hand swept over the tray, and a bottle of kohl powder toppled over, sprinkling glittering midnight over the embellished silver.

"You certainly are edgy today." Abul grinned wickedly. "Would that have something to do with the wedding in the royal palace?"

"What wedding?" Mehrunnisa asked, lifting her nose in the air. "Oh, Prince Salim's wedding."

Abul sat down next to her.

"Yes, *that* wedding. Prince Salim is getting married for the second time. To the princess of Jodhpur, daughter of Udai Singh. He is known as the Mota Raja, the Fat King. I've seen him; it is an apt name. I wonder," Abul picked up a delicately fashioned glass bottle and pulled the stopper so that the scent of frankincense flooded the room, "if Princess Jagat Gosini is fat also."

Mehrunnisa slapped his hand lightly. "You will break the bottle." She vigorously attacked her long tresses. When all the knots had been loosened and her hair lay about her shoulders in a sheet of shimmering silk, she divided it into three bunches and began to plait it.

Abul raised an eyebrow. "Why are you so unsettled, my dear sister?"

"I am not! The prince has a right to marry anyone he chooses."

"True." Abul nodded. "And he is well on his way to assembling his own harem. Two weddings in two years, and he is only seventeen. He already has a child from the first wife, though only a daughter, but he will soon have sons for the empire if he keeps up this pace."

"So?" Mehrunnisa's hands moved swiftly behind her head. When the plait had grown, she flipped it over one shoulder and continued down the front. "Why should it bother me?"

Abul tilted his head back and laughed. "Everyone knows you go to visit Empress Ruqayya only so you can see the prince. Just what are you thinking? That you will marry him next? The prince would never marry *you.*"

Mehrunnisa flushed, crimson staining her face and neck.

"Why not?" She turned defiant eyes at him. "That is . . . I mean, if I wanted to marry him, what would stop us?"

Abul roared again, almost falling off his stool. He held up his hand and started ticking off reasons. "First, you are too young. You are a baby, Mehrunnisa. Nine-year-old girls do not marry royal princes. Second, all the princes will make political marriages, and they will marry only princesses. Why would he want to marry you?"

"I may be young now, but I will grow up. And Maji says not all royal marriages are for political reasons."

"But all Prince Salim's will be. At least, as long as he is still a prince. The Emperor's own *zenana* is filled with women connected to the vassal kings of the empire. That is how Akbar has managed to keep the empire together. You will never stand a chance." Abul grinned. "Besides, by the time you grow up, the prince will be a dissolute young man. Have you heard the latest news about him?"

"What is it?" Mehrunnisa asked eagerly, despite her reluctance to talk to her brother about Prince Salim.

"He has started drinking." Abul lowered his voice conspiratorially. "They say he drinks twenty cups of liquor a day."

"That much!" Mehrunnisa gasped, her eyes wide. She knew Salim had started drinking because Ruqayya complained incessantly about it. The prince had always been temperate, but a few months ago, while on campaign near Attock to put down the Afghan rebellion, Mirza Muhammad Hakim had suggested that wine would ease Salim's fatigue. Now he was addicted, according to Ruqayya, who when she was upset about something was not always a reliable source. But here was Abul saying the same thing.

Mehrunnisa was silent for a few moments, her fingers tracing the engraving on a silver jewelry box.

"What does that have to do with me?" she asked finally.

"My dear Nisa." Abul's voice had taken on a mocking tone again. "If Prince Salim is going to marry you, he will have to wait. Who knows— in a few years he may be dead of drink. Then you would have to marry either Murad or Daniyal to be empress. It is a good thing the Emperor has two other sons who could be of service to you."

Mehrunnisa lifted her chin and looked down at him. "We are not talk-ing about my life," she said with dignity. "Go now. I must get ready. The Empress has commanded my presence."

"Yes, *your Majesty.*" Abul bowed to her, laughing, and backed from the room as though in the presence of royalty. Mehrunnisa picked up an ivory comb and threw it at him. It missed Abul, bounced off the door frame, and fell on the floor. Abul grinned, put his thumb on his nose, and waggled the rest of his fingers at her. He disappeared just as she was reaching for an enamel casket.

Mehrunnisa turned back to the mirror, frowning. Why was it so inconceivable that she could marry a royal prince? After all, her father was a respected courtier; the Emperor valued his advice. And the Mughal royals married whomever they wished to marry.

She changed her clothes swiftly, barely waiting to glance into the mir-ror. The Empress did not like to be kept waiting. The *zenana* would be rife with gossip about the new princess, the dowry, her father, what Salim thought or did not think of her. Every little detail would be picked over and analyzed and inflated, all with great enjoyment. Mehrunnisa won-dered how this new princess would fare in the women's quarters. The first wife was a little mouse, letting out a few imperceptible squeaks here and there, barely ruffling life in the imperial harem. This one, it was said, had more iron in her spine. It would be interesting to see her interact with Ruqayya. And if one day—not if, when—Mehrunnisa became Salim's wife, this princess would be the one to watch.

Mehrunnisa had no idea how all these dreams were going to come true, only that they should somehow, if for no other reason than to irri-tate Abul because he had made fun of her.

She picked up her veil, draped it on her head, and went out of the house with Dai, who had once been her wet nurse. Maji was busy with her new brother, Shahpur, born a few months earlier. In the outer court-yard, Mehrunnisa climbed into the palanquin that would carry her to the royal palace to congratulate Empress Ruqayya on her newest stepdaughter-in-law.

* * *

THAT SAME YEAR Salim married again, this time to Sahib Jamal, the daughter of Khwaja Hasan. The next year, at Lahore, Salim's first wife, Princess Man Bai, gave birth to a son named Khusrau. The Emperor was overjoyed at the birth of a new heir to the throne. Garden parties, galas, and festivities marked the week after the child's birth.

From Lahore, in the autumn of 1588, the imperial court shifted to Srinagar, the capital of Kashmir, for the first time. Kashmir had withstood Mughal occupation for long but had finally fallen to the imperial forces the previous year.

Srinagar charmed the entire royal party. The city was set in a valley amid the Himalayan mountains. The air was pure and heady, like *amrit*, drink of the gods. The lower hills, clad in autumnal colors of fiery reds and browns, rolled gently down to golden fields of ripening wheat, broken only by the silver glitter of the Jhelum River snaking through the valley. Behind, snow-clad mountains reared their majestic heads to the vast blue sky.

Upon the court's return to Lahore the next year, Akbar promoted Ghias to *diwan* of Kabul. The appointment as treasurer was a great privilege, for Kabul, although provincial, was a strategic outpost in the northern Mughal Empire for trade and defense. Kabul lay in a triangular gorge between the steep and forbidding Asmai and Sherdawza mountains, and crowning the lower hills surrounding the city was a long, winding mud wall interspersed with towers.

Ghias and his family moved to Kabul. His new duties kept him awake late into the night, as he went over the books from the treasury. Mehrunnisa usually came to him wanting to hear about his day's work, the people he had met, what he had said to them and why. Sometimes she would sit by him quietly with a book. Sometimes he would turn to her with a column of numbers to add, or talk to her about the trouble the clerks gave him, or complain that the accountant of the army had come up short again on revenues. On one winter night as the cold seeped through the stone walls of the house, Mehrunnisa and Ghias sat huddled together for warmth. She was leaning against her father's back, her feet stretched toward the coal brazier, when Ghias suddenly said, "A new Hindu priest has come to the city. I heard him reciting the *Ramayana* under the *banyan* tree to passersby as I came home. They tell me he knows most of Valmiki's opus by heart."

Mehrunnisa whipped around to him, her eyes bright with excitement. "Bapa, can we go listen to him? Is it in Sanskrit?"

Ghias grinned. "Your Maji would die a thousand deaths if you went out. Perhaps we should ask him to come home?"

She clutched his arm. "Oh, Bapa, yes, please."

"I will talk to your Maji."

The next day Ghias talked with Asmat, but she was worried. How old was the priest, she asked. Would it be right to bring him into a house with young girls? What would people say?

"But, Asmat, the children have a wonderful opportunity to learn. We must not deny them this," Ghias said.

Asmat frowned as she pulled absently at a lock of her hair. "Ghias, we must be careful not to teach the girls too much. How will they ever find husbands if they are too learned? The less they know, the less they will want of the outside world. Mehrunnisa already insists that she should be allowed to go out with you."

Ghias smiled slowly. "I know. She asks why a woman has to stay in the house when a man can go and come as he pleases."

An apprehensive look crossed Asmat's face. "Do not encourage her, Ghias. We must be careful, so people do not think our daughters are too arrogant to make good wives."

"I will not. I promise. But it is a pleasure to have at least one child who interests herself in my work." Ghias kissed away the worry lines from his wife's forehead. "They will be confined behind the *parda* soon enough, Asmat, for the rest of their lives. What little we can give them, we must."

Asmat looked up at her husband. "Even I want to listen to the priest. Can I, Ghias?"

"Of course. We will all gather around him."

So the Brahmin priest came to the house four nights a week. He was a thin, spare man, with ribs that stood out in his chest, and a shaven head with a small pigtail at the back. Even in this cold, he was clad in a chaste *dhoti* and not much else. He had a saturnine face that grew in mobility as he recited the verses from Valmiki's *Ramayana* in his tuneful voice. When she had time, Asmat joined her daughters behind the thin silk curtain that separated them from the men. Mehrunnisa usually sat at the front, against the curtain, its folds molding against her face. She had to be behind the *parda* for the sake of propriety, but she asked the priest questions and listened as he gravely answered her, turning to speak to her as though she mattered.

And the days passed. The children were all taught the scriptures, arithmetic, geometry, astronomy, and the classics. When those studies were done, Asmat made sure her daughters also learned to paint, sew, embroider, and oversee the servants. While they were at Kabul, Prince Salim's third wife, Sahib Jamal, gave birth to his second son, Parviz. Ghias returned home at the end of a day to find his wife and daughters seated on low divans busy with their embroidery.

"The messengers have brought news from the court." He held out the letter.

Asmat glanced through the elaborate Turkish script, the language of the imperial court. Babur, Akbar's grandfather and the first Mughal emperor of India, had adopted Turki, his native tongue, as the official language to keep in touch with his ancestry through Timur the Lame. That practice had continued through the generations. Both Asmat and Ghias had been unfamiliar with Turki upon their arrival in India but had taken great pains to learn the language. Around the courts, the nobles spoke Arabic and Hindi, which was Sanskrit based, with a liberal borrowing of Persian words. Asmat and Ghias now spoke all these languages fluently. At home, their conversation was a strange amalgam of Persian, Hindi, and Arabic, the children tending more toward the languages of Hindustan rather than the native Persian of Asmat and Ghias.

"Let me see, Maji," Mehrunnisa said.

Asmat handed her the letter. Mehrunnisa read it rapidly, then returned to her embroidery. Prince Salim had another son. Two heirs to the empire already. Mehrunnisa had not heard from the Empress in all the time they had been at Kabul. Ruqayya was a poor correspondent, with little patience to even dictate to a scribe. In any case, the Empress could not be expected to write, so Mehrunnisa wrote to her every now and then. News of the harem came from other courtiers' wives to her mother. They said that Princess Jagat Gosini, Salim's second wife, was a feisty girl with a stubborn chin and a strong back, who would not be cowed by anyone. But there was no sign of a child yet. That kept her somewhat subdued.

Mehrunnisa stuck the needle into the cloth and laid it aside, staring out of the window at the snow-clad mountains. Leaving the court had been difficult, but it was only for a few years, Bapa had said. There were new adventures here, new friends to make, new places to see. Here she had met Mirza Malik Masud for the first time. He was her foster father; he had found her as a baby under a tree and returned her to Bapa and Maji. Mehrunnisa had been timid with the merchant with his weather-beaten, sunburnt face, but he had put her at ease immediately. "I am like your Bapa, *beta*," he said. "You cannot be shy with me." He had brought a gift for her, a bolt of thin gold muslin for a veil, the weave so fine the cloth could be pulled through a ring. After the awkwardness of the first meeting, Mehrunnisa spent hours listening to his tales: of highway robberies, of camels that refused to budge when ghosts possessed them, of tents that flew away in the wind, leaving the caravan naked and shivering under a cold night sky. She became so comfortable with him that she was sorry when he left, but he took with him her promise to write every month.

Bapa was much revered at Kabul; people came from far to see him, to ask his advice, to listen with respect. They always left a little gift for him on the table: an embroidered bag weighted at the bottom, or, in season, mangoes, brilliant yellow and honey sweet, or even the horse one nobleman had led to the front yard. They were privileges attached to the post

of the *diwan*, Bapa said—privileges they all enjoyed. But, Mehrunnisa
sighed softly, it was nothing like the imperial *zenana* with its beautiful
women and its petty jealousies and thrilling intrigues. She missed
Ruqayya's caustic tongue and quick wit. How did the Empress interact
with Prince Salim's proud second wife?

"When are we going back to Lahore, Bapa?" she asked suddenly.

Ghias looked up from the official documents in his hand. "When the
Emperor wishes. I have no say in the matter. Why do you ask?"

"No reason." Mehrunnisa picked up the cloth and bent toward her
embroidery. Restlessness rose over her like tide on a beach. The older
she became—she was now fourteen—the more Bapa and Maji imposed
restrictions on her. Do not go out too much; keep your voice down; pull
your veil over your head when a strange man, one not of the family,
comes to visit. These restrictions would be part of her life from now on,
for she was a woman. But cloistered as they were, the women of the
imperial *zenana* still managed to step beyond the harem walls. They went
to visit temples and gardens and to sightsee. They owned lands in the
empire and talked with their stewards without any commotion. Ruqayya
advised Akbar on grants of gifts or *mansabs* or his campaigns. Though
she was behind the veil, she was still a voice to reckon with. Nowhere
else in the empire did women have such freedom. A mere nobleman's
wife could never hope for such liberty. The sheath of royalty gave the
women of the imperial harem an emancipation a commoner could never
hope to achieve.

Mehrunnisa clicked her tongue in irritation when she saw that her
stitches had flowed over the pattern of champa flowers. She pulled the
needle out of the pink thread and, using one end, undid the stitches one
by one. It was ironic, really, because the royal *zenana* was a sign of the
Emperor's wealth and position, his most important possession—more
important at times than the treasury or the army. Although physically
shut from the rest of the world, it still slid tentacles into every aspect of
the empire.

She had gained all this perspective from being away from the *zenana,* and from growing older, for now her movements were more curtailed. At fourteen, she was already considered a woman ready for marriage.

Perhaps it was for the best that they were away. With distance must come a deeper desire. But Bapa had to, he must, return to court. Then she could watch Ruqayya, a mere woman, exert her power over the minions who scurried at her commands. Then Mehrunnisa would see Salim's wives for herself. And Salim? He had to notice her too, or how else would she become Empress?

THREE

Baba Shaikhuji, since all this
Sultanate will devolve upon thee why
Hast thou made this attack on me?
To take away my life there was no need of injustice,
I would have given it to thee if thou hadst asked me.
                    —W. H. Lowe, trans.,
                    Munktakhab-ut-Tawarikh

THE SOFT STRAINS OF A *SITAR* FLOATED DOWN FROM THE BALCONY into the reception hall at the Lahore fort. Thin muslin curtains, hung on arches, billowed in the breeze that swept through the outer courtyard. Within, wisps of bluish gray smoke from incense censers swirled upward, spreading the aroma of musk and aloewood around the room. The white marble floor gleamed dully in the lamplight, bare of furniture except for one satin-covered divan in a corner, flanked by bright Persian rugs.

Prince Salim lay on the divan, head propped against a velvet bolster, a goblet balanced precariously on his chest. He watched as slave girls clad in the finest muslin swayed and undulated to the music, their anklets tinkling as they moved. The low insistent drum of the *tabla* joined in with the *sitar*, and Salim turned his head to look up at the enclosed balcony, where an entire orchestra was assembled. His gaze then dropped to the pretty faces surrounding him.

The ladies of his *zenana* sat around the prince, gorgeously attired and delicately perfumed, their toilette so complete that not one hair was out of place. The ladies were unveiled. They were the reason why the musicians were sequestered: if the ladies of the harem appeared without the *parda* in front of their lord, no other men could be present. Salim was surrounded only by the members of his harem: wives and concubines, slave girls and eunuchs.

49

The room blurred into a drunken haze. Salim lifted a languid finger and beckoned to a slave girl. She hurried to his side and, bowing gracefully, poured more liquor into his jade cup. Salim raised it to his mouth and drank greedily, the alcohol fumes tickling his nostrils. In his haste, he spilled the rich yellow liquid on his *qaba*.

Jagat Gosini, Salim's second wife, touched his arm.

He glared at her. "What is it?"

"My lord," she said gently. "Perhaps you should try these grapes."

Salim's glance softened as he looked at her calm face. He opened his mouth and allowed himself to be fed like a child with a few plump, purple grapes, but they were like sand on his tongue. Five years of drinking had spoiled his appetite for food. He pushed her hand away impatiently.

To his right sat Man Bai, whom he had given the title of Shah Begam, chief princess of his harem. After all, she had provided him with his first son, Khusrau. Jagat Gosini made a sign to Man Bai. As Salim turned to Man Bai, she tried to tempt him with some sweets.

A petulant frown creased Salim's brow. He stared moodily into the distance, tapping his now empty jade goblet on the marble floor, ostensibly keeping time with the music. Suddenly he threw his cup against a sandstone pillar. It crashed and broke into tiny, green, wine-tinged pieces. Startled, the musicians stopped playing, and the princesses froze in their places.

"Your Highness—" Jagat Gosini tentatively put a hand on his arm. Salim pushed her away and staggered to his feet.

"Why doesn't the old man die?" he yelled. "He has ruled for thirty-five years. It is time for the next generation to sit on the throne of Hindustan."

Silence followed.

Salim weaved unsteadily up and down the carpet, his hands clenched into fists, his face red. He had been content until now to be heir to the throne. But during the last few months, his courtiers had pointed out, quite rightly, Akbar's extreme injustice in remaining steadfastly alive while Prince Salim was mature enough to take over the duties of state.

Salim's legs gave way, and he collapsed on the floor. Attendants came rushing to help him. He waved them away with a drunken gesture and lay there, looking up at the ornate ceiling of the hall, abloom in lotus flowers embossed in gold trim.

He had everything he could want: handsome looks; virility, which had been proved twice by the birth of two sons; several wives; and an equal number of concubines. Yet, he had nothing without the crown. He should rebel, as Mahabat Khan and the others had suggested. That would teach Akbar a lesson.

As soon as the thought came to his mind, Salim groaned. Akbar was too strong an Emperor. It was unlikely he would give up his throne without a fight. But why not? Akbar had come to the throne of the empire at the tender age of thirteen. He, Salim, was now twenty-two, and surely mature enough to handle the duties of state.

Salim drummed his fists on the floor in frustration. Akbar could live for many years, and when he eventually died, it would be too late. Salim would come to the throne an old man. What use would that be? He curled up on the carpet, and hot tears rolled down his face.

Jagat Gosini made a sign for everyone to disperse. The musicians and attendants bowed and left in silence. She went up to her husband. "Sleep now, my lord," she said in a soothing voice. "You are tired."

Salim lifted a tearful face. "When will I be Emperor?"

"Soon, my lord. Come, you must rest."

Salim let himself be led to the divan. He lay down heavily, still sniffling. The lamps were extinguished, plunging the room in darkness. Under the soft touch of his wife's hand, the prince cried himself to sleep.

SALIM OPENED HIS eyes and gazed around the unfamiliar room. Why had he slept in the reception hall? He moved slightly, then sank back on the divan with a groan. Hammers pounded on his brain. His mouth was dry, rank with the smell of stale liquor. He licked his lips and shouted, "Water!"

The previous night came rushing back to him. Something had to be done. Salim rose and staggered to his rooms. He sat waist-high in a tub of warm water, deep in thought, as the steam leached out the aches and pains and alcohol from his body. Should he do what Mahabat and the others had suggested—no, dropped hints about? But how could he do that to his own father? A father who doted on him and loved him, whose eyes lit up when he saw Salim? Yet, what was he, Salim, without the throne?

Salim scooped water with his hands and splashed his heated face. No, it had to be done. Mahabat said Humam was reliable, that he would fix it so Akbar would not be hurt too much, just incapacitated. Then Salim could be Emperor. . . .

A few hours later, Akbar's personal physician, *hakim* Humam, came to the prince's apartments. Salim dismissed all his attendants. The *hakim* and Salim remained closeted for an hour. Then the *hakim* left, carrying in his right hand a heavy embroidered bag, usually used for gold *mohurs*.

Salim stood at the door to his apartments, watching Humam leave. He almost shouted out at the last minute to stop the man, then changed his mind. He was not strong enough yet, and his mind was too fuddled by the morning dose of opium. Perhaps, Salim thought dully, sinking down to the marble floor and leaning against the doorway, nothing would happen after all. Neither Salim nor the *hakim* noticed one of Akbar's servants lounging against a pillar in the main courtyard.

A few days later, the royal palace was rife with gossip. The Emperor was unwell from a bout of colic, and it seemed he would not recover. The royal physicians could do nothing to ease the Emperor's suffering.

News of Akbar's agony was brought to Prince Salim in an inner courtyard of the *mardana* late one afternoon as he fed the pigeons. The eunuch who brought the message coughed to attract his attention. Salim did not look at him, heard what he had to say, and then dismissed him with a nod. A pigeon gently nudged his clenched fist. Salim opened it and let the wheat fall to the ground. He watched the pigeons scramble in the dust. Was it true that the Emperor was gravely ill? Or was it just an exaggeration, as all matters of the royal palace were exaggerated? What if Akbar died?

Salim straightened up and said, "Hoshiyar."

A eunuch stepped forward from behind one of the pillars. Hoshiyar Khan was the head eunuch of Salim's *zenana*, the most important man in it other than the prince. It was he who ran the harem with metronomic efficiency, settling squabbles between the various women: wives, concubines, slaves, maids, cooks. He also doled out their allowances and advised them on their investments.

Like everyone, he had his instructions not to disturb his master during the afternoon sessions, but he was never too far from the prince. Hoshiyar listened, bowed, and left the courtyard. Salim watched him go. What was done was done. Humam had assured him Akbar would live. Now he had to attend to other matters.

Through Hoshiyar, Salim sent spies to the palace of his brother Prince Murad to check on his activities. Murad, now twenty-one years old, was also a candidate for the throne, as was Daniyal. The laws of primogeniture did not prevail in Mughal India as they did in Europe—all three of Akbar's sons had equal rights to the throne.

The spies reported that Murad was in no fit state to contend for the crown. The prince was a drunkard, barely lucid for a few hours every day. He had no ambition; wine and the women of his harem had propelled him to past caring. Daniyal was as yet too young to pose a threat. Neither of the two princes would inspire confidence in the nobles of the court, so their support would naturally go to Salim.

IN HIS BEDCHAMBER, Akbar suffered in silence, not daring to voice his fears. Pain racked his body, and sweat drenched his face. But the physical agony was nothing compared with the dull ache in his heart, as though something large and heavy were sitting on his chest. The previous day, one of his trusted retainers in Salim's service had asked for and been granted an audience. What he had to say filled Akbar with unbelievable distress.

The Emperor moved restlessly in his bed. How could he believe such an infamous charge against his beloved son? But the facts all pointed to it. His condition had steadily deteriorated day by day. He was a robust forty-nine years of age, temperate in his habits, and he had always enjoyed good health. Yet, the colic was persistent, the pains increasing every day. Now he lay in his bed, a ghost of his former self.

As he moved again, muttering to himself, Ruqayya rose from her seat at the far end of the room and then sank back, signaling the approaching attendants to move away. She sat down heavily, turning her face from her husband, unwilling to see him like this. Salim was not her son, not born of her, but she had known and loved him since he was a child. His actions defied belief, defied all reason. But worse, much much worse was Akbar's grief. If the colic did not kill him, the sorrow would, and all those years when the whole harem and the Emperor had prayed for a male heir, when they had rejoiced at Salim's birth, would mean nothing. They had all failed in their duty to make him a good man.

Even as she thought thus, another thought came to her mind—that perhaps Akbar himself was responsible for Salim's drinking and his laziness. Ruqayya had many times warned the Emperor that the prince needed responsibility, that he spent too much time in the *zenana* and not enough among warriors and men of learning. But Akbar would not listen to her, for sending Salim on campaign or out to study with *mullas* would mean sending his son away. How could Salim repay Akbar's affection thus?

An attendant padded silently onto the room on bare feet and bent to the Empress's ear. She listened, then rose and went to the Emperor's bedside.

"Your Majesty, *hakim* Humam is outside."

"Send him in."

Ruqayya motioned to the eunuchs by the door to let the *hakim* enter. As she was pulling a veil over her head the Emperor said with an effort, "Thank you."

Tears welled in her eyes and flowed down her plump cheeks. She clasped the pale hand between her two warm ones. "I would do it a hundred times, my lord," she said simply.

Humam entered the room and bowed. Akbar lifted a feeble hand and bade him come closer. The *hakim* went up to the bed and knelt by the Emperor.

"Your services are no longer necessary to us."

Humam lifted his head in surprise. Akbar glared at him.

"But, your Majesty, I have served you and will always serve you, with my life if necessary," Humam said, trembling. He had never seen the Emperor in such a mood before. Akbar was known for his calmness and his ease of temper, and now Humam was frightened.

"Enough!" Akbar roared, with strength born from anger. "Leave our sight, and no longer show your shameful face to us."

Two attendants swiftly came and pulled the *hakim* away from Akbar's bedside. Humam hung his head, paid obeisance to the Emperor, and backed out of the room.

Empress Ruqayya watched Humam go, wondering if he knew how lucky he was to have his head still. If it had been her decision, Humam would not have seen another sunset, but the Emperor had been adamant about not punishing the *hakim*—as though, Ruqayya thought, putting Humam to death would be an admission of Salim's culpability.

For the next week, Akbar's life hung on a thread. Then, slowly, with the help of his physicians and his devoted wives, he recovered. But the Emperor was not the same: he became quieter, more reserved, and soon the court noticed that the relationship between Akbar and the heir apparent had greatly deteriorated.

AS THE DYING sun heralded the end of yet another day, Ghias Beg carefully laid down his quill on the inkpot and rested his elbows on the desk, letting the golden rays play over his work. He watched as the approaching gloom chased the light over the barren mountains, until one by one they disappeared from his view. Only then did Ghias turn from the window.

In front of him lay a royal *farman*, an edict from the Emperor himself. In it Akbar congratulated him on his services to the empire as *diwan* of Kabul for four years, and finally summoned him back to the imperial court at Lahore.

Four years, Ghias thought with a flush of happiness. Four long years of hard work. His father would have been proud of him. Ghias had initially resisted being sent here, although only inwardly, for no one would have dared disobey or even question the Emperor's command. Ghias had not wanted to leave the Emperor to go to Kabul, important as the post was. He had grown fond of Akbar, reverent almost, and thought that being away from court would mean sure death to his career.

But that was not so. Ghias spread out the *farman* again under his hands, his eyes skimming over the black-ink Turki and the heavily embossed royal seal in one corner. Instead of forgetting him, the Emperor seemed to have carefully watched him these four years through spies and regular reports from Kabul. It was a comforting thought for Ghias, because he had worked hard and put effort into the job with a dedication that was paid back not only by the Emperor's accolades but by the gratitude of the people of Kabul.

Anklets tinkled by his door, and Ghias smiled. So much had happened in the past four years. Abul and Muhammad were both married now. It had been a little early for Muhammad, but Ghias had hoped to settle his wild ways with the marriage. Unfortunately, that had not happened. If anything, Muhammad had grown more distant, more unreachable. Ghias sighed. Perhaps if there were a child . . . fatherhood would surely bring some calmness. Once Muhammad was settled, a very good *rishta* had come for Abul, and he too had been married. But before that, Saliha had been married to a nobleman named Sadiq Khan. It would not have been right to marry the sons with an unwed of-age daughter still at home. Saliha's new family was a good one, and Ghias was not upset at leaving his older daughter in their hands when they returned to Lahore.

As for the other girls—Mehrunnisa, Manija, and Khadija—they continued their education as usual, along with Shahpur.

Mehrunnisa—ah, she was now sixteen and seemed to live up to her name, Ghias thought. Sun of Women—she was a beautiful child, physically as well as in spirit. In all their years of marriage, Asmat and he had never shown undue partiality to any one child, but with Mehrunnisa it was difficult not to do so. Her smile, her laughter, the mischievous glint in her blue eyes filled Ghias with a paternal contentment. If it were socially acceptable to have a daughter live at home all her life, Ghias would choose Mehrunnisa to be by him without hesitation.

Ghias suddenly sobered at the thought. Mehrunnisa was sixteen. Where had time flown? She was now old enough to be married.

THAT NIGHT, WHEN the servants had bowed their way out of the room after extinguishing the lamps, Asmat and Ghias lay side by side in a comfortable silence.

Asmat spoke first. "It is time we think of Mehrunnisa's marriage."

Ghias turned to look at the shadowed face of his wife. "Yes. She is already sixteen."

"We shall miss her," Asmat said softly.

Ghias felt for her hand and held it fast, choosing his words with care. He did not want to communicate the sudden emptiness that had descended on him at Asmat's words. "She will be an asset to us and to her future husband. We have brought her up well."

"It must be a brilliant marriage, Ghias. Someone who will understand her needs, encourage her spirit. I know she will make a good wife."

"And so it shall be, my dear. I will contact my friends for a suitable husband, and when I find him I shall request permission from the Emperor." As with any marriage that took place in the vicinity of the court, Ghias had to request—at least formally—permission from Akbar.

With that, Ghias fell into a restless sleep.

Across the courtyard, Mehrunnisa lay awake on a cotton mattress in her room. Somewhere in the night, a dog barked at a passing stranger, then yelped with pain as a stone found its mark. Mehrunnisa lay still, hands clasped on her stomach, her mind revolving with thoughts. Back to Lahore at last. Back to the court, to the imperial *zenana*, to the Empress with her quick mannerisms and her biting sarcasm. But most of all, most of all, back to Salim.

Mehrunnisa turned on her side, pillowed her head on her arm, and closed her eyes, a smile on her face as sleep claimed her.

THEY EMBARKED ON their long journey back to Lahore, where the Emperor held court. As Ghias rode his sturdy mountain horse, its measured hoofbeats brought memories of another day, so long in the past, when they had made their first trip through the Khyber Pass into Hindustan. Life had been uncertain then, each succeeding day void of security. The winter's cold had bitten into their tired bodies. Now he went at the Emperor's invitation. At the end of each day, they settled into thick canvas tents, slept on feather-stuffed mattresses, rested their heads on silk-covered pillows. His sons rode beside him—men now, no longer children—and the women of his family traveled in a *howdah* set atop camels.

Upon reaching Lahore, Ghias hurried immediately to pay his respects to Akbar. When he straightened up from the *konish* to look at the Emperor, a mild shock coursed through him. Akbar's hair was almost completely white, and though his face was the same, calm and kind, a hint of sadness touched his eyes. Ghias glanced quickly at Prince Salim, who stood next to the throne. The same sadness appeared to echo through him. So it was true, Ghias thought. He had heard rumors about the Emperor's illness and *hakim* Humam. Such things never stayed secret.

"You have done the empire a great service at Kabul," Akbar said.

Ghias turned to him. "Your Majesty is too kind. I only did my job."

"Still," Akbar continued, "we are pleased with your work."

At a sign from Akbar, an attendant came forward, bearing a large gold tray on which reposed a jeweled sword and a garment of honor. Ghias knelt. Akbar lifted the jeweled sword and the coat and presented them to him.

The imperial harem watched the proceedings from an overhead balcony screened from view. As soon as the short ceremony was over, Ruqayya Sultan Begam spoke from behind the screen. "Your Majesty, please ask Mirza Beg to send his wife and his daughter Mehrunnisa to wait upon us."

Akbar looked at Ghias.

"It shall be done, your Majesty." Ghias turned toward the balcony. "They will be honored to hear that you have commanded their presence."

He moved back to his place in the *darbar*, glad to be at Lahore again. At the end of the morning audience, the Emperor's face crumpled suddenly with fatigue. Ghias saw Prince Salim reach out a hand to his father, then withdraw it when Akbar turned away. It was done so quickly that only a few courtiers saw it happen. The court bowed as the Emperor left, followed by Prince Salim. Ghias returned home, thinking about the *darbar*. During the next few weeks he would talk with the other nobles to find out as much as he could about the Humam incident. Was it true? Or just a fabrication by courtiers who did not like Prince Salim? What a burden the crown was, he thought. Kings had always fought brothers and fathers and sons for it.

WHEN MEHRUNNISA ENTERED Ruqayya's apartments the next morning, a game of chess was in progress between two of Akbar's concubines. A few ladies sat around them in silence, following the game. Incense burned in gold and silver stands, swirling blue smoke around the room and perfuming the air with sandalwood. Slave girls and eunuchs stood or knelt around other women, offering wine and sherbet, plying peacock feather fans. A bird tweeted, and Mehrunnisa turned to the sound. One of the Emperor's concubines lay on a divan, elbows propped on a velvet bolster, a yellow and red lovebird perched on her fingers. She made kissing sounds to the bird, and it promptly put is beak forward for a kiss. Its reward was a sliver of almond. The bird chirruped happily and flapped shorn wings. Mehrunnisa turned away, wondering whether she should attract the Empress's attention.

Just then, Ruqayya noticed her and beckoned from her divan, where she sat smoking a *hukkah*. Mehrunnisa walked slowly to the Empress, suddenly feeling shy. She had not seen Ruqayya in four years; it seemed a long time. Ruqayya's hair was now liberally sprinkled with gray, and a few more wrinkles creased her round face, but the eyes were the same as ever—dark, lively, darting around the room incessantly.

"So you are back?" Ruqayya said by way of a greeting.

"Yes, your Majesty. We returned yesterday," Mehrunnisa replied, falling back into the relationship as though she had not left. Ruqayya possessed the talent to put everyone at ease, from the most menial servant to Akbar himself. A talent she should learn too, Mehrunnisa decided. One day Salim would value her as much because of it.

"How was Kabul? I hear your father has distinguished himself there."

Mehrunnisa opened her mouth to answer, but before she could, a curly-haired little boy toddled into the room and flung himself onto Ruqayya's lap.

"Ma, sweets," he said peremptorily, stretching out a chubby hand.

Mehrunnisa looked at him in surprise. Ruqayya had no children, so who was this boy? To be sure, there were hundreds of "mothers" for every baby born in the *zenana*, but she had never before seen any child wrap the autocratic Padshah Begam around his little finger as this one had.

Ruqayya's face was wreathed in smiles. She leaned over to the silver dish at her elbow and fed the *burfis* to the boy herself, unmindful that his sticky fingers were clutching her *choli*, smearing *ghee* all over it and her bare midriff.

"Meet my son, Mehrunnisa." Ruqayya smiled at her over the little boy's head. "This is Khurram."

"Your son?" Mehrunnisa blurted out, unable to stop herself in time.

"Yes, he is mine. All mine." Ruqayya wrapped her arms around Khurram. He squirmed in her lap. She kissed the soft curls on his head and let him go. As he ran out of the room, followed by his attendants, she turned to Mehrunnisa and said defiantly, "I may not have given birth to him, but he is nonetheless my son."

"Of course, your Majesty," Mehrunnisa mumbled.

"Tell me about your stay in Kabul." Ruqayya lay back on the divan and picked up the mouthpiece of the *hukkah*.

For the next hour, Mehrunnisa talked in a low voice so as not to disturb the chess players, prodded every now and then by a question from the Empress. Before she left, Ruqayya had returned to her normal good humor. She reached out and touched Mehrunnisa's face lightly. "You have turned into a beautiful girl. How old are you now?"

Mehrunnisa told her.

"Well, it's time you got married, my dear. Soon you will be an old maid." The Empress waved her hand in dismissal. "Come tomorrow at the same time."

At home, Mehrunnisa learned about Khurram from Asmat. He was Salim's third son by his wife Jagat Gosini, and he had lived the last two years in Ruqayya's apartments, believing *her* to be his mother. Akbar had named him Khurram, "Joy," because his birth had brought much happiness to the court and the aging Emperor.

Upon his birth, Ruqayya Sultan Begam had demanded custody of Khurram. Akbar, unable to deny his wife anything, commanded that the child be weaned from his mother and put in the care of his Padshah Begam Ruqayya. But why this child, Mehrunnisa wondered. Salim had other sons, but Ruqayya had wanted this one, born of Salim's second wife—the iron princess, the one who had always defied Ruqayya's authority. Even as her mother talked on, Mehrunnisa smiled to herself. Ruqayya was cruel, merciless, and dangerous. Princess Jagat Gosini should have taken more care to appease her when she had first entered Salim's harem. Now, for her arrogance, her child had been whisked away from her.

*   *   *

A FEW MONTHS passed. Mehrunnisa visited the imperial harem every day after finishing her studies, eagerly leaving her books. Her relationship with the Empress had changed subtly. Ruqayya no longer treated her like a child. She let Mehrunnisa stay in the room when her stewards came to visit, bringing with them the accounts from all the lands the Empress owned in the empire. "Listen and learn, Mehrunnisa," she said. "A woman must not be completely reliant on a man, either for money or for love."

Ruqayya also began to depend more and more on Mehrunnisa, especially when it came to Prince Khurram. The Empress guarded the little boy jealously and would allow no one to come too close to him in case they stole his affections. One of the noblemen's wives was his appointed nurse. Each morning, she rose at sunrise and came to the *zenana* to start her duties, leaving only at night after Khurram had been put to bed. But some days she could not come because of her responsibilities to her husband and children. On those days, the Empress grudgingly let Mehrunnisa take charge of Khurram, and as time passed, she came to trust her more.

The usually levelheaded Ruqayya was obsessed with the child, to such a point that his mother, Princess Jagat Gosini, was permitted only brief weekly visits. Mehrunnisa usually stood to one side and watched as Jagat Gosini came to see her son under Ruqayya's alert scrutiny. The princess ignored Mehrunnisa, as she did the other waiting women, but finally Mehrunnisa came face to face with Prince Salim's most influential wife.

Khurram had been in a particularly boisterous mood one afternoon; he refused to take his nap and insisted on playing. The Empress's nerves had frayed with his incessant chatter. She sent Khurram out with Mehrunnisa to the gardens attached to her apartments, with a reminder to keep him in the shade.

They sat together in the verandah, watching as the sun made rainbows around a fountain in one corner of the garden. In another corner, a huge *peepul* spread its dense branches. A few *zenana* women sat under the *peepul*, *ghagaras* gathered over their knees. They were piping henna patterns on their feet and legs, drawing intricate curved designs with the thin black paste. Mehrunnisa saw one woman lean over to another and bare her shoulders, pushing her *choli* down her arms. Then, using a cone-shaped leaf filled with henna, she drew a pattern across one shoulder, curved it down into the woman's cleavage, and drew it up the other shoulder. When the henna dried and was washed away, the woman would have a forest of red flowers glowing on her skin. She was one of the Emperor's slaves and would dance that night for Akbar, clad in very little but henna designs. The Emperor, busy as he was with matters of state, always had time to enjoy his inventive slave girls.

For those few minutes they could be rewarded with jewels of unimaginable beauty and value, grants of lands and estates—enough to make them comfortable for the rest of their lives. They did not all have Empress Ruqayya's advantages. Ruqayya had known Akbar all her life, for they were cousins. They had grown up together, knowing they would marry one day. The Empress never talked of her early days of marriage to the Emperor. Had he looked at her then with lust, perhaps? Had he sought her with a hunger no other woman could satisfy? Or had their relationship always been thus: comfortable, steady, strong, with an implicit trust that nothing could shake?

There was only one other woman in Akbar's harem whose intimacy with him came close to Ruqayya's: Salima Sultan Begam, who was Akbar's uncle Gulrukh's daughter, and who was first cousin to Ruqayya, too. Akbar was Salima's second husband, and Mehrunnisa knew, from rumors in the *zenana*, that Ruqayya had given her blessings to the marriage. The relationship between the two women was one of utmost friendliness and respect. They had known each other all their lives, too, but there was no jealousy, no spite. They divided Akbar's affections, with a larger part—unsaid and unacknowledged—going to Ruqayya, for she was a wife of longer standing. But unlike Ruqayya, Mehrunnisa did not think she could bear to share Salim with anyone else, no mater how well she knew or loved her.

Mehrunnisa watched as Khurram got up and went running to a flower bed. He picked up a stick and began digging around the poppies, throwing clumps of dirt over his shoulder. She looked down at her hands, bare of henna. On her wedding day, she too would have designs on them. And one day, she would dress her body in henna for Salim. She flushed and put her hands behind her back.

A shower of dirt fell over her, and she looked up. Prince Khurram was still digging furiously in the dirt. He howled when she rushed over and tried to pick him up.

"Let me go, Nisa. Let me go! I command you."

"Your Highness, please, you cannot play in the dirt. You know it is forbidden. Please come back to the verandah."

"No!" he yelled again, screwing up his small face to cry.

Mehrunnisa set him down hurriedly. Khurram's cries would wake the whole *zenana*. "All right, let us do something else. What would you like to do?"

"Play a game with me, Nisa."

Anything to keep him from bawling. "What shall we play, your Highness?"

"Hide-and-seek," Khurram said promptly. "I go hide."

Mehrunnisa groaned. Khurram's idea of hide-and-seek was to crawl behind the short hedges lining the stone pathways or climb the big *chenar* trees in the courtyard—anything that would get him dirty. And would get her dirty too, she thought ruefully, glancing down at her impeccably washed and ironed *ghagara* and *choli*. But she had to obey him. He was the prince.

"I shall count to fifty. Go hide, your Highness." Mehrunnisa turned to one of the pillars, leaned her head against the cool marble, closed her eyes, and started counting.

". . . Forty-eight, forty-nine, fifty. Ready?"

"Yes," a little voice piped up.

Mehrunnisa smiled when she saw the heron's feather on Khurram's turban bobbing along the hedge to her right. She went down on her hands and knees on the opposite side and started crawling, calling out as she went, "Where are you, your Highness?"

A few minutes later she was hot and filthy. Her *ghagara* had grass stains; her hair had escaped from its pins and clung damply to her forehead. Mehrunnisa wiped her sweating face, leaving a streak of dirt on her cheek. She would have to pretend to search for him a little longer, she thought, dragging herself along the damp grass.

Khurram giggled, and Mehrunnisa turned to peer at him through the hedge. When she turned back, she first saw a pair of feet clad in jeweled kid-leather slippers. Her gaze traveled slowly upward, taking in the pearl-studded pale blue *ghagara*, jeweled hands clasped in front, thin muslin veil billowing in the breeze. The woman's face was classic in its beauty. Her complexion was a rich brown, her eyes a glittering ebony under bow-arched eyebrows, her mouth well formed; the whole was set off by high cheekbones.

Mehrunnisa scrambled to her feet in a hurry, almost tripping over her long skirts. "Your Highness, I did not see you coming."

"Obviously," Jagat Gosini said. "Who are you?"

"Who are *you?*"

Both turned to see Prince Khurram standing up on the other side, his plump arms resting on his hips. Mehrunnisa smiled involuntarily; it was a pose Ruqayya often adopted when she was irritated. She turned to look at Jagat Gosini.

A look of pain crossed Jagat Gosini's face for an instant. Then she drew herself up and said, "I am Princess Jagat Gosini."

Princess Jagat Gosini, not your mother, Mehrunnisa noted wryly. What was she doing here, anyway? Ruqayya would be furious to hear of an unannounced visit.

Khurram, absolutely indifferent, pointed imperiously to the arched exit of the gardens. "Go away. I am playing with Nisa."

"I have come to see you, Khurram." Jagat Gosini lifted her skirts and skipped over the hedge. When she had crossed the stone pathway, she put out a hand.

Khurram dodged her outstretched hand and ran across to Mehrunnisa. He clutched the skirt of her *ghagara* and said, "Go away, or I shall tell my ma."

"No, please . . . I shall go." Her eyes lifted with a malevolent glance to Mehrunnisa. "You are to say nothing of this to the Empress, do you understand?"

"Yes, your Highness," Mehrunnisa murmured.

"Who are you? Where is Khurram's nurse?"

"Mirza Ghias Beg is my father, your Highness."

"Oh?" The well shaped eyebrows lifted. "I have not heard of your father. Send for Khurram's nurse immediately."

Mehrunnisa's face grew hot. She took a deep breath to steady herself and chose her words carefully. "Your Highness, the Empress will send for us as soon as her nap is over. We must go inside now."

Jagat Gosini nodded. "Remember, not a word to the Empress." She held up a warning finger. "If you say anything, I will make your life miserable."

"I can only obey your Highness's commands," Mehrunnisa said. She let her hand fall to caress Khurram's curly head and watched warily as Jagat Gosini's face twisted with hatred and grief. Any brief sympathy she might have felt for Jagat Gosini had vanished with those unfeeling words. The princess might not know who her father was, but she would remember Mehrunnisa. Khurram clung even tighter to her legs, and Mehrunnisa bent to pick him up. He put his head on her shoulder and watched his mother with curious eyes.

The princess turned around and stalked out of the gardens. Mehrunnisa drew Khurram to the shade of a *neem* tree and sat down. The prince laid his head in her lap and soon fell asleep. Mehrunnisa stared at the haze dancing over the bright yellow sunflowers. She had finally talked to Salim's second wife. It was said in the *zenana* that Jagat Gosini was very powerful in Salim's harem, that she had the prince under her thumb. But she was certainly too arrogant and lacking in common courtesy.

Perhaps she could change all that, Mehrunnisa thought slowly. So far, Salim had not seen her since their return from Kabul. He came to Ruqayya's apartments only once a month, in the evenings after she had left to go home. And she herself had been in no hurry to meet the prince, either. For the past few months, Mehrunnisa had watched and learned about the workings of the harem from the *zenana* ladies. She had political conversations with her father at the end of his day's work. She talked with her mother when she visited other palaces in the imperial harem, and all the time she absorbed information about *zenana* life, Salim's likes and dislikes, and the situation at court. Ghias, impulsive most of the time, had yet managed to impart some of his patience to his daughter, which she used with a supreme confidence in her abilities.

But now the time had come to captivate the prince, Mehrunnisa thought, goaded into action by Jagat Gosini's cruel words. She glanced at her reflection in the nearby pool. Many people had told her she was beautiful, but would that be enough for Salim? Her brows came together in thought as she picked a blade of grass and ran her fingers over it.

She looked over at the women under the *peepul* tree. The slave girl now had her entire back and the backs of her legs covered with henna designs. She lay on her stomach, her arms spread out, letting the black paste dry on her body. It was power; these women knew how to have it and to hold it. From Ruqayya she had learned the value of conversation, of exuding comfort. In these other women of the harem, Mehrunnisa had seen the assurance that only physical beauty can provide.

Ten minutes later, she smiled and looked down at the curly head in her lap. Perhaps Jagat Gosini would be more careful when both her husband and her son were at Mehrunnisa's feet.

EVEN AS MEHRUNNISA sat dreaming in the imperial gardens, Ali Quli Khan Istajlu was announced to the Emperor in the *Diwan-i-am*. He entered the Hall of Public Audience slowly and bowed low as he reached the throne, the back of his right hand touching the floor. He then raised his hand up to his forehead until he stood erect in front of Akbar.

As the Emperor inclined his head, Ali Quli glanced surreptitiously at the Khan-i-khanan, the commander-in-chief of Akbar's army, and his mentor at court. Abdur Rahim nodded. Ali Quli had performed the *taslim* well.

Ali Quli was new to Akbar's court. Like Ghias Beg, he had fled from Persia to India, but after the assassination of Shah Ismail II in 1578. Ali Quli had been a *safarchi*, a table attendant to the Shah. But even then he had known that was not his calling; being a warrior was. He reached Multan and joined the forces of the Khan-i-khanan, who was then on his way down the Indus to lay siege to the king of Thatta, Mirza Jani Beg. After six months of hard fighting, Thatta surrendered to the imperial forces, and Ali Quli distinguished himself in the battle. Abdur Rahim, much impressed by Ali Quli's valor, had promised him an introduction at court. Now the soldier stood in the august present of the great Emperor.

"Is this the brave soldier you have told us so much about, Abdur Rahim?" Akbar asked.

"Yes, your Majesty."

Akbar looked at Ali Quli. He was in his early thirties, tall, broad-shouldered, and strong, his skin ravaged by countless suns, a fearless look in his eyes.

"We are pleased with your dedication and loyalty to the throne," Akbar said.

An attendant brought Ali Quli the robe of honor and a jeweled sword. Akbar also granted him a small *mansab* of two hundred cavalry and infantry. Overwhelmed by the imperial gifts, Ali Quili fell to his knees and thanked the Emperor.

Akbar was pleased. "We have yet more honors to bestow upon you, Ali Quli. We hope you will remain with the imperial army for many more years."

"I will, your Majesty," Ali Quli said fervently. He bowed again and backed out of the *Diwan-i-am*.

The Emperor watched him leave thoughtfully. He knew many men like the young Persian: brave, adventurous, though essentially restless. Abdur Rahim, a man not usually given to effusiveness, had been profuse in praise of the young man. But how much longer would Ali Quli serve his crown?

The soldier needed stability, an anchor that would keep him in the Mughal Empire. Marriage would provide that anchor.

Akbar's eyes roamed over the silent assembly. Which of his courtiers had a daughter who would make a suitable bride for the Persian soldier?

The Emperor's gaze passed over, returned, and finally rested on one man. He searched through his vast memory for details of the courtier's family. Then Akbar nodded happily, well pleased with himself. It would be a good match. Later that afternoon, he would talk to his Padshah Begam Ruqayya; she would tell him whether he had made the right decision.

The Emperor was looking at Ghias Beg.

FOUR

The daughter, who had been born to Aiafs in the desert . . . was
educated with the utmost care and attention. In music, in
dancing, in poetry, in painting, she had no equal among her sex.
Her disposition was volatile, her wit lively and satirical, her spirit
lofty and uncontrouled.
> —Alexander Dow,
> *The History of Hindostan*

"Mirza Ghias Beg, his imperial Majesty, Emperor Akbar,
commands your presence," the Mir Tozak, Master of Ceremonies,
intoned.

Court was in session at the *Diwan-i-khas*, the Hall of Private
Audience. Ghias came forward and performed the *konish*, placing the
palm of his right hand on his head and bowing to the Emperor. The *konish* indicated that the saluter placed his head in the hand of humility and
gave it to the royal assembly, showing his readiness to obey any service
demanded of him.

Ghias straightened up and remained standing. No one was given the
privilege of sitting in the Emperor's presence, and Ghias would have considered it sacrilegious to do so.

"Mirza Geg, we have called you here for a special purpose."

"Your wish is my command, Padshah."

"Do you have a daughter of marriageable age?"

Ghias looked at Akbar in surprise.

"Her name is Mehrunnisa, your Majesty," Ruqayya called out from
behind the screen.

"Ah, yes. Mehrunnisa. It is a good name," Akbar said. He turned to
Ghias. "There is a brave young man at court named Ali Quli Khan."

"I remember the soldier well, your Majesty," Ghias replied cautiously. So this was why the Emperor had commanded his presence.

"We have decided to honor him, Ghias. And what better way to do so than to give him the hand of your daughter in marriage? It will be a good alliance. You are both Persian and share the same ancestry and history. We wish for the marriage to take place."

"Yes, your Majesty."

He knew that the Emperor's wishes were as good as a command. There was nothing to do but agree. His search for an appropriate bride-groom for his darling Mehrunnisa was over. Ali Quli had impressed Ghias on the day he had been presented at court. Pushing aside doubts that suddenly and involuntarily came rushing to his mind, Ghias bowed his head.

"I shall immediately start proceedings for the marriage, your Majesty."

GHIAS RODE HOME in the gathering dusk, thinking of his audience with the Emperor. As his horse ambled down the well-known path home, Ghias let his mind wander again as it had done all day since his morning audience with the Emperor. He did not doubt the matter had been insti-gated, at least in part, by the Padshah Begam Ruqayya. She had betrayed her interest by speaking up in court. Surely the Empress would want the best for his daughter? Around Ghias, the twilight was tinted gray-blue with smoke from cooking fires. The spicy tang of wood smoke brought sudden memories of the day he had stood at the base of the tree where he had left Mehrunnisa, thinking he would never see his daughter again. Now, after all these years, she was to leave him again.

The evening call for prayer, the fourth of the day, rang from atop the mosques around Lahore as Ghias entered the front courtyard of his house. In an inner courtyard, Asmat and their children were already on their knees, facing west toward Mecca. Ghias dismounted, threw the reins to the waiting groom, and hurried in to join them.

They lifted their hands in prayer and silently mouthed the sacred verses, bowing to the ground at the end. Ghias watched as Mehrunnisa, Khadija, Manija, and Shahpur rose from their knees and walked inside the house. Darkness was falling fast, and the servants moved around noiselessly, lighting oil lamps inside the house and in the courtyard. He called out to Asmat.

She came to him, the bells of her anklets jingling as she walked. "Why were you late today? The call for prayer has already been made."

"I had an interesting audience with the Emperor."

Asmat looked at him questioningly.

"He has commanded our daughter for Ali Quli."

Asmat sat down on the stone bench in the garden. "Who is he?"

"A soldier, a very brave soldier, who helped the Khan-i-khanan in his conquest of Thatta." Ghias hesitated before adding, "Ali Quli is from Persia, like us, and he was a *safarchi* to Shah Ismail II."

Asmat's eyebrows met in a frown. She was silent for some time, and then said slowly, "Then he must be considerably older than Mehrunnisa."

"Asmat, the Emperor has commanded us." Ghias took her hand. "I saw Ali Quli presented at court. He has distinguished himself in battle and is now a favorite of the Emperor. By asking for Mehrunnisa, the Emperor is doing us a great honor. He wants the two Persian families to be united."

"But a common soldier, Ghias," Asmat protested. "What would he know of the classics, and poetry, and music? Would he be the right choice for a daughter we have so carefully reared, one who is so proficient in the literary arts, so well educated and so . . . delicate?"

"Asmat." Ghias turned to her. "It will be a good alliance. I am sure Ali Quli will be kind to Mehrunnisa, that he will look after her well. What more can we ask of a *rishta?*"

Asmat pulled her hand out of his, her face flaming with anger. "Listen to yourself, Ghias. Is this what we wanted for Mehrunnisa? Is this what we have talked about? Are you so blind to your daughter's needs that you cannot see this will not be a good alliance? It is your responsibility to make sure she is happy."

"Enough," Ghias roared. "Send Mehrunnisa to me now."

Asmat rose and stood looking down at her husband. Her voice was quiet. "Do not raise your voice at me, Ghias. I have never gone against your wishes before in all the years we have been married. But to send our child away to such a home . . ."

Ghias put his arms around her and pulled her to him, his head against her stomach. The scent of musk enveloped him. "I am sorry." His voice was muffled. He raised his head to look at Asmat. But she looked away from him, her arms held stiffly at her sides. She had voiced a concern he had not dared even to think about, and he had shouted at her for it. "You know that I cannot disobey the Emperor. Ali Quli is to be our son-in-law, and we must start treating him with the respect he deserves. Send Mehrunnisa to me."

Asmat nodded and moved away from the circle of his arms. "It will be as you say, my lord."

Deeply angry, she went into the house. Was it for this Mehrunnisa had come back to them? Even as this thought came to her mind she knew that what Ghias said was true. The moment Akbar had expressed a wish for a union between Mehrunnisa and Ali Quli, the matter had been decided. There was nothing Ghias could do. Neither of the two families would dare refuse the Emperor. Still . . . a soldier for Mehrunnisa?

MEHRUNNISA WALKED SLOWLY toward her father. He sat with his face in a shadow, a thoughtful expression on his brow. She stopped a few paces away, wondering why he had called for her. Her mother had seemed upset, barely looking at her when she gave Mehrunnisa the message from Ghias. Her eyes had been bright, as if she were crying.

Mehrunnisa stepped up to Ghias and put a hand on his shoulder. "Bapa . . ."

"Ah, you are here, *beta*." Ghias turned and caught her hand. He patted the bench next to him. "Come, sit down. I have something very important to tell you."

Mehrunnisa sat down and looked into his face. Ghias was smiling, but his smile seemed too forced; it did not reach his eyes. A feeling of dread rose in her, and she tried to shake it off.

"Mehrunnisa, I have found a bridegroom for you," Ghias said abruptly.

"Oh." Her hands left her lap to grasp the edge of the bench, her fingers clutching, slipping against the smooth stone. This could not be happening. Was she to be married already? What of Salim?

"He is a very handsome man, a brave soldier, a prince among princes."

Mehrunnisa glanced up quickly, hope filling her. A prince? Surely, Ghias could not be talking of . . .

"His name is Ali Quli Khan Istajlu. Like us, he is from Persia. It is our good fortune that the Emperor himself has commanded this marriage. We are again given an opportunity to serve him. . . ." Ghias continued in the same vein, but Mehrunnisa heard him no more.

She stared unseeingly into the darkening garden. She was to be married to a common soldier. Gone were the dreams of being an Empress, of ruling the great Mughal Empire. How absurd her fantasies had been. They had been childhood dreams, better left in childhood.

Somewhere, far away, she could hear the lamplighters greeting each other in the street. The once pleasant perfume from the opening *rath-ki-rani*, Queen of the Night flowers, now hung stifling in the humid night air. The crickets had begun their incessant chirping, sounding unnaturally loud in the silent courtyard. Her father droned on in the background.

"Mehrunnisa?"

She was suddenly aware that Ghias had finished talking and was looking at her expectantly. "You have not said anything, my dear."

"Can I say no?"

Ghias frowned. "Have you been talking with your mother?"

"What does Maji have to do with this? I am the one who is to be married to a soldier," Mehrunnisa said bitterly. "Why? . . . " *Why could it not be Salim?*

Ghias stared at her until she lowered her eyes. "It would seem I was too indulgent with you, Nisa, have given you too many liberties. But in this matter there will be no argument. It is not your choice who you marry. I am telling you of the *rishta;* most fathers would not even have done this."

With every word, Mehrunnisa felt shame and guilt flood over her. She had addressed her Bapa without respect. Ghias had never before spoken to her like this; he always hid his anger well.

"I shall do whatever you want."

"Don't you want to know more about your bridegroom, my dear?" Ghias asked.

She shook her head. "No."

A flash of pain crossed Ghias's features, so Mehrunnisa forced a smile on her face and added, "I do want to know, Bapa. Perhaps later. All this . . . it is so sudden."

Ghias leaned over and kissed her forehead. "Yes. It is not every day a girl gets such a wonderful proposal of marriage. We are very lucky, *beta.*" He drew back. "Now go see that dinner is readied. I am hungry."

Mehrunnisa wanted to fling her arms around her father's neck and plead with him. Was it decided already? Just like that? Was the *rishta* fixed? Was there no turning back from it? When she looked at her father, his expression was forbidding. She could ask other questions—about her husband-to-be—but not these. She rose tiredly from the bench. Her father's voice stopped her. "You can tell your Maji that I will call upon Ali Quli tomorrow to discuss the marriage."

"Yes, Bapa."

Mehrunnisa stumbled to the verandah in a daze, her heart filling with despair. She turned back to glance at her father.

Ghias sat motionless on the bench, his shoulders hunched, a dissatisfied look on his face.

THE NEXT DAY, Mehrunnisa went to the royal palace as usual to pay her respects to Ruqayya Sultan Begam. It seemed everyone knew of her pending engagement to Ali Quli. The guards at the *zenana* gate, tough

Kashmiri ladies, smiled at her knowingly. The eunuchs giggled and called out Ali Quli's name as she walked through the courtyard, and the slave girls smirked as she passed. Mehrunnisa ignored all the well-meant jibes and went swiftly to the Padshah Begam's palace. Ruqayya was being attended to by three slave girls, who were massaging her body with perfumed oils.

"So, what do you think of your bridegroom?" Ruqayya demanded, lifting herself on an elbow.

"I have not seen him yet, your Majesty."

"Of course not. No self-respecting girl sees her husband before the engagement. But tell me, what do you think of my choice?"

"*Your* choice, your Majesty?" Mehrunnisa lifted surprised eyes at the Empress.

"Yes." Ruqayya laughed with abandon, her plump face round with glee. "Have I not made a good selection?"

"Yes, your Majesty," she replied in a low voice. So the Empress was behind the decision. Why? And why had Ruqayya not told her of this earlier?

"It is high time you got married, my dear. Ali Quli is a little older than you are, but he will mold you into the perfect wife. And he is a soldier. Perhaps when he goes on campaign, he will leave you here with me," Ruqayya said.

Now Mehrunnisa knew why Ruqayya had made such a choice. Her instincts, although charitable, were also somewhat selfish.

"I shall always be at your command, your Majesty."

"Yes." Ruqayya lay back and closed her eyes. She reached out for Mehrunnisa's hand. "Now you shall always be with me. It is a good *rishta*, Mehrunnisa. The Emperor himself wants it."

"I thought you . . ." Mehrunnisa started.

"What the Emperor wants, I want." Ruqayya looked hard at her. "Are you unhappy? Is there someone else your heart fancies?"

"No, your Majesty. Of course not," Mehrunnisa said quickly, turning away.

Ruqayya's sharp gaze burned through her back. The Empress was very shrewd.

"Mehrunnisa," Ruqayya said gently. "This is for the best."

Mehrunnisa said nothing, busying herself with folding a veil that lay nearby. Ruqayya would never guess. It was unthinkable to the Empress that Mehrunnisa would want Prince Salim.

A few days later, Mah Banu, wife of the Khan-i-khanan Abdur Rahim, standing in as Ali Quli's mother, came to Ghias Beg's house with gifts for the bride and her family. Servants brought in brass trays loaded with silks, satins, and jewels of all kinds.

Mehrunnisa sat through the engagement ceremony in a stupor, a gold *zari*-embroidered pink veil covering her face. One look at her future husband had been enough. Ali Quli had come striding into the room full of battlefield bravado. He was a tall man, much taller than her father, but to see them side by side, one would think they were the same age. Ali Quli was only six years younger than Ghias. But there the resemblance ended. Ali Quli was every inch a soldier from his sunburned skin, unkempt beard, and harsh laugh to his callused hands more used to holding a mace or sword than a book of poems.

She watched her dreams slipping away as Ghias Beg solemnly promised to wed her to the brave soldier Ali Quli Khan Istajlu. All through the ceremony her father studiously kept his gaze from meeting hers.

PRINCE SALIM LIFTED his turban and wiped his forehead with a camphor-doused handkerchief. There was not even the slightest breeze. He put a hand up to shade his eyes and looked at the sun. Two o'clock—the middle of the afternoon. He closed his eyes wearily. Why had he allowed himself to be persuaded into this?

"We shall be there soon, your Highness."

Salim turned to Jagat Gosini. "Why couldn't you have chosen the evening? It is much cooler then."

"Now is the best time, my lord. Her Majesty, Ruqayya Sultan Begam, will be taking her nap, and we can spend some time alone with our son."

"All right," Salim mumbled, dragging his feet. He had drunk too much wine in the morning as usual and was feeling queasy in the heat. His head ached. The attendants who followed the royal couple were talking too loudly; their laughter grated on his nerves.

He would not have agreed to his wife's suggestion if the Emperor himself had not hinted that he was being remiss in his fatherly duties. Salim grimaced. The Emperor was not as quick to point out his responsibilities to his other two sons, Khusrau and Parviz, only to Khurram. For it was Khurram whom Akbar saw most often, since he spent most of his time in Ruqayya's apartments.

Since Akbar's near-fatal brush with colic two years earlier, the Emperor could hardly look at Salim without suspicion. And though Salim felt remorse every time he considered that his father might have died as a result of Humam's overzealousness, discontent still plagued him. He still had an undeniable, deep yearning to feel the weight of the crown on his head. Salim tried to be with his father and learn from him, but between them hung the slivered threads of a shattered relationship, fragile as a broken cobweb. Between them also were Salim's courtiers—Mahabat, Qutubuddin, Sayyid—men he had known since childhood, men he had known better than his own father. It was hard to resist them, or their influence.

Salim's shoulders slouched as the entourage entered the silent courtyard outside Ruqayya's apartments. He caught the flutter of white muslin through the corner of his eye and stopped short, lifting his head for a better look.

Ya Allah! Was he in Paradise? Words from the Holy Book came unbidden to his mind: "The believers shall find themselves reclining upon couches lined with brocade, the fruits of the garden nigh to gather; and will find therein maidens restraining their glances, untouched before them by any man or Jinn, lovely as rubies, beautiful as coral."

She was all that and more. He stared at her, his gaze riveted, every-

thing else fading around her. His attendants, chattering among themselves, fell silent, and glanced at him with curiosity. Jagat Gosini lifted a
hand to Salim's arm, but he was already moving forward, leaving her
standing under the wide stone arch.

Salim tiptoed into the courtyard. He was afraid to make any sudden
movement, afraid that she would fly away, and he would wake to find it
all a dream.

The girl sat on the edge of a goldfish pond, her feet dangling in the
water. It was a heat-smothered day, but the courtyard was cool. The
stone floor was chilled by a running stream of water underneath, falling
into pools dispersed artistically around the courtyard. Lotus flowers and
lilies bloomed white and red in the reservoirs, and huge *banyan* trees provided shade. The hush was broken by the soothing drone of bees and the
musical tinkle of water rushing through the channels.

Salim moved forward softly until he was by her side. He stood looking
down at a glossy black head of hair and long eyelashes against a
porcelain-smooth cheek. A pink rose lay against her nape, its stem lost in
her hair. It perfumed the air around them.

"Who are you, beautiful lady?"

Menhrunnisa looked up, startled.

Salim fell headlong in love with a pair of surprised blue eyes.

Mehrunnisa rose hastily, splashing water on Salim. A deep flush
spread over her face and neck as she stood before him, slim and proud,
her back straight.

Salim looked her over from the top of her head to her feet, the nails
painted red with henna and still wet from the pool. His gaze moved slowly
up, skirting the pleats of her long *ghagara*, spangled with shimmering white
stars, past her waist hidden under the folds of a white chiffon veil, over
the curve of her shoulders. Blood rushed to his ears as he saw the pulse
fluttering at the slender throat partially hidden under a shroud of hair.

"I beg pardon, your Highness," Mehrunnisa said in a low voice, so low
that Salim had to strain his ears to catch the words. The musical tones
enchanted him even more.

He reached for her hand, but she pulled away from him, turning her face as she did so.

"Don't you know who I am?" he demanded.

"Yes, sire."

"Your Highness." Jagat Gosini came up to Salim, her face set in unyielding lines.

"Who is she?" Salim asked, still looking at Mehrunnisa. She had turned back to him now.

"The daughter of some lowly courtier, I believe," Jagat Gosini said. "Who is your father, girl?"

The two women stared at each other, neither willing to break eye contact. Mehrunnisa smiled, a quick curving of her lips. "But your Highness knows who I am. We met once in these gardens."

"Did we?" the princess said disdainfully. "I do not remember."

"Ah, but you must remember, your Highness." Mehrunnisa's voice was brittle, each word enunciated carefully. Again that insult to her Bapa. Somewhere in her mind was the advice of caution, of not speaking rashly to Jagat Gosini. But anger overcame all that advice. "I look after Prince Khurram, Empress Ruqayya's son."

"*My* son!"

Mehrunnisa turned toward Ruqayya's apartments, the windows shaded under the *banyan*. "Yes, forgive me. Your son, of course. It's only that he calls the Empress 'ma.' "

Salim watched this interchange in bewilderment, looking from Mehrunnisa to Jagat Gosini. An admiration rose in him for this beautiful woman who sparred so brilliantly with his wife. She had courage. Few people dared to talk with his second wife in this manner. Who was she? How had he not seen her before?

He said quietly to Jagat Gosini, "Leave us, my dear. I wish to talk with her."

Jagat Gosini flushed and drew herself up. "We must go to our son now, your Highness."

"Go. I will meet you later."

But the princess stood where she was.

Salim nodded with a sigh, realizing what he had just said to her. He watched as Mehrunnisa bowed to both of them and turned to leave. "What is your name?"

Mehrunnisa shook her head and walked away from them.

Salim took a step toward her, then stopped, torn between her and Jagat Gosini. He would find her again. Every woman in the royal *zenana* was accounted for. If she was not a member of the harem, the guards would know who she was and where she came form. A petal from the rose in her hair lay on the ground. Salim bent and picked it up, cradling it in the palm of his hand as though it were a precious jewel.

The petal fell from Salim's hand into the pool. He watched as a gold-fish came to nibble at it curiously.

"We must go in, your Highness." Jagat Gosini's voice was quiet.

Salim turned to her. "Was it wise to argue like that with the daughter of a lowly nobleman, Jagat? You are a royal princess; you should know better."

"Why do you defend her? Who is she to you? You do not even know her name," she cried, her voice trembling with outrage.

Salim rubbed his jaw, watching his wife's distraught face. "This is interesting, my dear. I wonder why you are so upset with a woman you don't even know. Come, let us go see Khurram."

Khurram was not delighted to see his parents. He had been waked from his afternoon nap to be paraded in front of near strangers, and as a consequence he was irritable and noisy. Salim sat in Ruqayya's apart-ments in a stupor, thinking only of Mehrunnisa. He did not notice his wife glancing at him thoughtfully from time to time.

Finally, in the evening, he went back to his own apartments. And there he found out her name from Hoshiyar Khan. He said it aloud to himself, elongating the "r" sensually. Mehrunnisa, he thought. Surely she was the Sun of Women. What woman could outshine her beauty?

That evening, Jagat Gosini surpassed herself in providing entertain-ment for her lord. The best *nautch* girls were sent for, and they danced superbly, swaying and undulating seductively in front of the prince. Driven to a frenzy by his one glimpse of Mehrunnisa, Salim groped and grabbed at the girls, thinking one, then the other, to be the angel of the morning. All the while Jagat Gosini watched, filled his cup with proper wifely concern, and made sure that the prince's *hukkah* had enough opium. By midnight, Salim was so muddled he could not even recall Mehrunnisa's face.

An hour later, he toppled over from the divan and sprawled out on the floor, asleep before he hit the rug. The music stopped, the lamps were extinguished, and a cool cotton sheet was brought to cover the sleeping prince.

Princess Jagat Gosini stopped at the door of the reception hall and held up her lantern. She was still furious with Mehrunnisa. The girl had belittled her, behaved beyond her station in life. What was she trying to do now? Wasn't it enough that she had the care of Khurram? Did she want Salim too? Dread, cold as a winter night, crept over her when she thought of how Salim had looked at Mehrunnisa. He had been oblivious to everything else around him. The princess shivered. Nothing would come of this meeting today, she promised herself.

She turned and went out, plunging the room in darkness.

FIVE

*When his eyes seemed to devour her, she, as by accident, dropt her
veil; and shone upon him, at once, with all her charms. The
confusion, which she could well feign, on the occasion, heightened
the beauty of her face.*
> —Alexander Dow,
> *The History of Hindostan*

A BREEZE WHISPERED THROUGH THE GARDEN, RUSTLING LONG-
fingered leaves on the mango trees. The muslin curtains on the window
rippled inward gently, letting a shaft of moonlight into the room.
Somewhere in the distance, a hyena howled at the white orb suspended
in the midnight sky.

In her bed, Mehrunnisa lay awake, staring at the gray and black shadows on the ceiling. Khadija slept next to her, her back against
Mehrunnisa's shoulder, her presence comforting in the narrow bed. In
the cobbled street beyond the gardens, there was the sound of a horse's
hooves. An owl hooted softly from its perch on the mango tree, its keen
eyes searching the garden for mice.

Mehrunnisa's thoughts crowded out the sounds and the smells of the
summer night. For the first time, she had come face to face with Salim.
There was an aura of royalty around him. It was there in his rich silk *qaba*
embroidered with rubies, the thick rope of precious white pearls around
his neck, the gorgeous aigrette with an emerald on his turban, the diamonds on his fingers and on the buckles of his shoes—all as glorious as
the sun that shone upon them in the courtyard. And more than that,
Mehrunnisa thought, was Salim's princely bearing. His tone, his manner, had been gentle and polite.

The setting had been perfect; she couldn't have planned it better herself. This was how she had dreamed Salim and she would meet. He had even looked at her with the wonder and awe she had imagined in her plans to captivate the prince.

Mehrunnisa sighed and turned over, trying to find a comfortable spot on the bed. She had finally captured Salim's attention. But why now? After she was already committed to another man?

How different they were from each other. In her mind, since she was eight, she had painted Salim in splendid colors. He was kind. He was charming. He was passionate. And she thought he was all of those things, even in the brief meeting. For he had wanted to send Jagat Gosini away that he could talk with *her*. A feeling of triumph rose in Mehrunnisa because the arrogant princess had been insulted with quiet finesse by Salim. So he did not like her, either; that was another thing they had in common.

She had been thinking of Ali Quli when Salim came upon her. She could not imagine the life she was to have with him. A soldier's wife, perhaps always alone at home, waiting for him to return from his campaigns, never knowing when he left whether he would live or die. Then—that brief moment when time seemed to stop, and she looked at up Salim.

As day broke over the city of Lahore, Mehrunnisa finally fell asleep, her dreams colored by Salim, his charming smile, and above all his royal majesty.

At home, preparations were being made for her wedding to Ali Quli. When there was an event in the house, custom came home; a nobleman had no need to go in search of it. Cloth merchants came with their wares, spreading out bolt after bolt of silks, muslins, and brocades in reds and blues and greens. The next morning, Mehrunnisa sat with Asmat in the front room as the merchants whipped out fabric in clouds around them. "This one, *Sahiba*," they said. "Your daughter will look like a princess in blue to match her eyes." Asmat and Mehrunnisa smiled at each other under their veils; how did they know of the color of her eyes? From the servants?

Over the next few days jewelers came, too, velvet boxes bound tightly in white cloth, to lay out the gold and silver necklaces, anklets, headpieces, earrings, bangles. "Do you like this pattern, *Sahiba*? Or this one? Any design, only two days to make." The *bawarchis* came to hire themselves for the three days with samples of their cooking: golden wheat *halwas* sprinkled with saffron and sugar; lamb and chicken *pulavs* scattered with sultanas; rust-colored *gulab jamuns*, plump with sugar syrup; rich brown goat-gravy curries; and slivers of roasted silver fish, marinated in lime and garlic.

Through all this, Mehrunnisa waited for Salim to call for her, never really believing that she would marry Ali Quli. After the first day passed, she told herself that it was only one day. Surely he had to find out who she was, whose daughter she was. The next day, each time the servants went to answer the front door, she expected to see a guard or a eunuch from the royal palace. Then she realized that of course he could not call for her. Etiquette must be followed. He would talk with Emperor Akbar, and Akbar would call for her Bapa, and Bapa must talk to her. So she waited for Ghias to come home from court each evening. How would Bapa approach the subject? Would he be ecstatic? Of course he would be ecstatic; his daughter would marry Prince Salim. It would be an unexpected honor for him, for all of them, through her.

The days passed thus, sluggishly, every minute straining to eternity. Bapa did not come home looking especially happy. No summons came from Salim. Her hopes died slowly, crushed and withering as time went by. The wedding preparations went on as usual. Miserable, she did not go to the imperial harem to visit the Empress.

Two weeks after the meeting with Salim, Ruqayya Sultan Begam sent an impatient summons.

When Mehrunnisa arrived at the palace, the Padshah Begam scolded her soundly. "Why did you not come to visit me before, child?"

Mehrunnisa stood silent, with her head bowed.

"Is it because of Salim?"

She lifted eyes to her. No doubt Ruqayya had heard of the encounter through Salim's retinue, for she herself had not breathed a word of it to anyone.

"Oh, yes, I know," Ruqayya said sharply in response to Mehrunnisa's unasked question. Then her tone softened. "Come here, child."

Mehrunnisa sat down near the Empress.

"Salim was naturally enamored of you. But believe me, he thinks of it no more. His memory is very short, for some things. And if he saw you again, he would not remember."

Mehrunnisa's heart sank. Was what Ruqayya said true? It must be. That was why Salim had not called for her—not because he was busy with other things, but because he simply did not remember.

"There is nothing you can do, my dear," Ruqayya continued. "Remember that you are promised to another man." Ruqayya put a finger under her chin and tilted her face. "His Majesty would never sanction a breakup of your engagement. Never. Do you understand?"

"Yes, your Majesty," Mehrunnisa said in a low voice. She turned her face away from Ruqayya. What use were all these admonitions? All that mattered was that Salim did not want her.

The Empress clicked her tongue and looked hard at her. "Somehow, I do not believe that you do. Be careful, Mehrunnisa. Your family's honor depends upon you."

THE MINA BAZAAR was in full swing at the royal palace. For three days every month, the harem palaces were thrown open to traders and merchants, who were allowed to set up stalls to display their wares. Since the ladies of the *zenana* went unveiled to the Mina bazaar, only women were allowed to sell the goods; the merchants sent their wives and daughters to keep shop on their behalf.

The ladies of the imperial *zenana* shopped, haggled, and bargained to their hearts' content, and the Emperor joined them in their activities. The bazaar gave the harem ladies a sense of freedom and much pleasure, so Akbar named the event Khushroz, "days of joy."

Prince Salim swayed from side to side in his corner of the Mina bazaar, his eyes dull. He stretched himself and flexed his arms. A shout of laughter came from a jewelry stall, and Salim turned toward the sound, more out of reflex than curiosity.

The Emperor stood there, his arms around two pretty concubines, who were squealing with laughter as the lady of the stall tried to haggle with him for a pair of emerald bracelets.

Salim's wives stood near him, gazing wistfully at the gaily festooned stalls.

The prince gave them an irritable glance and then called to the chief eunuch of his harem. "Hoshiyar, go with my wives and help them select some satin and gold cloth."

"Yes, your Highness." Hoshiyar Khan bowed, turned, and raised his hand to guide Salim's wives, his face impassive. He looked thoughtfully at the prince, wondering at his listlessness. The prince had not been himself for a few weeks now—not since his encounter with the girl in Empress Ruqayya's apartments.

Hoshiyar made sure to keep himself informed. Through his acquisition of knowledge, he had worked his way up the ranks to his current position with cunning and a ruthlessness that helped him get rid of any rivals. In the *zenana*, the ladies treated him with respect and a little fear, for anything Hoshiyar knew to their detriment invariably found its way to Jagat Gosini. Hoshiyar bowed to only one woman: the woman who ruled Salim's harem, Princess Jagat Gosini. He was her eyes and ears outside the walls of the harem; within it, her right-hand man. Intelligent creature that he was, Hoshiyar recognized intelligence in the princess and never tried to undermine her in any way. She would make a powerful enemy. Now she worried about Mehrunnisa. Why? Salim seemed to have forgotten her—but not completely; he was floundering, grasping for something out of his reach. And not really knowing what it was.

"Oh, and take the others with you. I wish to be alone," the prince said.

The servants scampered off with glee. Salim turned slowly and walked toward the gardens.

On the way, a vendor yelled out to him, "Your Highness, look at these beautiful birds."

A young girl sat at a stall surrounded by brass cages, each containing a variety of colored birds. She was quite pretty, her coarse features brightened by her smile. Salim eyed her with appreciation. Taking advantage of his interest, she brought forward a mynah with a bright yellow bill.

"Now isn't that pretty, your Highness?" she tried to cajole, stammering as she did so.

Salim grinned, watching her bravado disappear. She had been bold in calling to him, but now that he stood in front of her, she was suddenly shy. "How much?"

"A special price for you, *huzoor*." She batted her eyelashes becomingly. "Just five rupees."

"Three," Salim said, smiling.

"Oh, *huzoor*," the vendor sighed, putting away the cage. "I wish I could sell it to you for three rupees, but the cost of living is so high. . . ." She suddenly brightened. "I will take four for it."

"Only if you throw in the two pigeons," Salim said, pointing at two pristine, unspeckled Persian pigeons.

"Done."

Salim brought out four silver rupees from his cumberbund and handed them to the girl. He wanted to give her more for such a fine performance, but it would spoil their little game. He looked around for Hoshiyar, who as usual was not far from his side, despite Salim's order to go wait on his wives.

He handed the mynah to Hoshiyar, took out the Persian pigeons, and held them to his chest. They cooed softly in his arms. He rubbed his cheek against their feathers and descended the stone steps into the garden. The noise from the bazaar seemed to fade away. The green lawn stretched out in front of him, luminous with morning dew. Bees droned over the flowers, their wings iridescent in the warm sunlight.

His eye was caught by the red roses on the border in heavy bloom. Their thorns had been trimmed by the royal *malis*, each painstakingly removed by hand to protect the royal family. Salim bent down, and the sweet aroma of sun-fired roses filled his nostrils. He straightened and looked around for Hoshiyar, who was nowhere to be seen. He then saw the veiled girl seated under the dense shade of the *chenar* tree.

"Hey, you!"

She rose and walked up to the prince.

"Hold these for me." Salim handed her the pigeons and went off to pluck the roses. When he came back, the girl was standing there, eyes downcast, holding just one pigeon.

"Where is the other bird?" he demanded angrily.

"Your Highness, it flew away."

"How?"

"Like this!"

To Salim's amazement, the girl lifted her hands, her blue glass bangles falling back with a tinkle on her wrists, and released the second bird. It flew away into the distant sky. He turned back to her, enraged. She was watching the pigeon. His memory stirred. Where had he heard that voice before? A slight breeze swept through the garden, and the veil molded her face.

"Mehrunnisa!"

"Your Highness, I apologize."

Salim waved an impatient hand, letting the roses fall to his feet. "Never mind the bird. Why did you run away from me the other day?"

"I could not stay."

"Why not?" Salim reached for her hand and held it. Her fingers were long and slender, the nails henna-tipped, the skin as smooth as pearls. They stood smiling at each other with no words, just happiness. Salim reached out and pulled her veil from her head. He took a deep breath and expelled it slowly. Suddenly, he ached to touch her everywhere, to feel her skin against his, to hear her voice and her laughter.

"You are the most beautiful woman I have seen, Mehrunnisa."

She tilted her head at him. An errant breeze lifted a lock of her hair and blew it across her mouth. "But you have so many beautiful women in your harem, your Highness. Surely there is one there who surpasses me in beauty?"

Salim tilted his head to the other side, his tone matching the lilt in her voice. "That is simply not possible. What are you doing here alone in the garden? Why are you not at the bazaar?"

"It tired me."

"As it did me." Salim raised her hand to his lips and rubbed his fingers over the back slowly. His touch then strayed down her wrist, rippling over the bangles.

'Your Highness, his Majesty desires your presence." Hoshiyar was standing at the top of the stone steps.

They turned to see the eunuch, his eyes hooded and watchful.

"Tell him I am busy. I shall be there in a few minutes," Salim said.

"Now, your Highness," Hoshiyar said gently. "His Majesty does not like to be kept waiting."

Salim turned to Mehrunnisa. "Will you wait for me? I will be back soon."

"Where would I go, your Highness? If you have commanded me, I can only obey."

He leaned close to her, his eyes bright with amusement. "This from the girl who released my pigeons. I do not command, Mehrunnisa. I request. Please wait, so I can come back to you."

As he left, Mehrunnisa turned away, so she did not see Hoshiyar gazing at her thoughtfully. Rubbing his chin, Hoshiyar followed his master to the Emperor's side.

Mehrunnisa sat down on the stone bench under the tree and pulled her veil back over her head. So he had not forgotten her.

A slow smile spread over her features. She had seen him come into the garden well before he had seen her. She had crouched into the tree, thinking that as he stood in the glare of the sun he would not be able to see her under the shade of the *chenar*. Mehrunnisa drew her knees to her chest, hugged her arms around them, and watched Salim. At that moment she did not care that he had forgotten her, that he did not know who she was. It was enough that fate had given her this one chance. Startled when Salim called upon her to hold the birds, she rose to go to him without thinking. While his back was turned, she deliberately let one of the pigeons loose, wanting to see how he would react. Now, Mehrunnisa sat against the backrest of the bench, playing Salim's every word and gesture over in her mind: the look in his eyes, the feel of his mouth on her hand . . .

She heard the sound of approaching footsteps and looked up with a smile that faded when she saw Ruqayya Sultan Begam entering the garden, attendants in tow. Please, Allah, the Empress should leave before Salim returned. Ruqayya left her servants and came to her.

Mehrunnisa stood up and bowed.

"What are you up to now, Mehrunnisa?" Ruqayya sat down and patted the bench.

"I have no idea what you are talking—"

"Yes, you do. Listen to me. Salim may outwardly be a man, but inside he is a child. He is always searching for his ideal mate." Ruqayya paused and stared hard at Mehrunnisa. "I can see you know the prince's character and are taking advantage of it."

"Your Majesty," Mehrunnisa protested hotly. "That is unfair. I am doing nothing of the sort. The prince is interested in me. Why shouldn't I . . . encourage that interest?"

"Because you are as good as married, that's why," Ruqayya said firmly. "And his Majesty will not sanction an end to your betrothal."

"Why not?"

"My dear, you were away from court when the incident took place. Prince Salim tried to poison the Emperor through one of the royal physicians."

"That is not true—it is just a rumor."

Ruqayya smiled grimly and said, "Are you doubting my word?"

Mehrunnisa shook her head.

"It is true. And it is the reason why the Emperor and Salim have been at odds for the past two years." The Empress took Mehrunnisa's hand in her own. "The Emperor will not go back on his word, if for nothing else, simply because Salim has proved to be such a disappointment."

"Why is Prince Salim a disappointment to the Emperor? I thought he loved him well." Mehrunnisa's voice was subdued.

Ruqayya sighed and sat back. "He does. Too well perhaps. We all love Salim. We wished for him, prayed for him, and when he came it was as though Allah had smiled on all of us. But over the years . . . the Emperor and Salim have not been able to agree on most matters. The prince wants a crown that is his, and he is unwilling to wait for it. He listens too much to his cohorts, too little to us. He is restless, dissatisfied with his life."

"Perhaps his Majesty should give the prince more?"

The Empress shook her head. "What more can a royal prince, an heir apparent, get from his father? Salim is too young to wear the crown, too rash in acting out his wants. The poisoning incident still rankles with his Majesty; he feels betrayed by this child he so wanted, so cherished. It is something even I do not understand, Mehrunnisa, so you cannot be expected to. Do not lay your hopes on anything but your marriage to Ali Quli. Remember this, my dear: your actions in the future could well undermine your father's standing in court. You do not want that to happen, do you?"

"Of course not, your Majesty. But how would it affect my father?"

"Mehrunnisa, Mirza Beg has promised to marry you to Ali Quli. The Emperor will not agree to go back on his word, and if you persist in encouraging Salim, your father will have to shoulder the blame."

Silence stretched between the two women as the Empress watched the play of emotions across Mehrunnisa's face.

"What shall I do, your Majesty?" Mehrunnisa asked finally.

"YOUR HIGHNESS, THE Empress is talking with Mehrunnisa right now," Hoshiyar bent and whispered in Jagat Gosini's ear.

"Good. Let me know what happens."

Hoshiyar turned to leave, but the princess caught his sleeve and pulled him back. "And Hoshiyar, not a word of this to anyone, do you understand?"

Hoshiyar bowed. "Yes, your Highness. I shall be discretion itself."

Jagat Gosini nodded and turned to her husband. Salim was sitting next to Akbar in the center of the bazaar, his feet tapping to an unheard rhythm. So her lord wanted to rush back to the gardens to meet with his latest paramour. Her glance flickered to the juggler in front of the Emperor. He twirled three flaming torches in the air and manipulated them deftly, flipping them first under one leg, then the other. The ladies of the *zenana* exclaimed aloud, clapping their hands when the juggler finished. He bowed and made way for the snake charmer with his basket of cobras and his mongoose on a leash.

Jagat Gosini rubbed her forehead. There was something about Mehrunnisa she did not like and—if she could admit it— something about her she feared. A wry smile crossed her face. Born of royal blood, a princess in every sense of the word, Jagat Gosini had been brought up to think of herself as someone special. Then, when her marriage was arranged with Prince Salim, her expectations had been fulfilled. For Salim would be Emperor, and she would rule the *zenana* as his Padshah Begam, and one day Khurram would ascend the throne of the Mughal Empire. Now it seemed that a new threat to her ambitions loomed on the horizon.

If Mehrunnisa came to the *zenana*, there would be a conflict for power. This much she knew. The girl had a vicious tongue and no sense of etiquette, no notion of how to behave in the presence of royalty. And if Salim persisted in mooning about her, she, Jagat Gosini, could well lose the advantage she had so carefully built up over the years. She was not willing to give that up without a fight. It had taken time to gain supremacy over Khusrau's and Parviz's mothers, but she finally had done it. When Salim became Emperor, she *would* be the Padshah Begam.

Someone touched her shoulder.

"The gardens are empty, your Highness."

"Thank you, Hoshiyar." Jagat Gosini moved away from the group around the Emperor with a grim smile.

*   *   *

PRINCE SALIM WAS finally granted permission to leave the Emperor's presence. He hurried to the gardens and found them deserted. Hoshiyar followed him there.

"Where is she, Hoshiyar?" Salim asked, turning to the eunuch. "She said she would wait."

"It has been some time, your Highness."

"Where can I find her?"

Hoshiyar hesitated, searching through his mind for an appropriate reply. The princess would be furious if she knew, but then, why not tell the prince . . .

"Answer the question, Hoshiyar. Do you hesitate because my wives are jealous?" Salim asked, a flash of understanding in his eyes.

"At Ruqayya Sultan Begam's apartments. She comes to visit the Empress."

Salim smiled at the eunuch. "Good. You must realize that *I* am your master. You report to me, not my wives. Is that clear?"

"Perfectly, your Highness," Hoshiyar replied with a straight face.

This time Mehrunnisa did not slip easily from Salim's memory.

THE LONG HOT Lahore summer had waned into a welcome autumn. The sun sank lower in the sky, and by afternoon its dying rays were touched with a hint of coolness. All the windows in the royal palaces were shut to the outside air, and within the rooms, coal braziers blazed cheerfully.

It had been two weeks since Mehrunnisa's encounter with the prince in the gardens. She still came to visit Ruqayya during the day and did not know that in the evenings, most evenings, Salim came to see his step-mother, hoping to meet her there. The Empress did not talk to Mehrunnisa of Salim's visits or of Salim or of their talk in the gardens. Ruqayya just watched, slyly, enjoying the drama around her. Then one day, just as Mehrunnisa was leaving to go home, the Empress persuaded her to stay longer. Her servants had told her Salim was going to visit again that evening.

"May I step outside for a few minutes, your Majesty?" Mehrunnisa asked. The room was stifling. Smoke from the braziers swirled in unending circles around the ceiling, combined with the heavy sandalwood incense with which the Empress liked to perfume her apartments.

"Go, child." Ruqayya waved a languid hand at her, lying back on a divan. Today, they must meet, Salim and Mehrunnisa, and in her presence so that some sense could be drummed into them. This infatuation, though exciting for the whole harem, was pointless. The Emperor would never sanction it.

Mehrunnisa bowed to the Empress and went out of the rooms slowly. The sun was sinking in the horizon, setting the western sky past the towers and minarets of the city ablaze in shades of gold. From the mosques came a faint call for prayer in the musical voices of the muezzins. *Allah-u-Allah-u-Akbar* . . .

Mehrunnisa knelt on the floor of the veranda to pray. Then she rose, touched her head against a cool sandstone pillar, and closed her eyes. She was so tired. At home and here in the imperial harem, she had to pretend that nothing had happened. Ruqayya never spoke of the incident in the gardens, though she watched Mehrunnisa incessantly.

She took a deep breath and leaned out over the verandah into the chilling evening air. At least Maji and Bapa did not know of all this. But the pretense was taking its toll on Mehrunnisa. She hardly ate or slept, and dark circles ringed her eyes during the day, fatigue drawing her face into a pale shadow.

Through all this were thoughts of Salim. Mehrunnisa smiled involuntarily. The first meeting in the *zenana* gardens had happened so swiftly; she had been unprepared for him. The second meeting during the Mina bazaar had been what she had wanted until the Emperor had called him away. And he had left saying, *wait for me, Mehrunnisa.* How sweet her name sounded on his lips.

"Mehrunnisa?"

She froze against the parapet. It could not be . . . Mehrunnisa straightened and turned slowly, knowing who had called her name.

Salim stood in front of her.

The verandah was deserted except for them. The cold evening air had driven the last of the dawdlers to the coal braziers indoors.

They looked at each other in silence. Salim looked tired too, Mehrunnisa thought, wanting to smooth away the lines on his forehead. She reached up to pull her muslin veil over her face.

"Don't," Salim said, putting out a hand, then drawing back as though afraid to touch her. "Let me look at you, please."

She hesitated, then let her hand fall to her side. Let him look at her, as she would him, unhindered by the veil. This would be the last time. Even as she watched him, Salim, suddenly bold, tilted her face with the tips of his fingers and bent down to touch her lips with his.

A fire blazed to life within Mehrunnisa. No man had kissed her before; no man had touched her with such exquisite tenderness. Today, now, Salim was just a man who with love in his eyes had met her lips with his in a token of ultimate affection.

And she was bound to another.

Mehrunnisa drew back and pushed Salim away. "I cannot, your Highness."

"Why not?" Salim asked, laughter in his eyes.

Why not indeed? Overcome, she reached to touch his jaw, tracing her finger down to his chin, then up the other way. With a sigh, Mehrunnisa put her hands around his face and brought it to hers. She laid soft kisses on his brows, his closed eyes, the cheekbones jutting just under them. She followed around his mouth with her breath, inhaling the clean scent of him, and finished by laying her face against his.

"Now I must return the favor," Salim said hoarsely, capturing her hands in his. With exquisite tenderness, he pressed first one, then another to his mouth. Then he bent to where her neck joined her shoulder, his face a few scant inches from her breasts. Mehrunnisa groaned and let her head fall back. Every nerve was alive to his touch. Her skin quivered under his tongue. She enclosed him in her arms, rubbing her chin against his hair. How was it she knew what to do, even though she had never done this before?

Salim was the one who broke this embrace. As the evening glowed golden around them, they stood watching each other, their breaths coming in harsh gasps. "You smell of roses."

"My mother . . ." Mehrunnisa stuttered. What was it he had said? What was she trying to say? "My mother makes rose water for our baths."

Salim stared at her with an intensity that made her shiver. "You will come to me soon, Mehrunnisa. I know your father is Mirza Ghias Beg. I will ask the Emperor to send a formal proposal to your house tomorrow—no, today." He grinned impishly. "What would you like for a wedding gift? A menagerie of birds you can set free?"

But she was another man's property. She should not have done this, not have kissed him with such ferocity. But for these past few weeks he had obsessed her every thought. Why, Allah, did they have to meet like this if nothing was to come of it? Why even bring him into her life if he was not to be hers? She spoke tiredly. "I am to be married in a few weeks, your Highness."

Salim frowned. "No one told me. But," he reached for her hand, "that can be no problem. I will ask the Emperor to dissolve your engagement. You will be mine soon, Mehrunnisa."

Mehrunnisa pulled her hand out of his grasp. "No, your Highness, please do not do that. My father has promised my hand in marriage. To go back on his word would shatter his reputation. Please . . ."

"It cannot be that bad, Mehrunnisa. The Emperor himself has commanded many marriages dissolved, let alone engagements. A word from him—"

"No, your Highness," Mehrunnisa cried out, Ruqayya's words of warning ringing in her ears. She still did not believe Salim to have been responsible for plotting Akbar's death. Not this Salim who stood before her, surely. It was a rumor, grown ugly and huge through the years, arms and legs added haphazardly with each telling. Yet, the estrangement between father and son was common knowledge. There was no easy way out. Sudden tears sprang to her eyes—for the loss of Salim, fear for her father's reputation, dread of her future life, everything.

The prince reached out and rubbed a tear away from Mehrunnisa's smooth skin. "Go now, my darling," he said softly. "I will fix everything. And don't worry."

At his command, Mehrunnisa picked up the skirts of her *ghagara* and fled down the marble verandah, her bare feet skimming the stone. She knew Salim stood where she had left him, looking after her, but she did not turn to him one last time.

MEHRUNNISA RAN OUT of the palace, calling for her chaperone, Dai Dilaram, who had once been her wet nurse. Dai came out of the servants' quarters where she had been gossiping, took one look at her distraught charge, and hurried her home.

On the way, Mehrunnisa sat motionless in the palanquin. Matters had progressed too far for her to handle on her own. After her talk with the Empress, she had finally begun to think. What Ruqayya said was true: if her engagement was broken, it would bring great dishonor on her father. And the last thing she wanted was to cause pain to Ghias. She had been blind to what was happening around her, so determined to captivate Salim, that she had flirted with him without thinking of the consequences. Even just now . . . but that had been irresistible, the need to touch him. And now Salim was determined not to forget her. What if he went to the Emperor? Her father would be disgraced and held in ridicule. People would say that he had deliberately sent his daughter to the *zenana* so that Mehrunnisa could bewitch Salim. And rumors would circulate that Ghias Beg was not a man of his word, that he was not to be trusted.

Mehrunnisa's heart lurched at the thought. There was only one thing to be done. She must tell her mother. Asmat would know how to handle the situation. But Salim . . . his kiss . . . no, her mother had to know—

not about the kiss, but everything else. Even as the palanquin reached the outer courtyard of Ghias Beg's house, Mehrunnisa was dreading the encounter with her mother, for if Asmat knew, sooner or later her father would come to know too.

THAT NIGHT, ASMAT heard her daughter's story in shocked silence. She talked with Ghias, and they decided that the best thing would be to approach the Padshah Begam. The next morning Asmat went to Ruqayya and complained of the young prince's behavior.

The Empress was very concerned to hear how far matters had pro-gressed. She had thought it to be a mere flirtation on Salim's part, know-ing her stepson's mood swings well. She sent a message to the Emperor.

Akbar arrived at her apartments that afternoon, and Ruqayya wasted no time in telling him of Salim's latest fling. While they were talking, the prince entered Ruqayya's apartments unannounced.

"Your Majesty, I have a request." He hurried to his father and sat down at his feet. In his haste, Salim had not followed court etiquette. Upon entering the Emperor's presence, everyone had to perform the *taslim* or the *konish*, irrespective of age, status, or kinship to the Emperor.

"You forget your manners," Akbar said angrily.

Salim performed a half-hearted salutation.

"Well, what is it?" Akbar demanded.

"I would like to marry the daughter of one Mirza Ghias Beg, your Majesty. Her name is Meh—"

"That is not possible," Akbar cut Salim short. "She is engaged to be mar-ried, and we have given our permission. We cannot go back on our word."

Salim stared at his father. Why did he care if Salim married a courtier's daughter? He forced himself to be polite. "But your Majesty, that can be easily overturned if you order it."

"No, Salim. The engagement took place by our command, and we shall not break our word." Akbar turned away from his son as he spoke.

Salim knew he was dismissed. He rose slowly, bowed to his father, and walked out of the room on leaden feet. He wanted Mehrunnisa, desperately even; he had not slept much last night. Every thought, every dream had been colored by her face, the feel of her in his arms, the touch of her skin. She consumed him. But he would not beg for her from his father. Salim knew he had done wrong, once, all those years ago. Now, it seemed Akbar would not meet him halfway. He had tried time and again to show his repentance without actually admitting what he had done. If only the Emperor could have indulged him in this one matter . . . for in this short time, Mehrunnisa had come to mean more to him than any other woman he had known. Outside the door, he leaned against the wall, resting his head on a cool marble pillar. *Mehrunnisa.*

As Salim left, Ruqayya watched the Emperor's face crumple in sorrow. Suddenly he seemed older than his years. Akbar sighed and bowed his head. "We shall talk to Mirza Beg."

WITHIN THE WEEK, trumpets sounded the arrival of Ali Quli at Ghias Beg's house. The men of the house—Ghias, Muhammad, Abul, and Shahpur—waited in the front yard for the bridegroom. Ali Quli had no family in India, so the Khan-i-khanan, Abdur Rahim, rode with him, the women of his house behind them in palanquins. In her room, Mehrunnisa sat with her head bowed under the weight of the gold *zari* embroidered red wedding veil. Her hands were patterned in henna, her body golden with sandalwood paste, her eyes outlined in kohl. The women around her— neighbors, friends, and cousins—kept lifting her veil to exclaim at her beauty. They laughed at the tears in her eyes, for it was the right attitude for a bride who was to soon leave her paternal home. Asmat bustled around, calling to the servants to bring in fresh pots of *chai* and trays of *laddoos* and *jalebis*. She did not look at her daughter. This last week, no one had talked to Mehrunnisa much. Maji and Bapa did not tell anyone of what had really happened. People were just informed that the wedding was being rushed at the Emperor's orders. Even Saliha had not yet come from Kabul for the festivities; she was still on her way.

So Mehrunnisa sat waiting during the long hours before the actual ceremony. She forced her mind to empty itself of all thoughts. She seemed to have let Bapa down even though she had done right in telling her parents. Empress Ruqayya had commanded her to stay at home and not to visit until she was married. From Salim, of Salim, there was no news.

The wedding ceremony was brief, but the feasting went on all night. Ali Quli took Mehrunnisa home as the hired musicians played their trumpets and beat on their *dholaks*. When she left to climb into the palanquin in the outer yard, Mehrunnisa clung to Ghias Beg until he had to push her away from him. "She is fond of all of us," he said to the watching Ali Quli.

Ali Quli laughed heartily, baring his teeth. "As she will become fond of me soon, Mirza Beg."

Asmat and Ghias flinched. Then, without a look back, Mehrunnisa entered the palanquin. She kept her gaze away from her family as the bearers lifted the palanquin on their shoulders and jogged slowly out of the courtyard.

In the seclusion of the bridal chamber, Ai Quli lifted the veil and looked upon Mehrunnisa's face for the first time. Involuntarily, his hand went out to touch her face. He traced her bridal makeup of tiny painted white dots that ran from over her eyebrows down to the curve of her cheeks. She was trembling; Ali Quli ignored it. He could not believe his good luck. He had thought the marriage would cement his alliance with Ghias Beg, but never had he imagined his wife would be so beautiful.

While Ali Quli marveled at his good fortune and enjoyed his wedding night, Prince Salim drowned every coherent thought in cups of wine.

SIX

She aspired to the conquest of Prince Salim and succeeded, by a dexterous use of her charms and accomplishments at an entertainment, in casting a spell over him. But she was married to Sher Afkun, a Persian noble of the highest courage and valour.
—Beni Prasad, *History of Jahangir*

THE DAY HAD DIED A FEW HOURS AGO, PULLING ALL LIGHT INTO THE flat horizon beyond the fort at Lahore. As the earth swung away from the sun, the streets glowed in small pools of light—more shadows than light. The bazaars were empty, the shopfronts shuttered, the brick houses along the banks of the Ravi closed behind their high walls and towering tamarind trees. At night few people walked the streets. Even here, at the seat of the Emperor's court, it was unsafe to wander alone, for the night brought out thieves, murderers, ghosts, and demons.

Ghias Beg sat on the steps of the inner courtyard where the women of his house resided. It was paved in gray-flecked granite slabs and surrounded by a deep verandah from which doors opened into various rooms. Ghias sat silent, letting the worries of his day melt away. Arjumand slept in his arms, her face against the crisp white cotton of his *kurta*, her skin smudged already by the raised embroidery over the front. He looked down at her. Her thumb was in her mouth, her little legs dangling over his lap, the other hand clutching at his chest through the *kurta*'s opening. Her *ghagara* had ridden up to her knees, and he smoothed it back down, his fingers slipping through a small rent in the silver *zari* border.

She looked like Mehrunnisa, he thought. She had the same thick black hair, tied behind her head now but reaching beyond her waist when let loose. The same mischief in her eyes, gray like a storm-filled sky; the same delighted laughter when she was pleased; the same furrowing of her brow when she was denied something she wanted. She was just like Mehrunnisa. But she was not Mehrunnisa's.

Ghias gently pulled Arjumand's thumb from her mouth. She resisted, then, deep in sleep, allowed him to do so. What an unhealthy habit it was in a six-year-old child. But try as Abul had, neither he nor his wife had been able to break Arjumand of this habit of comfort. Arjumand was Abul's daughter, and now she slept in her grandfather's arms. Ghias looked over at the courtyard where the two women knelt.

Mehrunnisa and Asmat worked in silence, their hands dipping into the *rangoli* powder in little clay saucers by their side. Torches in sconces on the pillars of the courtyard threw swaths of light over them, skipping over the shadowed part where Ghias sat. They had started work on the *rangoli* pattern two hours ago, and now the flat stones of the courtyard bloomed with colors and patterns. Jasmine drawn in white rice flour, delicate closed buds and fresh-blown flowers; long-fingered mango leaves in colored green powder; hibiscus in deep reds; lotus in silk-pinks; triangular *peepul* leaves, sharply veined in sandstone brown.

Mehrunnisa sat back on her knees, her hands colored to the wrists with the chalky powders. "It looks like an impossible forest, from someone's wild dreams."

Asmat smiled as she filled in the green of a mango leaf, the powder escaping her fingers in a precise pattern, not straying outside the chalk outline they had drawn earlier. "The more colorful the *rangoli*, the more welcoming we are to Manija's new family. This is a Hindu custom, this laying of rice powder patterns on the floor, but very appropriate for Manija's wedding."

Mehrunnisa rubbed her forehead to ease a sudden flash of pain, leaving a streak of blue over her eyebrow. "What is her husband like, Maji?"

"His name is Qasim Khan Juviani. I saw him only briefly at the engagement ceremony. Your Bapa says it is a good family. He is a poet, Manija tells me."

Mehrunnisa bent over the clay saucers again and scooped some yellow powder into her hands. "A poet. And what does he compose?"

"Love poetry. He sent Manija a poem yesterday." Asmat's voice took on a little lilt. "His eyes thirsted for the sight of her, his heart beat in cadence with her footsteps, his every breath cried out her name."

Mehrunnisa laughed, the sound tripping in the warm night air. "And we paint an enchanted forest on stone to welcome the women of his family. What would he say if he saw this *rangoli*?"

"Volumes, I imagine. But he will never come this far into the women's quarters; you know that."

"Manija is getting married," Mehrunnisa said, after a pause. "First Khadija, then Manija. It seems hard to believe."

'Your Bapa and I would like to have you all with us, as Abul and Muhammad live with us now. But daughters belong to someone else, right from their birth. We are only temporary guardians of girl children, *beta*," Asmat said. "They grow up; they marry. They go to their real homes. They have children of their own."

At her mother's words, Mehrunnisa glanced over to where her Bapa sat. Ghias shifted Arjumand in his arms, making her more comfortable. Then Mehrunnisa looked down. Though she tried very hard to stop it, a tear rolled softly down her cheek and splattered onto the *rangoli* pattern, like a dew drop on a mango leaf, turning the dry powder under it a deeper shade of green. Mehrunnisa turned away from Asmat, hoping she had not noticed, not wanting her to see how those words had suddenly emptied her heart. *They have children of their own.*

It had been four years since her marriage to Ali Quli. But their house was silent of the pleasant noise of children. It was also just a house, not a home, for Ali Quli was rarely there. Five days after the wedding he had gone out on campaign with the Khan-i-khanan. For eight months after that, there was silence: no letters to her—just news from runners. When her husband returned, he was a stranger: a man she had known for five days. He was not a bad man, Mehrunnisa thought. He did not beat her, was not openly cruel to her as other women's husbands were, as if their wives were dogs, unclean, untouchable, fit only for the most carnal satisfaction. This pain Ali Quli did not give her, but his silences were almost more painful. It was as though he did not care.

Then, that first year of the marriage, after Ali Quli's return, Mehrunnisa's monthly blood did not come. The sight of food made her nauseated; the smell of champa flowers made her gag; headaches pounded her brain. She slept only little, in brief snatches during the day. Then one day, as she sat in a warm bath, the water pooled crimson around her body. The pain from that miscarriage had been like being pulled apart by elephants, slowly, limb by limb, until only a numbness was left.

The shame of it stayed with her longer, as months went by and she did not become pregnant again. Once, Ali Quli had said to her, "It is because you are unfaithful to me. Do you think of another man?" Mehrunnisa had stared at him in shock. Was it true? Did thoughts of Salim take away her body's ability to nurture another man's child? But she did not think of Salim. At least not all the time. Not every day. Now and then, when she was tired, when her brain would disobey her, she thought of him. Of the first meeting in the Empress's gardens, of the second at the bazaar. Of the third . . . the kisses . . . the last time she had seen him.

"*Beta.*" Asmat put a hand on Mehrunnisa's shoulder and turned her around. When she saw the tear on her cheek, she wiped it away with the end of her veil. "It will happen, *beta.*"

Mehrunnisa forced a smile to her face. She did not want pity from anyone, not even Maji. These last four years, they had all pitied her—Muhammad, Abul, Khadija, Manija. Muhammad and Abul both had children. Khadija, married only six months ago, was already pregnant, her body rounding in anticipation of the child. "I think," Mehrunnisa said slowly, wanting to wipe away the sympathy in Maji's gaze, "I think it will happen soon, Maji."

Asmat touched her daughter's face with gentle hands. "How long?"

"Two months."

Asmat laughed, put her arms around Mehrunnisa, and kissed her. "You did not tell me. Why did you not tell me? We must celebrate."

"No, Maji, please," Mehrunnisa said, drawing back, worry drawing lines over her forehead. "Not yet, not so soon."

"Why? This is a time to be joyous. A marriage in the house, another grandchild—what more could I ask for? We must tell your Bapa."

As Asmat raised her hand to beckon to Ghias, Mehrunnisa stopped her. "No, Maji. I do not want to tell anyone yet. We must wait. I would not have told you—"

Asmat dropped her hand and looked at Mehrunnisa. "Not even me, *beta?* How can you not tell your mother? Does Ali Quli know?"

"No."

"Why?" Asmat asked. Then she said again, "Your husband must know. This is not something to hide. It is an occasion to rejoice. A child in the family, perhaps even a son. Your husband *must* know."

Mehrunnisa shook her head, wishing she had not told Asmat. How could she explain her fear? How could she say that every day she watched for blood, that she took short baths in clear water and never looked down, not wanting to see the water color?

"I cannot tell him. Not yet."

Asmat turned from her daughter and filled in another leaf, moving away as she did so. "Mehrunnisa, Ali Quli must know of his child. Your husband must always know more than we do, for you belong to him now, not to us. It is his home you grace, your every thought must be of him. Just as I think of your Bapa."

"But we are not like Bapa and you, Maji," Mehrunnisa cried out, her voice trembling. "This is a different marriage."

"Yes, I agree to that. But it is a marriage. There is no way out of it. Perhaps your Bapa and I did wrong in the early days. Perhaps we should have married you to another man, one who would have understood you better. But there was little we could do in the face of a direct order from the Emperor. At least Ali Quli has not gone in search of another wife. In that he is like your Bapa."

Mehrunnisa stared at Asmat, treacherous tears filling her vision again. "Bapa never married again because his world is filled with you, with us. I matter very little to Ali Quli. I take up very little space in his world. Why do you defend him? It is me you must worry about. You are my mother, not his. Have you given me away so completely to him that you care no longer about how I am?" Even as the words escaped her, Mehrunnisa knew she should not have spoken them. Asmat bent down over her work, not looking at her. Her eyes were closed as though in pain. Mehrunnisa wanted to apologize, to wipe away that pain. She did not believe that she was lost to her parents. She knew that they thought of her all the time, more than her husband did. But they had to present a face, even to her. Asmat had already broken several rules of etiquette by speaking as she had about Ali Quli, speaking—four years later—of Ghias and Asmat's regret at having married Mehrunnisa to Ali Quli. Such matters were simply not discussed. If fate had decreed a marriage, then the marriage would be feted and celebrated and would survive, no matter what.

"I wish," Asmat said softly, and Mehrunnisa leaned over to listen to her mother. "I wish for a child for you, Nisa. Because you want a child. Because it will make you happy. If I could stop other women from asking you constantly why you do not have a child, I would. If I could somehow fill your lap with a child, I would."

"Maji, I should not have spoken as I did to you."

"No." Asmat shook her head slowly. "That is all right, *beta*. But—" She looked at Mehrunnisa again, her expression calm. "When you go home tomorrow, you must tell Ali Quli. He should have been the first to know. There must be no sense of impropriety in what you do, Nisa. No one should be able to point a finger and say that what you did was wrong. Appearances must be maintained at all costs."

Mehrunnisa sighed. There were always strictures in society: how one must live, eat, even what to talk about and what to keep silent on. When she had been younger is had been easier, sheltered as she was under Bapa and Maji. But now, as a married woman, she came under very close scrutiny. Even as Mehrunnisa was thinking this, Asmat said again, a smile lighting up her eyes and spreading laugh lines around her mouth, "But there is going to be a child. We are like two old women with imagined fears. Be strong, *beta*. Perhaps even I do not understand what anxiety you undergo, for I have not experienced this. But I will pray to Allah for the life of your child, for the happiness it will bring you."

"Don't tell Bapa, Maji," Mehrunnisa said quickly.

"He will understand, *beta*. Whether you want me to tell him or not, he will understand. And one day, just as he now holds Arjumand, so too will he sing your child to sleep."

They both looked to where Ghias sat. He was asleep now, leaning against the pillar, his granddaughter sprawled over him. The day's work and the night's tranquility had crept over both of them. Mehrunnisa bent down again, glad her mother did not fuss over her, for if the unthinkable happened, she would be ashamed of the fuss. She was glad Asmat did not insist she stop painting the *rangoli,* or go and lie down. When her hands and her mind were busy, she did not have time to think—of what might have been. Maji had always been practical. There was too much else to do to spend hours in idle contemplation of how life could have turned out, if not for this or for that.

The next morning dawned too early for Mehrunnisa, who slept for only a few hours. She and Asmat worked steadily through one more *pahr* of the night: three hours. Long before that, Asmat rose to wake Ghias, take Arjumand from his arms, and usher them both to bed. When she came back, the two women finished the *rangoli* in silence. Every now and then, Mehrunnisa saw her mother look at her with concern when she put a hand to ease the strain on her back, or sucked on a tart wedge of dried mango Asmat had brought for her from the kitchens. When they were finished, the whole courtyard was ablaze in color. "Now sleep, Nisa. You must be tired, and with you the child will be tiring too," Asmat said. Then she drew Mehrunnisa into her arms, and they stood there for a while, Mehrunnisa with her head against her mother's shoulder. She could smell the wilted jasmine flowers in Asmat's hair and hear the steady beat of her heart, and she felt a comfort she had not felt in a long time.

When Mehrunnisa left her father's house, the milkman was at the front doorstep with his cows. Her veil pulled over her head, she stopped to watched as he massaged a cow's engorged udders, then showed his terracotta pot to the maidservant. When the suspicious servant had peered into the pot to ensure that there was no devious half inch of water at the bottom to increase the volume of milk, he put the pot between his knees, spoke softly to the cow, then with practiced hands squeezed the udders. As the milkman and the servant talked, Mehrunnisa slipped away from them and walked back to her husband's house, four male servants a few steps behind her.

Maji said Ali Quli must be told, so she would do so. For all that she was tired from the previous night, for all that her back ached and a sour taste tinged her tongue, Mehrunnisa felt an easing inside her. Talking with Maji had abated her fears. Now things would be different. Ali Quli and she would have a child, this child that was inside her. The questions about her would stop. Ali Quli would be proud of her, and together they would make a home. Not like Maji's and Bapa's, but a home nonetheless. Now she would no longer have to watch other women with their children and feel as though the ache would consume her. She too would have a child, so she could grow old and fretful and have that child indulge her whims. Mehrunnisa laughed. The sound was like water in a stream, a happy sound.

When she reached her house, she went through the courtyard to Ali Quli's room. Qasim, his manservant, lay snoring across the front of the door. Mehrunnisa bent and shook him by the shoulder.

He woke with a shout from an unfinished dream and stared at her. "*Sahiba*, when did you come back? The *Sahib* does not expect you. I will let him know—"

"No need," Mehrunnisa said.

"But, *Sahiba* . . ." Qasim scrambled to his feet and hopped around like an injured cat. "It is best . . ."

By then Mehrunnisa had thrown the door of Ali Quli's room open. She stopped abruptly. Ali Quli slept in the bed in the center of the room, his leg thrown over a slave girl, one arm encircling her, his chin buried in the curve of her bare shoulder.

Mehrunnisa felt as though she had been shot at with a matchlock, a huge part of her blown apart at the sight of her husband with the slave girl. Ali Quli woke then, slowly, and looked at Mehrunnisa standing at the door to his room. He slapped the slave girl on her rump to wake her and said, "Get out."

The girl woke, saw her mistress, hurriedly pulled on her *choli*, and fled out of the room, slipping past Mehrunnisa with downcast eyes. When she had gone, Mehrunnisa slammed the door on Qasim's curious face.

Ali Quli propped himself on an elbow and said, "She was just a slave girl, Mehrunnisa. Be thankful I do not take another wife."

"And when would you have time for another wife, my lord?" Mehrunnisa asked, bitterness staining her voice. "When would you see her? When would you talk to her? Another wife would take too much time away from your campaigns. She would be demanding, want new clothes, want you to admire her in them."

"As you do." Ali Quli sat up on the bed, pulling the blue calico sheet over his hips.

Mehrunnisa slid down the door to the floor and put her face in her hands. "I ask for so little from you. But this, in my own house—this is too much. I do not complain when you go to the *nashakhana* or visit the *nautch* girls. Why in my own house, in the bed I have slept in?"

"A bed that is not fruitful," Ali Quli yelled, rage suffusing his face. "How dare you talk to me like this? Question my motives? I married you because I was ordered to by Emperor Akbar. Does he now have to order you to bear a child?"

Mehrunnisa looked at him, struck dumb by his words. *But I carry your child. I come to tell you the news that I carry your child, and I find you in bed with another woman.* Why did it hurt so much? She knew of his dalliances with the *nautch* girls, knew that sometimes he even took the slave girls of the house into his bed, but this was the first time she had actually seen it. Maji said she must tell her husband. Even Maji could not want her to tell him under these circumstances.

"I'm sorry," she said slowly. "Perhaps it is better you have another wife."

Ali Quli laughed as he lay back on the pillows and put his arms behind his head. Behind him the sun streamed through the latticework frame of the windows. He watched her distraught face through half-closed eyes. "Perhaps I will."

A fighting spirit rose in Mehrunnisa. His mockery was too much for her. This was the first real conversation they had had in four years, almost the first time they had talked for so long. She said, her words brittle, "Would you like me to choose her for you, my lord? What is it you want? Long hair, a slim body, eyes a poet would laud? A good family? Perhaps her father should be an important minister at court? Surely an alliance like that would bring you good fortune."

Ali Quli whipped out of bed, tying the ends of the sheet around his waist. He strode over to Mehrunnisa and grabbed her face in one of his large hands. His face close to hers, his morning breath souring the air around them, he said in a hoarse whisper, "You talk too much for a woman, Mehrunnisa—as if you were a queen, as if you expected to be a queen. Yet where is the gold in your veins? Who are your ancestors? What lands did they conquer? Where are the monuments to their lives, the tombs of their deaths? And who is your father? A Persian refugee. A man who fled his country with the clothes on his back, shredded by the time he got to India."

Mehrunnisa wrenched at his hand with both of hers, but he held her too tightly, his grip bringing an ache to her jaw. It was difficult to talk, but she managed a few words. "You are also Persian, my lord. Do not forget that. If my father found refuge in India, so did you. Under the same circumstances."

"But I am a soldier, Mehrunnisa. I fight in battles. I kill other men. There is iron in my blood. And what is your father? Nothing better than a lowly *vakil* who works with numbers."

Mehrunnisa mustered all of her strength and tried to push Ali Quli off. But he was much stronger. Suddenly, just as suddenly as he had leaped from the bed, he let go of her face and sat back. Their knees now touched. Mehrunnisa rubbed her cheek, knowing his fingers would have left their mark on her skin. She could not go to Manija's wedding—people would talk. Maji and Bapa would be deeply concerned.

"My father is the *Diwan-i-buyutat*—the Master of Works in charge of the imperial buildings," she said, "not some lowly *vakil*. You know that. It is because of his position at court that you enjoy privileges. A raised *mansab*, command of an army division—all these are because of him." She knew she should not be talking to him like this, that women did not talk to their husbands thus. Maji never had to Bapa, at least not in Mehrunnisa's hearing. But at this moment she despised Ali Quli, cringed at the thought that she was carrying his child, never wanted to see him again no matter what recriminations it brought upon her. How dare he insult her Bapa? Who was *he* to insult her Bapa?

Ali Quli made a sudden movement with his hands, and Mehrunnisa cowered, hating that she did so. But he had never yet hit her, and he did not now. "I know you think you married beneath yourself," he shouted. "Your Bapa and Maji think so also. Because I came here without a family, because the Khan-i-khanan's wife had to stand in as a mother for me during the wedding ceremony. Because I was a *safarchi* to the Shah. A table attendant. For four years I have withstood this treatment from your family."

"Bapa and Maji have never said a word," Mehrunnisa cried.

"They did not need to. Their mannerisms, their looks, their actions around me speak volumes. Yet, who are you, Mehrunnisa? You behave as though you were royalty. But what silks and velvets covered your mother's bed when you were born? What trumpets played and cannons boomed the news of your birth? What *bawarchis* sweated over *chulas* to make delicacies that sweetened the mouths of people who came to ask after your birth? What beggars did your father clothe and feed as an indication of his joy at your coming? What can you claim of these festivities? A bare tent, a winter storm. A mother who almost died giving birth to you. A father who decided you would be better brought up by someone else."

Mehrunnisa stared at him for a long time, the pain of his words searing through her as if her skin had been slowly set on fire. Somewhere through that agony she realized how ironic it was that his words were almost poetic when he was most angry. When she spoke, her voice was toneless, devoid of energy. "Why don't you divorce me, my lord? All you have to do is say *talaq, talaq, talaq* in front of two witnesses."

Ali Quli shook his head. "No. Your father, though I think of him only as a *vakil*, still has some use. It would seem that being Ghias Beg's son-in-law commands respect. So," he leaned forward and touched her face, gently this time, "it is not as easy as you think. Nothing in life is. We will be married for the rest of our lives, my dear Mehrunnisa. Think about it: for the rest of your life you will be nothing but the wife of a common soldier. Pray Allah I get a promotion soon, or you will never be able to hold your head up in your illustrious family."

With that he rose from the floor, bent to move Mehrunnisa to one side, opened the door, and left the room, calling out as he did, "Qasim, get my *chai* ready."

Mehrunnisa sat still, looking down at her hands. She had not had the opportunity to tell Ali Quli why she had come to his room so early in the morning. Around her she could hear the household stirring as the maids drew water from the courtyard well, as the sweepers swept the stone corridors of the verandah. She had no feeling any more, no sorrow, no heartache, just a dullness.

As she sat there the first pain came. Just like the others, it stormed down her lower back and belly, like a hand gripping her in a vise. Mehrunnisa closed her eyes as the pains flooded through her. Now she would not have to make up an excuse for not attending Manija's wedding. Now Maji would not ask why she did not come. She clutched her hand to her front, doubling over on the floor, her face flat against the cool stone. Another child gone, barely inside her, barely alive, now gone. *It could not be so.* It was unimaginable—this life without a child, this life Ali Quli had sketched out for her as the barren wife of a common soldier.

Her lips moved in a soft prayer, even as tears blurred the room and her breath stuck in her chest. *Please Allah, not again, let me keep this one. Please.*

But then there was the warm swamp of blood between her legs.

* * *

BY THIS TIME, 1599, the Mughal empire stretched vast across the map of Hindustan, embracing Qandahar and Kabul in the northwest, Kashmir in the north, Bengal to the east, and south to Berar. The *khutba*, the official proclamation of sovereignty, was read before the noon prayers every Friday in the melodious voices of the muezzins from mosques around the empire. *All hail Akbar Padshah, lord most mighty.* In Central India, the Emperor had managed to subdue even the Rajput kings, valiant warriors and a fierce, proud race. As each kingdom was conquered, its daughters, sisters, cousins, and nieces were given in marriage to the imperial family, cementing newly formed alliances and ensuring against further rebellions.

One kingdom still held out. Udaipur lay southwest in Rajput land—a rugged, harsh land of low-lying mountains, bare plains, and scrub. Water and rain were a distant memory; the scorching Thar desert lay to the north. But Udaipur, under a brutal burning sun, stood on the banks of the Pichola lake. Around it, replete with the waters of the lake, the land was fertile, green, and lush, surrounded by the bare hills of the countryside. Here Rana Pratap Singh had ruled with a stubbornness and arrogance that could only come from being a Rajput—proud of being from an unconquerable people, and angry at the presumption of anyone, even a great Emperor, at thinking of *his* land as part of a larger empire.

Rana Pratap Singh died in a hut on the banks of the lake. Through the windows of his shack he could see the brick and mortar walls of the palace a previous Rana had commenced building, but during his reign there had not been enough peace to complete the palace. His sons stood around him as he lay on his hay-stuffed mattress, vowing to continue Pratap Singh's fight against Akbar, swearing that until every last breath left their bodies they would not give up their land to be swallowed by the widespread Mughal empire. As the eldest of his seventeen sons and his heir apparent, Amar Singh, came through the doorway to pay his last respects to his father, his turban caught on one of the slats of the roof and was wrenched off his head. So Pratap Singh, that mighty Rana who had staved off the Mughal Empire, died with this image in his mind: that his son, turbanless and so relaxed, would live a life of ease. That he would not rule for very long. That he would lose this beloved kingdom.

EMPEROR AKBAR SAT by the window in Ruqayya Sultan Begam's apartments, the leather-bound and gold-embossed copies of the *Akbarnama* in his lap. He touched the raised surface of the engraving on top. Abul Fazl had said that the three volumes covered his reign, the first two consisting of the history of his rule, the third—the *Ain-i-Akbari*—an account of daily life. His fingers skimmed over the unfamiliar letters of the first page. Akbar's grandfather had written the *Baburnama*. His father's reign was covered by his aunt Gulbadan Begam's *Humayunama*. Now this: a first-hand account for posterity of his rule. Flowery, full of praise, and sometimes pompous in his attempts to please, Abul Fazl had yet managed to capture the essence of his life.

Outside the windows, the palace guard walked through the night, his melodious voice singing out the hour. "Two o'clock and all is well!"

The Emperor laid the *Akbarnama* next to him on the divan and slowly unwound his turban, wrapping the piece of embroidered silk into a ball as he did so. It was late and time for him to sleep. Tiredness crept over him as he undressed slowly, unlacing his *qaba*, replacing his silk pajamas with cotton ones and a loose, white cotton *kurta*.

He blew out the oil lamp by the window. When his eyes had adjusted to the darkness, he went up to the bed and stood there, looking down at the two shapes. Empress Ruqayya slept aslant on the bed, and Prince Khurram had his little arms tight around her neck. The cotton sheet that covered them had slipped off, so the Emperor bent and pulled it over them gently.

Murad. His son's name flashed through his mind, and he sat down, letting the tears come for the first time since he had heard the news. After all those years of wanting sons, being blessed with three, now he was left with only two. Murad was dead.

Akbar had sent Murad a few months ago to oversee the campaign in the south, hoping and praying that command of the imperial army would take his mind off drink and drugs. But that had not happened. Like Daniyal before him, Murad was a weak leader, unable to control the men. Petty fighting had broken out among the army commanders. Then news had come to Akbar that Murad was very sick and dying from excessive drinking. So the Emperor had sent Abul Fazl, head chancellor of the empire, to nurse him back to health. But Fazl arrived too late. Murad had fallen into a coma, and on the fourth day after Fazl's arrival, on the second of May, 1599, he died.

Fazl found the imperial army scattered, the men disillusioned and weary. The Emperor, with scarcely any time to grieve Murad's death, had appointed Fazl chief commander, to give him the authority to rally the forces. And now, Fazl had written to Akbar requesting his presence in the Deccan.

Akbar bent his head. There was always so much to do and so little time to think. Only during the nights did he have the privacy and silence to allow those thoughts to come. Unlike Salim, he had not known either Murad or Daniyal well. They had come to him in their childhoods guarded by nurses and ayahs, whisked in and out of his presence during ceremonial occasions. He had paid careful attention to their upbringing though, but from afar, giving them the best tutors, the best nursemaids, the best of everything a royal prince should command. Yet, both Murad and Daniyal were too fond of drink and the women of their harem. Now Murad was dead. Salim disappointed him. Daniyal drank too much.

He was an Emperor with three heirs, two left now, in neither of whom he had much confidence.

As he sat there a gentle hand reached out and rubbed the side of his neck.

"Come to bed," Ruqayya said softly.

Akbar leaned into her hand, breathing in the essence of *santuk*, which Ruqayya used on her skin. He turned to her, his face still wet with tears for his son. She was sitting up in the bed.

"Come," she said again, holding out her arms to him.

The Emperor rose and went into her embrace. They stayed like that for a long time, his head against her breast, his tears coming fast now. She rocked him, smoothed back his hair from his forehead, wiped his tears. Then they lay down together on either side of Prince Khurram, arms still wrapped around each other, Khurram in the warm circle they formed.

"We must leave for the Deccan, Ruqayya," Akbar said softly, comforted by her as he always was. He had known her all his life. Ruqayya was his cousin, daughter of his uncle Hindal. They had gown up together, knowing they would marry one day. From her he had had no expectations. When she had not borne him children, it had not mattered. For it was Ruqayya he always wanted, not any child she might give him. Therefore, when she asked for Salim's third son, Akbar had gladly taken Khurram from Jagat Gosini and given him to her, not asking why this son, why not another, why now after so many years. What Ruqayya wanted from him, she got. It was as simple as that. And now Khurram was seven, too old to sleep in Ruqayya's bed. But he wanted to, and she wanted him to; so when Akbar came to spend the night with Ruqayya, all three of them slept in the same bed.

Khurram shifted in their embrace, moving his little body to a more comfortable position. In his sleep, he clutched with one hand the front of his grandfather's *kurta* and with the other a stray lock of his step-grandmother's graying hair, pulling them closer to him.

Ruqayya leaned over Khurram's head and kissed the Emperor's cheek. "If Mirza Abul Fazl has requested your presence in the Deccan, your Majesty, then you must go there. He would not ask for you if it were not important. Bijapur and Golconda, if you were to conquer them, would be valuable additions to the empire."

'Yes," Akbar said, still softly, not wanting to awaken Khurram. "We have been on campaign there for five years, with no success."

"It will happen, your Majesty. At least the Uzbeg menace that had brought us here to Lahore has now ceased to exist with the death of King Abdullah Khan. There are no responsibilities anymore at the northwestern front of the empire."

Akbar turned to lie on his back and stare up at the shadowed ceiling. "What about Udaipur? Rana Pratap Singh is dead, and his son Amar Singh is now Rana. He is still getting used to his new obligations. If we strike now, Udaipur will be part of the empire before long."

"Perhaps you should wait for a more opportune moment to lay siege on Udaipur, your Majesty," Ruqayya said.

Akbar looked at her, seeking her eyes in the darkness. "We cannot wait too long, Ruqayya. It has been two years since Rana Pratap Singh's death. Any longer, and Amar Singh will have an opportunity to establish himself too well."

"You respected Rana Pratap Singh."

"He was a brave man, a king worthy of the title," Akbar said somberly. "Udaipur is the only Rajput kingdom we have been unable to conquer. We admired Rana Pratap Singh for that. To be able to withstand the imperial army time and again . . . but as much as we admired him and kept away from annexing Udaipur after the death of Pratap Singh, the time is now right to do so. It is not just for political reasons. You know that, Ruqayya. Amar Singh's men regularly plunder and loot trading caravans carrying goods from the east to the western ports. At least within the empire, our subjects must travel freely and without fear. As long as Udaipur remains independent, that will not be so."

"And who will you send to command the Udaipur campaign, your Majesty?"

"Raja Man Singh. He will be a good leader."

Ruqayya put a hand to Akbar's face. "Send Salim, your Majesty."

"Without Raja Man Singh?"

"No, with him. Let Salim have primary command of the imperial army. He needs the responsibility."

A long silence stretched between them. Then Akbar said slowly, "Will Salim be capable, Ruqayya?"

"There is only one way to find out, your Majesty. If he is to be Emperor after you—and Allah forbid it happens too soon—he must be prepared. After the Humam incident, his value has dropped among the nobles of the court. They must have confidence in him. Without confidence, they will not support him when he comes to the throne," said the Empress.

A deep sadness came over Akbar at her words. He had tried very hard these last eight years not to think of the poisoning incident. He had never talked even with Ruqayya about his fears that Salim might somehow have been responsible for it. Now he did, finally. "And were we right to dismiss the *hakim*?"

"Yes, right about the *hakim*. But about Salim, we will never know, your Majesty. Yet, you must not think he does not love you, has little affection for you. In some ways, he was still a child, easily led by his supporters, unthinking of consequences. I cannot believe he wished for your death. You must not think so. These past years have shown his repentance. So send him to Udaipur and show him you trust him. From that will come a new friendship between you."

Akbar pulled Khurram closer to him, feeling his little body warm in his arms. "Salim gave us Khurram. This little child brings us so much joy, Ruqayya. As Salim did when he was born." He looked at his wife. "How is it you are so wise? Where does that wisdom come from?"

She laughed softly in the dark night, pulling the sheet to cover them all: Emperor, Empress, and Prince. "From you. Because of you. Salim is our child too; we must nurture him, cherish him, and, if he has done wrong, forgive him. Now you must sleep, your Majesty."

So they slept, wrapped around each other. Before his eyes closed, Akbar prayed silently that Ruqayya was right. He was heartsick at Murad's death, at the prospect of a deteriorating relationship with his two remaining sons, at the little time he might have left on this earth to consolidate his beloved empire and hand it safely into the hands of Salim.

A few weeks later, the imperial court and the *zenana* moved to the Deccan with the Emperor. Ghias Beg and Asmat left with the court. The bazaars emptied, and most of the traders moved with Akbar. The nobles shut their houses and followed the court.

Ali Quli was sent to Udaipur under Prince Salim's command. He chose not to take Mehrunnisa along. She was left alone at Lahore.

SEVEN

*At the time when he (Akbar) went in prosperity to the provinces of
the Deccan, and I was ordered against the Rana, he came and
became a servant to me. I gave him the title of Shir-afghan (tiger-
throwing).*

— A. Rogers, trans., and H. Beveridge,
ed., *The Tuzuk-i-Jahangiri*

THE TWO MEN RODE SIDE BY SIDE AHEAD OF THE ARMY. THEY WERE
mounted on frisky Arab steeds, one black with ivory socks, the other
dark gray with a startling white mane. Prince Salim turned to his companion, jerking his horse to obedience with one hand.

"That is a fine horse."

Ali Quli bowed from the saddle "I bought it from an Arabian trader,
your Highness. It comes from good stock. If you wish for my horse, I
would be honored to present it to you. Please, take it if it pleases you."

Salim looked appreciatively at the strong lines of the steed, with its
sleek muscular flanks and lustrous white mane. It was certainly unusual.
How had Mehrunnisa's husband acquired this animal?

"If my brother Daniyal were here, he would have immediately appro-
priated your mount. He is very fond of horses."

"Your mount is spectacular, too, your Highness," Ali Quli said. "You
have excellent taste in horseflesh."

Salim nodded, wondering at Ali Quli's effusiveness. Why was he tripping over himself to be so obsequious? Salim had asked for the soldier to
be part of his army, wanting to see for himself the kind of man
Mehrunnisa had married. And he had picked him from the ranks to
accompany him on the last leg of their journey. He pointed into the distance with his jeweled whip. "We are almost there."

"Have you decided on a plan of action, your Highness?" Ali Quli asked.

"Yes. As soon as we are settled, armies will be sent to establish out-posts. I thought of Untala, Mohi, and Chittor as starting points. From there, the lieutenants will send out sorties on sudden raids. We must mount a continuous barrage on the Rana, to tire him out and force him to surrender."

"The Rana's forces will not withstand the imperial army's assaults. Your Highness," the soldier hesitated for a brief moment, "have you found commanders for the imperial outposts?"

"Not yet." Ah, that was why Ali Quli was being so unctuous. Salim turned to look at him. "I can see that you wish to go."

"I do, your Highness," Ali Quli said eagerly. "I shall make you proud."

"Doubtless," Salim said. "Your military exploits are legendary. But you please me with your company, Ali Quli. I wish for you to remain here. Other commanders will be found for the imperial forces."

"As you wish, your Highness," Ali Quli said.

Salim watched disappointment write lines over his face. Another question lingered on his tongue, but he held himself back. It had been a long time, many many years, but he could still remember how laughter had built inside him when Mehrunnisa released the pigeon during the Mina bazaar. No one else would have dared to so do in his presence. But she had let the bird go, her slender hands singing in the air as they fol-lowed its flight, and then she had looked at him with a mocking glance. *Now what, your Highness?*

Salim looked away. To the east a slow wind kicked up brown dust in puffs, engulfing the trees and shrubs in its path. He pulled the cloth of his turban over his nose and mouth. *Mehrunnisa.* It was a lovely name, fit-ting her in every way. He had been with her for only brief snatches of time, yet it seemed like a lifetime. He did not even think of her all the time. Only her name was etched in his memory; her face came to him in dreams, slipping away before he woke. There were so many women in his *zenana,* from so many countries, and yet none was like her. And this man who rode by his side was her husband. He went home to her every evening. Did he treat her well? Did she love him? An unexpected pain flared through him at the thought.

"Do you have children, Ali Quli?" he asked suddenly.

"No, your Highness. Allah has not seen fit to bless me. My wife is barren."

Salim turned away from him, bile rising to sour his tongue. A lot of men talked like this about their women. *This* was the man she was married to, so callous about her with a stranger? "It cannot be all that bad," Salim said. "Perhaps you should take her to a *hakim*. They can do wonders."

Ali Quli stared at him insolently. "Unfortunately not for her. She is very beautiful, your Highness. A lovely woman, but one, it seems, incapable of giving me children. If only you could see her . . . but it is forbidden, alas."

Salim tightened his grip on his reins, yanking at his horse as he did so. He itched to whack Ali Quli in the face and wipe that sneer from his mouth. He said through clenched teeth, "You must not talk thus of the woman who graces your home, Ali Quli. It is impolite."

"But perhaps," the soldier turned to Salim with a speculative gleam in his eyes, "your Highness has already seen my wife before."

Salim whipped his head around. "Why do you say that?"

Ali Quli shrugged. "Just a thought, your Highness. Mehrunnisa used to visit with Empress Ruqayya in the imperial harem."

"No."

Ali Quli bowed again. When he raised his head, his expression was contrite. "I beg pardon, your Highness, for suggesting that you might have seen my woman. And if you change your mind about the command of the imperial outposts, please do think of me."

What did the one have to do with the other? Still furious, Salim lifted his hand in dismissal, and Ali Quli fell back. He urged his horse into a gallop, racing through the brush and scrub, mud stinging his eyes. No children. What did that matter? For him it would have been enough to have Mehrunnisa in his *zenana*, to know that he could lie by her side at night, that he could watch her sleep. For four years he had pushed away thoughts of Mehrunnisa. She was another man's wife; she would never belong to him. And as time passed, he thought she must have forgotten him. Now, seeing Ali Quli, all those aches had come back, startling him with their intensity. He should send the soldier out on campaign, not keep him by his side. What good would that do? Every time he saw Ali Quli, he would be reminded of Mehrunnisa. But every time he saw Ali Quli, disrespectful as he was, Salim would perhaps learn a little more about her. Now he knew she had no children. Maybe later he would find out other things about her—little pieces of information he could hoard and keep with him even if he could not have her.

Anger flared in him again. Why hadn't the Emperor granted him permission to marry Mehrunnisa? It would have been so easy for Akbar to agree, yet he had not. Somehow, Salim's rage at this one decision of his father's never seemed to subside. Added to it now was a sense of futility about the Mewar campaign. When Salim had started out from Lahore, he had been full of ideas about the attack on the Rana. But during the journey all those plans dissipated into thin air. Mahabat and Koka pointed out that there would be long, weary months at some military outpost without the harem or basic comforts. It was much better to send out the imperial forces under his able lieutenants and direct the operations from Ajmer.

Salim agreed, but with some reluctance. His father had sent him to oversee the campaign, to prove himself worthy of the crown. And yet, as Mahabat said, when would he get that crown?

When the entourage reached Ajmer, Salim settled down in the comfort of the royal palaces to await news from the warfront. The days passed pleasantly as he played king, accepting homage from the crowds of local residents who turned out to see their prince.

THE INACTIVITY SOON palled, and Salim decided to go up to Nagaur, north of Ajmer. Farther north was the Thar desert, and in the forests on the southern fringes, near Nagaur, lay the imperial hunting grounds, well known for their large stock of cheetahs. Salim set up camp near the town. The royal party hunted daily, rising early in the morning and spending the entire day in the forests.

One day, the royal entourage returned to camp, victorious and tired, dragging along with them the carcasses from the hunt. The call for the evening prayer rang out, and they all fell to their knees, facing west toward Mecca. The prayer over, Salim rose from his prayer rug and walked outside his tent.

A groom came running up to him. "Your Highness, a tigress and her cubs have stayed near the camp. They must have been frightened by the drummers from the hunt."

"Lead me to them." Salim, excited, grabbed his musket and followed the groom. They passed Ali Quli, who was resting nearby, leaning against a tree trunk.

"Your Highness, it is unwise to leave the camp alone," he called out.

"Come with me then, Ali Quli," Salim shouted as he disappeared into the woods.

Ali Quli hastily stuck his dagger into his cummerbund and ran after Salim and the groom. In a few minutes he caught up with them. They walked as quietly as possible through the dark forest. The sun was low in the west by now, and the trees formed a thick canopy overhead, shutting out what little light there was. An unseasonable thunderstorm had drenched the hunting ground two days ago, and the undergrowth still smelled dank and damp. The groom struck a match and lit the torch he was carrying.

"Here, your Highness," the groom whispered, pushing aside a bush to let Salim pass.

They had come upon a small clearing. The groom held up his torch, and the darkness receded to the edges of the clearing. In the center, four tiger cubs, each not bigger than a man's hand, played alone. They turned and looked at the newcomers with inquisitive, unblinking golden eyes. One of the cubs came running up to Salim and pawed at his boots fearlessly. Salim laughed in delight, picked up the cub, and held it to his chest. The cub had a tangy smell, with a smear of blood from some ani-

mal streaked over one ear where its mother had not licked it off. Salim
rubbed his fingers along its neck, and the cub purred in contentment, its
bright eyes softening.

Ali Quli peered worriedly into the gloom. "Your Highness, the tigress
must be close by. Please be careful."

Salim paid no attention to him, stroking the gold and black lines that
arrowed down the cub's back.

Suddenly, a pair of incandescent eyes gleamed out of the darkness, and
a low growl sounded from the bushes directly ahead of Salim. He looked
up, startled, his heart thumping against his ribs. Crouched in front of
him, ready to spring, was a large, angry tigress. She had come from
nowhere, making no sound until now, giving no indication of her presence. Salim looked around wildly for his musket. It lay on the ground, a
few feet away; by the time he reached it the tigress would be upon him.
He looked toward the tigress, holding the cub in numb fingers.

Ali Quli watched his prince, the words he wanted to say stuck in his
throat. The cub, sensing the tension and excited by the smell of its
mother, twisted and mewed in Salim's tight grasp. The tigress growled
louder from deep inside her body. Ali Quli cleared his throat and said
softly, "Let the cub go, your Highness."

Salim did not hear him. He was mesmerized by the fluorescent gaze of
the angry mother.

The groom stood nearby, rooted to the ground, his torch spilling an
eerie glow over the clearing. It lit up the three men standing immobile
and the equally still crouched animal in the far corner.

Ali Quli slowly felt for his dagger. As he clasped the handle the tigress
sprang with a loud roar.

Salim went cold with terror. He tried to look away but could not. His
feet would not move; in any case, he knew instinctively that he could not
outrun the tigress. He watched stupefied as the tigress launched her huge
body from the ground, teeth bared, mouth open, coming toward him.
Time dragged to an inching halt as the animal pawed through the air,
closer and closer . . .

Suddenly, a man hurled himself on the tigress, just a few feet from the prince. The tigress fell to the ground heavily, Ali Quli on top of her. Salim watched motionless as Ali Quli and the tigress grappled together. Then, galvanized into motion, he dropped the cub, ran for his musket, picked it up, and held it to his shoulder. But he could not fire for fear of hitting the soldier.

The furious tigress lashed out with a powerful arm and sank her claws into Ali Quli's shoulder. He shouted in pain and with his free hand tried to stab at the muscular body on top of him. She wrenched him into the air, and the soldier crashed back like a cloth doll. As the huge mouth filled with sharp white teeth came toward him, blocking his line of vision, Ali Quli raised the dagger and with supreme effort plunged it to the hilt into the tigress's heart. Blood spurted out, pouring on his hand and down his clothes, as the tigress collapsed with a loud roar.

By this time, the entire camp had gathered around, alerted by the commotion. Still holding the musket, Salim scrambled over to Ali Quli. He lay motionless on the ground, half under the animal's body. Salim made a sign to his attendants, who rushed over to pull the tigress off Ali Quli and help him to his feet.

The prince embraced the soldier. Ali Quli winced as the prince's arm went around his shoulder, where flesh hung in bloody strips.

"I owe you my life," Salim said, the words coming hoarsely from his mouth.

"Mine is always in your service, your Highness," Ali Quli replied, almost fainting from the pain.

"Take him away, and see to his wounds."

As his servants put Ali Quli onto a makeshift stretcher and carried him back to camp, Salim let the musket fall to the ground and stood still, breaking out into a wild sweat. His brocaded *qaba* stuck to his chest, drenched with Ali Quli's blood and the tigress's blood. He peeled the cloth away from his skin shivering violently. The tiger cub he had held came back and sank its teeth into the leather of his right boot. It had not yet realized its mother lay dead just a few feet away. Salim looked at the cub and then at the body of the tigress. It had been stupid of him to pick up the cub; he should have known the mother would be nearby.

The problem, Salim thought wearily, bending to pick the cub up by the nape of its neck, was that Raja Man Singh had efficiently taken over command of the Udaipur campaign, leaving, as usual, little for Salim to do with his time. From far away in the Deccan, the Emperor kept himself informed of the campaign. Letters and missives passed between the Raja and Akbar; they rarely consulted Salim.

The cub wriggled in his grip, and he cradled it to his chest, watching with disgust as it licked at the blood on his *qaba*. He walked back to the camp and there gave orders for the four cubs to be put in his private menagerie.

The next morning, Salim rose and prayed for the well-being of the man who had saved his life. Then he issued a royal *farman*, proclaiming that from this day, Ali Quli Khan Istajlu was to be given the title of Sher Afghan, or Tiger Slayer. It was the least he could do. In the light of day, he realized he did not want to be in debt to this man of all men: the man who had married the woman he loved, the man who cared so little about her.

Salim laid his seal on the *farman* and blew on it to dry the glossy ink. Ali Quli had saved his life, but his new title and all the honor that came with it would benefit Mehrunnisa. He touched the rough paper. One day, after many hands had held this, Mehrunnisa would hold and read the *farman*. He felt a sudden urge to write one line to her, one line she would understand came from him. So he picked up his quill again and, under the scribe's writing, wrote "May you be forever peaceful." When the ink had dried, Salim called a servant to take the *farman* to Ali Quli. With it went his message to the woman he had seen only thrice, the woman he could not forget.

"WITH THE ROYAL treasury in your hands, you will rule the empire, your Highness."

"Shhh . . ." Prince Salim put his goblet down on the silver tray at his elbow with a clatter. He gave a swift glance around. The royal attendants

were arrayed around the room at some distance, standing against the pillars. The men had their hands behind their backs, feet planted apart.
Their faces were impassive.

Salim sighed with relief and picked up his goblet again. He frowned
over the rim at the three eager faces. Mahabat Khan, Qutubuddin Khan
Koka, and Sayyid Abdullah smiled encouragingly back at him. The four
men were seated on low divans in the reception hall of Salim's apartments at the royal palace in Ajmer. The room was large, with vaulted
ceilings and stone arches opening to the gardens outside. Salim and his
three most trusted and loyal cohorts huddled around the center. All
three men were about Salim's age, having literally grown up with the
prince.

Mahabat Khan was lean, wiry, and compact. His well-weathered skin
was darkened by the sun, drawn tight over the skull, with black eyes
shining intelligently from a clean-shaven face. His hair was well oiled and
slicked back, curling slightly at the ends. His energy was seemingly
boundless; and true to character, Mahabat sat at the very edge of his
divan, upright and alert. Mahabat had been brought into the royal palaces
at ten years of age to provide male companionship for Salim. A few years
later he had been appointed to the Ahadis, the royal personal bodyguards
of the imperial family.

Qutubuddin Khan Koka had also been brought up in the royal
zenana. Koka's mother, Shaikh Salim Chisti's daughter, had been Salim's
first wet nurse, and the two boys had grown up as foster brothers, drinking the milk of the same mother. Always tending to plumpness, in the
passing years Koka had let himself go. He lounged comfortably on his
divan, stroking the luxuriant moustache that grew unchecked over his
face. Most people tended to take his calm and unruffled demeanor and his
good humor for granted, unaware of the sharp mind behind the facade he
took great pains to present to the outside world.

Sayyid Abdullah had joined the prince's household after Salim's first
marriage and had quickly risen through the ranks to his private circle.
The prince had been initially drawn to Sayyid by his wit and charming

manner. He was very handsome: tall, and broad-shouldered, with a hooked nose, well-defined eyebrows, and a strong mouth. Sayyid was very careful of his personal appearance, determined to improve on what nature had given him so abundantly. But what Salim found most engaging was his absolute and blind devotion to him.

Indeed, Salim thought, these three men were his closest cohorts along with Muhammad Sharif, who was not here today, having been laid up with a fever. Physically, the four men could not have been more dissimilar. In contrast to the other three, Sharif was short, with stubby hands and legs, a receding hairline, a neatly clipped moustache, and cold, calculating eyes. But what had brought them together was their loyalty to Salim—loyalty that had been tried and tested over the years. Sometimes, though, they were overzealous, as when they had encouraged him to rebel against his father in 1591. Now they were suggesting that he storm the treasury at Agra and confiscate the empire's wealth.

He looked at them thoughtfully. Perhaps there was no harm in listening to what they had to say. For once his mind was as keen as a butcher's knife; Mahabat Khan had insisted against his regular morning dose of opium and then asked for a secret conference. Salim had listened to the three men in silence, an idea beginning to germinate in his mind.

A year had passed since he had arrived at Ajmer—a very dull year. He had been feted and pampered in the beginning, but as time passed, the commoners hardly stopped their chores to wave back at him before carrying on.

And the siege on the Rana of Udaipur was not progressing well at all. Somehow the wily Amar Singh had successfully managed surprise attacks on all the outposts and sent the imperial army scattering. No real harm done, but it took time and money to gather the forces again and replan the offensive.

A month ago, Raja Man Singh, his brother-in-law, had been recalled to his governorship of Bengal by the Emperor. It seemed that Usman, the last of the Afghan dissidents in India, had rebelled again, and Man Singh was sent from Mewar to quell the rebellion. The Afghan threat had plagued the empire for years now; they had driven Akbar's father from Hindustan. So the slightest sign of trouble from Bengal was taken very seriously.

But, Salim thought irritably, it left him without a strong commander in his forces. The Emperor had not chosen him to command in the first place; sending him here had just been a token gesture. Now he was not willing to go out into the battlefield and rally the forces. That meant his presence was no longer necessary at Mewar. But where else would he go? Certainly not to the Deccan; the Emperor would promptly put him in command of another long and tiring campaign under *his* nose this time.

As Salim was mulling over his problems, Mahabat Khan came to him with his request for a private audience. Until now, Salim had felt the throne secure for himself, especially since Murad was dead and only Daniyal was left in contention. And then Koka languidly pointed out that Prince Daniyal was in the Deccan with Akbar. Who knew how close they had become?

Salim grew cold at the thought. Would his father pass him by and leave the empire to Daniyal? Could he afford to take that chance? All these years he had wanted—no, yearned desperately—to be on the throne; and it seemed as though after all that, Daniyal, who had equal rights under the law, would take away his life's ambition. At that point he started listening to what his friends had to say. Capture the treasury and the empire would indisputably be his, for the life of the empire lay in its rich treasury.

Salim finally looked up from the amber wine in his goblet. "How can I capture the treasury at Agra? It is well guarded."

Mahabat, Koka, and Abdullah smiled at one another.

"There is only a skeleton army left at Agra," Koka said slowly. "The rest of the imperial army is here, or in the Deccan with the Emperor."

Salim shook his head. He was being asked to rebel a second time against his father. And this time, there would be no turning back. At least with the poisoning incident, Akbar had merely been suspicious; he had had no real proof. But capturing the treasury—that would be an open act of mutiny.

"The time is ripe, your Highness," Abdullah urged. "We must act now. Who knows how long the Emperor will live? It may be years before he dies and you ascend the throne of Hindustan."

"Why wait, your Highness?" Mahabat Khan chimed in. "His Majesty has clearly stated that he wishes you to be heir. If you capture the royal treasury, the Emperor will acknowledge you as the next king and retire from court life."

Salim shook his head again. "I don't know whether it will work. This is a big step to take."

"The right step, your Highness." Koka smiled under his moustache, sensing victory. "You reached manhood ten years ago. But does the Emperor admit it? No. Instead, he treats you like a child. He gives you no responsibility."

"He did send me to subdue the Rana of Udaipur," Salim said haltingly.

"A lost cause, your Highness. His Majesty should have sent you to the Deccan. But he went there himself, not trusting your command," Mahabat replied.

Salim bit his lip. "I cannot," he moaned. "What if the Emperor finds out before we reach Agra?"

"We will travel in the greatest secrecy, you Highness," Koka said. "We can send out word that you are confined to you bed with an illness. No one will know you are not here. Think of the riches of the royal treasury."

Salim's head jerked up from his cup. He could see the huge vaults at the fort. Thick strands of swan-white pearls, glittering rubies, diamonds and emeralds. Teak chests spilling with gold and silver coins, all sitting at the treasury, gathering dust. At the last counting, the treasury accountants had put the figure at two hundred million rupees.

But . . . this was surely wrong. The Emperor would be devastated when he heard of Salim's rebellion. The prince bent his head. As he did so, for a brief moment, he remembered Mehrunnisa. She must be a beautiful woman now. Ali Quli never talked of her anymore, not even in passing. Salim sometimes almost asked, then stopped himself. How did one man ask after another man's wife? Yet, if things had been different, she would have been *his* wife. A defiant gleam came into Salim's eyes. "You are right. It is time. The Emperor cannot treat me as a child any longer." He turned to the three men. "We leave for Agra tomorrow. Go prepare for the march."

"As you wish, your Highness." The three men smiled at one another and bowed out of the room.

EIGHT

*The Prince, advanced by this favor and swelling with Pride,
resolved . . . to go on the journey, answering he would treat of no
Peace until he were in the field with his Army. . . . The ambitions
of this young Prince are open, the Common talk of the People; yet
his father suffers all . . .*

—William Foster, ed., *The Embassy of
Sir Thomas Roe to India*

WINTER CAME TO LAHORE VENOMOUSLY COLD, CARRYING WITH IT A
touch of frost from the north and the mountains. All through the rest of
the year the city had baked in the heat of a blazing sun. The monsoons
were late, then they did not come at all, and the Ravi did not flood its
banks—instead, it lay parched at its edges, shallow and slow like a giant
python in the heat. It was six months since Emperor Akbar had moved
his court to his campaign in the Deccan, taking with him, it seemed, all
the life from the city. It had been a brutal summer. Now, as the earth
tilted away from the sun, dry, chilly winds whistled through the almost
deserted streets and lanes.

Only a few people braved the cold and the wind in one bazaar street
that hugged the ramparts of the Lahore fort. Beggars huddled around
rubbish-heap fires, rags gathered around their shivering bodies. A vendor
broiled fresh ears of corn over a coal brazier, and then brushed over them
a chilli-and-cumin powder mixture to bring fire to cold bellies. A few
intrepid men and women hurried through, shawls drawn tightly over
their heads and shoulders.

One woman walked slowly through the bazaar, her head bent, trying
not to attract the attention of the men who passed. There was little to
see, though, for she was clad in the deepest blue. Her veil was of thick,

137

impenetrable muslin and fell in heavy folds almost to her feet. The swirls of her *ghagara* swept the cobbled street and muffled her footsteps. It was only when an errant wind breezed through that her clothes molded to her body. Then the men looked with ravenous eyes at the curve of her breast, at the dip of her waist, at the sway of her hips. But they did not approach her, knowing, without really being able to see, that she was not a common woman.

But Mehrunnisa did not notice them. She stopped at one side of the bazaar and looked up at the red brick walls of the fort that rose to the blue-black sky above her. On the other side of these walls was her home. She put out a veil-clad hand and touched the pitted bricks, feeling the cold seep into her palm. For six months, since the Emperor had left, since Prince Salim had left, since her husband had left, she had roamed the bazaars of the city. Ali Quli would be horrified if he knew. Even Bapa and Maji would shudder. From Ali Quli would come *Like a woman of the night, as if you had no protector, no husband. Other wives don't do this; they stay at home where their men keep them. Why not you?* From Bapa it would be *You must take care, beta. It is an ugly world out there.*

And yet, Mehrunnisa could not have stayed at home without anyone to talk with, no one to visit, nothing to do. The imperial harem had moved away also, some with the Emperor to the Deccan, some back to Agra. Mehrunnisa had wandered into the bazaars with the servants at first, but they were always loud, quarreling, puffed with pride at their positions, and she had spent all her time trying to pacify them. Then she had forbidden all but two male servants from coming with her, and they had to follow at a discreet distance. They would keep her safe. The shop-keepers gave her curious glances but asked no questions; the gold *mohurs* in her hand kept them silent and grateful. It was, after all, the only thing she had to occupy herself with now that the city slept in the wake of the royal court.

A tempting aroma filled the air, and Mehrunnisa turned to watch a vendor as he roasted peanuts and chickpeas, his metal spoon clanking against the sizzling *tava*. Suddenly feeling cold, she went up to him and offered him a few coins. His mouth broke into a wide grin, showing yellow, tobacco-stained teeth, as he picked one coin from her hand, his grimy finger lingering longer than necessary on her palm. Mehrunnisa grimaced under her veil. It *was* an ugly world, but as long as these men looked and did not approach her, it was a small price to pay for such freedom. The vendor scooped the peanuts into a paper cone, twisted one end, and gave it to Mehrunnisa. She took it from him, careful this time not to let her hand touch his. Then, the cone warming her skin, she went down the street to the *chai* shop on the corner.

The rest of the bazaar was shut. It was too cold for the shopkeepers to linger in their stores, too cold for shoppers to visit and haggle, too cold to do anything but drink *chai* and smoke *beedis*. Mehrunnisa went into the teashop and sat down on a bench. The owner, a fat unsmiling man nodded briefly at her, then shouted, "Mohan!"

A little boy came scurrying out from behind the shop, flapping his arms to keep away the chill, clad only in a tattered pair of shorts and a *kurta*. He went up to his master and waited until he had poured some tea into an earthenware cup. This he took slowly and with great concentration to Mehrunnisa. As he neared her, a customer leaned into him, and a few steaming drops spilled onto his hands. He looked up at her, his eyes huge in his small face. Mehrunnisa reached over and took the cup from his hands. "We won't say anything about the spill." She knew he would be beaten if the *chai* seller found out. The boy wiped his hand on the front of his already stained *kurta* and took the money from her. "Thank you, *Sahiba*."

Mehrunnisa sat in the shop listening to the men around her talk, sipping the heavily sugared *chai* spiced with cinnamon and ginger. Two days ago, there had been a letter from her husband, the first in all this time. In it, he had recounted his tale of saving Prince Salim from the tigress. He was now called Sher Afghan. Tiger Slayer. It was an impressive title. Salim would never forget him or what he had done; the name would be a reminder. Mehrunnisa laid the cup down on the wooden crate that served as a table and watched the steam condense in the air. Suddenly, she yearned to know whether Salim knew that Ali Quli was her husband.

She leaned back against the soot-blackened walls of the *chai* shop. Ali Quli had said little else about the incident in the jungle, but she could picture it. Impetuous, rash Salim, rushing to pick up tiger cubs, aware that the tigress would be nearby. But he would still do it, even though he knew that a mother always protects her young.

A piercing, brief pain flashed through her chest and brought sudden tears to her eyes. She let them blur her vision, then slip unnoticed down her cheek. A mother. How sweet that word sounded. For her the hardest part was to fend off the constant, prying questions and advice. *Why? Take this powder mixed with milk every night. Fast on the night of the full moon. Be submissive.* The pain was sometimes almost physical in its intensity. Her arms ached to hold her child.

"*Sahiba!*"

A firm hand on her shoulder jolted Mehrunnisa out of her thoughts. She looked around to see one of her maids crouched next to her. Her heart faltered. What had happened?

"What is it, Leela?" she asked, rising as she spoke. There was a dense silence in the *chai* shop. All the men were looking at them. Mehrunnisa pulled the girl up and they hurried out of the shop, leaving her *chai* still sitting on the crate.

"*Sahiba*, it's Yasmin. Her time has come, but things are not right."

Mehrunnisa stopped and stared at the trembling maidservant. She was still very young, perhaps not even ten years old, but the servants did not keep note of their time of birth or death, so there was no way of knowing. Leela was still a child.

"What is wrong?" she asked.

Leela shook her head, pulling Mehrunnisa by the hand toward the fort. "I do not know, *Sahiba*. The *hakim* is busy; there is no midwife to be found. I think they will not come because Yasmin is not married. She needs help, *Sahiba*."

Mehrunnisa still stood unmoving in front of the *chai* shop, looking down at the grimy street, the cobblestones smudged with winter dirt.

Yasmin was one of her slaves, bought for a few rupees. She too was young, and pretty, with looks that had caught Ali Quli's eye. Mehrunnisa had ignored the situation as long as she could until Yasmin's belly had started to grow. Then she was left alone in Lahore, with nothing to do but watch her husband's child in another woman's body.

"Come, *Sahiba!*"

Leela now knelt in front of Mehrunnisa, a tear-smudged face against her hand. What did this child care about another slave in the household? They were not sisters, not related. They had only known each other for the last year. Yet, she pleaded for her life. Mehrunnisa turned away briefly and stared down the bazaar street. Then, her face unreadable, she looked down at the child in front of her.

"Come," she said, putting out a hand. The men in the shop leaned over their *chai* to watch as they fled down the street, hand in hand, Mehrunnisa's veil swirling in a blue cloud around her. Her two servants, who had been smoking *beedis* by the shop, hurriedly flicked them to the side of the street and raced behind their mistress.

When they reached the house, Mehrunnisa saw most of the servants gathered in a crowd in the front courtyard, their faces hostile. Some of these women were mothers themselves. Surely they would have more knowledge of childbirth and birthing than she did? Why did they not go to help Yasmin? It was nothing but prejudice and sloth and a small kind of meanness. Yasmin was an orphan with no protector, pregnant without being married. They had ostracized her for the last six months. And Mehrunnisa had allowed them to, angry herself, in a deep deep pain that this woman should carry her husband's child, while she could not keep one within her for more than a few months.

She pulled off her veil and glared at the huddled servants. Commands came out like musket shots. "Get hot water! Go look for a *hakim* or a midwife! No, no argument, tell them I have commanded their presence. Some clean bedclothes, sheets, towels, everything. Milk the goat for the child if it will not take to its mother's breast. Now!"

"It is of no use, *Sahiba,*" one old servant spoke up. "She has screamed for too long; the child is surely dead by now inside her. And she—she will not last long either. Better not to waste time."

"Why was I not informed before?"

They all shrugged and looked away at the walls, at the cloudy sky, at the floor, not wanting to meet the blue fire in Mehrunnisa's eyes. Just then, from behind the servants' quarters, Yasmin screamed again. Mehrunnisa shivered. It was a low feral wail, unreal, inhuman. The sound stretched thinly through the house and wrapped itself around them before dying out.

Snapping her fingers at the servants, Mehrunnisa picked up the skirts of her *ghagara* and ran to the quarters behind the house. They had put Yasmin in a shed where the hens were kept when her pains first started. Mehrunnisa entered the shed and almost gagged as the stench of stale blood rose to her nostrils. A red stain blossomed on the straw under the girl, seeping into the mud floor, the hens squawking and pecking curiously nearby. Bile shot up from her stomach, and Mehrunnisa ran back outside, throwing up the *chai* she had drunk. Still heaving, she wiped her mouth, covered her face with her veil, and went back inside.

Yasmin lay motionless on the hay, her lower body uncovered, her stomach distended toward the thatched roof. Her arms flopped at her side, and her head was turned to Mehrunnisa, eyes huge and frightened. Sweat soaked through her hair and pooled in a dark circle on the pillow.

Mehrunnisa put a hand on her forehead. "It will be all right, Yasmin."

A flicker of recognition flashed in the girl's eyes. "Sorry . . ."

Mehrunnisa shook her head. For what? She had had no choice. They were all—this slave girl, the servants, Mehrunnisa herself— the property of her husband. How could this girl have denied him anything?

"Leela," she said to the child, who had followed her inside and now stood near the door. "Take the hens out and clean out this shed. Open the windows a little to let the air in."

Just then another contraction racked Yasmin's body, and the shed filled with her low howl. Her stomach shuddered and quivered, the child inside straining to come out, her body trying to expel it, neither effort successful. Mehrunnisa washed her hands in the pail of cold water used for the hens and knelt in front of Yasmin's splayed legs. Something was wrong. Why did the child not come? Even if it were dead, it had to be removed or Yasmin would surely die. Mehrunnisa had watched enough births at home and in the imperial *zenana* to know what happened. She had seen the *hakims* and midwives battle to bring life back to the child, to the mother. With the fingers of one hand, she probed between Yasmin's thighs, watching her face for signs of pain. But Yasmin was beyond pain.

Mehrunnisa touched a rounded curve and drew back, her fingers coated in blood. The baby was already half out, but she had not been able to see it in the semidarkness of the hen shed. Almost dreading what she was to discover, she reached down again. Her hands slipped over a tiny smooth round bottom. Still kneeling there, Mehrunnisa closed her eyes. Sweat beaded her forehead even in the chill of the shed. The child was coming out bottom first. What could she do? Was there any way to turn the baby? *Allah, come to our aid.* Another contraction started, and Yasmin cried out again.

Mehrunnisa felt the baby force itself against her hands.

"Leela!" she called to the wide-eyed child who had just shooed the hens out of the shed. "Go and hold up Yasmin. Make her sit up. Don't argue; do as I say."

Then, when a nearly fainting Yasmin sat looking at her, Mehrunnisa said, "The next time a pain comes, I want you to push hard. As hard as you can. Do you understand?"

Yasmin stared at her blankly. Leela said, "I will help her, *Sahiba.*"

Mehrunnisa turned back to the child. When Yasmin's body shuddered again and she opened her mouth to let out an unearthly wail, Leela leaned into her and said urgently, "Push, Yasmin, push."

As the girl strained, Mehrunnisa reached inside, grabbed hold of one slippery leg, and gently pulled it out. The other leg was still folded near the head. Feeling inside Yasmin's body, Mehrunnisa caught the other leg. A few minutes later, it too came out. Almost too easily, Mehrunnisa thought, for now the head, the hardest and largest part of the child, was yet to be delivered. A servant came in with a copper vessel of warm water and some cloths. She dipped a few towels in the water and wiped the little body. It was too cold and bluish gray; the umbilical cord was shriveled. Mehrunnisa kept the baby wrapped in warm towels, waiting for the contractions, praying it would come out safely. She, who had seen difficult births only from afar, seemed to know instinctively what to do. Where that strength or that knowledge came from she did not know.

Thirty minutes went by before the child slipped out into Mehrunnisa's exhausted hands. Yasmin lay back on her bed of straw, a pulse barely beating on her thin wrists, blood drained from her face. Surprisingly, the bleeding seemed to have almost stopped.

Mehrunnisa looked down at the slippery, bloody, bawling infant cradled in her arms. It was a boy. He husband had his heir . . . through another woman. It was a child he would never acknowledge.

By this time, the rest of the servants had crowded outside the door of the shed, peering in curiously. The midwife came too, led by one of the grooms. Mehrunnisa nodded toward Yasmin. "Clean her up, and clean up the child too. There will be a reward for you."

Then she crawled to one corner of the shed and leaned against the wall, watching as the midwife wiped and swabbed at Yasmin, massaging her uterus back into shape, applying poultices to heal her skin. The baby too was cleaned and brought to Mehrunnisa. She sat there, holding the child, watching him sleep. Her hands were still caked with dried blood, his blood, his mother's blood. She traced his hairline with one finger, dabbed at the little nose, put his tiny curled fist against her lips. A huge pain came sweeping through her as she held the baby. When would she have one of her own?

The midwife fed Yasmin some chicken and beef broth, took her payment, and left. Still Mehrunnisa sat there holding the child. Would Yasmin live?

She put her head against the baby's tiny one and closed her eyes. Among all the filth and blood of the shed, the smooth smell of newborn life rose and surrounded her. The baby slept in the crook of her arm, so tiny, so content, so unaware of his fate. What if she never had children? At the heel of that terrible thought came another, stronger idea. If Empress Ruqayya could command a child away from a royal princess, why shouldn't she from a penniless, orphan maidservant? She could always pension Yasmin off and send her to some remote village. She would never talk. Mehrunnisa had brought the child into this world. He must belong to her.

PRINCE SALIM REINED in his horse, turned, and held up a hand for silence. Behind him, the sun glanced off the spires and minarets of the city of Agra.

"We will rest tonight," Salim announced, raising his voice. "Tomorrow, we shall storm the fort. Set up camp here."

Mahabat Khan came riding up, his lean, brown face taut with worry. "We must proceed to the fort immediately, your Highness. No time must be lost."

"Look at the men." Salim gestured. "They are in no condition to go into battle."

Both men turned to look at the soldiers with their dust-grimed faces and dark circles under their eyes, their horses foaming at the mouth from the long, hard march. No one had slept much in the past few weeks. They had left in the middle of the night from Udaipur. Salim's servants had been told to inform the army that he was ill and in bed, but that excuse would have worked for only a short time. Sooner or later, some commander would want to see him personally, and the pretense would be revealed. As they traversed the breadth of the empire toward Agra, Salim prayed that the news of his flight would not reach the Emperor until it was too late. Then all this—the hard riding through scorching days when the sun burned harsh on their skins; the brief rest stops to eat, rub down the horses, and feed them; the few precious hours of sleep—would come to naught.

"We shall lose the element of surprise if we stay here tonight, your

Highness. The governor, Qulich Khan, will have time to prepare for a siege. We must proceed," Mahabat said firmly.

"But when Qulich Khan sees us approaching with an army, he is sure to be suspicious," Salim replied, running a hand through his hair. It was dusty. He had not bathed in a week; there had been no time. "We are all tired from the march. How can we defend ourselves if Qulich attacks?"

"Not so, your Highness," Mahabat said. "What is more natural than a royal prince entering the fort with his army? He will not suspect anything."

Salim looked at Mahabat and then back at his army, struggling to make the decision required. Finally he said, "Let us march on, then." The soldiers wearily lifted their shields and spears and mounted their lagging horses.

The sun was setting in the western sky as they neared the fort. The Agra fort, built in red sandstone, was ablaze in crimson. It seemed quiet. There were no signs of undue activity. Salim relaxed in his saddle and allowed his shoulders to fall back. Mahabat was right. Qulich had not heard of their arrival. He would simply march into the fort and take over the treasury. Nothing could be simpler.

They reached the Delhi gateway, the western approach to the fort. Salim's fatigue began to disappear, and his spirits lifted. He knew that there was no turning back now; he would either capture the treasury or spend his life fleeing from the imperial army. The trip had been made in the greatest secrecy, but Salim knew that there were no secrets from the Emperor. Akbar had built a mighty empire, and one of the bastions of that empire was his superb spy system. Their only hope was to reach Agra before the Emperor could inform Qulich Khan of their intentions.

Now it seemed his wishes had been fulfilled. Everything appeared to be quiet and normal. The huge wooden gates were shut and the drawbridge drawn up, but that was not unusual. He held up his hand and reined in his horse at the moat.

Salim turned to Mahabat and nodded.

"Open the gateway. His Highness, Prince Salim has arrived!" Mahabat yelled out to the guard at the tower.

The huge gates swung open in silence, and the drawbridge was let down on well-oiled wheels. Salim spurred his horse forward eagerly.

Just then, a small entourage came out, led by the governor.

"Welcome to Agra, your Highness." Qulich Khan bowed to the prince. "Please accept these gifts on behalf of the city." He gestured toward the attendants behind him, who carried large silver trays piled with satins and silks. "It is indeed a great honor for us . . ."

A sudden noise distracted Salim. He looked up. Cannons had been silently wheeled to the ramparts. They lined the battlements, their black, ugly mouths pointed at his army. The bulwark of the fort, which had looked benign a few minutes ago, was filled with soldiers bearing muskets. Qulich Khan's intentions were clear.

"Your Highness, we can easily take the fort. There are not many soldiers," Mahabat said in an undertone.

Salim shook his head. The time had not yet come to clash with the imperial forces. His men were tired and could hardly keep upright in the saddle. By contrast, Qulich's army looked well rested and ready for battle. Koka and Abdullah came up to add to Mahabat Khan's pleas. Qulich Khan was finishing his speech, and Salim was struck by his last sentence.

"What did you say?" he asked the old man.

"Her Majesty, the Dowager Empress Maryam Makani, wishes to welcome you, your Highness," Qulich Khan repeated.

His grandmother! Salim felt his face go hot. He could not go in front of Maryam Makani while he was in revolt against his father. Suddenly, he felt like a child again; he could remember Maryam Makani's imperious voice as she scolded him for mischief. That decided it. If his grandmother wanted to see him, he had best leave before she turned a thirty-one-year-old man into a child with her quelling stare. Salim thought quickly. He had to get out of this situation with as much grace as possible.

"I have just arrived at Agra to make sure that you are taking good care of the imperial treasury, Qulich Khan."

"Your Highness's concern is understandable."

Was that sarcasm in his voice? Salim dismissed the thought and went on. "I leave Agra in your hands, and I am sure that you will guard the fort in a responsible manner. Tell my grandmother I regret I cannot wait upon her at this time."

Qulich Khan bowed. "You can rely on me, your Highness. I will serve the Emperor with my life if necessary."

"Good. Good." Salim turned to his men. "Let us continue on our way."

The army retreated. As he was leaving, Salim looked back at the fort. Within its walls lay the imperial treasury filled with riches that would have given him his dream. Qulich Khan stood at the gates, his arms folded across his chest, a grim look on his face. He bowed again to the prince. Salim nodded and turned back.

Disappointed and weary to the bone, Salim with his army reached the banks of the Yamuna river at Agra. His plans had failed. Akbar would hear of this, and he would be furious. The Emperor might even be on his way back from the Deccan.

Salim rubbed at his temples tiredly. Again he had failed, as he seemed to fail at everything he tried. Somehow the governor of Agra had known he was coming. And if he knew, the Emperor must know too. The last thing he wanted was a confrontation with his father. He had to leave Agra and go somewhere safe. He watched the river flow past, and a thought struck him. He could go to his estates at Allahabad and plan his next course of action from there. Right now, he could not think; he just needed to rest. Salim called Mahabat Khan and commanded a barge to carry him down the Yamuna to Allahabad. The army was to follow by land.

As Salim's barge departed down the river, one man stood thoughtfully in the gathering dusk, watching as the barge was swallowed up in the darkness.

Ali Quli turned and walked away slowly.

Faced by the imperial army in Agra, he had realized the magnitude of the folly he was about to commit if he betrayed his Emperor. He could not follow the prince to Allahabad. It was not cowardly of him to desert

Salim at this time, merely prudent. And the Emperor was still much stronger than the prince. It was simply a matter of choosing the right leader, and he chose the Emperor. He had no intention of spending his entire life following the prince in his recklessness.

While Salim's army was preparing for the march to Allahabad, Ali Quli slipped unnoticed into the city and went to his father-in-law's house. A week later, he sent a message to Mehrunnisa at Lahore, commanding her presence at Agra.

AKBAR PACED HIS apartments, hands clasped behind his back, an angry flush on his face. He reached the end of the room and turned abruptly, his silken sash flying out around him.

The Emperor stalked up to the silent figure. "We cannot agree to the prince's terms." His voice shook with rage.

Khwaja Jahan cringed. "Your Majesty, the prince is truly repentant. He wishes for a reconciliation."

Akbar glared at Salim's emissary. "If he wanted our forgiveness, he would not put conditions on our clemency. Why has he come with a large army to beg our pardon? He must disband his army and come to us with only a few attendants." Akbar paused and said, "Take this message back to him. We shall see him alone, without his army. And we will not grant immunity to his followers."

"Yes, your Majesty." Khwaja Jahan bowed. He backed away slowly.

Akbar spoke again, "Tell the prince that he must obey our orders. If he cannot do so, he can return to Allahabad. We will not grant him permission to wait on us."

Khwaja Jahan bowed again and let himself out of the room.

When the door shut behind him, Akbar sat down heavily and ran his fingers through his hair. Why was Salim rebelling against him? Salim had tried to capture the royal treasury at Agra, and he might well have succeeded if Akbar had not had an efficient spy system. Upon hearing of Salim's march from Ajmer, the Emperor had warned Qulich Khan. Now his errant son had set up court at Allahabad. The news was that he was playing king, granting *jagirs* to his followers and issuing *farmans* and titles to his loyal supporters.

The Emperor had to come rushing back from the Deccan from his siege on the fort of Asir. Fortunately, the fort had fallen just before news arrived of Salim's duplicity. So Akbar had sent two runners to Agra and followed almost at their heels, winding up his affairs in a hurry and leaving Abul Fazl to carry on the rest of the campaign.

After six months of negotiations with Salim's emissary, Khwaja Jahan, Akbar had finally agreed to meet with his son. But Salim had imprudently come to Agra with an army of seventy thousand cavalry and infantry, as if he were on campaign.

Akbar stared unseeingly out of the window. After he had spent so many years carefully nurturing his son, Salim had rebelled— and all this, for the throne of the empire.

The Emperor was still in his apartments when news was brought to him of his son's response. The prince had decided to return to Allahabad. He did not wish to disband his army.

Akbar dismissed the messenger with a frown. Something would have to be done about Salim. Who was the best person to advise him?

His brow cleared. Abul Fazl, of course. Apart from his duties as head chancellor, Fazl had also been tutor to the royal princes. Perhaps he could talk some sense into his son. The Emperor called for the royal scribes. An imperial *farman* was sent posthaste, commanding Fazl's presence at court.

"THE EMPEROR HAS called for Abul Fazl, your Highness," Mahabat Khan said.

Salim looked at his courtier in dismay. "Are you sure?"

Mahabat nodded. "The runner was spending the night at a wine house and talked too much. One of our men heard the news."

Salim slumped down on the cushions of his throne. He had ordered a black slate throne carved at Allahabad and called himself Sultan Salim Shah in defiance of his father's command to disband his army and come to him unarmed.

Many months had passed since that mad dash to Agra to capture the treasury, a few more after that fateful attempt at reconciliation with Akbar. Now, the Emperor was going to call upon Fazl. Why Fazl? What good would that do? Abul Fazl had never liked him, but he was one of the Emperor's closest confidantes, the man to whom he had entrusted the care of his sons. He had sent Fazl to the Deccan to look after Murad, who had died soon after his arrival. Now he wanted to bring him back to attend to another son. Akbar was devoted to Abul Fazl, even more so since he had finished the *Akbarnama*, bestowing great honors on him for that work. But Akbar had not read three volumes of the *Akbarnama*. He had merely looked at them with awe.

This great Mughal Emperor was illiterate; he could neither read nor write. However, that had not stopped Akbar from cultivating the acquaintance of the most learned and cultured poets, authors, musicians, and architects of the time—relying solely on his remarkable memory during conversations with them.

Salim sighed. So much . . . the Emperor always did so much with his time. He slept but little, only four hours every night, and each day was filled with state duties, time at the harem, time with the court musicians and painters and poets. And he, Salim, found it hard to even run his little kingdom within the empire.

"Why has the Emperor called for Fazl?" he asked.

"To resolve this dispute between yourself and his Majesty, no doubt," Mahabat replied.

"Abul Fazl will only make matters worse. He has never been my friend. He has always spoken against me to the Emperor," Salim said. "If he comes to court, I shall not be able to see my dear father again. The Emperor will never allow me to wait on him."

A short silence followed. Mahabat, Koka, Abdullah, and Sharif looked at one another significantly. Fazl's arrival at court would be disastrous for them, too. They were already facing charges of sedition, and the Emperor's army was itching to lay hands on them. Fazl might convince Akbar to forgive Salim, but their own heads lay on very uneasy shoulders; unfortunately they could claim no kinship to the Emperor.

"What shall I do?" Salim asked. "We can return to Agra, and I shall beg forgiveness from his Majesty."

"No, your Highness," Sharif said firmly. "We have to let some time pass before you return. Right now . . . ," he hesitated, "the Emperor is very upset and will not be reasonable."

"But there is no chance that he will relent before Fazl gets here. And that man will only make matters worse," Salim said again. He knew why a reconciliation with Akbar was not prudent right now for his courtiers. But he would protect them from his father's wrath. They had thrown in their lot with him; he could do no less. However, Fazl would not help. This Salim firmly believed. He would only be a disruptive influence. What was the alternative?

"Then he must not go to Agra," Koka said in his slow manner, his pasty face lit by cunning.

Salim looked at him in surprise. "What do you mean? He has been commanded by the Emperor. He will return to Agra from the Deccan."

"True. But the journey from the Deccan is very . . . ," Koka hesitated delicately, "shall we say, hazardous, fraught with danger? Who knows," he rolled his eyes to the ceiling, "Fazl may never complete the trip."

Salim stared at him, his pulse racing. Did he dare do what Koka was suggesting? It would be dangerous; he was already in trouble with Akbar. But it seemed he had no other options. It was this or nothing else. The risk that Fazl would reach Agra safely and further poison his father's ear, and perhaps convince him to leave the throne to Daniyal, was too great. He looked around quickly; they were alone in the reception hall. All the attendants had been dismissed.

Nevertheless, he lowered his voice and leaned toward his men. "You are right. After all, we live in dangerous times. Robbers and thieves infest our highways. A little accident, a small mishap, and, who knows?" He spread his hands.

The five men smiled at one another.

"Who is the best person for the . . . ah . . . job?"

"Bir Singh Deo, your Highness," Mahabat replied promptly.

"The Bundela Rajput chieftain from Orchha?" Salim frowned. "Isn't he in revolt against the empire?"

"Yes, but Bir Singh is a mercenary. If we make it worth his while, he will undertake any job for us. Besides, it is well known that you are at odds with the Emperor, and Bir Singh likes to fight the interests of the empire."

"If you think he is the right person—," Salim began, reluctantly.

"He is, your Highness," Abdullah cut in. "No shadow of suspicion should fall upon you, and therefore the . . . ah . . . assassin must be someone unconnected to your court."

Salim rubbed his chin. "You are right. Fazl is a minister of state, and the Emperor will not take his death lightly,. He will surely hunt down his killer." He looked up. "Can we trust Bir Singh? What if he betrays us?"

Mahabat smiled; it was actually more of a grimace. "He cannot. Even if the Emperor forgives him for this deed, there are others for which he is equally guilty. He knows he cannot escape with his life. He will go back into hiding in Orchha. After all, the Bundelas have lived there for years, successfully avoiding the imperial forces."

Salim stared at his courtiers. There was no turning back now from this decision. All he had done so far paled in comparison to this command of his, but it was essential.

"Send for Bir Singh. There is no time to be lost."

ABUL FAZL WAS informed of the plot to kill him, but he made no change in his route. His reasoning was simple: Akbar had commanded his presence posthaste. So he increased the number of his bodyguards and set out. Fazl and his men were attacked three times and fought off their assailants. A fourth time, when Fazl was passing through the village of Sur, the Bundelas set upon him and his men again. Heavy fighting ensued. Fazl managed to stave off the assassins but, injured and bleeding, was forced to lie down under a tree to rest. There, the Bundela chief found him, conscious but in great pain, and sliced off his head.

NINE

My intention . . . is to point out that no evil fortune is greater than
when a son, through the impropriety of his conduct and his
unapproved methods of behavior . . . becomes contumacious and
rebellious to his father, without cause or reason . . .
> —A. Rogers, trans., and H. Beveridge,
> ed., *The Tuzuk-i-Jahangiri*

THE EMPEROR SAT MOTIONLESS IN HIS DARKENED APARTMENTS, silken curtains drawn across the windows. Tears ran down his cheeks, soaking into the brocade collar of his *qaba*.

Akbar closed his eyes and leaned back on the velvet bolster. He had been looking forward to Fazl's arrival. Instead, two runners had brought him news of his death. Akbar had lost a dear and valued friend in Abul Fazl. But more than that, it seemed as though his son had had a hand in the murder. Could it be possible? Had Salim planned Fazl's death?

Akbar raised a trembling hand and wiped his tears. His soldiers had found Fazl's beheaded body under a tree. The minister was not even allowed to die with dignity. Now his spies told him that the head had been sent to Salim. How could his son cold-heartedly murder his father's friend? Rebellion was one thing, but murder . . .

Akbar buried his face in his sleeve. Three days had passed since the news of Fazl's death, and he had shut himself up in his apartments, seeing no one, talking with no one, not even with the ladies of his harem. What had he done to deserve such sons? Murad was dead, Daniyal was a dissolute youth given to drinking and opium, and Salim . . . he had done more to break his father's heart than either of his brothers.

He rose slowly from the divan and went to the window. With shaky hands, he unlatched the clasp and opened the latticework shutters. It was midafternoon; the sun rode high in the sky, bleaching everything to a glaring whiteness. Heat exploded into his face, and the Emperor stepped back, glad for the sensation after these last three days of numb-ing sadness. It was so hot that every breath seared his tired lungs. From here, Akbar could see only the heat-broiled plains beyond the Yamuna river, dotted here and there with stunted trees. But somewhere out there, in the dust of the plains, its sandstone buildings decaying, lay the city of Fatehpur Sikri. The city he had built for Salim.

Akbar had been twenty-seven when Salim was born. He had ruled the empire for fourteen years by then, already an old king. A king married many years, one possessed of vast lands and varied people—with no one to leave them to. A ruler with no heir. He had seen many sons born to his many wives by then. Some were dead at birth—perfectly formed, the *hakims* had told him, fingers and toes intact, hair dense on their heads, bodies rounded in their mothers' wombs. But the little chests lay silent without a heartbeat. Some had died in infancy after he had held them in his arms, watched them suckle with vigor at the wet nurse's breast, smile at his face.

With an empire to care for, it had been almost easy to forget these ghost sons of his, Akbar thought. Coming to the throne as he had at thir-teen had cultivated in him a deep sense of responsibility for his people, to every single person around him: the women of his harem, the soldiers of his army, the noblemen of his court. A king could not and did not give in to personal sorrow. Yet, an ache gnawed away at him. Akbar had searched for solace from every direction: religious, spiritual, physical. He had visited saints and gurus and physicians, hoping one or another would be able to tell him why he had this great empire and no one to bestow it upon. To tell him he *would* have the son he so longed for.

And in this search he had gone to Shaikh Salim Chisti. The Shaikh was a Sufi saint who lived in a cave at the outskirts of Sikri, a small village of little distinction sixteen miles from Agra. And there in his cave, Akbar, Emperor of Mughal India, had drawn off his pearl-and-diamond-studded slippers and sat on the bare ground next to the Shaikh. Three sons will be born to you, your Majesty, the Shaikh had said. Three brilliant sons. Your name will not die; your empire will flourish. Allah wills it.

Hamida Banu, Akbar's Hindu wife, had become pregnant around this time, and on August 31, 1569, Salim came bawling and kicking into the world. Just as the Shaikh had promised.

And so, Akbar thought, leaning out of the window again, his hand to his eyes against the glare, he had built an entire city at Sikri. And called it Fatehpur—Victory—Sikri after the conquest of Gujarat.

He could not see the city from where he stood at his apartments. The sun washed out the lines of the horizon, and Fatehpur Sikri was too far away, but he remembered every detail of the planning. Akbar's architects and engineers had balked at his commands. It was too far away from Agra, the capital of the empire. But Fatehpur Sikri *was* to be the capital of the empire, Akbar had responded. No one of any eminence lived there. They would, when the Emperor himself resided at the city. No water source, your Majesty, they had said. Dig a lake, was Akbar's order. And so it had been done. A vast lake had been dug and filled with water. In 1571, two years after Salim's birth, foundations had been laid for a mosque and an imperial palace in Sikri.

The imperials court had resided fifteen years at Fatehpur Sikri. With each passing year, as the waters of the lake dwindled, as the rains failed time and again, as the dust swallowed the red sandstone buildings of the city and turned everything a dull brown, Akbar knew the time had come to abandon the city. He had moved the court to Lahore to oversee the menace on the northwest from the king of Uzbekistan.

The city he had built for his son lay abandoned. He had never gone back there again.

But there had been exquisite memories, cherished even now, when he was so bewildered by Salim's actions. One year, when Salim was four, Akbar had taught him to swim in the lake. The servants had cordoned off a small section in the water with velvet ropes. It was early one morning, just before the sun rose. The sky around them was aglow in red-gold tones. Salim howled for five days.

"No, Bapa, I don't want to swim. I hate the water. It frightens me."

"But kings are not frightened, Shaiku Baba," Akbar said, smiling. He called him thus: Shaiku Baba. His given name was Salim, for the saint Shaikh Salim Chisti. Shaiku Baba was an endearment, again for the saint.

"No! I will not go. You cannot make me go. I don't want to go."

"Tomorrow, Salim," Akbar said sternly. The boy had to learn to obey orders.

"I will not come."

But that morning, he stood shivering and petulant at the bank of the lake in the early dawn light, sleep still creasing his face, his pouting lips blue from the cold. For Akbar taught him also that kings always kept their appointments and followed orders. If one did not know how to follow orders, one would not know how to give them.

Akbar was already in the water, a *dhoti* ballooning about his waist, the cool morning air bringing goosebumps on his arms and chest. "Jump, Shaiku Baba!" he called out.

Salim's nurses huddled around him, their faces covered, but Akbar could sense their displeasure as they glared at him through the muslin of their veils.

"Jump, *beta!*"

A nurse took off Salim's clothes until he stood naked in front of his father, his arms around himself. His ribs stood out sharp and rigid under his skin. His legs were long and skinny. His hair was dense and lush to his shoulder blades. He did not cover himself but just stood there gazing at his father with defiance.

Akbar almost sent him back to the palace at that moment, the look of fear in Salim's eyes melting his resolve to teach him to swim. But it would not do to be too kind. Salim had to learn. So he said, "Do you want to be a great king?"

Salim nodded, still clutching his arms around himself, his eyes not leaving his father's face.

"Then how can you fear something as simple as water?"

Taking three running steps to the edge, Salim jumped from the pier, flying out over the water into Akbar's arms.

And now, his spies told him that little boy was responsible for Abul Fazl's death. The Emperor sat down heavily on the floor, the heat still blasting from the open window above him. Salim had clung to him once in the water, his bravado deserting him. Even today, Akbar could feel those small arms around his neck, Salim's legs wrapped tight around his waist, his tear-stained face buried in his shoulder. Once, when he was a child, Salim had listened to him. Now he listened no longer. Like Fatehpur Sikri, their bond seemed to have been left to dry out in the sun, to be overcome by dust and dirt and cobwebs. He had abandoned the city he built for his son; now his son had abandoned him.

The Emperor lifted his head slowly. He was becoming so very tired these days. Everything fatigued him. The royal physicians could find nothing wrong, but he saw it in their eyes. *Old age. The end of a life well and fully lived.* Akbar sighed. He would have to put this affair behind him and reconcile with his son. Salim was the natural heir to the throne. Perhaps in the short time he had left on this earth, he could instill some character in Salim and make him a worthy Emperor.

Akbar rose and walked to the imperial *zenana*. He went first to his Padshah Begam's palace. She was waiting for him; even as he left his own apartments, servants had fled to Ruqayya to announce his arrival. He found her there with Salima Sultan Begam, another of his favorite wives. Salima and he had grown up together; they were first cousins and had been close friends before Akbar married her. She had initially been married to Bairam Khan, the regent when Akbar came to the throne at thirteen, too young to rule the empire himself. When Bairam died, Akbar married Salima to give her a home and to recapture their childhood friendship.

With Ruqayya and Salima, Akbar was more at ease than anywhere else, even at the royal *darbars*. They were his comfort. Now, true to character, they sat with him and talked of *zenana* affairs until he was ready to talk. When the Emperor was finally ready, his grief poured out in broken sentences: sorrow at Fazl's death, and pain at Salim's part in it. But he said nothing of a reconciliation. Salima, who had known Akbar all her life, left the next day for Allahabad. She knew, and Ruqayya knew, that Akbar wanted to see his son again. It was time. And so, as they always had, with an unspoken agreement between them, the two women went about setting the Emperor's world right again.

SALIM AND AKBAR met in the *Diwan-i-am*, in front of the entire court. It had been three years since they had seen each other. Even so, the Emperor insisted upon a public meeting. The Hall of Public Audience was packed to capacity with courtiers and onlookers. News of the strife between father and son had spread through runners and travelers to the farthest corners of the empire. Almost every person present had a vested interest in seeing how the meeting would advance; the empire's fate depended on this moment.

Behind the throne, the harem balcony was filled with the ladies of the *zenana*. For once, they too were silent, watchful, wondering. Right up front, near the screen, sat Ruqayya Sultan Begam. To her right was Salima, who had brought Salim home to his father. No one knew what she had said to the prince or how the encounter had progressed, only that she had convinced him to return—and without a large army. Also, when Salim first came to Agra, he had come to the harem to pay his respects to his grandmother, Maryam Makani, so the ladies had already seen him. Only one person associated with the royal *zenana*, but not actually part of the *zenana*, had not seen him in many, many years.

Mehrunnisa stood silent behind Ruqayya's divan, close enough to the screen to look through it with ease. It was still a few minutes before the prince's arrival at court and she felt as though she had been holding her breath till this moment. Mehrunnisa looked down at the marble floor of the *zenana* balcony, wondering if he had changed. Had time been kind to him? Had he aged? Had this mad dashing around the empire in search of futile goals weathered him?

It was all stupid, so stupid, she thought, to be led astray by men like Mahabat and Koka and Sharif. At least now he was returning to his rightful place by his father. Pray Allah he would stay there. Maybe then she could see him every now and then. Even that would be enough after all those years of starvation for the sight of him. She grimaced and looked up as the trumpets blared, announcing Salim's arrival. It was she who was stupid, married to one man all these years, and all these years still thinking of another . . . Perhaps if Ali Quli and she had had a child, things might be different. Mehrunnisa put a hand on her stomach softly, remembering that winter afternoon in Lahore in the hen shed. Yasmin had lived . . . and not wanted the child. Still, Mehrunnisa did not take him. She wanted, yearned desperately for a child—but her own child, not the fruit of some other woman's womb. So she gave the baby back to Yasmin and sent her away. Mehrunnisa bent her head, still touching her stomach. Would she ever have children?

Just then the Mir Tozak announced Prince Salim, and she looked up.

Salim walked slowly into the *Diwan-i-am*, followed by a few courtiers. Mahabat Khan and Koka were conspicuously absent from his entourage. Mehrunnisa watched as Akbar rose from his throne and walked down the few steps to the center of the court. The Emperor's eyes brimmed with tears. He held out his arms, and Salim, who was bending to perform the *konish*, straightened and came into his father's embrace. The court watched in silence as the two men hugged each other.

Salim stepped back from Akbar with a shock. It had been three years, and his father had aged immeasurably. The shoulders he embraced were bony, the Emperor's hair almost all white. Worry lines patterned his forehead.

"Bapa, I will surrender four hundred of my war elephants to you."

"We have missed you at court." The Emperor's voice broke in mid-sentence.

At a signal from Akbar, attendants brought forward robes of honor and jeweled swords.

"Come closer, Salim."

Akbar took off his jeweled turban of state and placed it on Salim's head. A hush came over the entire assembly. Salim raised his hand in wonder to the unfamiliar burden on his head, his fingers smoothing the jewels on the imperial turban. How sweet the weight was.

"You do me a great honor, Bapa," Salim said softly, so only the Emperor could hear.

Akbar stared at him for a long time, and Salim met his gaze unwaveringly. He wanted to touch his father again, to embrace him again, to apologize for the madness of the last few years. But there was no forgiveness in Akbar's look, just sorrow and disapproval.

"The empire must have an heir, Salim. There is no one else."

"Is that the only reason you asked for me to return to Agra, your Majesty?" Salim asked, wrath flaring in him.

"*We* did not ask you to return," Akbar said.

"No." Salim put his hand up to the turban again and adjusted it so it sat firmly on his head. "You did not ask; I know that. May I have permission to leave your presence, your Majesty?"

Akbar nodded. Salim took off the turban and laid it reverently in his father's hands. He bowed and backed slowly from the *Diwan-i-am*, past the courtiers in the front tier, the noblemen in the second, the commoners in the third, the war elephants standing in a row in the outer courtyard. Everyone was watching him, but he did not betray his feelings with any expression.

Until he left, the court was silent. Now, not having heard the soft exchange between the two men, the ladies in the *zenana* balcony burst into excited chatter, the nobles following them.

For with the laying of the imperial turban on his son's head, the Emperor had proclaimed, in no uncertain terms, that he wanted Salim to be his heir.

Mehrunnisa leaned back from the screen, her face flushed. Salim had not changed, not outwardly at least. She watched while the *darbar* dispersed as soon as the Emperor and Salim left the courtyard. Now there would be some peace in the empire. And Salim would stay here, at Agra, near his father, where he belonged. One of the ladies passing by made a sudden fleeting reference to a name, and Mehrunnisa's head snapped in her direction. A chill descended upon her. Even she had forgotten in her desire to see Salim. But all was not well, he must know somehow. Even she had forgotten Salim's son, Khusrau.

"THE EMPEROR WISHES me to return to the Mewar campaign." Prince Salim strode angrily into his apartments.

From their work, Mahabat Khan, Koka, and Abdullah looked up at him in dismay. Muhammad Sharif had been left in Allahabad as governor.

"When?" Mahabat asked, putting aside the *farman* he had been reading.

"As soon as possible." Salim signaled for a cup of wine.

"But why, your Highness? Both the Khan-i-khanan and Prince Daniyal are in the Deccan. They can easily travel to Mewar to command the imperial forces."

Salim gulped down the wine and held out his goblet for more. "You know that Daniyal is a poor leader. He drinks too much and spends too much time in his harem. I must go and instill confidence in the army, uplift the spirits of the men. Those are the Emperor's words, not mine."

"Your Highness," Abdullah said urgently, "You cannot leave Agra at such a crucial time. I beg forgiveness for what I am about to say, but the Emperor is not in good health . . . he is old and . . ." Abdullah let the sentence trail away.

Salim knew what he was about to say. Akbar's death was imminent; if Salim left Agra now, he would be too far away to claim the throne if Akbar died. He drummed his fingers impatiently on a little rosewood table. What did that matter? The Emperor had proclaimed him heir. Though he did not want to go, at least it would be something to do.

The homecoming had not turned out to be all he wanted. Salim and Akbar spent more time together than they had before the rift, but things were still not as they had once been. Too much had happened—the attempt on the treasury, Fazl's death. The only time they really felt close to each other was in the royal *zenana*, when the ladies were there to dispel any tension.

The three men around the prince watched him carefully. Didn't he realize his position in court? Salim's power play and his impatience to wear the crown had alienated him from most of the powerful nobles at court. Assured of his right to the throne, the prince had not attempted to befriend the courtiers. Now, while he was in a tenuous relationship with his father, the nobles were openly assembling against him.

"I realize that it is not prudent to leave now," Salim said. "But my father has commanded me, and I dare not disobey him. Besides, there can be no fear of my claim to the throne. The Emperor himself has publicly announced me to be his heir. Daniyal is no real threat. Who else can there be?"

"Prince Khusrau, your Highness," Qutubuddin Koka spoke up for the first time.

Salim looked at him in shock. "Khrusrau? My own son?"

"Yes, your Highness. I have heard that both Raja Man Singh and Mirza Aziz Koka have been gathering a coalition to support him."

Raja Man Singh, brother of Salim's first wife, Man Bai, was Khusrau's uncle. He was still at Bengal, having quelled the Afghan rebellion, but even from that distance he had friends at court.

Mirza Aziz Koka was Akbar's foster brother and lately Khusrau's father-in-law. Koka's mother had been Akbar's wet nurse. Aziz Koka and Man Singh, father-in-law and uncle to Khusrau, were definitely interested in seeing the sixteen-year-old youth ascend the throne to the Mughal empire. He would be easily controlled by these statesmen.

"The Emperor will never countenance putting Khusrau on the throne. It would defy the laws of natural succession. Besides, how could my own son even think of rebelling against me?" Salim cried. He looked away, the irony of his words not escaping him. What was Khusrau doing but following his father's example? But it was not as simple as that.

Khusrau he had barely seen during his childhood; he had been brought into Salim's presence briefly on special occasions to be shown to him, and then whisked away to his nurses and attendants. Salim did not even like this son of his very much, mostly because he had never really known him.

"It is wise to be circumspect, your Highness," Mahabat Khan said. "Mirza Koka has been entertaining courtiers for many days now, doubtless asking for their support. In light of these events, it would be best not to proceed to Mewar."

"I cannot believe Khusrau will rebel against me even before the crown is upon my head. But what shall I do? I cannot disobey the Emperor," Salim said. Yet, how could he leave with this new threat rearing its head?

"Perhaps you could pretend to go to Mewar. Once you are away from the capital, we can delay our march. . . ." Mahabat's eyes gleamed. "We can always invent some excuse, your Highness."

Salim looked at the three men. They were right; he could not leave the capital now.

The prince set out with his army and arrived at Fatehpur Sikri, a day's march from Agra. There, in the city his father had built to fete his birth, the city his father had hoped would live as the capital of the Mughal Empire, he set up camp. He had a sense of comfort in coming to Fatehpur Sikri. Salim had grown up in the palaces; he had played hide-and-seek with Mahabat, Koka, and Sharif here; it was his childhood home. But just as he could never hope to recapture the days of happiness with the Emperor, when the empire had not stood between them, so too were gone his hopes of an amicable relationship with Akbar. That trust could never again be recaptured. Under his cohorts' influence, Salim sent continuous messages to Akbar: the army was not well equipped, there were not enough cavalry to support the infantry, the elephants were ailing, and so on. He demanded a full complement of soldiers before he could progress to Mewar.

After one month, Akbar was disgusted by Salim's procrastination and sent him a curt message ordering him back to his estates at Allahabad, there to raise revenues to equip the army to his satisfaction. Salim agreed and returned to Allahabad.

SENSING THE EMPEROR'S discontent with Salim, Mirza Koka and Raja Man Singh redoubled their efforts to present Khusrau as an alternative heir to the throne. They had one big advantage: Khusrau was a charming, cultured, handsome youth, much beloved by the people, more popular than his father. Prince Salim was disliked, first because of his rebellion and second because of his hand in Abul Fazl's murder.

And so the next generation rebelled against its sire, just as Salim was himself doing. While father and son were watching each other's movements warily, another heir to the throne died.

Prince Daniyal, Akbar's only other surviving son, had been left in charge of the wars in the Deccan under the guardianship of Abdur Rahim, the Khan-i-khanan. Daniyal spent his days and nights in a drunken stupor, cavorting with his wives and slave girls. Akbar had sent a strongly worded message to the Khan-i-khanan to take better care of his charge. Afraid of imperial wrath, Abdur Rahim had ordered a dry spell for Prince Daniyal; he was to be given no drink or opium, healthy food was advised, and the prince was to be kept away from any intoxicants.

Daniyal was very fond of two things, his liquor and hunting. He had even named one of his favorite muskets the *yaka u janaza*, or "same as the bier," for to be shot with that musket meant to be carried out of the hunt on a bier. Finally that musket would carry him out of his palace at Burhanpur, feet first. Deprived of his drink and suffering acutely from withdrawal symptoms, Daniyal ordered his musketeer to bring him something to drink. The musketeer, in the hopes of pleasing the prince, smuggled in doubly distilled spirit in the musket. The remains of gunpowder and rust in the barrel of the musket mixed with the liquor, and upon drinking it, Daniyal fell severely ill. After forty days of suffering, the prince died.

* * *

WITH DANIYAL'S DEATH, Salim now saw Khusrau as a viable threat to his claim on the throne. What Salim had once thought to be conjecture on the part of his courtiers—conjecture that he had nonetheless heeded—seemed to be true. The Khusrau faction was growing strong. While Salim was at Allahabad, Khusrau and his supporters were at court near the Emperor, who was every day growing weaker.

The nobles at court openly started showing their loyalties, even those who had thus far kept doggedly neutral. The Emperor's death seemed imminent, and the next heir to the throne would compensate them amply for their support. Remaining neutral, while less dangerous than advocating the wrong man, was still not as rewarding. Secret meetings were held all over Agra to calculate the risks and choose the prince most likely to succeed, and then the nobles went to offer their support.

Two religious factions approached Prince Salim at Allahabad. First, there was the Sufi faction of the Naqshbandis, orthodox Muslims who did not support Akbar's liberal religious outlook. They sent Akbar's Mir Bakshi, or Paymaster General, Shaikh Farid Bukhari, as an ambassador to Salim, promising to champion his cause if he would promote traditional Islam upon his ascension. Their support was important, and Salim readily agreed to their demands. He already had the endorsement of the Sufi faction under Shaikh Salim Chisti.

The second religious faction of some strength in the country was constituted of Portuguese Jesuits. The Portuguese had been in India for a long time and had established missions in many cities in northern India. Their support was valuable in part because they controlled the major seaports of Goa, Surat, and Cambay, the main ports of access to the Arabian Sea. Any trade conducted with Europe or the Middle Eastern countries had to pass through the hands of the Portuguese. While land routes were still in use for trade, sea routes were becoming more and more important as means of revenue. The Jesuit priests remained neutral as long as possible, realizing that Khusrau was more likely to be sympathetic to their cause than Salim, but in the end they threw their lot in with Prince Salim, sensing that he would finally be victorious.

While Khusrau was scheming on how to deprive his father of the throne, Salim continued to enjoy his simulated monarchy at Allahabad. Khusrau's mother, Princess Man Bai, was deeply grieved at the rift between her son and her husband. She wrote many letters to Khusrau, admonishing him, pointing out his duty and obedience to his father, and pleading with him to give up his ambitions. But Khusrau turned a deaf ear to her arguments. The lure of the throne was too powerful. If he had to wait out his father's reign, it would be at least thirty more years before he could ascend the throne. Finally, Man Bai gave up and took an overdose of opium, plunging Salim's court into mourning.

When the news of his daughter-in-law's death reached Agra, the Emperor sent Salim gifts and a letter of condolence, but still the two did not meet. The Emperor was still insistent that Salim pack up and go to Mewar to oversee the campaign there, and Salim still stubbornly refused to go. Father and son remained at loggerheads over the issue, for the Emperor could not see Khusrau as a threat to Salim's right to the throne.

MEHRUNNISA GAZED UNSEEINGLY out of the window, a book open on her lap. Outside, the sun glanced off the Yamuna river, turning it into a placid sheet of silver. Bees droned lazily around the bright fire-orange bougainvillea that clung to the walls of the house. The city of Agra seemed to doze in the heat, but Mehrunnisa's mind was alert, moving quickly from thought to thought.

She had followed Salim's movements closely. Each step the prince had taken alienated his father, the nobles of the court, and now the commoners. A monarchy cannot exist without the support of the people, but Salim did not realize that. The prince was even alienating the royal *zenana*, whose members had always doted on him and supported him. But the ladies were grieved to see the Emperor a ghost of his former self. Akbar was dying, slowly but surely, his death precipitated by Salim's actions.

Mehrunnisa frowned. Mahabat, Koka, and Sharif were leading Salim into jeopardy, all because they wanted to rule the empire and could not wait. She had no doubt that when Salim came to the throne, it would not be he but his cohorts who would rule.

If she had been married to him . . . no, she would not take her thoughts there again, but they rushed to her mind nevertheless. If only she could have guided him, she would have taught him to wait and act at the right moment. After all, the throne was his. He was the undisputed heir to the empire. But now, Khusrau was being put forward as the next Emperor. That callow youth—how would he rule? He could not, of course, and that would mean a regency and civil unrest, and the empire would disintegrate.

A sudden noise distracted her. Mehrunnisa turned to see Ali Quli rush into the room, but she remained as calm and collected as usual. Her face betrayed none of her thoughts.

"What can I do for you, my lord?" Mehrunnisa asked quietly.

Ali Quli sank onto the divan next to her, his face flushed with excitement. He stared at his wife. "I have some news . . . good news."

She waited for him to continue.

"Mirza Koka and Raja Man Singh are supporting Khusrau as the next heir to the throne."

"I know."

"Well, I have decided to join them."

Mehrunnisa frowned. "Join the faction against Prince Salim?"

"Yes. The prince is imprudent and unwise. Khusrau will be a better emperor. Besides," Al Quli grinned, "he is a child, and we shall rule the empire." He rubbed his hands. "Think of the power, the army I shall command, the cavalry and infantry under me. . . ." His voice trailed off as he contemplated his honors.

"My lord—," Mehrunnisa hesitated, unsure of how to continue. "As you just said, Khusrau is but a child. If," she emphasized the word, "*if* he is made emperor, it will cause civil unrest in the empire. It is unnatural to pass by the legitimate heir to the throne. Khusrau's time has not come.

Besides, Prince Salim has yearned for the throne for almost fifteen years now. Do you think he will give up his claim so easily? The final decision lies with Emperor Akbar, and he will not abandon Prince Salim. It would go against the laws of heredity and succession to leave the empire in the hands of a young grandson when his son is yet alive."

"But if the Emperor dies? What then?"

"The Emperor will definitely name Prince Salim heir before he dies. His Majesty is well aware of his duties and responsibilities to the empire. If Khusrau fights the decision, there will be unnecessary bloodshed, and people will die fighting a lost cause, for Salim is the stronger of the two," Mehrunnisa replied.

"Khusrau has Raja Man Singh on his side. Do not forget that the Raja is probably the most seasoned soldier in the whole empire: a skirmish between Salim and Khusrau will only end in Salim's defeat."

"But what of the people? And the other nobles at court? Do you think they will allow interference with the laws of succession the Chagatai Turks have followed for centuries?"

"Well . . ." Ali Quli demurred. He had not thought of the other nobles. True, Mirza Koka and Raja Man Singh were two of the most powerful nobles at court, but there were others whose support was necessary. Ail Quli flushed. Why couldn't his wife be like other men's wives? They were ready to follow their husband's initiative without question; why not Mehrunnisa?

"Mirza Koka is even now canvassing the other nobles at court for their support. They will certainly favor our cause," he said defiantly.

"Khusrau will clearly lose," Mehrunnisa said, wanting to shout at him for being so obtuse. If Ali Quli had been less of a soldier and more of a statesman, he would have seen the situation as impossible. How could a man who was so brave in battle be so stupid in all other aspects of life? Short of killing Prince Salim, there was no way that Khusrau would ascend the throne, and even if he did, he would not hold it long. "It is best to remain neutral at this time. We must wait and see how the events progress, my lord."

"No!" Ali Quli said. "I have decided. My support will be for Prince Khusrau. That is the end of the matter."

As he was leaving he turned again. "I did not come to you for advice, Mehrunnisa, merely to inform you of what I was doing. Even that seems to have been unnecessary—" He held up his hand as she opened her mouth. "Keep quiet and listen. Confine your interests to the house and the children you are supposed to have. This is man's work. Just because you cannot fulfill your responsibilities as a woman does not mean you can interfere in this issue."

"Don't talk to me like that," Mehrunnisa said. His words tore at her heart.

"I will talk to you as I wish. I am your husband. I know your father is a powerful courtier; I know he is respected by the Emperor. But it is under my roof you live. You are my wife, not anymore your father's daughter. Is that clear?"

She stared angrily at him, despising him at that moment more than she ever had, every childhood lesson on being obedient to her husband forgotten. Ali Quli bent over her, took the book from her hands, and kissed her palms, one after the other. " It is good to see that you do not cringe at my touch."

He stalked out of the room.

When he had gone, Mehrunnisa fell slowly onto the carpet, holding her hands in front of her. She spat on them and rubbed them furiously on the pile, erasing the memory of his touch. Then she collapsed and lay there, her hair shrouding her face. Her tears came unchecked, blocking her breathing, tiring her immeasurably. An hour later she was still lying on the carpet, its pattern imprinted on her wet cheek. There was no turning back from this marriage, no escape from this life. It had to go on. She had to go on: one step in front of another, a smile on her face on family occasions.

Mehrunnisa turned and lay on her back, staring up at the ceiling. She touched her belly lightly through the top of her *ghagara;* then she put her hand inside and touched her skin. Five weeks now—and every day she watched for blood. Five weeks, and she had not told Ali Quli.

Her hand still on her belly she thought of the man she was tied to. Three years ago, when Prince Salim had left Mewar to try and capture the treasury, Ali Quli had walked away from him at Agra, leaving the prince to go to Allahabad with the army. That had been a prudent move. It would have been unwise to defy the Emperor for the prince—even though in her heart, for all his mistakes, her loyalty skewed toward Salim. And it still was unwise to defy Akbar. For Mehrunnisa knew, from her conversations at the royal *zenana* and from the hints the ladies dropped, that despite all Salim might have done in the past, Akbar firmly supported him over Khusrau. To the Emperor, Khusrau was still very much a nonentity, a child, more a pest than a real threat. He could not countenance putting Khusrau on the throne over Salim, so he ignored him, even though the young prince was at court. But, Mehrunnisa thought, Salim still needed to be here at Agra to show himself. It was foolish to be away from the capital at this time.

Mehrunnisa rose from the floor as a sudden wave of nausea hit her. She ran outside to the courtyard and threw up her morning meal of *chappatis* and ducks' eggs. Her stomach churned as she wiped her mouth against the foul smell. She stayed in the courtyard for a long time, not caring that a passing servant would see her leaning against the pillar, trembling and shivering. *Please Allah, please, let this one live. Let me fulfill my responsibility as a woman. Let me be a woman.* For she knew she would never be considered one until she had a child.

Two weeks later, Prince Salim returned to Agra from Allahabad, as though in response to a silent summons from Mehrunnisa. He was received again in the *Diwan-i-am* by the Emperor. Again, Akbar took off his imperial turban in front of the whole assembly and placed it on Salim's head. It was a warning to onlookers, especially to Raja Man Singh and Mirza Aziz Koka and eventually to all of Khusrau's supporters, including Ali Quli. Akbar was ailing—of that there was no doubt—but he had risen from his sickbed to greet Salim in front of everyone.

This open show of affection sent the Khusrau faction into near panic.

TEN

This annoyed Akbar more; but his excitement was intensified,
when at that moment Khursaw came up, and abused in
unmeasured terms his father in the presence of the emperor. Akbar
withdrew, and sent next morning for Ali, to whom he said that
the vexation caused by Khursaw's bad behaviour had made
him ill.

—H. Blochmann and H. S. Jarrett,
trans., *Ain-i-Akbari*

IN 1605, SUMMER CAME TO AGRA IN A BLAZE OF BRIGHT DAYS.
For months the Indo-Gangetic plains baked in the heat of an unforgiving
sun. Rivers dried to a mere trickle, exposing huge, sandy, pebbly beds on
either side. Fishermen despaired of making a living, and farmers watched
the empty, cloudless skies with anxious eyes as the paddy fields became
parched, leaving the seedlings yellow and limp. Even the river Yamuna,
which flowed through the city in wide, smooth, clear-glass curves,
became sluggish and muddy for want of the rains. The summer monsoons were late as usual; this year it seemed they would not come.

At the royal palaces in Agra, life went on with a semblance of normal-
ity. A hush had descended over the empire since Prince Salim's return to
Agra two uneasy months earlier. Akbar took to his bed more often now,
rarely attending the daily *darbars* at the *Diwan-i-am*, and when the
Emperor did make an appearance, he shocked courtiers and onlookers by
the increasing pallor of his face and his gaunt, stooped bearing. The end
was near. Even Akbar seemed to know it. So he made Salim sit next to the
royal throne on a special *gaddi*, on his right, proclaiming his claim to the
empire. Standing farther down, much farther down, was usually a fuming
Khusrau.

The hot summer days passed slowly, listlessly. Within the *zenana* walls, gossips chattered at every corner—maids, slave girls, guards, eunuchs, ladies-in-waiting, ancillary aunts, cousins, daughters, wives, and concubines. No one even bothered to be circumspect anymore. Yet, all their lives depended on who ascended the throne. If it was Salim, his immediate harem of wives would rule the *zenana*; if Khusrau, then his wife, the daughter of Mirza Aziz Koka. It was a thought to be shuddered at. Surely Khusrau's time had not come. And among all these women sat Ruqayya Sultan Begam. As Akbar's Padshah Begam, she had the most to lose. Not only would her husband die, she would be relegated to the position of a Dowager Empress. There would perhaps be small luxuries still to be enjoyed—she would be allowed to keep her royal palace, her servants, even her income—but there would be no power any more. It would be an empty title, an impotent palace, and with it would come decreasing respect.

All that would go to Salim's chief wife, Princess Jagat Gosini.

Only Mehrunnisa knew how much the Padshah Begam loathed the idea of Jagat Gosini taking her place in the imperial *zenana*. Mehrunnisa watched Ruqayya pine for her husband, for her position in the *zenana*, and for Khurram, who spent large parts of each day by his grandfather's bed, reading to him, talking with him, or merely holding his hand as he napped. It was heart-wrenching to see young Khurram so gentle with Akbar, whom he knew better than either of his parents. During Salim's absences on campaign at Mewar and at his estates at Allahabad, Khurram had continued to stay with Ruqayya in the harem.

Mehrunnisa kept away from the intrigues as much as she could, even though she visited the *zenana* every day. Of Salim she saw very little, for outside his public appearances at the daily *darbar*, he did not come to the *zenana* very much. Everyone—even the emperor, it seemed—was waiting for something to happen. And that something happened one scorching summer day as the sun sloped in the west, sending burning rays into the city of Agra.

Irritated by the constant tension between Salim and Khusrau, Akbar commanded them to set up an elephant fight in the main courtyard of the Lal Qila. The courtyard was a large ground of flattened mud, bare of vegetation, in the northern corner of the fort. By three o'clock in the afternoon, the courtyard was packed with spectators and supporters of both the princes, dressed in their best finery. Jewels blazed on ears, arms, and wrists. The men, commoners and courtiers, filled three sides, and on the fourth side a marble pavilion stood raised from the ground, long and cool. The stone of the pillars and the floor was inlaid with flowers and leaves in lapis lazuli, carnelian, and jasper. It had sharply angled *chajjas*—eaves that rushed rainwater down and away from the flat roof of the pavilion, and four octagonal towers topped with beaten copper that gleamed orange in the light of the dying sun. The Emperor's throne, also of marble, was built into the pavilion under the *chajjas*, protecting him from the water and the heat. One end of the pavilion was covered with a fine marble netting, the stone mesh slimmer than a woman's finger in some places. The entire screen had been built from a single slab of marble. This was where the imperial *zenana*, safe behind the screen and therefore unveiled, had come for the event.

Mehrunnisa stood a little behind Ruqayya Sultan Begam, her hands clasped in front of her. Ruqayya sat in her usual arrogant style, leaning back on the divan cushions, the pipe of the *hukkah* smoking gently in her hand, her eyes watchful as ever. To her right sat Princess Jagat Gosini. The two women had barely acknowledged each other's presence when Ruqayya came into the pavilion. Jagat Gosini had risen along with the other women. But there was resistance in every bone and with every bend of her head to perform the *konish*, and she seemed to make it clear that one day, very soon, it would be Ruqayya who would do this for her. Mehrunnisa, Jagat Gosini seemed to ignore.

Now the Empress leaned forward to look at Akbar through the screen, and with her Mehrunnisa looked too. For once the Emperor looked rested; he had had a good night. When he smiled, as he did at the twelve-year-old boy sitting next to him, his face lit up with its old charm, and Mehrunnisa sensed Ruqayya relaxing by her side. Seeing his grandfather smile at him, Prince Khurram reached out for his hand and kissed it. Akbar's eyes filled with tears as he shakily patted Khurram's head. The prince leaned into the Emperor. Then, as a gust of wind blew dust into the royal verandah, Khurram's nose twitched, and he turned away to sneeze.

Behind the screen, the hands of both Ruqayya and Jagat Gosini went to their blouses, and they both pulled out silk handkerchiefs.

"Ma!" Khurram said, looking toward the harem, holding his hand to his nose.

"Here, *beta*." Ruqayya signaled to a slave girl, who proffered her handkerchief to the prince through the gaps in the marble screen.

Khurram blew his nose, tucked the silk into the sleeve of his short coat, then said, "Thank you, Ma."

Mehrunnisa watched as Jagat Gosini flinched and slowly put her handkerchief back into her blouse. The princess was trying not to attract attention, but every woman in the harem enclosure had seen that involuntary action in response to Khurram's sneeze. Jagat Gosini sat frozen, her face immobile, washed with hatred. In the past few years, as Akbar and Salim seemed to come to a tentative accord and then break from each other again, the Emperor had asked Ruqayya to let Khurram spend more time with Princes Jagat Gosini as a gesture of goodwill. Ruqayya had agreed, but only reluctantly, still fiercely possessive of the boy she had brought up as her own. So Khurram knew that Jagat Gosini was the woman who had given birth to him, while Ruqayya was "Ma." He was a respectful child, so he treated the princess with courtesy, with affection, with respect. But his love belonged to Ruqayya, and as the months passed, Jagat Gosini was also painfully aware of this.

Mehrunnisa turned to the courtyard as trumpets blared Prince Salim's signature tune. He rode in on a white horse and went up to the imperial throne. When he was directly under the Emperor, Salim bowed from the saddle. All the ladies craned their necks to look at the prince.

"What is Salim's elephant's name?" Ruqayya demanded in a loud voice.

"Giranbar, your Majesty." Both Mehrunnisa and Princess Jagat Gosini spoke at the same time. The princess's eyes flickered briefly to Mehrunnisa; then Jagat Gosini turned away with a flush as Ruqayya pointedly raised an imperious eyebrow at her.

"Ah, Giranbar," Ruqayya said. "I remember seeing the elephant at the stables a few weeks ago. He is big and strong. Salim says he eats ten kilos of sugarcane each day. He will surely win the fight. He has not lost yet, you know."

"Yes, your Majesty, but Prince Khusrau's elephant, Apurva, is also unbeaten," Mehrunnisa said.

"No, no," the Empress said, shaking her head stubbornly, "Giranbar must win. Apurva will lose today."

Mehrunnisa looked thoughtfully at the back of Ruqayya's head. For some reason, the court, the commoners, and the imperial *zenana* all expected that the outcome of this fight would determine who was the rightful heir to the throne. And Ruqayya wanted Salim to win. It was what Akbar wanted—and so, despite the fact that Jagat Gosini would usurp her position in the imperial *zenana* if Salim came to the throne, that was what Ruqayya wanted. These last two months had been slow and uncomfortable. They were all waiting for something. Waiting for Akbar's death. Waiting to see who would win the throne. Waiting—yet not wanting the Emperor to die, for either possibility seemed frightening.

The heat did not help, Mehrunnisa thought, as she stared out of the screen. Outside it was bright. Inside, where she stood, it was cool, dark, and stifling. A sudden pain jabbed her lower back, and she put a hand to it. *Not again.* It was early yet, so she had not told Ruqayya, had not wanted to ask for permission to sit, though her body ached for that rest. The pain returned: one short stab where her spine met her hips. She leaned against a nearby pillar, feeling as though she would suffocate, try-ing to appear normal, trying not to draw attention. For if any woman looked at her she would know what Mehrunnisa was going through.

Mehrunnisa caught her breath and waited for the pain to reappear. It did not. She stood upright again before Ruqayya should turn to demand why she was lounging about. But Mehrunnisa did not notice Princess Jagat Gosini look sharply in her direction, once, twice, then a third time, before swinging her head back to the sound of the trumpets that heralded Prince Khusrau's arrival. In those brief looks, Jagat Gosini had seen the small swelling of Mehrunnisa's belly, had seen her face drain of color, had watched her falter on her feet.

"Another one. Good." Jagat Gosini said this so softly that even her slaves did not hear her. She looked through the screen at the prince.

Prince Khusrau rode up to the Emperor, dismounted, and bowed. Akbar nodded only briefly to him, and the prince turned away, his face red but determined. Then, with a stiff bow to Salim, Khusrau rode over to the other side and reined in his horse.

A loud roar went up from the crowd as the two elephants were led in by their mahouts. Mehrunnisa saw Prince Salim glance at Apurva, then turn worriedly to Mahabat Khan, who stood near him. She wanted to tell him to wipe away the worry lines; Apurva looked big and fierce, but Giranbar looked more so. It would be an exciting fight. The crowd hushed into silence as the referee of the fight, clad in red and gold livery, rode up to the imperial balcony.

"Your Majesty, we await your signal."

Akbar turned to Khurram. "Would you like to give the signal, Khurram?"

"Yes, Dadaji," Khurram replied eagerly. Then, turning to the referee, he said, "Where is the reserve?"

"He is being led in, your Highness," the man replied. Just then, the Emperor's elephant, Rantamhan, was brought into the enclosure. The rules of the elephant fight dictated, somewhat loosely and mostly based on the Emperor's whim, that if the fight was won too easily by one elephant, then the reserve would come to the assistance of the loser of the fight. Rantamhan was the reserve elephant, not as big as either Apurva or Giranbar, but with enough battle scars to prove his fighting prowess.

"Let the fight begin!" Khurram shouted.

The crowd roared with delight. Salim and Khusrau edged their horses closer. Giranbar and Apurva were led to the center of the courtyard and faced each other across a low mud wall, built that morning for this purpose.

The trumpets blew, and the mahouts, specially trained in the fight, urged the elephants forward. The two beasts rushed through the mud wall, clashing into each other with a deep thud. They retreated, and then, prodded by the mahouts, turned to clash again. Soon, Khusrau's Apurva was dizzy and teetering from the hits. Immediately, Akbar's elephant was urged into the fray.

Salim's noblemen, seeing Rantamhan entering the arena, jumped up and down in anger. They whooped out "No help to Apurva" and threw sticks, stones, and anything they could find at the elephant to dissuade it. One of the stones hit Rantamhan's mahout, who began to bleed from the head.

Chaos reigned over the entire courtyard as the men howled curses and threats at Rantamhan. Khusrau broke away from the group around the elephants and rode up wildly to Akbar's throne.

"Your Majesty, please tell the prince's men to desist from interfering. Apurva has a right to be helped by Rantamhan," he cried, his face twisted with anger.

Akbar turned to Prince Khurram. "Go to your father and tell him to restrain his attendants, or we shall stop the fight and appropriate all the elephants."

"At once, your Majesty." Khurram jumped down from the pavilion and ran into the field.

"Thank you, your Majesty." Khusrau turned his horse to leave.

"One minute, Khusrau," Akbar called out. When the prince was facing him again, Akbar beckoned him closer.

"Remember your position in court, Khusrau. You are a royal prince. It is highly unbecoming to ride up and complain about your father like this. Where is your respect for your elders?"

Khusrau flushed. "I apologize, your Majesty."

"As you must. Go now, and don't let us see you until you have learned your manners." The Emperor stared straight ahead.

Mehrunnisa saw Khusrau glance around to see who had been listening to his exchange with the Emperor, then his neck stiffened as he looked toward the *zenana*. What the harem knew, the whole city—no, the empire—would know by tomorrow. Khusrau turned his horse around savagely and galloped to his attendants.

When Khurram reached his father with the Emperor's message, Salim was trying to control his attendants. But the men were too excited and would not stop. By this time, the entire courtyard was noisy and resounding with the words "No help to Apurva." The commoners joined in the fray, yelling, screaming, fighting with each other, and generally enjoying themselves. No one watched the elephant fight.

An enraged Giranbar first chased Khusrau's elephant Apurva away, and then turned on Rantamhan, the royal interloper. Rantamhan, no match for Salim's elephant, fled to the banks of the Yamuna. There, seeing that Giranbar, now uncontrolled by his mahout, was still following, he jumped into the river. Finally, after an hour, attendants were able to separate the elephants by bringing boats between them and stopping the enraged Giranbar.

Long before this, Mehrunnisa saw the Emperor rise from his throne and leave for his apartments, sick and disgusted with the public display of hatred between his son and his grandson.

As Akbar left, the women in the *zenana* enclosure rushed to the doors. One woman pushed Mehrunnisa in her haste. She tripped and then steadied herself, forcing a smile in response to the apology. A sudden pain surged through her body. Mehrunnisa walked back to the palaces, her back stooped from the pain, cramps imprisoning her belly. And she waited for the blood to come again.

THE UNHAPPY EMPEROR lay in bed that night with a raging fever, his heart heavy at the enmity between Salim and Khusrau. If the rift was allowed to continue, civil war would break out in his cherished empire— an empire he had spent forty-nine years building. There was no question of Khusrau ascending the throne; he was too young, and it would be dangerous to leave the empire in the care of a regency. Salim was the rightful heir to the throne, and Akbar did not want to meddle with the laws of succession.

But the Emperor's intentions would have to wait. For Akbar was critically ill, falling into bouts of delirium and slipping in and out of consciousness. The royal physicians were helpless, and it was clear to everyone that the end was near.

A FEW DAYS passed. Prince Salim, at his palace at Agra, a few miles downstream from the royal fort, rejoiced in his victory over Khusrau. It was sign from the heavens, he thought. He would be Emperor of Mughal India. The words reverberated in his mind like a delicious song not yet worn out. But it was a happiness tempered by sorrow, for Akbar was on his deathbed. Salim went more often now to see the Emperor. At first, Ruqayya and the other ladies of the harem were distrustful of the visits. They watched keen-eyed for signs of fatigue in Akbar, for irritation at his son's presence. Slowly, they grew less suspicious. Salim sat for hours by his father's beside, reading to him when he wanted that, being there when his eyes opened from a fitful sleep, returning to his palace late at night after the Emperor had bade him go. "Do not worry about Khusrau," Akbar said to him one afternoon. "I will not, your Majesty," Salim replied, determined that he wouldn't. The elephant fight had had its repercussions. He had no doubt that he would win the crown. What could Khusrau do, after all?

But Salim underestimated both his son and his son's associates. While the prince spent time at the Emperor's palace, Khusrau's followers began to plan in earnest.

Mirza Aziz Koka, as Khan Azam, or First Lord of the realm, was made acting vice-regent of the empire during Akbar's illness. To ensure his son-in-law's position, Mirza Koka secretly dismissed Akbar's old retainers and filled the posts in and around the fort with his own men. But Khusrau was still insecure.

"Is this enough?" he asked his father-in-law, worry written over his young forehead. "My father commands a large army. He will fight us."

"There is one other thing we could do," Mirza Koka said slowly. "We could capture the prince on his next visit to the Emperor. That way, we will face no danger from Prince Salim's army."

Khusrau clapped his hands in delight. "That is a wonderful plan, Mirza Koka. But," the glee faded from his face, "I don't want my father killed. He won't be in any danger, will he?"

"No, your Highness," Koka said reassuringly. "We will simply imprison him until you are crowned Emperor."

Khusrau nodded. "Good.'

Mirza Koka watched him thoughtfully. Did the prince really think he could hold the crown while his father was still alive? He would have to arrange a small accident while Salim was in prison. Then the crown would be theirs forever.

THE NEXT DAY, just as Salim was about to disembark from his royal barge on a visit to the Emperor, a young man came running out of the fort.

"Your Highness, your Highness, please turn back. There is great danger here."

Mahabat Khan immediately pulled Salim back into the boat and, shielding him with his body, asked the man, "What danger? Speak up."

"Mirza Koka plans to capture and imprison you within the fort, your Highness," the man gasped, out of breath. "He has dismissed all of the Emperor's servants. The fort is filled with supporters of Prince Khusrau."

As he finished speaking an arrow whizzed past Mahabat Khan's ear. The man fell to the ground, clutching his bloody arm.

Mahabat pushed Salim down and covered him with his own body. He yelled to the boatmen, and they hurriedly pushed away from the pier. The prince forced Mahabat aside and looked over the rim of the boat. He saw the archer, now visible over the ramparts of the fort, raise his bow and take deliberate aim at the informant on the ground. Then Mahabat shoved him to the floor of the boat again, and they rowed back to Salim's palace. There, Mahabat called for the guards and escorted Salim inside.

SALIM WALKED INTO his apartments on trembling legs, his mouth dry. An attempt had been made on his life by his own son. How could Khusrau stoop to such a level? Was the crown worth such disloyalty? For a brief moment, guilt washed over him. He, Salim, had once wanted the throne with the same intensity as Khusrau. In fact, he still wanted it— only now it was rightfully his. But Khusrau's actions defied all reason. To kill his father in cold blood, in the open, in the daylight—how would he have justified Salim's death to the empire?

"Bring me some wine," he roared at a passing servant.

The servant scurried off.

Salim looked up and saw Jagat Gosini. She bowed to her husband. "You are back early, your Highness. I hope his Majesty is keeping well."

"There has been a plot to capture me. I barely escaped with my life," Salim said.

A frown crossed the princess's face. "By whom? Who would dare plot on your life?"

"Khusrau," Salim said wearily as he sat down on a divan.

The servant appeared, bearing a large silver tray with a wine flask and goblets. Jagat Gosini waited quietly while Salim drank his wine. She was troubled. If Khusrau had the arrogance to attempt to capture his own father, what would he try to do to Khurram? Her son was still at the fort in Agra. Ordinarily the Padshah Begam Ruqayya would have looked after him—this much Jagat Gosini admitted only in her private thoughts— but with the Emperor ill, all of the Empress's attention was centered on him.

"Your Highness, Khurram is with the Emperor. Do you think . . ." She hesitated. "Do you think he is safe there?"

"Khusrau would not do anything to hurt his own brother," Salim said.

The princess shook her head slowly. If Salim posed a threat to Khusrau's bid for the throne, Khurram did too. He was also a royal prince and had as much claim on the throne as Khusrau.

"But still . . . ," she said, persisting, "I would feel more secure if he was with us."

"Send for him, then," Salim said. "Leave me now. I wish to think."

"Yes, your Highness." The princess went to her rooms, had her writing materials brought to her, and wrote to her son.

Khurram steadfastly refused his mother's command. He insisted upon staying with his grandfather in his last days, and nothing she could say would change his mind. When Jagat Gosini received his reply, her heart hardened briefly. This was all Ruqayya's doing, as usual. If the Empress had let her bring up her son, as was natural, he would have listened to her now. One day she would pay back the Empress, and that day *would* come, no matter what.

MEANWHILE, MIRZA AZIZ KOKA was not idle. He had the informant killed as soon as Salim fled and then, realizing that he could not capture the prince, called Raja Man Singh. One attempt had failed; the two men knew they would not be given another. Something else had to be done. The two courtiers decided to hold a conference, to which they invited all the nobles of the court. There, they put forward Khusrau as the heir to the throne and asked for support. It was a bold move, but the only thing they could do now. Everything had to come out into the open.

While the conference was taking place, a spy at Agra fort came running to Salim with the news that the cannons atop the ramparts were pointed at his palace and were being made ready to fire. Salim panicked, the assassination attempt still fresh in his mind. In a hurry, without thinking, he ordered his effects to be packed and the horses readied for an immediate departure to Allahabad. It took all of Koka's, Abdullah's, and Mahabat Khan's persuasive abilities to get Salim to stay back at Agra. A departure at this juncture would prove fatal. Akbar could die at any time, and if Salim was not on the spot, Khusrau would immediately be crowned Emperor. Finally, Salim saw reason in their arguments. He had been temporarily overcome by fear. For all he had done and felt in his life, Salim had never been afraid. Now he knew fear, and it came coupled with a deep pain at Khusrau's actions. The attempt on his life brought a sudden and sobering realization that Khusrau was serious about his bid for the throne.

Salim agreed to stay at Agra, but he would not let Mahabat, Koka, and Abdullah convince him to send emissaries to the conference to court the nobles and persuade them to his side. He had done all he could. Now, if he were to be Emperor, it was in Allah's hands.

Meanwhile, the conference was progressing badly for Khusrau. While some of the nobles were still uncertain as to where their loyalties lay, one group was particularly vociferous in dissent. The Barha Sayyids, an ancient Mughal family connected with the imperial house, loudly protested the accession of Khusrau. They argued that Salim was the natural heir to the throne and that to promote Khusrau was to interfere with the laws of Chagatai succession. The Chagatai Turks determined their ancestry through Gengiz Khan the Mongol. The current imperial house was descended not only from Timur the Lame but also from Gengiz Khan.

In the face of such stiff opposition, the conference broke down. The Barha Sayyids were an important powerful family; to oppose them would have been dangerous. So the nobles refused to support Khusrau, and Sayyid Khan Barha, the head of the clan, rode to Salim to inform him of the outcome.

Mirza Koka now realized his tenuous position and hastened to Salim's palace to beg his forgiveness. Salim, magnanimous in victory, forgave Mirza Koka. But while Khusrau's father-in-law deserted him, his uncle Raja Man Singh was not deterred; he secreted Khusrau out of the fort at Agra and went into hiding. The plan was to take him by boat to Bengal, where Raja Man Singh had his estates.

* * *

THE MESSAGE CAME in the middle of the night. The searing, breathless summer days had finally broken as dense indigo clouds rolled over the horizon. A cool, welcome breeze swept through the brick-paved streets, and windows were thrown open to the evening. Sluggish pariah dogs in the bazaars lifted their heads up to gulp down fresh air. In the gardens, lawns glowed and flowers bloomed. Even the earth seemed to smile. Finally, after so many months of dry heat, the summer monsoons had arrived. As night fell, the hot, pale moon that had hung motionless in the sky was blotted by clouds. *Charpoys* and cots were dragged to outside verandahs and rooftops for the night's rest. The city slept in anticipation of waking to a drenching, life-giving shower.

But even as dreams were colored by the rains and relief from the heat, a lone messenger pounded his way through the silent streets, riding hard to the palaces of Prince Salim. An hour later, Salim rode into the main court-yard of the imperial palace. He pulled up his horse, jumped down, and threw the reins to the waiting groom. As he raced through the corridors to the Emperor's apartments, Salim noticed that the servants and slaves lining the way seemed to bow much more deeply than they had before. His heart pounding, Salim burst into Akbar's room and stopped at the door, staring at the silent, still figure on the bed in the center of the room.

Two oil lamps flickered in the soft midnight breeze by the Emperor's bed. The windows and doors to the outside had been thrown open, and muslin curtains surged inward gently. In the shadows were people— many people; Salim saw them from the corner of his eye. A tinkle of ban-gles drew his attention to the far corner of the room, and he recognized the round shape of Ruqayya's head. Next to her, bent over the cushions of the divan, soft sobs escaped from another of Akbar's wives, Salima Sultan Begam.

Just then the Emperor stirred.

"Has the prince come?"

Salim's heart wrenched at the rasp in his father's voice. He went up to the bed, grasped Akbar's hand, and kissed it.

"I am here, Bapa."

"Shaiku Baba." Akbar's eyes swam with unshed tears. He shakily reached out for Salim's head and smoothed his hair.

Salim stared back at his father, forcing back tears himself. Akbar had always called him "Shaiku Baba" as a child. It had been many years since his father had called him by any term of endearment, especially this one.

"Rest now, Bapa," Salim said softly. "I will be here till you fall asleep."

Akbar smiled. "Now there will only be the eternal rest. But before that, I have to do something. . . ." He turned to his attendants.

Two eunuchs came forward with the Emperor's robes of state and his scimitar. At a signal from him, the robes were wrapped around the prince, and Akbar's scimitar, the Fath-ul-mulk, was girdled around his waist. Then the Emperor relaxed back onto the pillows.

Salim fell to his knees, buried his face in his hands, and began sobbing.

"Do not cry, Baba," Akbar said with an effort. Then, drawing in a deep breath, he continued: "We entrust in you the care of the people of this great empire, all the wealth in the treasury, and its administration." The Emperor's voice died to a whisper, and Salim leaned forward to hear his father's words. "Take care of your mothers. All the harem ladies now depend on you . . . look after them." Akbar waved his hand around the room at the weeping attendants. "Take care of the servants; they have attended us well. Fulfill your responsibilities—" The Emperor fell into a fit of coughing.

"I will, Bapa," Salim said, tears coursing down his face. "I will do whatever you tell me."

They stayed like that for a few minutes, Salim with his forehead against his father's hand, the Emperor lying back on the bed, peace written over his face. Then the prince rose and circled his father's bed three times. For all their differences, no one had loved him with as much devotion as his father had, and Salim felt a brief pang for the many years they had spent estranged from each other.

He sat there by Akbar's side all through the cool night, holding the Emperor's hand. When the monsoon clouds finally let loose their bur-

den of rain and a feeble sun broke over the eastern horizon, Salim felt his
father's breathing slow to nothingness and his father's hand cool in his.

THE NEXT DAY, Salim watched as last rites were performed for Akbar.
His body was washed twice, once in pure water and a second time in
camphor water, and covered with a clean white cloth. Three more
shrouds were wrapped around the Emperor, and then he was laid in a
sandalwood coffin. The Emperor had, a few months ago, commenced
building a tomb for himself at Sikandara, six miles from Agra. Here he
would rest for eternity. The tomb was as yet little more than a clearing of
land. Only the first level had been built. It was square, with arched verandahs, the central arch towering thirty feet from the ground.

It rained all morning when the Emperor's body was taken on foot to the
tomb. The paths were heavy with mud and sludge. Salim went with the
funeral cortege, barefoot and bareheaded like the other mourners. For the
last few kilometers, the prince replaced one of the official pallbearers. He
carried his father's bier on his shoulders and watched as it was deposited
in its final resting place. Salim knelt to kiss the cold marble covering
Akbar's grave. After the mourners had left, he stood outside in the rain,
the water mixing with his tears. When the tomb was completed, it would
stand as a monument to his father's greatness. Years from now, the people
of Hindustan would come here to pay their respects to a great Emperor.
And he, Salim, would look after this cherished empire as well as he could.
Future generations would deem Akbar's choice of heir the right one.

A week of mourning was ordered for the Mughal emperor.

Finally, after almost fifteen years of yearning for the throne of India,
Salim was crowned Emperor at the fort in Agra.

He gave himself the title Nuruddin Muhammad Jahangir Padshah
Ghazi.

Posterity would know him as Emperor Jahangir.

ELEVEN

By the boundless favours of Allah, when one sidereal hour of
Thursday, Jumada-s-sani 20th, A.H. 1014 (October 24th,
1605) had passed, I ascended the royal throne in the capital of
Agra, in the 38th year of my age.

—A. Rogers, trans., and H. Beveridge,
ed., *The Tuzuk-i-Jahangiri*

THE MORNING SUN PEEPED OVER THE ROOFTOPS, LIGHTING UP THE
street with shimmering bands of light. White turbans gleamed, silk *gha-*
garas glowed, and jewels glittered as the crowd pressed forward eagerly
past the row of soldiers. They had been waiting on the streets all morning, some even since the previous evening. It had rained again at night
and the people had taken shelter under jute mats and cotton umbrellas.
For many of them, this day, when an Emperor first made his appearance
in public, would come only once in their lives. They were willing to wait
for the moment, come what might. Finally, their patience was rewarded
as the royal entourage turned the street corner.

"Padshah Salamat!" the crowd roared. "Hail to the Emperor!"

Emperor Jahangir smiled. He sat upright on his magnificently
appointed horse, which wore a bridle of pure beaten silver, a saddle of
deep blue silk studded with rubies, and a white plume of goose feathers
on its head. The Emperor was followed by two of his sons, Prince
Khurram and Prince Parviz, and behind them Koka, Abdullah, Mahabat
Khan, and Sharif, his most important ministers of state.

As Jahangir rode slowly through the street a shower of jasmine and
marigold flowers came down upon him from the house balconies overhead. The petals swirled in the washed morning air, spreading perfume
around him. Jahangir dipped his hand into his saddlebag, drew out a

handful of silver coins, and threw them. The people roared appreciatively as they scrambled for the money, pushing against the soldiers who were trying to keep them in control.

All this was for him, Jahangir thought triumphantly. The people loved him. He was their Emperor.

A sudden hush came over the crowd as the sun glanced off their Emperor's person. He wore a long brocade *qaba* studded with ruby buttons, tight silk trousers, and jewel-encrusted shoes. A gold cummerbund encircled his waist; from it hung an emerald-and-pearl-studded dagger. Rubies, emeralds, and diamonds glittered on his hands. On his head sat the turban of state, fringed with milky white pearls and plumed with heron feathers held in place by a large diamond the size of a pigeon's egg. This was majesty in all its glory, and here was the Emperor of what was possibly the richest kingdom of the time. The crowd looked on in awe.

Jahangir smiled in delight. This was his first public appearance since his father's death. The coronation had been a short, hurried affair, partly because he was still in mourning and partly because of the threat from Khusrau, who was still in hiding with Raja Man Singh.

But now, finally, he was Emperor of Mughal India. The royal entourage passed slowly through the city of Agra, entering the fort at the Amar Singh gateway through three gates, each at sharp right angles to the other to confuse an attacking army. They rode up the steep ramp past the last gate bordered by sheer sandstone walls into the courtyard of the *Diwan-i-am*. The Emperor reined in his horse and stood for a moment, looking up at one of the balconies. It was filled with veiled ladies clad in colorful muslins. One lady stood apart from the others and to the front, a jeweled turban adorning her head. A slight breeze molded her veil to her face, and Jahangir saw a slow, proud smile widen her mouth. Jagat Gosini bowed deeply to him, and when she lifted her head, Jahangir bowed back from the saddle at his chief Empress.

Ruqayya was not at the balcony. She chose to spend her days in her apartments, still in mourning for Emperor Akbar. And since Ruqayya was not there, neither was Mehrunnisa.

Jahangir and Jagat Gosini looked at each other across the breadth of the courtyard. The imperial orchestra started to play. The leather-headed *dholaks* resonated with loud booms. The gold tassels on the musicians' trumpets fluttered in the wind. Large brass cymbals clanged in tune with the music. The sun danced off the sea of jewels in turbans and shimmered on the gold embroidery of *qabas* and sashes. "Long live Emperor Jahangir!" The cry resounded around the walls as the assembled nobles punched their fists in the air. "Hail to Empress Jagat Gosini!" the women in the balconies cried out in unison. Both of them raised their right hands to their foreheads and bowed, again and again. Jahangir smiled at Jagat Gosini, dismounted, and led the way through the courtiers to his throne.

COURT WAS IN session at the *Diwan-i-am* in the royal fort at Agra. The Emperor's throne, at one end, was set in a small balcony raised five feet from the ground, enclosed in a verandah held up by marble pillars. Two huge wooden elephants adorned the front of the balcony, on which stood slaves with fly switches. The nobles were assembled around the throne in three groups, each distanced from the Emperor according to its rank and status.

"Call Mirza Ghias Beg!" The Mir Tozak's voice rang out in the silent courtyard.

Ghias Beg came forward and performed the *taslim*. Earlier that week, Mehrunnisa had visited his house, and father and daughter had sat together in the garden after lunch in a companionable silence. Ghias had looked at her intently, wondering why a little smile lit up her eyes every now and then. Ah, she was beautiful, this child of his. More beautiful and kind and gentle than his other children—a fact he would not admit to. If only he could wipe away the sudden, fleeting sorrow that came upon her every now and then. Was it because she had no child? Ghias was a man, not used to gossiping in the women's quarters of his house or to hearing gossip about women's doings, but Mehrunnisa's childlessness hurt him deeply, because it must surely cause her pain.

"Tell me," he commanded, leaning over to kiss her forehead.

"Remember to perform the *konish* properly, Bapa," she replied. "I know"—she waved away his objecting gesture—"I know you have done the *konish* many times, and to the great Emperor Akbar himself. But these are new times, and with new times will come new honors, new rewards. Oh, Bapa, how wonderful this all is for you."

"We can only hope," Ghias murmured, smiling nonetheless.

Then they both sobered, thinking of Ali Quli. Mehrunnisa's husband had openly supported Prince Khusrau, who was now in deep disgrace. Ali Quli's follies would not touch Ghias, but they would affect Mehrunnisa as his wife. Only time would tell how.

The rectangular overhead *punkahs* in the *Diwan-i-am* swished back and forth, pulled by a rope on the ground. Ghias felt their cool breeze fan the back of his neck as he straightened up from the *taslim* in front of Emperor Jahangir. He remembered when, so many years ago, there had been such madness between Salim and Mehrunnisa. If anything had come of it, his daughter would have been an Empress. He waited for his emperor to speak.

Jahangir looked down from his magnificent throne. "Mirza Beg, I am pleased with your service to the empire and to my esteemed father."

"I only did my duty, your Majesty."

"And you did it well, Mirza Beg," Jahangir said, "From this day, you will be *diwan* of the empire along with Wazir Khan."

Ghias Beg felt his knees go weak under him. He had expected a new title, yes, but *diwan*? Allah must have smiled on him. He thought back to twenty-eight years ago, when, standing on a busy bazaar street in Qandahar on the outer fringe of the Mughal Empire with only four precious gold *mohurs* tucked in his cummerbund, he had wondered how he would support his family. Now he was treasurer of that empire. "Thank you, your Majesty. It is a great honor."

Jahangir nodded. "You will also be called Itimadaddaula."

"Pillar of the Government." Ghias bent his head, glorying in the moment. It would be hard to focus on the rest of the *darbar* after such an honor. Silently, he bowed again to the Emperor and backed to his place.

Jahangir turned and nodded to the Mir Tozak.

"Call Muhammad Sharif!"

Muhammad Sharif came forward. Sharif had been left at Allahabad as governor when the Emperor returned to Agra to be by his father's side. Sharif was made the chief minister of state and given the title of Grand Vizier and Amir-ul-umra.

Bir Singh Deo, the rebel chieftain who had murdered Abul Fazl on Jahangir's orders, now came out of hiding. He was given a *mansab* of three thousand horses and the title Raja. The Emperor did not forget even him. Fazl's death had been necessary to his plans, even though it had caused his father much pain. Part of being royal was making those decisions; who would live and who would die.

Finally, it was time to deal with the dissenters.

A hush came over the court as the Mir Tozak's voice rang out again. "Call Ali Quli!"

The courtiers parted and made way for Mehrunnisa's husband. A truculent Ali Quli came forward and performed the *taslim*.

Jahangir looked at him thoughtfully. What was he to do with this man? Ali Quli had deserted him at Agra and had joined up with the Khusrau faction. Should he put him to death for disloyalty? *That would free Mehrunnisa.* The thought came out of nowhere, with no warning. Now that he was Emperor, she could be his. He looked down at his hands, at the ruby and diamond ring Akbar had worn and then given to him. So many years had passed since that evening in the verandah outside Empress Ruqayya's apartments. They had both been young then— children really. But it was impossible that she remembered. Too much time had passed. He looked up to meet Ali Quli's unflinching gaze, aware that the whole court watched them. He had given this man the title of Tiger Slayer because he had saved his life in the forests near Mewar. It was a heavy debt to bear.

"I have decided to overlook your misdeeds, Ali Quli," Jahangir said. "You were misled by dissident elements in my empire, but your long years of bravery in the battlefield and your services to me speak on your

behalf. You are granted the *jagir* of Bardwan in Bengal. Prepare to leave
for your estates tomorrow."

A surprised chatter broke out in court. The Emperor had in effect pardoned Ali Quli. Jahangir nodded to himself. He had done right; Akbar
would have approved.

"Silence in the court!" the Mir Tozak shouted.

The nobles quieted as a servant approached the Mir Tozak. They had
a whispered conversation. The Mir Tozak went up to Jahangir.

"Your Majesty, Prince Khusrau begs an audience."

At his words, the whole court drew in a breath of surprise again. The
new Emperor's first audience was proving to be unpredictable and exciting. The courtiers would have a lot to talk about tonight at dinner.
Tomorrow the news would fly all over the empire.

Jahangir smiled to himself at the reaction. Only a few people knew
that Khusrau had been captured and brought into custody. He had
wanted it thus.

"Command him here."

Raja Man Singh and Khusrau entered the *Diwan-i-am*. Khusrau slunk
in behind the raja, his face red, unwilling to meet his father's eyes. Uncle
and nephew quickly paid obeisance to their new Emperor.

"Come here, Khusrau," Jahangir ordered.

Khusrau approached his father diffidently. Jahangir rose, descended
from his throne, and embraced his son in front of the court. The nobles
murmured their approval. The Emperor stepped back, still holding onto
Khusrau's stiff shoulders. What was he to do with this son of his? Now
that he had the crown firmly on his head, Khusrau no longer posed an
open threat to him—but could he ever be completely sure? He looked at
his son, and just for a moment Khusrau met his eyes with a look of pure
malevolence. Then the prince looked down.

Jahangir recoiled, let go of his son, and went back to his throne. He
forced his voice to be neutral. "You have betrayed me," he said aloud.
"The empire has witnessed a son's disloyalty to his father. Your actions
have shamed you, and now you are here to beg forgiveness. I shall grant

you that forgiveness; after all, you are my son. Let the court be witness to
the love and affection I bear for you despite your treachery."

The nobles nodded appreciatively.

Jahangir looked around at the Mir Bakshi, the Paymaster of the court.
"Give Prince Khusrau one hundred thousand rupees and a house to live in."

Khusrau fell to his knees and mumbled, "Thank you, your Majesty.
Your generosity knows no bounds. I am truly ashamed of my misdeeds
and beg forgiveness if I have caused you any distress."

Jahangir then turned to Raja Man Singh. The old general looked up at
the Emperor from under white bushy eyebrows, holding himself upright
with pride.

Man Singh had originally secreted Khusrau away from the fort with
the intention of taking him to Bengal, but once Jahangir had been
crowned Emperor, he realized that the effort was futile. Besides, the two
had found all roads closed to them. Jahangir had positioned guards along
the Yamuna river and on the way to Bengal, and Raja Man Singh and
Khusrau had been politely turned back. They had not been arrested,
however, but Man Singh took the hint and brought Khusrau back to
Agra to plead mercy from Jahangir.

The Emperor knew that he could not publicly shame Raja Man Singh
as he had done Khusrau. It would be better to placate him now. He
needed Raja Man Singh in Bengal, which was a hotbed of dissident activity and still a stronghold of Afghan rebels. The climate was damp and
unhealthy and seemed to foster discontent among the locals.
Consequently, the governor of Bengal had to be a strong statesman and a
brave warrior. Man Singh was both, and so was Ali Quli. Although the
two had previously collaborated on Khusrau's behalf, they could do little
to further his son's cause in Bengal while Khusrau was at Agra under
Jahangir's custody.

"Raja Man Singh, I forgive your role in Khusrau's revolt. It was understandable, given the nature of your relationship to him. As a sign of my
pardon, your *mansab* will be raised to two thousand horses, and you will
continue your post as governor of Bengal," Jahangir said, as the Mir

Tozak brought forward the *charqab*, a sleeveless vest, as a robe of honor, and a jeweled sword to present to the Raja.

"Thank you, your Majesty." Man Singh bowed to the Emperor and moved back to his place in the court.

Court was adjourned for the day.

JAHANGIR LAY ON his royal bed, staring up at the golden canopy. The first day of duties had passed.

Emperor! With a sudden shiver Jahangir realized once again the word pertained to him. With Khusrau in custody, he was undisputed Emperor. And he would stay so. It was an obligation that thrilled him, yet unnerved him. He would guard the responsibility well. As soon as Jahangir arrived back to the harem he had sent for his Grand Vizier, Muhammad Sharif.

"Muhammad, I want a twenty-four-hour guard posted around Prince Khusrau's apartments. No one shall meet him without my permission. Also, I want spies put in his service. Khusrau has not yet given up his quest for the throne; I could see it in his face at court. See to it that he is cut off from any communication from the outside."

"It shall be done, your Majesty." Muhammad Sharif's face broke into a malicious grin. His cold eyes suddenly gleamed. Muhammad and Prince Khusrau had been at odds even before Khusrau's revolt, and he was happy to have charge of the prince's custody. Jahangir could not have chosen a better jailer.

Now, alone at night, the attendants and wives dismissed, Jahangir said his title out aloud: "Nuruddin Muhammad Jahangir Padshah Ghazi." Nuruddin meant "Light of the Faith," Padshah denoted "Emperor" or "head of the house of Timur," and Jahangir meant "World Conqueror."

Janangir smiled. He was Emperor of the world, like the sun to his people. They depended on his bounty just as the farmer depends on sunlight. And he was the head of the house of Timur, the ultimate symbol of independent sovereignty.

The day had been very satisfactory indeed, Jahangir thought. All of his supporters had been publicly rewarded, and the dissidents had been punished . . . all except one: Mirza Aziz Koka, Khusrau's father-in-law. Jahangir clicked his tongue. Khusrau, always Khusrau. Something would have to be done about Mirza Koka. He could not reside here at Agra with Khusrau so near. Something would be done about Mirza Koka.

Jahangir closed his eyes as the room blurred into a haze.

"MIRZA AZIZ KOKA, Emperor Jahangir commands your presence."

The doors at the far end of the *Diwan-i-khas* swung open silently on well-oiled hinges.

The nobles parted to make way for Khusrau's father-in-law. Mirza Koka marched into the court, his head bowed, his cheeks burning.

Mahabat Khan and Muhammad Sharif, standing closest to the Emperor as a sign of their status in court, smiled slyly at each other. Behind the throne, the *zenana* ladies crowded in the balcony, hidden from view by a latticework marble screen. Mirza Koka, foster brother to Akbar, had grown up in the royal harem. He was a great favorite of the ladies, and they had turned out in full force to witness his trial.

Mirza Koka's footsteps echoed in the silent court. As soon as he was under the throne, he saluted the Emperor with the *konish* and waited, his eyes on the ground, for Jahangir to speak.

Jahangir looked at him, his nostrils curling with dislike. Mirza Koka had actively championed Khusrau's cause, and unlike Raja Man Singh, he had no merit as a soldier and therefore was of no use to the throne.

"Mirza Koka, you have greatly displeased me with your actions."

"I have begged for and been granted your Majesty's pardon," Mirza Koka replied, raising his eyes.

"Nonetheless, you have been summoned here for the council to decide your fate," Jahangir said sharply.

In Mughal India, the monarch was the absolute and immediate power, and everyone assembled knew that Jahangir was looking for an excuse to retry the old statesman. Everyone also knew why.

Janangir turned to Mahabat Khan. "Mahabat, what would be a fitting punishment for the crime that Mirza Koka has committed against his Emperor?"

"There can be only one, your Majesty, and that is death," Mahabat replied. "Mirza Koka is indeed guilty of a serious crime. The punishment should fit the deed. By that you will indicate to others who might be contemplating the same sin that they would be wise not to try and rebel against your august person."

"You are right. Mirza Koka"—the Mirza looked up at Jahangir— "I have decided your fate. You have been inconsistent to the monarchy. You have tried to put on the throne a callow youth, one who would have been unable to rule, all to further your own interest and power. You are guilty of a greater sin: you have alienated a father and son, you have interfered in the sacred relationship between me and my son Khusrau—"

"Your Majesty!"

A gasp went around the court. Who would dare to interrupt the Emperor? Rigid etiquette demanded that everyone remain silent when the Emperor spoke, and never raise their eyes to the throne unless directly questioned. The interruption surprised Jahangir too, and he stopped in mid-sentence, the words dying in his mouth. Mahabat Khan pointed silently to the *zenana* balcony.

"What is it?" Jahangir forced his voice to be pleasant.

"Your Majesty, all the Begams of *zenana* are here for the purpose of intervening for Mirza Koka. It will be better if you come to us; otherwise we will come out to you," a voice called out.

The voice was that of Salima Sultan Begam, his father's widow and one of his stepmothers. Next to Ruqayya, it was Salima who had held a special place in the late Emperor's heart. So Akbar had never reined in her impulsiveness, and it was too late to control her now anyway. Jahangir thought for a while. He would have to go to the *zenana* balcony; otherwise Salima was sure to make good her threat and come down. It would be the first time in an imperial Mughal court that a member of the royal *zenana* was seen by the nobles. And knowing Salima, she might also come down unveiled. That thought, more than any other, made the Emperor rise quickly from his seat.

As Jahangir got up, Mirza Koka breathed a sigh of relief and glanced up at the balcony. He could make out one of the ladies waving to him, and he smiled weakly in gratitude.

Jahangir entered the *zenana* balcony. The ladies bowed to him as he sat down.

"Your Majesty, you cannot sentence Mirza Koka to death," Salima Sultan Begam started.

"I can do what I want," Jahangir said gruffly and then added, "dear Maji."

Salima smiled at him. "Your Majesty, Mirza Koka is like an uncle to you. Although you may not be of the same blood, the late Emperor considered him dearer than a brother; they both drank the milk of the same mother. And when his mother died, the Emperor himself carried her coffin on his shoulders to show his respect for her. His Majesty would have wanted you to treat Mirza Koka gently."

Jahangir flushed. Would he ever be as good an Emperor as his father? It was perhaps natural that comparisons would be made at the start of his reign, so soon after Akbar's death. Even from the grave, Akbar reached out to influence him through the women he had left behind. They expected him to behave as his father had, to make the same decisions, issue the same commands. But he was not his father. . . . He bent his head. Ideally, Mirza Koka should die. There was no doubt about that. The fewer supporters Khusrau had in the empire, the better it would be. But Salima had asked him for a favor. . . .

Without looking at the Dowager Empress, Jahangir rose and went back to the court.

"Mirza Koka, the ladies of the *zenana* have supported your cause. Although I am not fully convinced of their reasons, they seem to have much love and devotion for you. For their sake," Jahangir looked up at the balcony, "and for the sake of my revered father, who had great love and respect for you, I shall grant you your life."

Mirza Koka fell to his knees. "Your Majesty is very kind."

"You shall be stripped of all your lands, your power, and your dignity. The city of Agra no longer welcomes you, Mirza Koka. Lahore is where you should be. I shall allow you to retain your title."

"Thank you, your Majesty." As the Mirza bowed again, Jahangir gazed at him thoughtfully. No, this was not a man he could ever trust again.

Jahangir left the *Diwan-i-khas*, and the hall emptied of nobles. In the *zenana* balcony, the ladies of the harem returned to their palaces, chattering excitedly among themselves. One woman stayed until everyone else had gone. Her veil still covered her; she had pulled it over her head when Jahangir had so unexpectedly come to the balcony at Salima Sultan Begam's demand. Mehrunnisa rose slowly, her body heavy and tiresome, and went over to the divan where Jahangir had sat. She touched the cushion against which he had leaned. Then she turned and went out of the balcony.

THE CARAVAN WOUND its way slowly along the banks of the Yamuna, following its curves of glistening silver. Ali Quli rode in front, mounted on his favorite Arabian steed. Behind him, twenty horses and camels followed, laden with goods and household articles. He looked back at the palanquin carried on the shoulders of four strong men, who jogged along in an internal rhythm all of their own, in perfect step with one another. Only thus would they not easily tire during the many hours they carried their burden. The curtains of the palanquin fluttered in the breeze, and a delicate hand came out to close them.

Mehrunnisa drew the curtains and leaned back against a cushion, feeling its feather-stuffed comfort in the small of her back. It would be a long journey to Bardwan in Bengal—longer still for her, as she was heavy with child. After so many years of marriage and so many miscarriages, she had again become pregnant. As though in response to her thoughts, the baby kicked, and she put a soothing hand on the spot.

A child at last. After all the waiting. When she had met with Bapa just before the Emperor's first court appearance, she had known of the child, four months inside her. But she had not wanted to tell him—not yet, not until she was certain. Maji, with her wise, womanly, motherly ways, had known—and had not insisted that everyone else know. Mehrunnisa was grateful for that. After the miscarriages, it was as though this child, if it were to come, was wholly hers. So for the first few months she told no one, washed the cloths of her monthly blood as though the blood had actually come, so the servants would not talk. This time, too, the pains had come to plague her in the early months. She had been miserably sick and nauseated, but Maji said it was a good sign. Mehrunnisa had slept a great deal during the days and nights, living in a semiconscious state for months, for when she was awake, her fears choked her. But the child, thank Allah, had stayed inside her. Then she had told Ali Quli.

"A son!" he had said.

"Maybe," Mehrunnisa replied, hoping and praying fervently that it would be so.

She peered out of the palanquin at her husband. He rode his horse well, his back military straight. Years of army training had left their mark on his physique; he was as trim and healthy as the day they had been married. But now, when they were to share the responsibilities of parenthood together, the age difference between them yawned wide. Mehrunnisa was twenty-eight, Ali Quli forty-five. And more than age separated them; their minds were distanced, too.

As she lay back on the silk cushions her thoughts drifted to the scene in their house when Ali Quli had come back from court after the Emperor's first public audience.

The minutes had ticked by as Mehrunnisa waited in her room, a piece of satin cloth in her hands. Ostensibly she was embroidering, but for hours she had not put in a stitch. Then there were sounds of arrival in the outer courtyard. Mehrunnisa pulled her veil over her head and ran to the balcony. She watched as Ali Quli dismounted and came into the house. He looked relieved, happy, and discontented all at once.

An hour passed, but Ali Quli did not send for her. Unable to bear the suspense, Mehrunnisa sent word to him to come to her apartments. He entered with a swagger, a bottle of wine in his hands.

"What is it?"

"My lord, what happened at the *Diwan-i-am?*"

"Is that why you asked for me?" Ali Quli growled.

She nodded.

"I was granted the *jagir* of Bardwan, and we are to leave for Bengal immediately." His teeth showed. "I told you not to worry. The Emperor is well cognizant of the debt he owes me. After all, I saved him from the tigress."

Mehrunnisa looked at him, eyebrows lifting. Not only was Ali Quli not punished, Jahangir had actually raised his rank and offered him an estate. Why?

"Why do you look so surprised?" Ali Quli said. "Not even the Emperor can do me any harm."

He wandered to the divan and flopped down. He took a swig from the bottle and looked at it reflectively. "This is bad; I will have to ask for wine from Kashmir."

"Did the Emperor say anything?"

"He gave me a speech about duty and loyalty." Ali Quli grinned again. "But I knew that he would come around. He owes me his life. If I had not saved him, he would be dead now and"—his face hardened—"Khusrau would be Emperor."

He threw the bottle against the wall, and Mehrunnisa winced as it shattered. The rich red wine seeped into the carpets.

"Khusrau would be Emperor, and I would not be exiled in disgrace to the *jagir* of Bardwan," Ali Quli yelled. "Bardwan! What is it but an insignificant holding? What do I know of farming and estate management?" He puffed his chest out. "I am a soldier. I have fought many battles. People sing praises of me everywhere, and what does the new Emperor do? He relegates me to the sidelines, to Bardwan."

Mehrunnisa smiled slowly, turning her face away from her irate husband. She had not been wrong about Jahangir after all. It was a masterpiece of diplomacy. Ali Quli was well known for his bravery in the battlefield. Executing him would have served no purpose. Besides, Bengal was a hotbed of discontent. Who better than a soldier to send there? In one stroke, Jahangir had exiled Ali Quli— unofficially of course—and sent a soldier to suppress his dissidents. There was no fear of Ali Quli's supporting Khusrau again, not while the prince was thousands of miles away in the custody of the Emperor. Jahangir had shown himself worthy of the throne. Akbar would have been proud of him.

That was when she told him of the child, to placate him, to make him feel that the exile would not be so harsh if they had a child. Now, with his desire for a son, Mehrunnisa was tormented. What if she did not give him a son?

So here they were, traveling to Bardwan. Not even Ali Quli dared disobey Jahangir's orders. He had consoled himself that Raja Man Singh would be governor of Bengal and that they would together concoct another conspiracy.

Before their departure Mehrunnisa had gone to the imperial *zenana* to see the Dowager Empress. Ruqayya had taken her to the *Diwan-i-khas* to witness Mirza Aziz Koka's trial, and Mehrunnisa accompanied Ruqayya because she had commanded her and because she wanted one last glimpse of Jahangir. That she would see him so close, she had not expected. Perhaps fate had deemed it so for the last time. Jahangir would never move Ali Quli back from Bengal to the imperial court—that much Mehrunnisa knew. A dull ache flared in her back, and she massaged it as best she could. She leaned back and closed her eyes. If not Jahangir, at least there was to be a child.

They reached the house at Bardwan as dusk fell over the city. As Mehrunnisa stepped out of the palanquin, a sharp pain shot through her back, unlike any other she had felt before. Her knees buckled, and a gush of wetness flooded from her body. Heart pounding, she put a hand between her legs over the silk of her *ghagara*, uncaring that she stood in the front courtyard in front of all the servants. It was too early: only eight and a half months. Was her treacherous body going to expel this child too? Her hand came away sticky with a clear fluid. She leaned against the palanquin, then collapsed on the mud floor of the outer courtyard. Not blood, thank Allah, not blood.

The female slaves picked her up and rushed her into the house, to a room at the back, and put her on a bed. Through the deepening pain, Mehrunnisa saw Ali Quli's frightened face at the doorway, before he disappeared, shouting for a midwife. They were new to Bardwan; a midwife was not easily found at night.

Mehrunnisa lay sweating on the mattress, still in her travel-stained clothes, the birth pangs coming faster and faster, sweeping over her until she lost sense of everything around her. How had Maji given birth to seven children? Was it easier if one loved one's husband?

When the midwife came at last, she found Mehrunnisa moaning on the bed, her lower lip raw and bleeding where she had clamped down on her voice. The night was long, filled with pain, and Mehrunnisa slipped in and out of reality, opening her eyes to see a room filled with strangers. The servants were new, the midwife a woman she did not know. Ali Quli would not come into the room, for this was women's business.

"Maji . . ." Mehrunnisa whispered over and over again, wanting the cool comfort of her mother's hand on her brow, wanting to tell her of the fears that ambushed her. It was too early. What if the child came out dead?

The midwife patted her on the shoulder. "It will be all right, *Sahiba*," she said. She was kind, Mehrunnisa thought, staring dazed at her calm face, clutching at her hand and holding it tight. But she was not Maji.

The slaves had drawn the curtains in the room, and it was stifling inside, filled with the steam of breathing and sweat. Lamps flickered feebly in the humid, fetid air.

"Open the drapes," Mehrunnisa gasped. "I cannot breathe. . . ."

One of the slaves drew the drapes aside an inch, and the cool night air surged into the room, a tangible presence. Almost immediately, the labor became easier. Fourteen hours later, Mehrunnisa lay back on the mattress exhausted as the cries of the newborn babe filled the room.

"A girl," the midwife said in a hushed tone, pitying the woman who lay on the bed. After all these years of marriage, this poor woman had given birth to a puny baby girl. What ill luck.

Mehrunnisa immediately held out her arms and hugged the baby tight. Ali Quli would be disappointed. The great soldier had only a daughter; there was no son to grow into manhood and emulate his father's deeds—or misdeeds. She glanced down at the wrinkled, pink face, at the tiny legs that had kicked inside her, at the cut end of the umbilical cord that had drawn nourishment from her body. This child would be her own, she thought fiercely, protective of the babe as she had never been of anyone else. Even if Ali Quli did not want the baby, she did. Then, greatly daring, not wanting to tempt the fate that had given her a child, she counted her fingers and toes. Ten fingers, ten toes. A button nose. Eyebrows that winged over a face riddled with dots of peeling skin from the womb. Hair thick and unruly, curling over her cheek. *Forgive me for my greed, Allah*, Mehrunnisa prayed softly. *Thank you for the child, and thank you for making her perfect.*

Warmth stole over her was as she held her daughter, disregarding the false sympathy from the midwife and the slave girls. Ali Quli roared from the other room when he was told the news: "A girl! Only a girl child!" But Mehrunnisa heard little of what he said.

As the baby opened her tiny mouth in a yawn before subsiding at Mehrunnisa's breast, she knew what her name would be.

Ladli.

One who was loved.

Ali Quli did not come immediately to see Ladli. Mehrunnisa, selfish and wanting to keep the baby to herself, did not mind that he did not come. And so, with the child nestled in the crook of her arm, Mehrunnisa slept for the next twelve hours, exhausted from the journey and the birth.

Ten days later, news came to Ali Quli and Mehrunnisa of the birth of
two more royal princes. Shahryar and Jahandar had been born within a
month of each other to two royal concubines. Notwithstanding their
parentage, the two princes were also potential heirs to the throne;
Mughal law did not differentiate between the progeny of wives and concubines. Emperor Jahangir now had five sons: Khusrau, Parviz,
Khurram, Shahryar, and Jahandar.

JAHANGIR STARED INTO the distance, his brow wrinkled in concentration. He was seated in the outer courtyard of his apartments. He had a
sheet of paper, an inkwell, and a quill by his side.

It was late afternoon in the month of December, one of the most pleasant times in Agra. The sun dipped in the western sky, and shadows from
the guava and mango trees, long past fruiting, lengthened in the courtyard. Musicians played softly in the verandah above the Emperor.

Jahangir rubbed his forehead thoughtfully. He wanted to be known as
a just and kind king. It was difficult to follow in his father's footsteps;
they were calling him "Akbar the Great" in the streets. The initial
euphoria of being an Emperor had worn off, and the enormity of his obligations now came crashing on Jahangir. Millions of people depended on
him. Akbar had left him a large empire, and its administration was no
trivial matter. True, Mahabat, Sharif, Koka, and Abdullah had taken
most of the responsibility on their shoulders; but it was up to him to keep
the empire together, to protect his people, and, in essence, to look after
their needs.

But this was what he had been born for. If Murad or Daniyal had been
alive, they could not, would not, have handled their responsibility well.
He would show the people that he was capable of carrying on his father's
legacy. They would come to love him as they had loved Akbar. One day,
posterity would view him as the Adil Padshah, the Just Emperor.

And to make sure that his enemies did not distort the characteristics
of his reign, he would keep a personal day-to-day journal. He would call

it the *Jahangirnama*. The journal would start with the day of his corona-tion. Like his grandfather, he would leave a legacy for the future in his own handwriting. But to start off . . .

He dipped his quill in the inkwell and wrote out the words *dasturu-l-amal*: the rules of conduct. Pausing every now and then to think, he slowly filled the page. *Sarais*, rest houses, were to be erected on roadsides for the convenience of travelers. Merchants' goods and caravans could not be searched without their permission. Hospitals should be founded in the larger cities, and trained physicians were to be appointed.

He hesitated, looked at the goblet of wine by his side, and then added to the list: intoxicating drinks of any kind were to be forbidden in the empire. It was ironic, he knew, but these were the rules for his empire, not for him.

A thrill coursed through his body; he was making history. These would be known was as the twelve edicts of Jahangir. Even though he had been born to royalty, expected to wear the crown, his dreams had been so long in coming that they might never have happened. It was luck, Jahangir thought, his hand trembling over the page—Murad and Daniyal had died, taking away two potential heirs. Luck—Khusrau had been put away before he could make a nuisance of himself. Luck—and despite everything he himself had done, Akbar had pardoned him in the end.

Jahangir took a deep breath and continued writing. He revised the law of escheat, which had formerly determined that upon a man's death, his property went not to his heirs but reverted back to the crown, and it was for the Emperor to decide where to bequeath it. In his *dasturu-l-amal*, Jahangir decreed that the right of the lawful heirs to a person's property would not be disputed.

The twelve edicts were sent out in the empire, and people marveled at the Emperor's kindness and justice. The news filtered back to the impe-rial palace. Carried along by the people's praise, Jahangir ordered that a Chain of Justice be strung up. The Chain of Justice was a golden chain, eight feet long, fastened at one end to the battlements of the fort at Agra and at the other to a stone post on the banks of the Yamuna. It was hung with sixty brass bells. Jahangir decreed that the Chain of Justice was to serve the common people; any person who felt that justice had not been served could come to the fort and shake the chain so the noise would attract the Emperor's personal attention.

Jahangir then invoked one of the symbols of sovereignty: the right to issue coins. On an auspicious day, he ordered gold *mohurs* and silver rupees to be minted in his name. A few days later, samples were brought to him in court, shimmering on black velvet. The gold coins seemed to set fire to his veins; here was another lasting moment to posterity. He would go, his bones and flesh would turn to dust, but hundreds of years later, this piece of metal would glitter in someone's hands. This was what it meant to be king. Almost reverently, the Emperor set the coins back on the tray, his eyes full of unshed tears.

Thus Jahangir enjoyed his new-found popularity and power. Muhammad Sharif, as Grand Vizier, found himself busy with duties of state—so much so that he no longer had the time to personally oversee the details of Prince Khusrau's imprisonment.

A grave mistake, as both he and the Emperor were to find out soon.

TWELVE

To accomplish their purpose, the discontented lords turned their
eyes upon Chusero, and hoped, by his means, to effect a revolution
in their state. . . . They roused his ambition by the praise of past
actions, and animated it by the fair prospect of present success.
                              —Alexander Dow, *The History of*
                                    Hindostan

"IT WILL SOON BE TIME."

Khalifa looked up at her husband and blushed. "Yes, my lord." Her voice was low and musical. "I have prayed for a son, a healthy boy."

Prince Khusrau frowned. "What use will a boy be? I will have no throne to leave him. My father has made sure of that." He gestured around the room bitterly.

Khusrau and Khalifa were in the prince's apartments. At first glance, it seemed that every affluence available to a royal prince was present. But only at first glance, Khusrau thought, hunching into dissatisfaction. The windows were hung with ivory silk curtains; the stone floor was carpeted with deep-piled, red and green geometric patterned Persian rugs; sandalwood tables inlaid with mother-of-pearl were laden down with terracotta curios; and huge gold vases were filled with yellow summer roses. But outside the main doors, two strong Ahadis stood guard, and as the breeze lifted the curtains, ugly black iron bars showed on the sills, mocking the room's finery.

"The day will come when the throne shall be yours, my lord. It is only a matter of time."

Khusrau turned to her, his young face twisted. He had married Khalifa because Akbar had wanted the union, but Khusrau had fallen hopelessly in love with the shy girl whose face he had seen for the first time on their wedding night. Her complete devotion to him, even to the point of living in captivity in his quarters, had won him over. "I want it now. It is rightfully mine; my father has no right to rule. Even Emperor Akbar wished it."

"Hush, my lord." Khalifa turned frightened eyes towards the door. "The Emperor will hear of your outburst."

"I do not care," Khusrau muttered in a lower voice. "How long is he going to keep me locked up? It has been six months already."

"Perhaps when the child is born, my lord. The Emperor will be pleased to see his first grandchild."

"I cannot wait that long. I will not have my son born in captivity." Khusrau jumped up from the divan and paced the room, hands clasped behind his back. He was quivering with outrage. The empire was his. His father had no business ruling his realm. And then to ignominiously chastise him in the *Diwan-i-am*, in front of all the courtiers, as though he were a child pulled up for recalcitrance.

Khusrau stopped at the window and gazed out. He could see the ladies of the *zenana* lounging in the shade, draped in colorful muslins and silks, their attendants flitting around them with goblets of cool sherbet. If she had so wanted, Khalifa could have been there, outside. Jahangir had given her the choice, and she had chosen to be with her husband.

An inner door opened quietly, and a man stepped into the room.

"Your Highness," he said, his voice a soft whisper.

Khusrau whirled around. Khalifa quickly pulled her veil over her face.

Abdur Rahim, the Khan-i-khanan, came into the room and bowed to the prince. He had been one of Khusrau's most avid supporters during his rebellion for the throne. As the commander-in-chief of Akbar's army, he had been in a position of power, and he had lent that power to Khusrau's abortive cause. Like many others who had supported the young prince, he preferred to be Khan-i-khanan under a younger, more naive ruler than under the older, more shrewd Jahangir, with his cunning advisers. It was from him that Ali Quli, too, had taken his loyalty to Prince Khusrau. Of all the people in the empire, the Khan-i-khanan was the one whom Mehrunnisa's husband knew best. Years ago, when the Persian soldier had first come to the empire, he had hired himself out as a mercenary to Abdur Rahim, and Rahim had introduced him to Emperor Akbar.

"I beg pardon, your Highness, but there was no way to announce my arrival without the Emperor getting to know of it."

"That is all right. What news do you have?" Khusrau asked eagerly.

"Plans have been made to free you from the clutches of the Emperor. Husain Beg and Mirza Hasan are standing by to support you."

"Excellent!" Khusrau smiled. His petulance disappeared, and in its place appeared the youthful enthusiasm that had beguiled so many nobles and commoners in the empire. "What are the plans?"

"Three days from now the Emperor is to leave on a hunting trip. He will have you locked up as usual in the tower when he leaves."

Khusrau nodded. How he hated that bare, stone-walled prison, where a single pane of glass let milky light into the room. When Jahangir left for extended hunting trips, Khusrau spent days in the tower; he was not even allowed his daily walks in the gardens.

"The imperial party will return late at night after the hunting trip. That will give us enough time to escape from Agra. You will have to leave in the morning, right after the imperial party departs," Abdur Rahim continued.

"But how shall I get out? The Emperor allows me no visitors and has strictly forbidden me to leave the tower," Khusrau said.

"You will have to escape *before* you are sent to the tower. The next day is your grandfather's birthday, your Highness. Perhaps you could request a pilgrimage to Emperor Akbar's tomb in Sikandara. I will be waiting with a large army on the way, and we will rescue you from your captors."

Khusrau shook his head slowly. "I don't know that it will be that easy to escape my guards, Abdur Rahim."

The Khan-i-khanan looked shrewdly at the young prince. "You will have to try, your Highness. This is the best time. The Emperor will be away. It will be many hours before he gets the news of your flight and takes action. The guards are already lax in their duties; I was able to come here undetected."

"What about the princess?" Khusrau asked suddenly, looking at Khalifa.

She shook her head from behind the veil. "You must go alone, my lord. You will travel faster that way. The Emperor will do me no harm, especially . . ." She touched her belly.

Khusrau nodded and turned to Abdur Rahim, his face troubled. "You must make arrangements to bring the princess to me once we have reached . . . where will we go?"

"To Lahore."

"Lahore?" Khusrau asked in surprise. "Why not Bengal? My uncle, Raja Man Singh, will help us."

"No, your Highness." Abdur Rahim shook his head firmly. "Your uncle and Mirza Aziz Koka have barely escaped the Emperor's wrath with their lives. Even now, spies are posted on them. The Emperor would know immediately if we set out to Bengal, and we would be captured on the way. If we proceed to Lahore and manage to capture the fort, we shall have a stronghold to work from. Once Lahore is ours, we can send for Mirza Koka and Raja Man Singh. Besides . . ." Abdur Rahim hesitated.

"Besides what?"

"If we do not succeed at Lahore, we can take refuge farther north. The Shah of Persia will not refuse aid if you ask him. We will have nowhere to go from Bengal if we are defeated there."

"You are right," Khusrau said, as the logic of Abdur Rahim's argument impressed itself on him. "Go make the arrangements."

The Khan-i-khanan bowed to the prince and then slid out the back door.

Khusrau turned to Khalifa. "Will you manage without me, my dear?"

"I shall be all right, my lord. Go with Allah; I will pray for your safety."

THE EASTERN SKY turned pink with dawn as Khusrau peered over the windowsill. In the distance, he could see dust swirling in the wake of the imperial party. They had left early in the morning while it was still dark.

Although it was only April, the approach of summer made the days already very hot, so early mornings and late afternoons were the only times any physical activity was possible.

Khusrau turned from the window, his heart pounding with excitement. It was time to act. The guards would soon be arriving to escort him to the tower. He glanced quickly around the empty room. Khalifa had been sent to the royal *zenana* for the night, as was usual when Khusrau went to the tower. He strode up the to the door of his apartments and knocked.

A sleepy guard cautiously opened the door. "Yes, your Highness?"

"I wish to go to Sikandara to pay my respects to my grandfather," Khusrau ordered imperiously. "Have the grooms saddle my horse."

"But . . . your Highness . . . the Emperor has not sanctioned any excursions . . . ," the guard stammered. "I must go ask the other guards—"

"Enough," Khusrau yelled, in his best imitation of an irate royal. "I will not hear excuses from a menial. The Emperor will have your head if you do not allow me to proceed on this holy pilgrimage. I shall complain to his Majesty of your disobedience."

"But, your Highness, this is not possible," the man said again. "I cannot let you go like this—"

Khusrau made a slicing movement with his finger across his throat. He said in a quieter voice, "Your life seems worthless to you. Is that so?"

"Your wish shall be obeyed, your Highness," the guard said, frightened. "Please excuse me."

Khusrau waved a gracious hand. "All right. Now go obey my command."

When the guard had left, securing the door behind him, Khusrau sank into a heap on the floor, sweat beading his forehead. Was it too much? Had he overacted? Did the guard believe him, or would he return with the Grand Vizier to question him further? A chill came over him. That should not happen, please Allah, he prayed silently, still seated on the floor. Once Muhammad Sharif came to the door, probably furious at being roused at this early hour, he would throw Khusrau into the tower immediately. When a soft knock sounded on the door, Khusrau jumped up, trembling, to await his fate. The guard stood there, his face drawn with fright.

"The horses are ready, your Highness."

The palace was still stirring from the night's rest as Khusrau ran to his horse. The waiting guards were his regular guards, appointed by the Grand Vizier. Khusrau glanced at them briefly, wondering if they knew they had less than an hour of life.

Sikandara, the site of Akbar's tomb, lay six miles from Agra. On the way, Khusrau's guards were set upon by Abdur Rahim's men and killed. Disposing of their bodies on the roadside, the prince rode to Sikandara with three hundred and fifty horsemen. There, he met with Husain Beg and Mirza Hasan. Against their protests, Khusrau stopped briefly at Akbar's tomb, knelt down, and offered prayers for the success of his mission. Then he mounted his horse and the rebels rode away north, heading for Lahore.

"DO MY SHOULDERS."

The slave girl obligingly moved up. Jahangir relaxed as her skillful hands kneaded out knots from his tired muscles.

The Emperor reached out for the goblet and took a deep draught of the wine. He set the goblet down and closed his eyes. The hunt had been very successful. Only two of his shots had gone awry; all the rest had found their mark. Here was another advantage of being king. The empire was now *his* empire, and the hunt seemed all the sweeter for it.

Nearby, a huge brass bath had been brought into the royal apartments. Eunuchs carrying copper and silver jugs brought hot water and poured it into the bath. When the massage was over, the Emperor would soak in the delicately scented warm water for a while and then dress for the evening's entertainment.

A hesitant cough caught Jahangir's attention. He opened a languid eye. Hoshiyar Khan stood at the door. The eunuch had served him well over the years, Jahangir thought. He knew that Hoshiyar wielded great power in his *zenana* and that he was especially respectful to Jagat Gosini, who was now his Padshah Begam. Although the Emperor rarely interfered in harem politics—he never had even when he was a prince—he was aware of what went on around him.

"What is it, Hoshiyar?"

"I beg your pardon, Majesty. But the Grand Vizier is in the outer hall. He wishes for an audience," the eunuch said.

"Tell him to wait an hour. He can talk to me during the entertainment."

"It is of grave importance, your Majesty. The Vizier insists it cannot wait."

There must be news from the Deccan. Jahangir had restarted Akbar's unfinished campaign, determined to carry on his father's legacy. But surely there could not already be good news from the war front? He got up, his heart thumping at this possibility of an early victory in a battle at which his father had spent so many unsuccessful years. He pulled on his red silk robe and quickly walked out of the royal apartments to the outer hall. Only men from the royal family were allowed into the *zenana,* so the Emperor went out to meet all visitors.

Muhammad Sharif was pacing the floor as the Emperor entered. As soon as he saw him, he went down on his knees and performed the *konish.*

"I see I have disturbed your Majesty's bath. I beg your pardon."

"What news? Have we won a victory in the Deccan?" Jahangir asked eagerly.

Muhammad Sharif lowered his eyes. "No, your Majesty. I come bearing ill news. . . ." He hesitated. "Prince Khusrau has escaped."

"Escaped!" A sudden fear grabbed at Jahangir's heart. "How? Did I not order you to post a twenty-four-hour guard around him?"

"Yes, your Majesty." Sharif was contrite. "But he has escaped. This morning, while you were away hunting, the prince demanded his horses on the pretext of paying respects at Emperor Akbar's tomb. There he was joined by the Khan-i-khanan, Husain Beg, and Mirza Hasan. At last count, they were accompanied by about four hundred cavalry."

"Why wasn't I told before now?" Jahangir thundered.

"I only found out a few minutes ago, your Majesty. The lamplighter went to the tower to light the lamps and found it empty." Sharif bowed his head.

"This is all your fault," Jahangir said. Khusrau was gone. When? Where? He had only been on the throne a short time; was he to lose it already?

"Yes, your Majesty. I am willing to take any punishment you will bestow upon me. Only . . . I beg one favor. Allow me to go in pursuit of the prince and bring him back to you."

Jahangir's gaze softened as he looked at his childhood companion and friend. He pulled himself up mentally. This was not the time to panic. Plans had to be made, and only he could give the orders. "Very well. You shall redeem your mistake by capturing Khusrau. Make plans to go to Bengal at once. Khusrau is definitely headed to his uncle Raja Man Singh's palace."

"I shall leave immediately, your Majesty." Sharif bowed and backed to the door.

"Wait," Jahangir commanded as Sharif was about to leave, his voice gaining strength as he spoke. "Send the spies out to check Khusrau's route. He may not after all be going to Raja Man Singh. Leave tomorrow, after the spies have confirmed Khusrau's intentions. Once you know, I want you to pursue Khusrau relentlessly. Bring him back to me, dead or alive. I will not countenance any more rebellion from my son. Do you understand?"

"Yes, your Majesty." Sharif smiled. Nothing would please him more than to bring Prince Khusrau's head on a golden platter to his Emperor. "May I leave now?"

Jahangir nodded absently. He watched Sharif back out of the room again. Suddenly a thought struck him. What if Khusrau refused to give himself up to the imperial forces? What if he fought with them instead?

Khusrau was now supported by the Khan-i-khanan, the commander of the imperial forces, a seasoned soldier and veteran of many wars. What if Muhammad Sharif was killed in the fray?

"Muhammad," Jahangir said sharply, stopping Sharif for the second time. "Send Shaikh Farid Bukhari instead. Ihtimam Khan should accompany him as the scout and intelligence officer. I wish you to remain with the court; your presence is necessary here."

Sharif flinched. He would not be given the opportunity to pursue the prince. "But, your Majesty—," he began.

"I have decided, Muhammad," the Emperor said sharply. Then he added, more gently, "You must understand your importance to me. We will leave together once Khusrau's destination has been ascertained."

"As you wish, your Majesty." It was useless to argue with Jahangir once his mind was made up. Muhammad Sharif bowed to the Emperor and left the harem.

Jahangir went back to his unfinished bath. He lay thoughtful in the warm water as the slave girls soaped his shoulders. Had Akbar felt this same pain, this betrayal from Jahangir? During one reconciliation at Agra, when Jahangir was at Akbar's side when he was ill, reading to him, the Emperor had stopped him. Putting a hand on the page, he asked, "Tell me, Salim, is the crown so important?" The question had come so suddenly that he could only stare at his father, thinking without saying so that the crown already sat on Akbar's head, that he had felt its weight for forty-nine years. How could he possibly know what it was like to hunger for the throne? Akbar had allowed the silence to stretch between them, then pointed to the page. "Start from that paragraph."

Now, Jahangir thought, looking down into the soapy water, he knew what it was like to be Emperor and to have a son who wanted desperately to be one. Jahangir had been king for a very short while. The crown was rightfully his. He was determined to protect his claim.

Spies were sent out in all directions to gather information about Khusrau's route. By the middle of the night, news was brought to the palace that Khusrau was headed toward Lahore. Shaikh Farid Bukhari departed in pursuit. The evening's entertainment was too much for the Emperor. He left halfway through it and toppled into bed. While Jahangir slept, slaves and eunuchs packed furiously. The imperial army at Agra was roused and ordered to prepare for a march.

The next morning, at sunrise, Jahangir left Agra at the head of an army. Less than twelve hours after the news of Khusrau's flight had been brought to the Emperor, he and his army were in pursuit of the errant son.

THIRTEEN

*They rode through the dead nobles, who filled both sides of the
road . . . Mahabat Khan, was seated behind the Prince, in order
to introduce the head to Khusrau, and tell him their names. And
as the corpses were dangling or swinging on account of the wind,
he said to Khusrau, "Sultan, see how your soldiers fight against
the trees."*

> —B. Narain, trans., and S. Sharma,
> ed., *A Dutch Chronicle of Mughal
> India*

THE WARM, HUMID NIGHT SWEPT OVER BENGAL IN A RUSH. IT HAD
rained for five days, in a heavy, muffling downpour that clogged everyone's lungs. The houses in Bardwan reeked of mildew and damp clothes.
Mosquitoes came out in droves, humming about people's ears, seeking
blood and flesh with a persistence that no amount of smoldering *neem*
leaves could diminish. Gossamer-thin white mosquito nets lay draped
like ghosts over cots and mattresses. Mehrunnisa lay on her bed, staring
up at the slow-moving rectangular *punkah* suspended from the ceiling. It
faltered, then stopped, the pull rope hanging slack under the doorway.
She waited as the humidity settled around her like a living presence, then
said softly, "Nizam."

Outside her room, the slave boy awoke with a start and, still half
asleep, began again to swing his leg from side to side, setting the *punkah*,
whose rope was tied to his toe, into motion again.

Mehrunnisa turned to Ladli, sleeping by her side, and peeled her head
away from where it lay pillowed on her arm. Sweat matted the child's
head and glistened on Mehrunnisa's skin. She wiped her arm and blew
on her daughter's hair. Ladli sighed and flipped over, arms and legs

askew. Mehrunnisa raised herself on an elbow and looked down at her daughter. The heat of Bengal seemed not to bother her. Ladli slept blissfully, her mouth open, her breath coming in a whistle, for her nose was blocked by a summer cold.

Mehrunnisa touched her lightly, her fingers not lingering long enough for the contact to draw sweat. She skimmed over Ladli's rounded calves and thighs, over the dimples on her knuckles, over the smooth skin of her chin. In the beginning, when Ladli had just been born, Mehrunnisa would stay awake nights just to watch her sleep. She had thought that need would soon wane. But now, six months later, it woke her sometimes with the same intensity. The wonder of her child never seemed to cease. *Thank you, Allah.* She leaned over to kiss Ladli's nose. Still asleep, the baby put her hand on her mother's head, and her tiny fingers curled tight around a lock of blue-black hair. Mehrunnisa smiled and gently disengaged the fingers.

The *punkah* on the ceiling creaked and then stopped again. Nizam must have fallen asleep again, Mehrunnisa thought. She looked up as the *punkah* started more furiously, swirling the air in damp circles around the bed. What was the boy doing? Just as she was mustering the strength to move, a figure loomed in the doorway. Ali Quli hesitated, then came rushing in, his footsteps loud in the almost silent night.

Mehrunnisa put a finger to her lips and pointed at Ladli.

Ali Quli stopped and beckoned to her. Mehrunnisa rose from the bed and slid out from under the mosquito net, lifting it just enough to let herself through. She tucked the net under the mattress again and then went to her husband. They stood at the window together, looking down at the garden below. The moon was on the wane but still shed enough silver light to let them see. Ali Quli pulled out a letter from the pocket of his *kurta.*

"News from Bapa?" Mehrunnisa asked, reaching out.

"No. From the imperial court. Prince Khusrau has escaped."

Mehrunnisa stared at him, her eyes darkening in the moonlight. "What?"

"You heard me. Prince Khusrau has fled to Lahore."

"To Lahore . . ."

"And not here, where his uncle Man Singh is. Stupid boy!"

"But the Emperor would seek him here first," Mehrunnisa said automatically. "It stands to reason that he went in the opposite direction. How did he get away? I thought he was under heavy guard."

Ali Quli grinned. "The Emperor sent most of the prince's supporters away, but he forgot the Khan-i-khanan. Mirza Abdur Rahim managed to rescue the prince from his guards. They are now on their way to Lahore." Ali Quli's voice rose as he spoke.

"Softly, my lord," Mehrunnisa said. Nizam was outside the door. Like all their servants, he had elephant ears. He could not be trusted. She turned away from her husband as thoughts flew across her mind. Khusrau had escaped with the Khan-i-khanan. The commander-in-chief of the imperial army was a man of much influence and had powerful supporters. Could he possibly pull off this coup? Was Jahangir so soon to lose the crown that had barely rested on his head? How had he taken the news?

"What has the Emperor done, my lord?"

"He has left Agra for Lahore with the imperial army. But they will never catch up with the prince. Khusrau travels light, with only his men. Lahore is right now without a governor. The city will be easily taken. Once it is secure, the northwest will be ours, and then"—Ali Quli laughed, not bothering to keep his voice low anymore—"and then the whole empire."

Mehrunnisa's heart plummeted. What he said was true. The Emperor had just dismissed Lahore's governor and sent another noble from court to take his place. He was still on his way. How would a leaderless city defend itself from an army led by the Khan-i-khanan himself? The Emperor should have dismissed him upon his coronation, not forgiven Abdur Rahim's role in Khusrau's revolt and reinstated him as Khan-i-khanan. Suddenly, another word Ali Quli had just spoken stood out in her troubled mind.

" 'Ours'? Did you say the northwest would be 'ours'?"

Ali Quli nodded, peering at the letter in the dim light of the moon. "I leave tonight. Pack my belongings; I must go to the prince's army immediately."

"What about Raja Man Singh?" Mehrunnisa asked. "And have you heard from the Khan-i-khanan?"

"No. But no matter. Raja Man Singh will support his nephew. And the Khan-i-khanan will definitely need my services."

Mehrunnisa looked at him. He was an idiot if he thought he could traverse the whole empire in search of Prince Khusrau and his army. How long would the trip take? Six months? Eight months? Much could happen during that time. If the Emperor captured Khusrau, Ali Quli's life would be worth nothing. A second offense against the Emperor would be unpardonable. Ali Quli didn't stop to think of those things, but he should at least have reflected on why they were in Bengal, so far from the imperial court—precisely to keep Ali Quli from consorting with Prince Khusrau. How could she convince him that he was making a mistake?

"Wait a while, my lord. It is better to hear from either of the two nobles before you make any decision. Let us wait to hear more news. Please."

"Wait, wait! That is all I do now!" Ali Quli shouted. His voice resounded in the room, and Ladli awoke with a wail.

Mehrunnisa ran over to the bed, untucked the mosquito net, and picked her up. "Hush, *beta*." She tried patting the child back to sleep. But Ladli had already been awakened by the sound of her father's voice. She gurgled at him.

Ali Quli turned away and headed for the door. "I have to go. I must be with the prince's army. What am I to do here?"

Ladli, seeing him leave, began to wail again.

"Keep her quiet," Ali Quli said. "And pack my clothes. I leave soon."

Mehrunnisa stared at him, furious. He could not, must not go. What would happen to them if he left? "Think, my lord. The Emperor spared your life once and sent you here. If the prince is captured again, he will not hesitate to take it. Wait until you hear from either Raja Man Singh or the Khan-i-khanan. What you do will reflect upon all of us—Ladli, me, even my Bapa."

Ali Quli glared at her from the doorway, deep furrows creasing his forehead. He looked so angry that Mehrunnisa thought he would raise his hand and hit her. She stood there unflinching, holding a wailing Ladli in her arms. Ali Quli turned and stomped out of the room. As he passed Nizam peeping around the door on all fours, he bent and cuffed the boy on his head, sending him yelping and sliding across the stone floor of the verandah.

"HOW MANY DAYS have we been here?"

"Eight, your Highness," Husain Beg replied.

Prince Khusrau turned to look down the desolate hill that sloped to the ramparts of Lahore fort. They had arrived at Lahore to find the fort barricaded and fortified against an attack. Even the terrain seemed as inhospitable as the people of Lahore. The ground was baked dirt; the trees and shrubs were stunted from a lack of water; the only relief in the dry colors of the land were gray rocks and brown boulders. During the day the sun raged, and at night the temperatures plunged to near freezing. The battle, the weather, and the lack of cohesion in his army were all taking a toll on his men.

"They will not hold out much longer," Khusrau said, hope his voice. But inside, his mind was dead, numbed by the fear that had been his constant companion these last few weeks.

"No, your Highness. Their supplies must be running out. Only—" Husain hesitated.

"We must take the fort before the imperial army arrives. I am aware of that," Khusrau said, sinking into his shoulders. "How did Ibrahim Khan hear of our arrival?"

"His Majesty sent him a message. Ibrahim Khan was already on his way to Lahore to take up his post as governor when we left Agra. He rushed to Lahore before us and fortified the city." Husain Beg looked shrewdly at his young commander's woebegone face. "There is one thing in our favor, your Highness. Ibrahim Khan's army is made up of servants and tradesmen. He did not have enough time to amass an army of soldiers. Besides, for eight days, we have surrounded the fort and not allowed in any food supplies. They will soon surrender."

"I hope so." Khusrau ran a grimy hand through his hair. He shaded his eyes from the harsh sunshine and peered down. Every day, Khusrau's army had set off mines near the ramparts, but each night, under cover of dark, Ibrahim's men had worked swiftly to repair the breaches. For servants and tradesmen, they had shown an amazing amount of loyalty and resilience, neither of which Khusrau was able to evoke in his men. It had been eight long days since they arrived at Lahore. And the fort had held out.

As he turned and walked slowly into the camp, the all-too-familiar fear came flooding back. Would they capture the fort before imperial reinforcements arrived? If they didn't, Khusrau would have no place to hide, no defense against his father's army. It was too late now to flee to Persia in hope of refuge; the imperial army would catch up before they crossed the border.

The prince kicked a wayward pebble and watched it tumble in the red dust. Had he acted too hastily, without enough planning? For that, too, it seemed late for remorse. Jahangir would not forgive him this time. It was said that a price had been put on Khusrau's life.

Khusrau shook his head from side to side, trying to ease the cricks in his neck that only rest—which had been almost unknown for these eight days—would erase. He would have to run from his father all his life, for to surrender meant sure death. Yet, there was some hope. His army now numbered over twelve thousand infantry and cavalry, all dissidents who had joined him as they had passed from city to city on their way to Lahore. Khusrau shuddered as he thought of the manner in which his army had behaved en route. They had plundered and looted the villages, raped the women, left sorrow and misery in their wake. And he had not been able to control them.

"Your Highness!"

He turned to see Husain Beg leading a runner.

"Your Highness, the imperial army led by Shaikh Farid Bukhari is a day's journey from here."

Khusrau paled, the blood rushing from his face. "They have made good time. What else?"

"Mirza Hasan is dead."

"How did he die?"

"The Emperor's men captured him at Sikandara, where he was gathering forces." The runner wiped his sweating face. "The Emperor ordered him to be trampled to death by elephants."

Khusrau bit his lip to choke back sudden tears. He had lost another supporter. Pulling himself together, he turned to Husain Beg. "We will have to take Shaikh Bukhari's army by surprise tonight. Where will they be pitching camp?"

"Near Sultanpur, your Highness."

"Your Highness . . ." The runner hesitated and then went on. "The Emperor himself follows at the head of a large army. He is a day's journey behind Shaikh Bukhari."

His father was right at his footsteps. No time was to be lost now. Khusrau's insides turned to sudden iron. He would die fighting if necessary, but he would not surrender.

"We cannot afford to be attacked from both sides. Prepare an army of ten thousand men. I will lead them into battle against Shaikh Burkhari. In the meantime, keep up the siege on the fort with the rest of the men. We should be able to vanquish at least one of the armies." Khusrau's voice took on a new strength as he spoke.

He sat on a rock outside his tent as the arrangements went on around him, wanting the men to see him and to know that he was there to lead them. All this would finally be worth it, he thought, when the crown sat on his head. He had heard that Jahangir was furious with him, that the ladies of the *zenana* cursed him for his waywardness, that the nobles at court, who had once supported him, now denounced his actions. It was lonely and frightening to be at the receiving end of such invective. But he was doing exactly what his father had done for fifteen years: hunger for the throne. Why, then, this outrage?

That night, as Shaikh Burkhari's army, only five thousand strong, were pitching camp at Sultanpur on the Beas river, they were attacked. Although taken by surprise, the imperial army fought hard. Khusrau's men outnumbered them by far, but the rebels lacked the discipline and training of the imperial forces. The two armies fought all through the night and into the next day.

THE AROMA OF ginger-spiced chicken and fragrant rice grown on the foothills of the Himalayas filled the imperial tent. Jahangir washed his hands and sat down cross-legged on the mat. He inhaled deeply as a slave set the silver plate in front of him, his mouth watering. Arranged against the outer rim of the plate were three silver *katoris* filled with steaming curries of chicken, lamb, and fish. In the center was piled a small mound of flaky rice, cooked just the way he liked it. A dollop of cucumber and tomato *raita*, smothered in sour yogurt, was on one side of the rice. On the other side were two wedges of green mango pickle, glistening red with chili powder and oil. The slave bowed and reverently rested two crisp rice-flour *papads* on the side of the plate before backing out of the tent.

Just as the Emperor bent over his plate, Mahabat Khan whipped open the flap of his tent and rushed in unannounced. "Your Majesty, Prince Khusrau's army is fighting Shaikh Bukhari's army. The Shaikh's army is outnumbered."

Jahangir grimaced. He had not eaten since the previous evening, and he was hungry. But this was the time for action. He scooped up a little of the rice, dipped it in the onion and tomato gravy of the chicken curry, and swallowed the morsel for good luck. Then he rose quickly.

"Hoshiyar, get my armor," he commanded, wiping his hand on a silk towel.

Hoshiyar Khan ran off to do his bidding.

"We must leave immediately for Sultanpur, your Majesty. No time can be lost." Muhammad Sharif ran into Jahangir's tent, fastening his armor.

"Is my horse saddled?"

"It awaits you outside, your Majesty."

Jahangir ran out, forgetting his armor. Mahabat Khan threw him a spear. Armed with only a spear and a dagger, he mounted his horse and led his forces to the Beas river. There was no time to think on the way, no time to worry about going into the battlefield almost naked. Jahangir could now reaffirm his manhood as he approached his fortieth year. This rush, this thrill at danger, had been so long absent from the Emperor's life. With just a brief glance around to affirm that Mahabat, Sharif, and the others were with him, Jahangir kicked his heels into his horse and rode at the head of his army into Sultanpur.

In the meantime, Shaikh Bukhari and the imperial army were fighting a losing battle. Just as all seemed to be lost, Ihtimam Khan, the *kotwal*, who had been appointed scout by Jahangir, arrived at the scene of the battle with another army, carrying Jahangir's standard and flags. At the sight of the royal standard, a rumor flew through the rebel forces that the Emperor himself had arrived at the scene of the battle. Abdur Rahim, the Khan-i-khanan, panicked and dropped Khusrau's standard. When the rebels saw the Emperor's standard and not Khusrau's, they thought Khusrau had been killed. In the confusion that ensued, Shaikh Bukhari, the Barha Sayyids, and Ihtimam Khan gained control of the rebel forces. Some were killed, and others fled the scene of the battle.

Khusrau, Abdur Rahim, and Husain Beg fled from the site with a small army, intending to proceed to Kabul and from there to seek refuge in Uzbekistan.

The Emperor crossed the Beas river and arrived at the scene of the battle to find that Khusrau's army had been vanquished and his son had fled. He left the rebels in the charge of Shaikh Bukhari and proceeded to Mirza Kamran's house outside Lahore to await news of Khusrau's capture.

* * *

KHUSRAU AND HIS cohorts rode hard from Sultanpur toward Kabul. They came upon the Chenab river two nights after the battle. It was late, and the boats were already docked on the piers. The boatmen had all gone home, except for one, who was just returning from a late fishing trip. He was brought to Khusrau.

"Prepare your boat to take us across," Khusrau ordered.

"Your Highness," the man stammered. "The Emperor had sent orders that no one is to cross the river without his permission. I will have to see the royal seal before I can take you to the other side."

"I order you to take us across," Khusrau yelled, losing his temper. He had not come this far to be thwarted by some commoner. It was imperative that they cross the river tonight. Waiting until first light would be too late.

"I cannot, your Highness. Please forgive me."

At that moment, Abdur Rahim brought a woman and two children to Khusrau. The boatman started when he saw them.

"Is this your family?"

"Yes, your Highness."

"Well . . ." Khusrau looked at the woman, brought out a knife, and ran his finger along the edge until two drops of blood pearled on his skin. "How would you like to see them dead?"

The boatman fell to his knees with tears in his eyes. "Please, your Highness," he begged. "Spare their lives. I will take you across. I beg of you, spare them."

"All right," Khusrau said curtly, turning away and wiping his cut finger on his *qaba*. "Go prepare the boat. Abdur Rahim, free this man's family. Tell the army to follow us as soon as we have crossed over to the other side."

While the boat was being readied, Khusrau sat on the banks of the Chenab, heels dug into the mud. His finger twinged, and he started shivering. When had he become so violent? *What* had he become? Fear, stress, and sleeplessness had turned him into a monster he could not even recognize. What would Khalifa think of him? At the thought of his wife, Khusrau put his head down and wept. Would he ever see her again?

And the child, their child—great gulping sobs rushed out of him.

As he sat there, arms wrapped around himself, Abdur Rahim came to tell him the boat was ready. Khusrau, Abdur Rahim, and Husain Beg boarded it, and the boatman started rowing them over. The Chenab flowed fast, and crossing was no easy task. Treacherous sandbars appeared unexpectedly, and only an experienced boatman could row across. The boatman, however, was smart. He had freed his family from Khusrau's clutches, and he had no intention of disobeying his Emperor's orders. He guided the boat toward a sandbank, where it stuck fast. For the next half hour, he pretended to try to extricate the boat. When Khusrau's attention was diverted, he jumped from the boat and swam to the bank, leaving the prince and his companions stranded in the middle of the inky river.

Khusrau yelled after the boatman, but his voice was swept away by the sound of the fast-moving waters. The prince cursed and kicked the side of the boat, nearly upsetting them all into the river. Finally he gave up. Brave in the battlefield, neither of the men had the courage to defy the currents.

As night wore on, the three men waited for assistance from the army. The river swirled around them in a melody of its own. One by one, tired from the events of the past few days, the men fell asleep.

Day dawned. Khusrau sat up sleepily and rubbed his eyes. When he opened them, the gold banner with the crouching lion did not at first register in his brain. Then sleep was chased away when he realized it was the Emperor's standard. The prince was surrounded on both banks by the imperial army. While he had slept in the boat the army had easily vanquished Khusrau's men on the banks of the Chenab. Now they stood at the side, waiting for the sun to rise. A few soldiers rowed over to Khusrau and captured him.

THE EMPEROR BENT down and breathed deeply into the heart of a brilliant yellow rose. He straightened up and asked, "When will they be here?"

"Soon, your Majesty," one of the attendants replied.

Jahangir nodded and continued down the garden path, his attendants following at a distance. Mirza Kamran had done a wonderful job, he noted with appreciation. Despite the dry climate, the garden was lush with greenery. Flowers bloomed in profusion, giving a delicate perfume to the air, and water gurgled pleasantly in the many channels that criss-crossed the lawns. Birds trilled merrily in large *chenar* trees, which cast shady spots around the lawns. It was very peaceful, even more so since the news of Khusrau's capture had been brought to him.

The door to the garden opened, and the sound of marching footsteps broke the silence. Jahangir turned and waited. Soldiers led Khusrau, Husain Beg, and Abdur Rahim up to the Emperor. All three prisoners were chained from hand to foot and to one another. Khusrau shuffled in between his two companions. The party halted in front of Jahangir, and they bowed in unison.

"Your Majesty, I bring to you Prince Khusrau, Husain Beg, and the Khan-i-khanan," Mahabat Khan said.

Jahangir looked grimly at Khusrau. Under his father's gaze, Khusrau broke down and started weeping, wiping his eyes with dirty hands that left streaks of grime on his face. Jahangir's upper lip curled in distaste. Why did Khusrau give him so much trouble?

"What have you to say for yourself?" he demanded.

Khusrau wept on, in loud, hiccuping sobs. The last few days had been too much for him. It was almost a relief to know that he had to make no more decisions, that the fight was over. Khusrau was only nineteen. For too long, covetous men in the empire had filled his head with tales of king-ship and power. He had not really had a childhood, and as he stood weep-ing in front of his father it seemed he would not even have an adult life.

"Your Majesty, forgive me . . . ," Husain Beg started. "I knew not what I was doing." He pointed at Abdur Rahim. "The Khan-i-khanan promised me riches if I helped the prince. I would never have disobeyed my Emperor otherwise. Please pardon me, your Majesty. I am and will always remain your most loyal servant—"

"Enough!" Jahangir held up a hand. "You are a coward and a disloyal servant. Your deeds speak of your character, and your punishment shall befit the crime."

Jahangir turned to Mahabat Khan. "Throw Prince Khusrau into prison. He shall remain chained. As for the others, the two villains will be put in the skins of an ox and an ass, then mounted on donkeys facing the tail and paraded around Lahore, so that all can see their disgrace."

Husain Beg fell to his knees, bringing Abdur Rahim and Khusrau down with him. Jahangir turned away in disgust, and the three men were dragged out of the garden, with Husain Beg's cries echoing in the still air.

The Emperor's orders were carried out. An ox and an ass were killed and skinned. The fresh skins, still bloody from their previous owners, were thrown on Husain Beg and Abdur Rahim, heads and all. As the two prisoners were led around the city the skins dried out in the heat of the sun, sticking to the bodies of the men and causing great discomfort and pain.

After twelve hours, Husain Beg died on his donkey, his skin suffocated and his body dehydrated by the dried-out ox hide. His head was then cut off, stuffed with grass, and sent by runners to Agra, there to hang on a stake at the ramparts of the fort as a lesson to other dissidents.

However, the Khan-i-khanan survived. Abdur Rahim had grown up in Lahore as the beloved son of the *diwan*, Bairam Khan. He was well known to the people and much loved by them. Against the Emperor's orders, people threw water on him to keep the ass's skin from drying out, and they offered him sherbet and fruits as he was dragged around the city. After two days, Jahangir ordered the release of the Khan-i-khanan.

* * *

THE REBELS DEALT with, Jahangir arranged to enter the city of Lahore in state. This would be his first visit as Emperor of Mughal India. A few days passed while the people of the city prepared for their Emperor. Jahangir spent his time at Mirza Kamran's house, holding court, walking in the lush gardens, and trying to decide a punishment for the rest of the rebels. He felt no remorse at the punishment meted out to Husain Beg and Abdur Rahim. Jahangir had pardoned Abdur Rahim once, upon his accession, but this time it was impossible to do so again. If he had died, his death would have been a lesson, simply and swiftly put. That Abdur Rahim had survived was a stroke of good luck; Jahangir was able to publicly pardon him. And having once been humiliated, the former Khan-i-khanan would not dare to lift his head again. The crown was now his, Jahangir thought grimly, and he had no intention of giving it up until he died. Which brought him to the rest of Khusrau's so-called army. The Emperor was lying in his canopied bed one night when an idea struck him. The next morning, upon awakening, he sent for Mahabat Khan.

"Mahabat, how many of Khusrau's soldiers have been captured?"

"About six thousand, your Majesty."

"I have been contemplating a suitable chastisement for these dissidents. Their punishment will fit their crime. They have dared to rebel against their lord and Emperor. For that, the sentence is death."

Mahabat bowed to Jahangir. "It shall be done, your Majesty."

"Yes," Jahangir said reflectively, "but in such a manner that their death will be a lesson to all those contemplating a similar sin. Their bodies should hang in full view of the people, and Khusrau shall see the result of his actions on his followers."

Mahabat Khan waited. He could tell that Jahangir already had a plan in mind. A grisly punishment was at hand, not only for the supporters of Khusrau but for Khusrau himself. When the Emperor spoke again, at great length, Mahabat Khan allowed a slow smile to spread over his features. This was even better than he had expected. The punishment was one that not only Khusrau would never forget, but posterity would remember.

For the next few days, there was intense activity in and around Mirza Kamran's gardens. Trees were cut down in large numbers, and their trunks were shaped into stakes with pointed ends.

Finally, the day arrived when Jahangir was to enter Lahore. It was a strategic city in the empire, one of great importance both administratively and from the point of defense. Had it not been for the Deccani wars, Jahangir would have liked to live at Lahore, where the temperatures were more moderate than at Agra. Fate and Khusrau, he thought that morning, had brought him to Lahore in haste, but he was determined to enter the city in state as an Emperor should. He rose slowly, an excitement building in him all morning as he bathed and dressed. Even the procession to Lahore would be eventful, for Khusrau was to be punished. The world would hear of it soon; future generations would speak of it for years to come. He waited outside Mirza Kamran's house for Khusrau to be brought to him.

"I am willing to forget your disobedience of the last few days. As a token of my forgiveness, you shall ride with me in the *howdah*," Jahangir said.

Khusrau fell to his knees. "Thank you, your Majesty."

His chains removed, the prince was escorted to the *howdah* on the elephant. Jahangir climbed in first, then Khusrau. The prince watched in surprise as Mahabat Khan climbed up behind and seated himself at Khusrau's elbow.

The royal elephant rose slowly at the mahout's command, and the entourage departed from the courtyard of Mirza Kamran's house to a fanfare of trumpets. As the elephant turned the corner into the road, Jahangir heard Khusrau draw in a sharp breath of horror.

Stakes were bored into the ground at regular intervals all along the road leading from Mirza Kamran's house to the gateway of the city. On each stake, a man was impaled. Some were still alive, writhing in agony. Bodies also dangled on ropes from the few trees that lined the road; those who had been hung had suffered a gentler death than their comrades who had been impaled alive on the stakes, all lined up to greet their erstwhile leader. As the royal procession passed, the men who were still alive cried out to the prince.

Khusrau buried his face in quaking hands. He recognized the men; they were all soldiers who had served with him. He had brought these men to their gruesome deaths. It was all because of him that they hung here in disgrace, that they were dying horrible deaths.

The Emperor watched the prince, his face grim. Then he pulled Khusrau's hands away from his face.

"Look," he commanded harshly. "Look at the fate of those ill-meaning souls who served you. It is your fault that they die so horribly."

Khusrau stared around him, his face white, tears rolling down his cheeks.

Mahabat Khan leaned over the prince's shoulder.

"Your Highness, allow me to introduce you to these men. This is . . ."

Khusrau listened, horror written over his face, while Mahabat Khan proceeded to "introduce" each of the dead men to him as the royal entourage passed along the road. The wind blew fiercely as the procession neared Lahore, and Mahabat Khan directed Khusrau's attention to the bodies swinging from the trees, flapping against the trunks.

"Prince, see how your brave soldiers battle with the trees," he said, malice dripping from each word.

The prince shut his eyes tight, and this time Jahangir let him be. Khusrau would not easily rebel again. The lesson had been taught. Finally, the procession reached Lahore, and Jahangir entered the fort, smiling only from his mouth. He threw silver rupees among the people, acting the role of the benign Emperor.

Khusrau sat by his side, pale and trembling, a wild, haunted look in his eyes, knowing that nothing in his life would ever be the same again.

THE SUMMER MONSOONS had begun, and all around Bengal, trees and grasses grew lush and wet. It rained day and night. The houses were constantly damp, mildew flourished, hairpins rusted overnight, termites greedily gnawed at the furniture, and mosquitoes went after their hapless victims with unerring accuracy.

Mehrunnisa turned with a sigh from the window. Bardwan was unlike the Gangetic plains. Here the rain did not bring new life to the countryside. It brought an overabundance of life: insects, earthworms, and even the trees and bushes seemed predatory. They grew wild and unchecked, with leafy, succulent fingers reaching out of every crack in the stone pathways to snag pedestrians.

Mehrunnisa and Ali Quli had been at Bengal for over a year, and there was no indication that they would ever return to court, no sign that the Emperor remembered them. Even so far away from the nucleus of life in the empire, Mehrunnisa had heard of the punishment meted out to Khusrau and his followers. It was a cruel punishment; yet, she approved of it. Nothing was more important than the crown, and if it meant taking a firm stand to discourage any further attempts on Khusrau's part, the message must have surely gotten through to the errant prince. He would not soon try another rebellion.

As for Ali Quli, he was still here too. If he had gone chasing after the prince to Lahore, he would not have escaped Jahangir's wrath. Mehrunnisa's words of reason had finally penetrated his excited mind. When the news had come of Prince Khusrau's capture—and it had come surprisingly soon, as bad news always does—Ali Quli had flung the letter at her. Mehrunnisa had read it carefully and stored it in one of her trunks.

She leaned back against the windowsill, her hands resting on the edge. It was frustrating having to hear news of court from runners and travelers, wrenching not to be there to see it happen, to experience it firsthand. If her husband had not been stupid enough to support Khusrau's first attempt at the throne, they would still be at court. At least, no one but she had known of his desire to go with Prince Khusrau this past time. The slave boy Nizam had been pensioned off to his native village; Mehrunnisa had thought it too much of a risk to have him around in Bardwan where he could, and would, talk sooner or later.

She went to the ivory-inlaid wooden box where she kept all of her precious letters and pulled out the *farman* that lay at the bottom of the pile. Her fingers traced over the Turki words. The ink was fading now; it had been many years since Prince Salim had written the *farman* giving Ali Quli the title of Tiger Slayer. Mehrunnisa's eyes lingered over the strange phrase at the bottom of the paper. *May you be forever peaceful.* She touched the words, blotting one, then another, with her finger. Had the prince written that? No, it could not have come from his hand, but from that of an overzealous clerk. Still, it was a strange phrase to put in an official document. She put the *farman* back in its place and piled her veils over the papers. The letters lay hidden again under lustrous silks of blue, green, yellow, and red. Then she rose and went back to the window.

A sudden feeling of restlessness stole over her. She would give anything for a visit to Lahore—even a short visit—to the seat of power, to court life and the intrigues.

But that would not happen, Mehrunnisa thought, grimacing as she dusted mildew from her hands. Ali Quli was still in disgrace, and where he went, as his wife she was duty-bound to follow. The only consolation was that Bapa wrote to her every month, taking time from his duties to fill page after page with his flowing handwriting. He told her of the court, of home, and, when he could, news of the Dowager Empress and the *zenana*. More than being at Lahore, Mehrunnisa wanted to be with her father, to sit outside under a star-studded summer sky and hear him talk, to show him Ladli, the grandchild he had not yet seen. The letters were not enough.

Mehrunnisa turned again to look out at the rain-lashed landscape, the trees pushed to their knees by the wind, leaves and grasses glistening a rapacious green. A shudder passed through her body. She felt she would never leave Bengal.

But even as she stood there, a thousand miles away at Lahore, Emperor Jahangir paced his apartments, deep in thought. Now that the Khusrau affair had been dealt with, it was time to turn his mind to more pleasant matters.

FOURTEEN

The passion for Mehr-ul-Nissa, which Selim had repressed from a
respect and fear for his father, returned with redoubled violence
when he himself mounted the throne of India. He was now
absolute; no subject could thwart his will and pleasure.
                                        —Alexander Dow,
                          The History of Hindostan

JAHANGIR SIGHED AS HE LAY BACK AGAINST THE SILK CUSHIONS, loosening the ties of his qaba so he could breathe more easily. He could not remember when he had eaten so much or had the time in the past few months to enjoy his meal. The lamb kebabs had been skewered to perfection; marinated in lime juice, garlic, and rosemary; and roasted over hot coals. He patted his stomach and reached over for the wine.

Jahangir looked at the ladies of the harem over the rim of his goblet. They sat around him, clad in colorful muslins, smiling when his eye alighted upon them. Which one would grace his bedchamber tonight, he wondered idly. It was wonderful to have them here at Lahore. He had left Agra in a hurry to pursue Khusrau, and the royal harem had not been able to accompany him. Almost four months later, he had ordered Prince Khusrau to escort the royal ladies to Lahore.

After their arrival, the imperial court went back to its usual routine. Jahangir first bestowed great estates and favors on all those who had aided the empire during Khusrau's rebellion. Both Mahabat Khan and Muhammad Sharif were granted larger *mansabs* and revenues.

A few months later, news had been brought to Jahangir of a rebellious uprising in Rohtas, in Bihar. He decided to send Raja Man Singh at the head of the imperial army to quell the rebellion. The Raja was ordered to resign his post as governor of Bengal, and in his stead, Jahangir appointed

Qutubuddin Khan Koka. He had not wanted to let Koka go to Bengal, but his foster brother had come to request the post, and he had relented.

The Emperor put down his goblet and beckoned. A pretty concubine, a girl of sixteen years and his latest addition to the *zenana*, rose hastily from her seat and walked up to him.

"Help me to the royal bedchamber."

"Yes, your Majesty." Her seductive voice sent a thrill through the Emperor's spine.

The rest of the ladies watched in silence as their lord and master walked out of the room, leaning on his chosen consort for the night.

STATE DUTIES WERE so tiring, Jahangir thought, as he listened with half an ear to the singsong voice of the Mir Tozak. The Emperor was holding court in the *Diwan-i-am*. Petitions were being read, *jagirs* and *mansabs* granted, and the yearly budget accounted for. Bright sunshine in the courtyard beyond the *Diwan-i-am* beckoned invitingly. He could have been in the royal gardens with the ladies of his harem, perhaps watching them frolic in the new bath he had installed. . . .

"Your Majesty?"

Jahangir was jerked out of his thoughts by the sudden silence. He gave the Mir Tozak an irritable glance. "What is it?"

"The *diwan* of the empire, Mirza Ghias Beg, begs an audience, your Majesty," the Master of Ceremonies said.

Jahangir nodded. "Bring him in."

Mehrunnisa's father came into the court and performed the *konish*. "Your Majesty, news has been brought to me of danger in Qandahar. The governors of Herat, Sistan, and Farah have attacked the city under the orders of Shah Abbas of Persia. Beg Khan, the governor of Qandahar, has sent a courier requesting assistance from the imperial army."

Jahangir frowned. "How is that possible? Shah Abbas is like a brother to me. Will a brother invade another brother's dominions?"

"Your Majesty, it is imperative that we send an army. Qandahar is a commercial center of great importance to the empire, the center of trading activity between India and the western countries. Besides, it is one of the biggest outposts of the empire. To lose it to Persia would mean putting Kabul and the rest of the northwest in danger."

Jahangir saw the force of Ghias Beg's arguments, but he could not believe Shah Abbas to be the instigator of the attack on Qandahar. Why, just a year earlier they had exchanged letters, and the Shah had congratulated him on his ascension.

"All right," he said finally. "Send the imperial army with the royal standards to Qandahar. Be sure not to act aggressively until the matter is cleared up. Convey a message to the Shah of Persia informing him of the attack. He will take appropriate action against his governors."

Ghias bowed and backed away. The Emperor's voice stopped him. "Mirza Beg," he said. "You will be rewarded for your service to the empire."

"I need no reward, your Majesty," Ghias said. "But I thank you."

Jahangir turned to Muhammad Sharif. "How do these governors dare invade our province without the permission of their own Shah?"

"Your Majesty, this is a new regime. Doubtless the governors thought that in the confusion arising from the change of reign from your exalted father to you, they could overpower Qandahar. It is through Allah's grace that your Majesty is present at Lahore and can personally oversee the campaign."

Jahangir nodded. "True. Inform the *zenana* that we will be putting off our trip back to Agra until the Qandahar problem is solved."

When the *darbar* was over, Jahangir returned to his apartments and went to his private courtyard with a bag of wheat. The pigeons came fluttering down from their roosts in the verandah, greedy, pecking at the golden grain in his hand. A hesitant cough sounded at his elbow, and some of the pigeons squawked and flew away, frightened by the intruder. Hoshiyar Khan stood at the Emperor's side. He silently proffered a sealed letter. Jahangir took it and waited until the eunuch had left. Then he broke the seal and unrolled the letter. It was from Bengal. Jahangir read it rapidly and then put it down next to him, leaning against the *neem* tree and squinting into the bright sunshine that reflected off the marble slabs of the courtyard. The spies in Bengal had done their job well.

"BEGAM *SAHIBA*, RUNNERS have brought mail from Lahore." The slave girl proffered a letter on a silver tray.

Mehrunnisa reached out even before she had finished speaking. "Bring it here."

News from Lahore at last. Almost three months had gone by since the last letter from her father. Ghias was usually prompt in his correspondence, but the added responsibility of overseeing the Qandahar affair had kept him busy. Mehrunnisa unrolled the letter, savoring the crackle of paper under her hands, and settled down to read it. As always, he headed the letter with the word "Safe." That was to tell her at a glance that all was right with them. In her hurry to reply to him, Mehrunnisa often omitted to put that one word on top of her letters, and Ghias invariably started his letters with a scolding to her for that. And thus this one, too, began.

"My darling Nisa," he had written. "I have your letter in front of me, and again you have left out the indication to me that all goes well with you in Bengal. I had to read through your whole letter to find it was so. I think you must have my stubbornness in not following your Bapa's instructions, for so my own Bapa also berated me for other things. But no matter; it makes me feel you are here, with me, when I get your letters. I can only think that in one month, you will hold this paper in your hands and read my words.

"How is Ladli? Has she grown? Does she speak much? The painting you sent of her is little consolation for your not being here in person. It is hard to tell whom she resembles. Is it you? Maji? May I even hope, me? Talk to her of us, *beta;* let her know us through your words when we cannot be where she is."

A small hand crept out to tug at Mehrunnisa's *ghagara*, and she looked down and smiled. Ladli sat on the ground, clutching her knees. Her inquisitive eyes looked up at her mother as she reached out for the letter with an imperious "Give."

"Not this, *beta*," Mehrunnisa said, holding the letter aloft. "You will tear it. Go play with the horse and cart Nizam made for you before he went away."

Ladli shook her head. "Give me." Then, when Mehrunnisa held the letter away again, her face crumpled into sham tears.

"Come here," Mehrunnisa said, putting the letter on a table beyond her daughter's reach. She pulled her onto her lap and sat back on the divan. Ladli lay on her mother's lap, her thumb seeking her mouth, her petulance gone. Mehrunnisa smoothed the hair from her forehead. This child had made the years away from Bapa and Maji bearable.

"This is from your Dada, Ladli. He is a big man, an important man, *diwan* of the whole empire."

Even without Ghias's command, Mehrunnisa had spent many hours telling Ladli stories of her grandparents. And also stories of the Mughal court, of the pomp and glamour surrounding the harem ladies, of money that flowed like wine, and wine that flowed like water. But most of all, she told Ladli of Jahangir, convincing herself that her daughter must know of the Emperor. One day, Mehrunnisa thought, she would take Ladli back to court to meet the ladies of the harem and Dowager Empress Ruqayya Sultan Begam.

She looked down at her daughter and began to speak. The tale was one oft told, but the child's eyes grew round with wonder. She did not talk much yet, but it seemed to Mehrunnisa that she understood, that she listened intently to her mother's stories. Twenty minutes later, Ladli was asleep, leaning against her mother. Mehrunnisa gently laid her on the bed and covered her with a cool cotton sheet. She went back to her seat and eagerly picked up the letter again.

"Mirza Masud visited Lahore again and spent a few months with us. He has aged very much in the past few years; his eldest son now leads the caravan. As usual, he asked after you, his favorite foster daughter, and insisted that I read all your letters to him. I feel as though we will not see him again unless we visit Persia. He thinks the trip is too difficult to undertake at this time of life. I will never forget the debt I owe Mirza Masud: dear Nisa, he brought you back to me. For that I will be eternally grateful.

"Muhammad has settled down somewhat now. I had thought marriage and fatherhood would subdue your eldest brother, but that was not so. There is a streak of wildness in him that I have not been able to tame. Did you know that when Prince Khusrau escaped from imprisonment to Lahore, Muhammad wanted to go with him? Even now, unless I curb his tongue, he speaks of his loyalty to the prince in public. This, considering Emperor Jahangir has been so magnanimous and generous to our family. We would not be where we are if not for the benevolence of his Majesty. Even your husband enjoys a great deal of liberty and wealth because of the Emperor's good graces. Thank Allah that you were in Bengal and far away, so he was not involved in the Lahore escapade."

A wry smile crossed Mehrunnisa's face. If only Bapa knew. But she had told no one, especially not Bapa. She did not want her husband to fall further in her father's esteem. Then she frowned and read through the passage about Muhammad again. What was this madness in him? There had never been any real bond between Muhammad and her; Abul was Mehrunnisa's favorite brother. Muhammad had always been restless, always yearning for what he did not have; now he wanted to support Prince Khusrau. Thank Allah Bapa had stopped him from doing anything rash.

"But enough of that. Here is some good news. The Emperor has seen fit to confer an even greater favor upon us by uniting the two families. Can you imagine that? His Majesty has requested the hand of Arjumand Banu for Prince Khurram. The union will bring great distinction to our family. To be tied by marriage to the imperial family—who would have thought we would have such privileges in India?

"The betrothal ceremony will take place in a few months, and your Maji and I will be overjoyed if you can attend the function. Come, darling Nisa, and bring Ladli with you. It has been too long since we have seen you. Here is a good excuse to travel; your husband will not deny you this.

I have enclosed a letter to him regarding this matter. It is unfortunate that your husband cannot present himself at court and pay his respects to the Emperor, but Allah willing, the discord will be cleared up in time. Until then, for this occasion in any case, you must come alone."

Mehrunnisa put the letter down with a flush. Just a few minutes ago she had been thinking of the Mughal court, and now she would be returning to court life if Ali Quli allowed her to go. She bent her head in silent prayer. *Please, please make him say yes.* She looked down at the paper again. Arjumand Banu was to be betrothed to Prince Khurram. Her niece to be married to the Emperor's third son, the little boy who had been the Dowager Empress's charge. And Arjumand was her brother Abul's favorite child, his precious jewel. Abul had once said to Mehrunnisa, "If you are to have a child, Nisa, have a daughter, one just like my Arjumand. She will fill your heart with immeasurable joy." Mehrunnisa looked over to where Ladli slept, her knees drawn to her chest. Abul had been right. And how did he feel about this marriage? He must be ecstatic. It was an unprecedented honor for their whole family, all because of Bapa. Little Arjumand—she was not even fourteen years old, and now she was to be a princess.

At one time Mehrunnisa had thought she herself would be a princess. Now that honor was to be Arjumand's.

Ali Quli reluctantly gave his wife and daughter permission to go to Lahore. A request from Ghias Beg was in essence a command; his father-in-law was too powerful at court to refuse.

He watched gloomily as the two departed with happy smiles on their faces. He would not miss them, but he did not want them to go either. Why should they enjoy themselves when he could not? The brave soldier was discontented with life. He was not made out to be a landholder. Raja Man Singh, Ali Quli's only ally in Bengal, had been sent to Bihar. The new governor, Qutubuddin Khan Koka, a staunch supporter of the Emperor, was not inclined to be friendly with him. But, he thought, as his wife and daughter left on their long journey to Lahore, there were others who would listen to him. There were always others.

*   *   *

"THEY ARE HERE!"

At the cry, Ghias Beg rushed down the stone steps into the courtyard. He waited impatiently as the bearers put down the palanquin. Then, unable to restrain himself, he went to help the passengers out.

His daughter's cool hand reached out to him from between the palanquin curtains. As soon as she was upright, Ghias hugged her and then moved back to look at her, still holding her hand in his grasp.

She lifted the veil from her face and stood there smiling at him. Motherhood had brought a new maturity to her face, but her skin was still smooth, her eyes a clear azure blue, and her hair, coiled down the back, as black as the midnight sky. She was as slim and supple as a young girl. He leaned over to kiss her forehead. It had been too long since he had seen this child of his.

"You look the same as the day you were married, Mehrunnisa."

She blushed, a deep rosy glow coming over her cheeks, her eyes bright with excitement. "Thank you, Bapa. I am so happy to be here." She hugged him again and said, concern in her voice, "But you have aged. Are you looking after yourself?"

"Aged? Me?" Ghias asked in mock reproof. Then, putting a hand on his hair liberally sprinkled with gray, he said, "You mean these? These, my dear, are signs of wisdom, not age. The *diwan* of the empire must look his part." He looked around. "Where is my granddaughter?"

"Here," a voice called out. Ladli ran up to Ghias as fast as her plump little legs could carry her and flung herself into his arms. He held her tight, his face glowing at the warmth in her embrace. He had never met this granddaughter of his; yet she came to him naturally.

"Do you know who I am?" he demanded as he drew back to look at her. She was a tiny child—almost a miniature of her mother—with her lush hair in two tight plaits on either side of her head, *his* eyebrows sailing over a broad forehead, and a determined little chin that she stuck out at him.

"Yes, you are Dada. Mama says you are a very big man," Ladli told him confidently, her words coming in a rush.

Ghias Beg roared with happiness, his eyes twinkling as he turned to his daughter. "She talks so much already. Full sentences, just like you, *beta*, always in a hurry to get the words out. So"—turning back to Ladli, who had an arm around his shoulders—"what else did she tell you?"

"Emperor Jahangir is handsome."

"Ladli!" Mehrunnisa said hurriedly. "Enough chatter. Go inside now."

"Let her be." Ghias turned to his daughter, and she cast her eyes down. He looked at her speculatively. If things had turned out differently, she might have been an Empress by now. . . . His thoughts were broken by Ladli, who was tugging at his beard to catch his attention. He turned to her.

"Where is Dadi?" she demanded in a peremptory tone.

"Inside, waiting for you." Ghias, still carrying Ladli, put an arm around Mehrunnisa's shoulders, and they walked into the house.

FOR THE NEXT few days, Ghias Beg's home was turned upside down to prepare for the betrothal. The Emperor himself would be a guest. A battalion of servants, armed with brushes and mops, descended upon the house. Every nook and cranny was cleaned; rugs taken out and dusted, floors waxed, windows washed, walls whitewashed, brass and silverware polished to a shine. Presents were prepared for the groom and the Emperor. The whole house was a potpourri of aromas and essences. In the kitchens, cooks were busy day and night preparing for the feast. Sweets and savories bubbled invitingly on cast-iron stoves. Fresh flowers brought in from the gardens brightened the rooms.

Finally, the great day arrived.

The men of the house assembled in the front courtyard in a line, with Ghias as the host right near the entrance. The ladies crowded the upstairs balconies, their veils pulled over their faces. All morning, scouts from the royal palace, ministers of state, guards, and other people attached to the court had come to the house, checking the arrangements and security, and giving orders until Mehrunnisa's mother had almost dropped into a faint. And the day had not yet officially begun.

Now, finally, royal attendants came running to the house. "The Emperor is on his way! Be prepared."

Mehrunnisa watched her father straighten his *qaba* and make sure his ceremonial dagger was securely fastened to his cummerbund. His face was expressionless, filled with dignity; but inside, she knew he was nervous. This was a great day for him; Arjumand would not be betrothed to Prince Khurram had it not been for Ghias's service to the empire. Next to Ghias stood Abul, his expression one of pride. Even Abul had aged, Mehrunnisa thought. She had not seen this beloved brother of hers for a few years, and gray hairs had taken hold of his head. But in many ways he was the same Abul, teasing her after a few minutes of awkwardness, tickling Ladli until she squealed with delight and insisted on being carried on his shoulders around the garden. Abul and Mehrunnisa had barely had time to talk these last few days, but he had said one sentence, with wonder in his voice, that had been enough to show her what he felt. "Arjumand will be a princess, Nisa. Think of that. My little Arju. A princess." Then, shaking his head as he left her, he had said, "What will I call her once she is married to Prince Khurram?"

But he was happy, Mehrunnisa knew. As were they all. Happy and in a daze, rejoicing at the honor that had come to their family.

A few minutes later, the courtyard resounded with the Emperor's orchestra.

A loud gasp of awe went through the courtyard as two glittering figures appeared. Even Ghias Beg, who had seen the Emperor in his robes of state, could not help drawing in a deep breath.

Jahangir and Prince Khurram rode at the head of the imperial cavalcade, followed by the courtiers. Diamonds, rubies, and emeralds sparkled in the bright sunshine from their clothes and persons. Everyone bowed low and performed the *taslim*.

Ghias straightened up and rushed to help the Emperor dismount.

Mehrunnisa leaned over the balcony for her first glimpse of Jahangir, her heart pounding against her ribs.

Ladli tugged at her *ghagara*. "Mama, I want to see the Emperor."

Mehrunnisa picked her up.

They watched in silence as the usual formalities were completed. The Emperor and Prince Khurram had dismounted. Ghias broke into his speech of welcome.

Mehrunnisa had lain awake last night wondering. Would Jahangir have changed? Would his new position have given him dignity? It certainly had, she thought now. He seemed calmer, more collected, much more self-assured. The crown sat well on his head.

In her eagerness, she leaned too far over the balcony ledge, and they almost toppled over. Righting herself and holding securely onto Ladli, she looked at Jahangir's face with hunger, drinking in every detail of his appearance: the sprinkling of gray that showed under his turban, the sun brilliant on his clothes, his low laugh of pleasure at something her father had said. She waited, her breath catching in her chest, for him to glance up at the balcony so she could see his face properly.

"Mama." Ladli put a hand to her face and turned her eyes from Jahangir. "Is that Prince Khurram? How beautiful he is!"

These were familiar words. Once, so many years before when Jahangir was Prince Salim, Mehrunnisa had thought *him* beautiful too. Her gaze flickered to Khurram in pleasant surprise. He had grown into a handsome boy; Arjumand was very lucky. He stood to one side, gazing around him uncertainly. Mehrunnisa smiled, remembering the curly-haired child she had once looked after. Khurram seemed overwhelmed and uncomfortable to be the focus of all the attention. Quite natural, since he could not have been more than fifteen. He fidgeted around on his feet, rubbed his smooth face, and glanced back at the palanquins being carried into the courtyard.

The ladies of the royal *zenana* descended one by one, led by a heavily veiled lady. Empress Jagat Gosini, no doubt, Mehrunnisa thought. Then she was sure. Jagat Gosini strode up to Khurram and nodded distantly as Ghias bowed to her.

It was a pity Ruqayya was not here. She had chosen to stay back at Agra when the royal harem made its journey to Lahore. Mehrunnisa

would have liked to meet the Empress again. She wondered idly who led
the royal *zenana* now that Jahangir was Emperor. Ruqayya must find it
galling to give precedence to Jagat Gosini and Jahangir's wives after three
decades of being supreme in the harem.

The formalities completed, Jahangir, Prince Khurram, and the ladies
entered the house. Mehrunnisa set Ladli down and turned to welcome
the *zenana* ladies.

THE BETROTHAL CEREMONY took place with great solemnity. The ladies
of Ghias Beg's household and the Emperor's wives sat behind a silk
screen watching the proceedings. Arjumand was at the very front, near
the *parda*, a gold-sequined veil covering her head. Mehrunnisa saw
Khurram glance once or twice at her niece. Each time he looked at her,
the ladies burst into giggles, and Khurram hurriedly looked away.
Mehrunnisa leaned over to hug Arjumand. "He is very handsome, my
dear," she whispered to her niece and was rewarded with a shy nod. The
men sat in the center of the room: the Qazi on one side, Jahangir and
Ghias Beg on the other. The Qazi registered the formal engagement of
Arjumand Banu Begam, daughter of Abul Hasan and granddaughter of
Ghias Beg, to Prince Khurram, son of Emperor Jahangir. Ghias signed
the contract and bowed to the Emperor as he gave him the goose-feather
quill. Khurram was in for a very nice surprise, Mehrunnisa thought. Her
niece was more beautiful than any other woman in the family. Once
Khurram saw her, he would be pleased.

After the ceremony, the rooms were cleared. The servants streamed in
with the dishes of goat and chicken curries; copper platters of whole river
fish roasted over coals with garlic and lemon juice; turmeric and saffron-
tinted *pulavs* sprinkled with raisins, cashews, and walnuts; and silver jugs
of *khus* and ginger sherbets. The men ate in one part of the room and the
ladies in another, long muslin curtains hanging between them.

From behind the *parda*, Mehrunnisa watched Jahangir. This man
would have been her husband if matters had turned out differently—and

today, it might well have been her son who would have had the chance of becoming the next Emperor of India.

She turned to look at Jagat Gosini. The Empress held court in one corner of the room, her ladies fluttering around her. There was no doubt who headed the *zenana* now. There was an imperious tone in Jagat Gosini's voice, an arrogant look on her face, and she raised her eyebrows disdainfully when something displeased her. Just like Ruqayya.

A slow smiled spread across Mehrunnisa's face. All this play-acting had aged Jagat Gosini. It had been all right in Ruqayya; the Dowager Empress had not been born beautiful, so she had had to use all her other skills to keep her place in the *zenana* and in Akbar's heart. But Jagat Gosini was beautiful—at least, she had been. Now she rarely smiled; her mouth was set in a thin, disapproving line, her face grim. How did Jahangir take all this? The Emperor was not usually drawn to morose, long-faced women. If she remembered correctly, he liked his women to be good-humored, seductive, and witty.

"This *burfi* is terrible."

Mehrunnisa looked up from her musings to see Jagat Gosini push away a plate of coconut-flaked sweets.

"I beg pardon, your Majesty. I shall send for some more," Asmat Begam said hurriedly, signaling to the servants.

"No, I do not want any more. Bring me a glass of wine," Jagat Gosini commanded.

Asmat bowed. "At once, your Majesty."

Mehrunnisa frowned, hackles rising along her spine. Ever since Jagat Gosini had come into the house she had been complaining. Either the food was not cooked to perfection, or the servants were lax, or something else. Her mother had been sent scurrying around to bring the choicest *pulavs*, curries, and sweets for the Empress. Asmat had not even had time to sit down and eat her lunch. She looked harried and tired; her hair had escaped from her usual neat plait, and her veil had fallen off her head. And Mehrunnisa knew how much trouble Asmat had taken with the feast and the preparations for the ceremony. She had hardly seen her mother in the last few days, catching only brief glimpses of her as she rushed about the house, cleaning it and personally inspecting the food.

Now the Empress was ordering her around as though she were a menial. Stiff-backed, Mehrunnisa rose from the divan and went up to her mother. "I shall bring the Empress her wine. Why don't you sit down for a while?" She pulled the reluctant Asmat to a divan and firmly sat her down.

"I want my wine," Jagat Gosini said.

"At once, your Majesty," Mehrunnisa said. "My mother is tired; I will be able to serve you better."

"Who are you?"

"Mehrunnisa, Ali Quli's wife." She moved away to pour the wine.

When she handed the goblet to Jagat Gosini, the Empress asked, "Where have I seen you before?"

There was drama in this moment. Mehrunnisa realized it and couldn't help making use of it. *Khurram.* All she had to do was say the prince's name, and Jagat Gosini would remember. She opened her mouth, then shut it. She let the silence stretch delicately between them as the Empress's brows began to contract, and then shrugged. "I don't know, your Majesty."

Jagat Gosini nodded with a flush, feeling that she had somehow been vanquished, and turned away to mull things over. Then her voice came, sharp and biting, "*Now* I remember you. You are married to that Persian soldier of ill repute."

Mehrunnisa glared at her, swallowing the words of bitterness that came rising up her throat.

"Tell me," the Empress murmured, snapping her fingers to gather the ladies of the harem. "The last time I inquired about you, there were no children. How long have you been married?"

Mehrunnisa ignored the question and said instead in a soft voice, "You inquired about me, your Majesty? A mere soldier's wife? Why?"

"I . . . the Emperor . . . we like to keep informed of our subjects. All our subjects, even the ones who betray the throne, as your husband has done. Now answer my question: how long have you been married?"

"Thirteen years, your Majesty."

"And no children yet? Your husband should take another wife, if he already has not—one who will serve him better."

"I do have a child, your Majesty," Mehrunnisa said heatedly, stepping away from Jagat Gosini and colliding with one of the harem ladies behind her. She dipped out of the circle, then pulled Ladli into it.

The Empress looked over the child and saw her brilliant gray eyes, the shock of thick hair knotted at her nape, the pink cheeks, the gap on her midriff where her miniature silk *choli* did not quite meet the top of her *ghagara*.

"A pretty child," she murmured. Then, slipping a pair of gold bangles off her wrists, she offered them to Ladli. "Here, take these."

Ladli screwed up her mouth, sensing her mother's unease, and shook her head violently. "Don't want them. You keep them."

Jagat Gosini's eyes glittered as she looked over Ladli's head at Mehrunnisa. "Only a girl child for your husband, my dear? And such an arrogant one. You must teach her humility. Commoners must never refuse a gift from royalty."

"But our family is going to be associated with yours, your Majesty," Mehrunnisa said. "Surely we are no longer common?"

"Only by my grace is your family to be united with ours, Mehrunnisa. Do not forget that," Jagat Gosini snapped. She pushed the bangles at Ladli again. "Take them, child. I command you."

Mehrunnisa leaned over Ladli and took the bangles. She said, "Thank you, your Majesty." She bowed and moved away from the circle around the Empress, head held high. When they were out of the room, she sent Ladli to play with her cousins, then ran to the back courtyard. There she leaned over the well in the hot sunshine and threw the bangles in, watching as they spun golden through the air before splashing into the water.

The gift was a demand of humility from Jagat Gosini; Ladli would never wear the bangles. She, and Mehrunnisa, did not need charity. Trembling with rage, she sat on the ground, leaning against the wall of the well. Her tongue had almost got her into trouble, had almost broken

Arjumand's engagement. Although Jahangir had probably commanded the union, a word from Jagat Gosini could easily have broken it. What a fool she had been. It would have dishonored her Bapa, Maji, Abul . . . as for Arjumand, she would never have been married. A royal prince's reject would not find many suitors.

Mehrunnisa sat there until her uncovered head grew hot in the sun. Then, composing herself, she went back into the house to help Asmat with the preparations and play the part of a good daughter.

Toward afternoon, when the sun was high in the sky and the heat was blinding, the courtiers and attendants slipped off into shaded cloisters in Ghias's gardens, there to take a short nap or rendezvous with lovers.

THE ROOM WAS cool and dark, *khus* mats had been pulled over the windows, and attendants sat outside, sprinkling water on the mats. The *khus* rushes grew on riverbanks, where they dipped their heady aroma into the air. Cut, woven into mats, and sprinkled with water, they released their perfume once more. The hot afternoon wind blowing over the Gangetic plains was miraculously turned into a cool, scented breeze as it wafted through the *khus*. All around the room the ladies lay supine on their divans, unwilling to move. This time of the day was enervating, no physical activity was possible, and the heavy lunch lulled them into a pleasant doze.

Mehrunnisa leaned against the cool stone walls of the room and closed her eyes. Her daughter was asleep next to her, with her head on her mother's lap. Ladli moved restlessly, and Mehrunnisa patted her back to sleep.

There was a hush over the room, broken only by the soft gurgling of the *hukkahs* and the muted conversation of the younger harem ladies. Blue smoke floated lazily up to the ceiling from the water pipes, mixing with the sandalwood of incense censers.

Mehrunnisa settled herself more comfortably against the wall and looked around. Jagat Gosini was asleep on a divan, her head pillowed on the velvet bolster. She lay perfectly still, hands crossed on her chest. In repose, her expression had softened, and she looked youthful, reminding Mehrunnisa of the day she had met the Empress in Ruqayya's gardens. She had much to thank Ruqayya for, she thought. Mehrunnisa had met Jahangir as a prince in her courtyard. But—and here she shuddered—if it hadn't been for Ruqayya's influence, she would not be married to Ali Quli.

Just then, the *khus* mat over the door was lifted, and harsh sunshine flooded the room. Mehrunnisa shielded her eyes and turned away. A man's figure blotted the light, his face not visible, but she recognized him almost immediately from his turban. The large white heron feather was Jahangir's favorite ornament. Mehrunnisa sat frozen in her place, her heart beating out every other sound. Her hand stilled on Ladli's shoulder.

"Your Majesty, you have come to join us," some of the ladies cried out. In a few moments the whole room was bustling as the ladies rose and bowed to the Emperor. They glanced surreptitiously at the small mirrors on their thumb rings to make sure their hair and makeup were in place. A few of the concubines rushed up to Jahangir and hung on his arm, coaxing him to their divans.

Jahangir laughed down at their bright faces and selected one concubine. Just as she was pulling him to her seat, Jagat Gosini spoke. "Come here, your Majesty."

Jahangir glanced at her, then gently disengaged himself from the girl's hands, leaning down to whisper something in her ear. She pouted and turned away. Jahangir shrugged, walked up to his Empress, and sat down next to her.

"Congratulations, my dear. You are to have a very beautiful daughter-in-law," he said.

"Thank you, your Majesty. We are indeed fortunate to be related to Mirza Beg's family," Jagat Gosini replied.

Mehrunnisa raised her eyebrows in disbelief. Was this the same bad-tempered Empress of two hours ago? Jagat Gosini had changed; she was simpering and flirting like an adolescent. But Jahangir seemed oblivious to her wiles. His gaze kept roving to the pretty young concubine, who was now lounging seductively on her divan facing Jahangir, giving him the full benefit of her charms. Nonetheless, Jahangir stayed by his Empress; he wanted to honor her on the day her son had become betrothed.

"Asmat, get the Emperor some wine," Jagat Gosini said imperiously, still looking at her lord. "Asmat!"

"I will do it, your Majesty," Mehrunnisa said from her corner, her cheeks flaming in anger. Asmat had gone to the kitchens much earlier. How dare the Empress treat her mother this way?

"What are you waiting for?" Jagat Gosini said, the dulcet tones turning harsh, still without looking at Mehrunnisa. Suddenly, her head snapped in Mehrunnisa's direction and she said quickly, "Get a servant to do it. Not you."

"But, your Majesty, there are no servants here. Only me," Mehrunnisa replied. She shifted Ladli's head onto a pillow, rose, and went to the tray by Jagat Gosini's elbow. The Empress shook her head and indicated the door, as if to say *get out*.

Determinedly not looking at her, Mehrunnisa poured the wine and held it out to Jahangir.

Her heart pounded as Jahangir reached for the goblet, but he did so without giving her a glance. Their fingers touched briefly. *Look at me.* He did not, his attention still caught by the concubine. With great deliberation, Mehrunnisa let go of the goblet and stepped back. Jahangir had not quite gotten hold of the goblet, and it fell to the floor with a clatter, spilling the wine on the divan and staining the edge of the Empress's *ghagara*. Mehrunnisa had stepped out of the way long before.

"Stupid girl! Don't you know how to serve wine?" Jagat Gosini got up and shook off her *ghagara*, glaring at Mehrunnisa. Mehrunnisa stared back at her steadily, but out of the corner of her eye she saw Jahangir look at her briefly, and then turn to look with more interest.

"I apologize, your Majesty. It will not happen again," Mehrunnisa said, a demure, innocent look on her face.

"It had better not. Go get some towels."

"Wait!" The Emperor's voice rang out through the room. He rose to his feet, stumbling as he did so. "Who are you?"

Mehrunnisa smiled at him, suddenly the consummate actress. In Bengal, Ali Quli ignored her and the coolies gazed at her stupidly. But here, among all these beautiful women, she, the mother of a child and old in the eyes of all men, could command the attention of the man who had everything. It was the best feeling in the world. "Mirza Ghias Beg's daughter, your Majesty."

Jahangir stared at her, his eyes drinking her in like a man who had long thirsted for water. She was here, right in front of him. The passing years seemed to melt away, leaving them in the corridor again. He knew who she was, of course, but he had to say something, and that was the first question that had come to mind.

He took a deep trembling breath. She had an aristocratic nose, rose-bud lips, and a slender frame. The court painters would die for a sitting. Her breasts heaved under the silk *choli*. She was blushing, the color lending her charm. She stood absolutely still, hands at her sides, fingers encircled with diamond and ruby rings.

Mehrunnisa raised her eyes to Jahangir's face and was jolted by what she saw. What had started out as a game to annoy Jagat Gosini was turning into something more serious. The people around them melted away into the fringes of her consciousness. She wanted to touch him, just to hold his hand and feel the warmth of his skin on hers. With him, this man she knew only from afar, she felt protected, safe, as though she did not need to fight battles. He would do that for her, like a safe harbor where she could rest her thoughts. Suddenly, she felt tired from all these years of living, of wanting him, of wanting a child, of getting only one of her desires after such a long time.

"Your Majesty, I am drenched with the wine. Send her to get me some towels," Jagat Gosini complained, trying to pull Jahangir back to the divan.

"Send someone else, my dear," Jahangir said, pushing away her arm.

"I want to talk to her." He turned to Mehrunnisa with a gentle voice. "What is your name?" But he knew her name; he had said it to himself many times. He just wanted to hear her say it.

"Mehrunnisa."

"Sun of Women." Jahangir rolled the words around his tongue. He looked over her contemplatively. "Yes, you are."

Mehrunnisa shifted under his gaze. She felt as though he were mentally stripping her of everything—her clothes, her emotions—and peering into her deepest secrets. Would he see the love? Would he see thirteen years of yearning? She saw that he had not forgotten her. That thought sent heat through her veins. It was easy for her to remember him; she had wanted him since she was eight. But for him to hold her in his memory . . . to ask her name even though he seemed to know it . . . yet, he had made no move to seek her out since he became Emperor. What did this mean? How could she have known that she still had this much power over him? What would Jahangir do? There was no father to thwart his wishes now.

"Your Majesty, Mehrunnisa is wanted in the kitchens. She has to give instructions to the cooks." Asmat Begam's voice broke into the silence.

They all turned to see her standing next to them, a respectful but watchful look on her face.

All of a sudden Mehrunnisa did not want to go. She would play this out to the end. The Emperor had the power to give her so much; why should she not take it? Her back stiffened, and Asmat, seeing the gesture and recognizing it well, said quietly, "Please, your Majesty."

"Send someone else, Asmat," Jahangir said.

"I beg pardon, your Majesty. But"—Mehrunnisa's mother hesitated—"my daughter is a married woman and—"

Jahangir turned and looked at Asmat, her words finally sinking in. He nodded slowly. "I understand. You are given permission to leave, Mehrunnisa."

Mehrunnisa bowed and moved away. She was uncertain, wanting to stay, not wanting to leave. She dragged her feet out of the room, feeling

Jahangir's and Jagat Gosini's eyes on her. She glanced back, and a shiver went up her spine. The Emperor was looking at her with lust, the Empress with implacable hatred.

She hesitated in the doorway. Asmat Begam put a firm hand on her back and pushed her out.

THAT NIGHT MEHRUNNISA lay awake in her bed. Asmat had not said a word except to send her to the kitchens with spurious instructions. A few hours later, afternoon *chai* was served, and then the royal party had gone back to the palace. The family had retired to their rooms early for some much-needed rest; there was no opportunity for conversation with her mother.

But Mehrunnisa could not sleep. Had she done right in trying to get Jahangir's attention again? Her previous ploys to capture him seemed childish now, especially when the stakes were higher. There was more, much more to gain . . . and to lose.

Jahangir fascinated her. Gone was the petulant prince she had known. In his place stood a strong man, one possessed of much power, charm, and cruelty. All his life, Jahangir had been accustomed to getting what he wanted. No one had denied him anything before, and as Emperor, no one could deny him anything now.

Mehrunnisa shivered. She rose, pulled a shawl over her shoulders, and went to the window. She stood staring down into the deserted courtyard. It was dark except for the small pool of light from a lantern hung on the doorway of the stables. What would the Emperor do now? Jahangir's sense of justice was legendary. People all over the country talked of his twelve edicts of conduct and the Chain of Justice. But equally legendary was his cruelty. The Emperor thought little of executing men en masse, inflicting on them the cruelest punishments and tortures. If Jahangir wanted Mehrunnisa, then Jahangir would get Mehrunnisa. But at what price? Mehrunnisa was a married woman and belonged to Ali Quli.

Mehrunnisa had tried not to give herself the luxury of self-pity at her marriage to Ali Quli, at their deteriorating relationship, at her childlessness for so many years, at the jibes and snickers because of it, or at having only a girl child at the end of it all. Now she thought that there were two parts of her: one for Ladli, whose every breath was precious to her, the other for Jahangir, the man she had dreamed of for many years. Neither precluded the other, and both, she realized now, were equally important. Neither could be denied, no matter how much she forced herself not to think of the Emperor.

She raised her eyes from the courtyard and looked over the walls of the house. The city of Lahore was asleep, but lights twinkled in the darkness from the street lamps. In the distance, she could see the ramparts of the Lahore fort bathed in the golden light of torches.

The situation was difficult, too difficult. Mehrunnisa sighed, turned back into the room, and crawled into bed. As her weight settled on the mattress, Ladli moved in sleep to fling a leg over her mother. Mehrunnisa lay awake for a long while, then forced her eyes shut. She had to sleep soon, or she would not be prepared for the lecture her mother would give her in the morning.

GHIAS BEG KICKED his heels into the horse's flanks to urge it into a faster pace. The Emperor had expressly sent for him. He was surprised and not just a little apprehensive about the summons. He mentally ran over the previous day's events. Had he done anything to displease Jahangir? He did not think so. Everything had gone smoothly. The Emperor had seemed pleased and been very generous in his gifts to Arjumand.

Still wondering, Ghias presented himself at the reception hall. When he entered, he found Mahabat Khan and Muhammad Sharif standing on either side of Jahangir.

"*Inshah Allah*, your Majesty."

"*Inshah Allah*, Mirza Beg. I was very pleased with the arrangements for the betrothal ceremony yesterday. The union between our two families will be advantageous to us both."

"Your Majesty is too kind," Ghias protested. "The honor is all ours, sire."

"Yes, yes. But I have commanded your presence for another reason." Jahangir looked at Ghias keenly.

But the *diwan* was completely in the dark. Asmat Begam had not mentioned anything to him the night before, believing the matter to be best left alone. He waited for his Emperor to speak.

"You have a married daughter?"

"Four married daughters, your Majesty, by the grace of Allah."

"I am talking of Mehrunnisa." Jahangir waved an impatient hand at his *diwan*. "She is married to Ali Quli."

"Yes, your Majesty." A little doubt crept into Ghias's mind. He looked at Jahangir.

"Ali Quli is a dissident. He teamed up with my rebellious son Khusrau during my father's reign in an effort to put Khusrau on the throne. I have magnanimously overlooked his faults and his disloyalty to me."

"Your Majesty is very kind. My son-in-law was mistaken and fell in with mutinous people. He was misled into actions against your person, and I know he is greatly repentant."

"Yes, yes, but nonetheless he has committed a great crime and must pay for his sins. Do you understand?"

"Your Majesty . . . I . . . Ali Quli is loyal to you now . . . ," Ghias stammered. Where was this leading? What had Ali Quli done in Bengal?

"Your daughter Mehrunnisa is very beautiful and charming. I had an amusing encounter with her yesterday. She will grace any man's household. In fact, she is fit to be a king's wife," Jahangir said distinctly.

Realization dawned upon the *diwan*. At last he understood the purpose for which he had been commanded to his Emperor's presence. The Emperor wished to invoke the *Tura-i-Chingezi*, the law of the Timurs. In effect, Jahangir wanted Ali Quli to divorce Mehrunnisa so that he could marry her.

A troubled look came over the statesman's face. The *Tura-i-Chingezi* was common enough, and it was a great honor for any man to be com-

manded to give up his wife to the Emperor. But Ali Quli was fractious
and disobedient. Ghias had secretly heaved a sigh of relief when his son-
in-law was sent to Bardwan, far from the imperial court, for he was sure
to get into trouble if he stayed near the Emperor. Now Jahangir wanted
Ali Quli to give up his wife. Ghias shook his head. Things were happening too fast, without warning. Mehrunnisa to be the Emperor's wife!
That meant riches for the whole family, and prestige and reputation. And
who knew—he might one day be grandfather to the next emperor. But
Ali Quli . . . always Ali Quli . . . too late now to correct any mistakes. The
diwan looked up and saw the Emperor waiting for an answer.

"Your wish has always been my command, your Majesty. I shall do
everything in my power to ensure your—and my daughter's—happiness." There was little else he could say.

Jahangir nodded happily. "You may go now."

Ghias left, and Jahangir fell into a satisfied reverie. Soon he would
sleep next to the beautiful Mehrunnisa, and upon waking he would see
that lissome form next to him . . . those gorgeous eyes would awaken
him. . . .

"Your Majesty." Mahabat Khan's voice broke into his thoughts. "I beg
your pardon, but—" Jahangir turned to him. "Is Ali Quli's wife really a
good choice? She has lived for thirteen years with the man and doubtless
harbors resentment against your Majesty for the punishment inflected
upon her husband."

"Your solicitousness for my well-being is gratifying, Mahabat. But if
you could have seen her yesterday as I did: beauty, charm, and grace, all
in one person . . . why, she is the essence of femininity and woman-
hood—" Jahangir stopped abruptly.

"Your Majesty," Mahabat urged. "Please reconsider your wishes."

But try as he would, Mahabat Kahn could not make Jahangir budge
from his position. The Sun of Women, Mehrunnisa, had bewitched the
Emperor, and he would not rest until she was his.

He too had lain awake last night thinking about her. When Jahangir
had offered Khurram's hand to Ghias's granddaughter, he had thought to

honor the *diwan*. But he remembered that Ghias was Mehrunnisa's father and that she too would be honored by the proposal. Somehow, the thought of seeing her at the betrothal had never crossed his mind. She was in Bengal, at the easternmost reach of the empire; yet she had traveled to Lahore for the ceremony. At the sight of her, a fire lit inside him, raging, consuming him with its intensity. All these years she had been a dream, a distant memory. Seeing her standing in front of him, he knew why he had fallen in love with her. Now there was no turning back. Ali Quli was disposable.

He had no regret at invoking the *Tura-i-Chingezi*. For unknown to even Mahabat and Sharif—and they did not know everything, although they thought they did—a letter had come to Jahangir a month ago. His spies recounted a tale told by a slave boy named Nizam. When Khusrau fled to Lahore, Ali Quli was prepared to join him. The *Sahiba* had stopped her husband.

Had she done it for him? And now, would she come willingly to his *zenana*? Doubt came flooding over him. But she must come. He bowed his head and closed his eyes. Please Allah, even if she did not love him, let her come. He would show her what she meant to him. Then he remembered the smile in her eyes, the reluctance with which she had left the room. Surely there was hope in those signs.

"WELL?" THE VEILED figure demanded. "What happened?"

Mahabat Khan gave a swift glance around and then pulled the woman into a bower of sweet-scented jasmine vines. A few feet away from them, the head eunuch of the harem, Hoshiyar Khan, paced the stone pathway bordered with terracotta *diyas*, their flames flickering in the close night air. Hoshiyar lifted his head every now and then to make sure no one was approaching.

Mahabat turned to the woman. "Your Majesty, I was not successful. The Emperor wishes to invoke the *Tura-i-Chingezi*. He has ordered Ghias Beg to write to Ali Quli."

Jagat Gosini drew in a sharp breath. "Did you remind the Emperor of that man's duplicity? That he had teamed up with Prince Khusrau?"

Mahabat spread his hands in a helpless gesture. "I did, your Majesty. But the Emperor used the information to his advantage. It is on the basis of Ali Quli's rebellion he is invoking the law. The Emperor is infatuated with that woman."

Jagat Gosini frowned. Mahabat watched her with care, wishing he could see the Empress's face more clearly.

Mahabat was well aware that the harem and the court had to work in tandem to run the empire. While one operated behind the scenes to influence the Emperor, the other worked at court in full view of the nobles. Together they would be powerful—so powerful that Jahangir would not have the slightest inkling that he was being gently led by the nose. It mattered little if the other courtiers knew or protested.

Mahabat grimaced. Ever since Jahangir had become Emperor, it had been more and more difficult to control him. It seemed that upon wearing the imperial turban, the once impressionable prince had developed very decided opinions of his own. Jahangir had sent out his edicts of conduct, had strung up his Chain of Justice, and was generally making a nuisance of himself by prying into the affairs of the empire. He was no longer as susceptible to their influence as he had once been. So when Jagat Gosini asked him to try to dissuade Jahangir from marrying Mehrunnisa, Mahabat had agreed. If the Empress was on his side, it would be so much easier to rid Jahangir of his fanciful ideas and bring the empire under their control once more.

"What now, Mahabat?" Jagat Gosini asked finally.

"All is not lost, your Majesty." Mahabat smiled slowly, his lean, sun-browned face creasing into wrinkles. "Ali Quli has to agree to the Emperor's command. And chances are that he will not."

"Do you think so?" There was a new hope in the Empress's voice.

Mahabat nodded. "Yes, I do. He is bound to get angry and rush off into some indiscretion or another. If he doesn't, we can give him a slight push. You see, your Majesty," Mahabat grinned, "Ali Quli is a soldier. He has no idea of diplomacy. The tactful thing to do would be to give up his wife to the Emperor. But Ali Quli is sure to rebel against the idea. We can only wait and see."

Jagat Gosini bit her lip, drawing blood but not tasting it. "If you say so. I am relying on you, Mahabat, to see that my wishes are carried out." Her eyes blazed at him.

"It shall be done, your Majesty." Mahabat bowed. "Now, I should leave. No one must see us together. But," he turned again to her, "if I may ask, why this interest in Mehrunnisa? Surely she can be no threat to you. This is simply like the Anarkali incident. We know that the Emperor's fancy often strays. . . ." He let the words trail away and looked at her.

They were both silent for a moment thinking of Anarkali, "Pomegranate Blossom," the name Akbar had given to one of his favorite concubines. In 1598, when the court was still at Lahore, Akbar had caught Prince Salim and Anarkali flirting with each other in the Hall of Mirrors. Anarkali was massaging Akbar's shoulders, and he had glanced up to catch her smiling at Salim in the reflection of one of the mirrors. The Emperor had been furious and immediately sentenced her to death, to be entombed alive brick by brick.

"This is more serious," Jagat Gosini said. "I can compete with a dead woman. The Emperor's so-called love for Anarkali was fanned by her death." She smiled wryly. "It is easier to fall in love with an image; when the woman is around every day, little irritations are bound to crop up, and love will wane."

"Then, by your own argument, it would be better not to stand in the way of the Emperor's wishes regarding Mehrunnisa. Let him marry her, and in a few months he will tire of her."

The Empress looked at Mahabat, wondering how much she could tell him. That she had to tell him something there was no doubt; he would not offer his help for nothing, and Jagat Gosini knew it was pointless to try and dissuade Jahangir herself. Finally, she said, "Mehrunnisa is some-how . . . different. Her presence in the *zenana* will be a threat to me—and maybe even to you."

Mahabat gave an incredulous laugh. "Me? How could she do that? You must be aware, your Majesty, that the Emperor has absolute confidence in me. We have been children together. It will take a lot to shake that confidence."

"Tell me," Jagat Gosini looked at him. "Does the Emperor realize that he was once before enamored by this woman?"

Mahabat shook his head somberly. Jagat Gosini's serious tone had finally penetrated. The Empress was afraid of this woman, and she thought that Mehrunnisa could create trouble for all of them. Although Mahabat could not see how that was possible, he had enough faith in Jagat Gosini to believe her.

"Well, then, he must not be reminded," Jagat Gosini said. "Go now, Mahabat. I see Hoshiyar coming toward us. Someone must be approaching the gardens."

"Patience, your Majesty. Time is on our side. We shall wait and see what happens." With that, Mahabat let himself out of the *zenana* gardens.

The Empress watched him until he disappeared through the brick arches at the far end of the gardens. She leaned on the stone backrest of the bench, shrinking into the shadows beyond the lamps. Mahabat had taken a great risk in coming to her, in coming into the *zenana* quarters. But somehow Hoshiyar had managed it, doubtless greasing a few palms so that eyes would be blind.

A *rath-ki-rani* bush bloomed behind her, releasing its sun-filled fragrance into the night, the perfume almost cloying at such close proximity. Jagat Gosini looked down at her hands. She had taken a risk too. If she had been found here with a man from the outside, it would not matter that she was the Padshah Begam or that Mahabat was a powerful minister, for they could not tell the truth of why they had met. Jahangir would have been furious. Her hands started trembling violently, and she wrapped her arms around herself. For the first time, Jagat Gosini had had to go for help outside the harem walls—and all because of Mehrunnisa.

Hatred, palpable as the heat of the day, fired through her. It was an illogical hatred—one sane part of Jagat Gosini's mind told her this much. But all the emotion she could not express in the *zenana*, because she was supposed to be calm and collected and wise, had found its home in Mehrunnisa. Jealousy: yes, that too—a rabid, all-consuming jealousy that her husband was so infatuated by this woman, that all these years apart had not dimmed his passion for her. There were many other women in the *zenana* who shared Jahangir's affections, yet he always seemed to have had a special fondness for Jagat Gosini. The only woman who threatened that fondness was Mehrunnisa, because Jahangir wanted her not for the title she bore—she was no princess—and not for her family connections—her father was, after all, and would always be, just a Persian refugee—but for herself.

There was also the fact that Mehrunnisa was Ruqayya's protegee. And no matter what logic dictated, Jagat Gosini swore to herself that neither of those women would gain ascendance over her. Hence the small lie to Mahabat about Mehrunnisa being a threat to him also. For had she not lied, Mahabat would not have helped her.

GHIAS BEG RODE home, his hand resting lightly on the reins, the horse picking its way back at an even trot. The Emperor's hints had put his mind in a turmoil. His daughter to be the Emperor's wife! The betrothal of his granddaughter and Prince Khurram was nothing compared to this.

He suddenly sobered. It was all very well to think of what might be, but again he was forgetting Ali Quli. Would he give up Mehrunnisa without a fight? They were an ill-matched couple—this had been sadly evident to him for years—but Mehrunnisa had never complained to him.

When the *diwan* entered his house, he was informed that a courtier was awaiting him in the reception hall. Ghias's eyes gleamed when he heard the man's name. He hurried in to welcome him, heard his request, and promised to do something about it. The man was suitably grateful, and a heavy bag of gold *mohurs* exchanged hands. After the man had left, Ghias sent for his daughter. He then emptied the bag on a satin cloth and lovingly ran his hands through the gold. He was counting the *mohurs* when his daughter entered, a smile on her face.

Mehrunnisa stopped short and frowned. "Where did you get those?"

"Ah, you are here, come sit down, Nisa." Ghias put the *mohurs* back into the bag and locked the bag safely in his strongbox. He was tucking his key chain into his cummerbund when he noticed the look on his daughter's face.

"What is the matter, my dear?"

"Where did you get the *mohurs*, Bapa?"

"One of the courtiers wants his son to get a position in the imperial army. I promised to put a word in the Khan-i-khanan's ear."

"I see. You took a bribe." Her voice was scornful, full of contempt and fear.

Ghias flinched. "Not a bribe, *beta*. That is such an ugly word. Let us just say . . . ah . . . payment for services rendered."

"A bribe," she insisted. "Bapa, how could you? Don't you realize that if the Emperor finds out you will get into deep trouble? Have you forgotten what led you to flee Persia?"

Ghias turned away from the accusing look in her eyes. What could he say to her? He felt a little ashamed that she had caught him. But surely she knew that all courtiers of some influence indulged in this? She was right: he had always taught his children to live with honesty, yet now he was doing something dishonest. There were excuses for it, of course—a thousand excuses he could call to mind if he wanted to. It was the way things were done. Life at court was this unending circle of give and take. You took from one person and gave something back—to that person, or another.

"The incident in Persia was different," he said finally.

"Not really. You had to leave because you ran up debts you could not pay. And you would not have run up those debts if you had not taken advantage of your father's position as *wazir* of Isfahan."

Ghias groaned. No one else in his family would have dared to talk to him in this manner, not even Asmat. But Mehrunnisa was different.

Right from the beginning he had doted on her, given her liberties he had not allowed any of the other children. Now she was rebuking him for something that was usual in the business of court life.

"You do not understand, *beta*." He took her hand and gestured around the room. "How do you think we are able to afford all this magnificence? As *diwan* I draw a comfortable salary, but it would not pay for all the entertainments and the dinner parties I am forced to give to maintain my position. Don't worry yourself about this. I have called you here for something else."

Mehrunnisa nodded reluctantly. "What is it?"

"I have just returned from an audience with the Emperor."

A wary look came over her face. She waited for her father to continue.

"Why didn't you tell me what had happened yesterday?" Ghias asked.

"There was nothing to say." Mehrunnisa's voice was low. "Besides, it was too late last night, and this morning you had left already. I thought Maji . . . what could I have said to you, Bapa?" she ended finally. "I met the Emperor. I saw him in the *zenana* quarters. That was all."

"That was enough. He has put a very difficult proposition to me," Ghias said. "He wishes to invoke the *Tura-i-Chingezi*."

The blood rushed from Mehrunnisa's face. "My husband would never agree, Bapa."

"And you?" Ghias looked at her. "What do you want?"

Mehrunnisa shook her head. They had talked of all things since she was a child, since she could talk almost, leaning on his knee, looking up at him, listening to her father's melodious voice. But one thing they had never talked about: Ali Quli and her marriage to him. Here was another wish she could not voice aloud, even to her Bapa. What she wanted was to be Jahangir's wife. Suddenly, with a force of feeling, Mehrunnisa knew this to be true. Not for his crown or his jewels or his power—well, for those a little—but for his smile, for the tenderness in his voice, for his passion for the empire. She wanted to be an object of desire for this man who gave body and soul to his obsessions. She wanted to feel that kind of love. But she only said, "I will comply with your wishes."

Ghias sighed. Again, she talked as he had taught her to, with a yield-ing to duty. It was a response he wanted to hear from her. As attractive as the Emperor's proposition was, and even though it was legal, something in Ghias and now in Mehrunnisa recognized this difference between wanting something and doing what was right. *He* could not reconcile himself to this when he took bribes, but from his daughter he wanted to see that honesty. It was illogical, Ghias knew, but that was how it was. If nothing else, in Mehrunnisa he would leave the model of the man he wanted to be.

"Your place belongs with your husband, Mehrunnisa. I wish things were different, had been different all those years ago—"

"Hush!" Mehrunnisa put a hand on his arm. "Do not berate yourself. You made a promise to Ali Quli and were obligated to honor it. It was Emperor Akbar's wish. My place is with my husband. It is for him to decide what to do with me. I shall immediately make preparations to leave for Bardwan."

Ghias looked at her in sorrow. His own daughter had to flee from her father's house, but it was the right thing to do. Perhaps time and distance would make the Emperor forget Mehrunnisa. Father and daughter sat in silence. To be Empress of Mughal India was an honor beyond their wildest dreams, but Ali Quli stood in their way. Thoughts rose to their minds simultaneously, thoughts that could not be spoken aloud, and the two looked at each other with the understanding that had always existed in their relationship.

Ghias rang the bell for his writing materials. It had to be done. Jahangir had hinted his wish to have Mehrunnisa, and it fell to Ghias's lot to write of this wish to his son-in-law.

Ali Quli was sure to refuse Jahangir. What would the Emperor's reac-tion be? Jahangir was still irascible. His new responsibilities as Emperor had not changed his childish whims. How would he answer this disobe-dience by one who had already been treacherous to him?

Ghias sighed again as he dipped his goose-feather quill into the inkpot and started writing. He filled the page haltingly, stopping to think long and deep for words of diplomacy and tact. He knew that no matter what he wrote, or how he wrote it, there was going to be trouble ahead. By Allah's grace, Jahangir would remember Ghias's long years of service and loyalty to the empire and would not wreak vengeance on his household.

The next morning Mehrunnisa left for Bardwan with Ladli. She carried with her the letter to Ali Quli. Ghias had not informed her of its contents, but she knew that he had written to her husband telling him of Jahangir's wishes.

Now, it was for her husband to decide.

FIFTEEN

What can I write of this unpleasantness? How grieved and troubled I became! Qutbu-d-din Khan Koka was to me in the place of a dear son, a kind brother, and a congenial friend. What can one do with the decrees of God?
      —A. Rogers, trans., and H. Beveridge,
        ed., *The Tuzuk-i-Jahangiri*

MEHRUNNISA GROANED ALOUD AS SHE STEPPED OUT OF THE PALANquin. Every muscle in her body ached, turned raw by the rocking motion of the palanquin. It had been a long journey to Bardwan, almost two months. Somehow, the trip to Lahore had been easier. At least she had had something to look forward to then. But the journey back had been both physically and mentally tiring. With every step away from Agra the feeling grew that she would not see Jahangir again.

She had not wanted to return to Bengal to face an irate husband, who would doubtless accuse her of trying to captivate the Emperor. Of course, that was true. But whatever she might feel for Jahangir, she had returned to Bengal to be with Ali Quli. And then there was the matter of her father's taking bribes. A dull ache throbbed in the pit of her stomach when Mehrunnisa thought of Ghias Beg. She knew that all the courtiers took bribes, but somehow she had thought her father above it. He had always seemed so honest, so untouched by the corruption in the Mughal court. His was one of the greatest minds in the empire, but even he was fallible . . . and human.

As a child she had seen Ghias talking with various men who had come to their house, and taking money from them or a basket of golden sunripened peaches or an Arabian horse, but she had never realized the significance of what she had seen. Now those memories came rushing back.

Mehrunnisa sighed as she straightened out her *ghagara*. Perhaps it was not wrong after all. But it wasn't right, either. She looked around at the deserted front courtyard of her house. Where was everybody?

The slave girls came running out of the house. "Welcome home, *Sahiba*."

"Where is your master?" she asked, fatigue slurring her words, as she lifted a sleeping Ladli out of the palanquin.

"He has gone hunting, *Sahiba*."

"I sent word of my arrival yesterday."

The servants carefully averted their heads and busied themselves with unloading the luggage from the pack horses.

Mehrunnisa wiped the sweat from her brow with a tired hand. This was the man she had come back to in such haste. And he was too indifferent to even be present at the house to welcome her back after an absence of almost five months. Perhaps it was for the best, she thought, dragging herself inside. She could rest now before the confrontation.

Ali Quli did not return from the hunt until late. The next morning, after he had bathed and eaten his breakfast, he went to his wife's apartments.

Mehrunnisa looked up from her book as he entered. "*Inshah Allah*."

Ali Quli grunted in reply. "Did you have a good journey?"

"Yes." They had nothing to say to each other beyond the greeting. Her hands suddenly became clammy, and she wiped them on her *ghagara*. How could she open the topic?

Ali Quli's voice broke into her thoughts. "What is this?" He pointed to the embroidered letter bag on a table.

"A missive from my father. He wished for me to give it to you." Her voice faltered.

Ali Quli picked up the letter warily. "Is there a problem?"

She shook her head. The previous night, Mehrunnisa had stood at her bedchamber window and looked out into the moonlight that painted shadows and silver over the low hills around the house. Two months had gone by since her father had written the letter. That was a long time.

Perhaps, she thought with a pang, the Emperor had already forgotten his order to his *diwan*. Why ruffle seemingly calm waters? Why not just tear up the letter and let things be? Then she remembered Jahangir's zest for the throne. For fifteen long years—sometimes with impatience, but mostly, because it had taken so long, with patience—he had yearned for it. She knew he would not easily forget her either. A shiver went up her back. Her husband would see the letter.

"It is best you read it, my lord."

Ali Quli ripped open the bag and pulled out the letter. Mehrunnisa's heart thudded loudly in her ears as the paper crackled in his hands. She watched him with care. Ali Quli's face became expressionless as he read. A deep color started on his neck and spread upward to his face.

He threw down the letter with shaking hands. "Do you know the contents of the letter?"

Mehrunnisa bit her lip. "I have a fair idea, my lord."

"How did the Emperor see you? You are my wife. You should have taken care not to reveal your face to him, instead of brazenly attracting his attention. Why were you near the Emperor in the first place?"

"It was during Arjumand's betrothal ceremony. I had to be present."

"I will never agree to this." Ali Quli glared at her, his face ugly in anger. "You are my wife and will remain so. Even the Emperor cannot command me to give you up. Emperor! Bah!" He threw up his hands in disgust. "If I had played my cards right, that weakling Khusrau would have been Emperor today, and I would have been the commander of the imperial forces instead of rotting in this hell-hole." He looked angrily at Mehrunnisa, and she stared steadily back at him.

"Lower your eyes as becomes a modest woman," he yelled. "I did not want to let you go to Lahore, and now see what has come of it. You wretch, I know all about your previous flirtation with the Emperor."

Mehrunnisa's eyes opened wide in shock. She felt as though she had been punched in the stomach. Yes, she had flirted with Jahangir as a prince, but only a few people knew. . . .

"Oh yes! You thought I didn't know," Ali Quli said, a deadly malice coloring his voice. "But I knew the day I married you that I was taking you away from Prince Salim. He wanted you then; I had you. He wants you now, and I still have you. I shall never forgive him for spoiling my hopes of a military career."

He turned to leave. Mehrunnisa looked down, her mind in panic.

Ali Quli spoke harshly from the door. "You are confined to your rooms. Do not leave here until I give you permission to do so. I will be away for a few days, and you are to stay here."

Mehrunnisa grimaced. This was the man she had married, and she was bound by duty to be his wife. He was going mad. Did he think he could take on the Emperor? Their family would be ruined.

"My lord," she said hurriedly, forcing her voice to be neutral. "Don't do anything rash. A simple no to the Emperor will suffice. It is ill advised to raise his anger."

"So you still have feelings for your old lover," Ali Quli mocked. "That is a fine way to talk to your husband." He gave her an evil smile. "We shall see how long he remains Emperor."

Mehrunnisa watched him go with foreboding, knowing it was useless to talk with him. Ali Quli would be senseless enough to try another rebellion. He rode off that very morning, looking secretive. Raja Man Singh was away from Bengal, but in this land of dissidents, there were plenty of others who were willing to listen to him. So far from the imperial court, and drunk with the heady feeling of freedom, he felt that anything was possible.

But Jahangir was no fool. Bengal was full of spies in the Emperor's service. All designs on the throne invariably found their way to the court and to the Emperor's ear.

JAHANGIR SAT IN the *jharoka* window overlooking the main courtyard outside Lahore fort. The *jharoka* was a special balcony built in the bulwark of the castle, where the Emperor gave audience to the public three times a day: morning, noon, and evening. Even when Jahangir was ill, he dragged himself to the *jharoka*. Early in his reign he had decided that people must see their sovereign; they must assure themselves of his well-being so that civil unrest would not start in the country.

Today, an elephant fight was in progress. Jahangir was reminded of the other elephant fight many years before. He had come out victorious, and Khusrau had been defeated. His mouth twisting, he turned and looked at the object of his thoughts.

Prince Khusrau sat by his father's side with a frown on his face. The spirit of rebellion has not left this boy, Jahangir thought. He would have to watch his son carefully. It was necessary to be thought of as a generous and just king; hence he had pardoned Khusrau publicly. That meant enduring his presence on public occasions like this one. He turned away from his son, not even willing to look at him anymore. Any affection he had felt for Khusrau was gone after the prince's numerous attempts to win the crown for himself. Now Jahangir could hardly bear to sit near him; waves of antipathy colored the air around them.

Jahangir sighed. He wished he could follow Mahabat Khan's suggestion and have Khusrau executed. He certainly would not miss him. But the ladies of the harem would harangue him continuously, and he would have no peace in the palace. However, something had to be done about Khusrau before he put up any serious resistance to his position as Emperor.

The two elephants rammed into each other with a loud thud. The crowd cheered, but the Emperor paid no attention, a deep, aching pain dulling his senses.

Ghias Beg had come to him earlier in the day with the information that Ali Quli had refused his command. Jahangir rubbed his chin, feeling sudden tears prick behind his eyelids. All this waiting had fatigued him. Every morning on waking he had thought of Mehrunnisa. Ghias had sent her back to Bengal, and when he had asked why, his *diwan* had said he was merely performing a father's duty. So Jahangir had said nothing. He would wait, with patience. Time would also tell him if that brief glimpse was enough to fix her in his love. It had—he hadn't stopped yearning for her presence. And then to get such a reply. How was it he did not even have the power to get the woman he wanted? How did a scoundrel like Ali Quli dare deny his Emperor? And he, Emperor of Mughal India, could do nothing. He had sent Ali Quli a direct order; it had been disobeyed. Already, there were rumors around court of his wish to have Mehrunnisa. Doubtless, Ali Quli's refusal too was the subject of gossip. He could not force Ali Quli to give her up. What else could he do?

At least the news from Qandahar was heartening. The imperial army had reached the outpost in the past month, and the attackers had fled upon seeing Jahangir's standards and flags. The Shah of Persia had sent an ambassador, Husain Beg, to the Mughal court to assure Jahangir of his friendship and to apologize for the behavior of his governors. The Emperor had been polite to the ambassador, accepting his apology with diplomatic heartiness. But he had not been deceived either by him or by his master. The attack on Qandahar had been orchestrated not by insubordinate governors but by the Shah himself, to test Jahangir's prowess in foreign policy.

Jahangir closed his eyes tiredly. Somehow, he had imagined that life would be easier once he was Emperor. But he had too many things on his mind, and he was constantly haunted by those blue eyes. That one glimpse of her, after so many years, was enough to bring back memories he had buried away deep inside. Now uncovered, they plagued him with longing and restlessness. And she was out of reach.

A messenger rode up to the *jharoka* and dismounted. He bowed and pulled a letter out of his cummerbund. Jahangir reached down for it immediately. He knew it was important, or else the messenger would have waited until he had adjourned to court. He read the letter slowly, his face growing grim. This was the final straw. He rose and walked back to the royal palace.

A few minutes later, Mahabat Khan and Muhammad Sharif, glancing up at the *jharoka* and finding it empty, left their seats in the courtyard and rushed into the palace.

"Your Majesty, I hope there is no bad news," Mahabat Khan said as he caught up with the Emperor.

"There is," Jahangir said curtly. "Ali Quli has been up to something. I have received news from Bengal that he is gathering forces in secret. Send an army to check on him."

"Your Majesty, perhaps it would be better to investigate the matter first," Muhammad Sharif said in a cautious voice.

"Why? The man has already proved that he is a dissident. He should have been executed for his crimes, but instead I pardoned him. He shall not escape now," Jahangir said, striding in front of his ministers.

"Sire . . ." Sharif coughed and cleared his throat, then, seeing the Emperor a few paces ahead, ran to catch up with him. "Your interest in his wife—the whole court knows of it. To suddenly order his execution now would be unseemly."

"What has this to do with Mehrunnisa? Do you think the people will accuse me of devious behavior just to gain her?" Jahangir stopped and turned to face the two men.

Sharif and Mahabat Khan remained silent. That was exactly what they thought, and what the whole country would think. It was a delicate situation, one that had to be handled with the greatest diplomacy. Besides, there was the small matter of the promise to Empress Jagat Gosini. Mahabat nudged Sharif.

"Your Majesty, please reconsider your decision," Sharif said, taking Mahabat's cue. "It would be better to investigate the matter first. Perhaps you could have the governor of Bengal pay Ali Quli a visit, or you could command Ali Quli to wait upon you. That way, the whole court will see your intentions as impartial."

"Hmmm . . ." Jahangir stroked his chin. "You may be right. I'm sure enough evidence can be gathered against this man. I will write to my foster brother, Qutubuddin Khan Koka, immediately."

As he turned away in dismissal, Jahangir allowed a small smile to come to his lips. Fate had thrown Ali Quli's life in his hands. As for Mahabat and Sharif . . . it almost seemed as though they were trying to dissuade him.

Why? They had no affection for Ali Quli; in fact, they disliked him actively. As for Mehrunnisa, they knew nothing of her. Yet, this was the second time Mahabat had voiced an opinion about her. Why?

The Emperor watched his two most powerful ministers back out of his presence. Mahabat's insistence made him suspicious, and only time would tell him why. There were more important matters, for perhaps he would have Mehrunnisa after all. There was hope. He could not have taken her by force from Ali Quli and justified his actions to the empire. But rebellion—that was different. Even posterity could not fault his actions now.

That evening, he sat down and wrote to Qutubuddin Khan Koka, the governor of Bengal. Koka was to summon Ali Quli and question him closely on his activities. If Koka was not satisfied, he was to send Ali Quli to court to answer directly to the Emperor. At all costs, he must meet with the soldier personally and make his decision. Jahangir added that if Ali Quli refused to come to court and Koka discovered any sedition, he was given full authority to punish him as he saw fit.

A few days later, the imperial court moved residence from Lahore to Kabul, to spend the approaching summer months in cool comfort.

IN BENGAL, QUTUBUDDIN Khan Koka received the Emperor's letter. He immediately relayed a message to Ali Quli to present himself.

Ali Quli ignored him.

Koka was furious. He was acting on Jahangir's orders, so indirectly Ali Quli had disobeyed the Emperor's summons. He gathered a large force of well-armed soldiers and marched to Bardwan.

THE AFTERNOON SUN stalked sentinel in the sky, sending the people below scurrying for cover. The hot rays beat down upon Bardwan, and all signs of life disappeared from Ali Quli's house. Shutters were drawn over the windows and laid over with *khus* mats. Horses stomped in the stables, twitching slow-moving flies off their backs. The grooms lay supine on the hay;

their only movement was to lift smoldering *beedis* to their mouths and then, exhausted by the effort, to lie back and watch the smoke swirl to the roof.

A messenger came running into the courtyard. Sweat poured from him, drenching semicircles under his collar and both armpits. "Call for your master," he gasped. "I bring important news."

One of the grooms bolted upright and raced for the house. Ali Quli came rushing out in a few minutes, buttoning his *qaba;* he had been waked from his nap. "What is it?"

"*Sahib*, the governor of Bengal, Qutubuddin Khan Koka, is on his way here."

Ali Quli frowned. What did Koka want? Was it possible he had got an inkling of his plans? Or was Koka coming to Bardwan because he hadn't responded to his summons? Either way, there would be a confrontation, and Ali Quli was determined to be prepared for it. The servants watched him in silence; the only sound was of the messenger panting. Ali Quli looked at the man.

"Take him to the kitchens and give him something to drink," he said curtly. He called for his eunuch. "Bakir! Send a message to the Amirs in the neighborhood that Koka is on his way here. They are to prepare their men for battle if necessary. I will give them the signal. Wait . . ." He turned to the messenger. "How far is the governor from Bardwan?"

"A day's march, *Sahib*."

Ali Quli nodded and turned back to Bakir. "Tell the Amirs to prepare themselves by tomorrow."

Bakir ran off to do his bidding.

Ali Quli walked back into the house. When he entered his apartments he found his wife waiting for him. The noise in the courtyard had drawn her to the window, and she had heard the exchange between Ali Quli and the servants.

"My lord, don't do anything rash. The governor may just be visiting you with a message," Mehrunnisa pleaded. If only he would listen to her. . . . But Ali Quli was past listening to advice; he had caught the scent of battle, and it drew him inexorably into its embrace.

"Go back to your apartments. I will handle this matter," Ali Quli said shortly.

"Please . . ." Mehrunnisa laid a hand on his arm. "If there is a difference of opinion, talk it over with the governor. He is an emissary from the Emperor."

He flung her hand away. "What do you care? After all, I stand between you and your Emperor, the man who will make you Empress." He glowered at her, and Mehrunnisa dropped her eyes to the ground.

"I see that I am right." He smiled sarcastically. "Do not worry, dear wife. I will live for many years yet; it may be too many for your liking." He pushed her toward the door. "Now go. I have plans to make."

Mehrunnisa left his apartments slowly. Somehow, she had a feeling this would not end well.

"ATTACK!" HE YELLED, his sword raised. At his command, the army marched on and on. . . . Ali Quli opened his eyes and stared at the dark ceiling. Where was he? He heaved a sigh of relief as the room came into focus. It had been a dream. He turned over and became aware that the sound of marching footsteps was very real.

He jumped out of bed and staggered sleepily to the window. He peered into the darkness, listening, but all was silent. As he looked down, someone struck a match to light a torch. What was going on?

Ali Quli shook himself awake, grabbed his sword, and ran downstairs. Bakir met him at the front door.

"What is happening?" Ali Quli demanded.

"I don't know, sire." Bakir unlocked the door.

The two men rushed into the courtyard. More torches flared, illuminating the space. The courtyard was deserted of all but the grooms. Ali Quli breathed more easily. It had been a dream, after all.

Three men stepped forward from the shadows. Ali Quli tightened his grip on the sword when he recognized them. Qutubuddin Khan Koka, flanked by two Kashmiri servants, Amba Khan and Haidar Malik, bowed to Ali Quli.

"*Al-Salam alekum*, Ali Quli," Koka said.

"*Walekum-al-Salam*," Ali Quli replied, still clutching his sword.

Koka spread his hands out. "I am unarmed and come in peace."

Ali Quli let his shoulders relax. A sudden movement caught his eye. One of the grooms had lit another torch and was carrying it to the far end of the courtyard. The gloom dispersed, and Ali Quli saw the imperial forces, in full armor, standing in orderly rows behind the governor.

He clenched his free hand into a fist and turned to Koka, an ugly look taking over his face. So this was the governor's idea of coming in peace? The courtyard swam in a red haze before his eyes.

Koka had stepped forward. He said, "I come from the Emperor—"

Ali Quli gave a loud shout. It was the sound of rage, of broken sleep, full of all the injustice he had suffered in the past few years. Still screaming like an animal in pain, Ali Quli jumped on Koka. Before the governor had time to react, he plunged his sword into Koka's stomach. Koka staggered back, reaching for his sheathed dagger. Ali Quli barged headlong into the governor and hacked wildly. Somewhere in his now deranged brain, he felt the satisfaction of making contact with Koka's flesh with each stroke of his sword.

Koka's guts spilled out, making a bloody mess on the floor. He put a hand to his stomach to hold in his bowels and fell to the ground. Out of the corner of his eye, Ali Quli saw Amba Khan rush at him with his sword raised.

Ali Quli turned on him. He lifted his sword and brought it down heavily upon Amba Khan, cleaving steel through Amba's hair. The force of the action nearly took off Amba's head, and he fell, dead before he hit the ground.

At the same moment, Haidar Malik and the rest of Koka's army fell upon Ali Quli. Surrounded on all sides by the enemy, Ali Quli fought like a cornered animal, twirling his bloody sword and frothing at the mouth. He managed to kill two men, but there were too many of them.

Suddenly he felt a red-hot pain and looked down to see a sword sticking out of his stomach. His energy seemed to drain away with the blood that flowed from his body. He tried to raise his sword but could not. The pain was too intense. Koka's army rained blows on him. His body seemed on fire and then . . . there was nothing.

MEHRUNNISA STOOD FROZEN at the window, her hand still raised to part the curtains. The stench of blood came up to her nose, and she gagged involuntarily, raising nerveless fingers to her mouth. She wanted desperately to look away from the carnage in the courtyard, but her eyes kept returning to it over and over again.

She watched in fascinated horror as Koka's men pounced on her husband's body and cut it to pieces, hacking wildly long after he was dead. They then turned on Bakir and the grooms. In a few minutes, the ground was drenched with blood, and dismembered arms and legs lay everywhere.

The men below had turned into savage animals excited by the smell and sight of blood. Their lust unsatisfied, they looked around for other victims.

"The house!" a man yelled.

As one, the men rushed toward the front door, pushing one another violently in their effort to get in. Mehrunnisa's mind suddenly snapped into action. She ran to her daughter's room and shook her by the shoulder. "Come, wake up. We have to leave."

Ladli awoke slowly and stared at her mother. "Is it morning already?"

"There is no time to talk. Let's go." Mehrunnisa pulled a sheet around her daughter, picked her up, and ran to the door.

Below, the soldiers had entered the house. Slave girls screamed as they were dragged out of bed and raped. Vessels clattered to the floor, curtains were ripped, and furniture was broken.

"The wretch had a wife," someone yelled. "Find her."

Mehrunnisa heard the words and froze where she stood.

"Mama," Ladli wailed.

"Hush!" Mehrunnisa said fiercely, clamping a hand over her mouth. "Keep quiet, or they will find us."

They were coming upstairs now. She could hear footsteps pounding up to the landing. She turned and went back to the rooms. Perhaps they could climb down a window and escape. She rushed blindly and bumped into something. Two hands clutched her arms in a hard grip. Mehrunnisa's heart plummeted as she looked into the bloodshot eyes of the soldier.

"Please . . ." But the words would not come beyond the plea.

He asked in a harsh whisper, "Are you Ali Quli's wife?"

Dumbstruck with fright, Mehrunnisa could only nod. Her heart skipped a beat. For the first time in her life she knew pure, mind-numbing terror. The man was splattered with blood from a deep gash over his right eye that was bleeding down his face and onto his hands.

"Come." He pulled her roughly.

"No!"

"Don't shout; the soldiers will hear you. Come—," he said again, as she pulled away from him. "I will protect you from them. You have to hide. They are bloodthirsty and will not rest until you are dead . . . or even worse."

The sound of footsteps neared. The man hurried Mehrunnisa and Ladli into the large trunk in one corner where she kept her veils. He had barely shut the lid and turned the key when soldiers pounded into the room.

"Is she here?"

"No, she must have fled from the house," the man answered. "She cannot have gone far on foot. Look outside."

But the soldiers seemed not to hear the man. They rushed about the room, pulling open cupboards, spilling the contents, running their swords through silk and linen. One kicked the wood chest, and the sound rattled around her. Mehrunnisa cowered inside, holding fiercely on to Ladli. Then suddenly, they all rushed out of the room, leaving a dense, welcome silence. Inside the dark trunk, Mehrunnisa clutched Ladli to her and heaved a trembling sigh of relief as she heard the sound of receding footsteps. After a few minutes, the man unlocked the trunk and peered in. "You can come out. They have left."

He helped them out of the trunk. As Mehrunnisa climbed out, Ladli whimpered, and she realized that she still had her hand clamped over the child's mouth. When she removed her hand, it left a red imprint across her daughter's face, blood streaking across her lips where her teeth had cut into skin.

"Who are you? Why did you help us?" Mehrunnisa asked, still shaking from shock.

"My name is Haidar Malik, *Sahiba*. I am a servant in the house of Qutubuddin Khan Koka. It would not have been right for the soldiers to harm you. Besides . . ." He hesitated. "The Emperor would never have forgiven me if anything had happened to you."

Mehrunnisa stared at him, a jolt running through her body. Was Jahangir responsible for the attack on Ali Quli? Surely not even the Emperor had the right to order the execution of an innocent man. But Jahangir could not have had anything to do with the mayhem; she had seen the events progress with her own eyes. Koka had barely started to talk when Ali Quli had plunged his sword into his stomach, seemingly without provocation. She shivered and clutched her daughter tight.

"I shall take you to the camp."

Mehrunnisa nodded and allowed him to lead her out of the house and through the deserted courtyard. She would have gone anywhere he wanted to take her. Thought was impossible now; too much had happened, too quickly, even before it registered fully in her mind. She followed Malik's tall figure through the deserted streets of Bardwan. He was carrying Ladli as though she were a sack of feathers, slung easily into his arms. Mehrunnisa looked around her at the shut bazaar fronts, the street lamps wavering in the humid night air. She heard the scramble of pariah dogs in the shadows and recognized no sight, no sound. All her effort went into walking behind Malik, one foot placed in front of the other in a mindless fashion.

When the sun rose in the eastern sky, she was sitting wide-eyed in Malik's tent, stunned and terrified. Her *choli* and veil were smeared with caked, dried blood where Haidar Malik had clutched at her. The odor brought bile rising from her stomach. A cock crowed in a neighboring house, and Mehrunnisa flinched. She started to tremble violently as she remembered how Ali Quli had died—like an animal brought to slaughter. There was little left of him now, little to show of the man who had once been her husband. Only Ladli. The child, with the resilience of youth, slept at her side, holding fast to her mother's hand. Malik had returned to the house after posting guards around his tent.

Physicians were summoned to tend to the fallen governor's wounds. A makeshift camp was erected in the courtyard, and the injured man was laid on a bed. Malik watched while the physicians sewed up Koka's stomach. If only Koka survived, he thought, turning away from his master's body, the lady in his tent would be safe. But the damage had been done, and though Malik kept vigil at Koka's bedside, the governor never recovered consciousness. Before his family could come to him he died, twelve hours after the battle.

ASMAT AND GHIAS BEG were in their courtyard garden; he seated on a stone bench, she standing beside him. Night had closed around them a long time before; yet, they waited in the dark with their thoughts, the letter still in Ghias's hands. It had arrived only that afternoon, but each word of the short message was imprinted on his brain. Someone named Haidar Malik had written the letter. Ghias looked down at the bright white sheet in his hands, not seeing the words. Mehrunnisa was with him, and Ladli too. Ali Quli was dead. Ghias shook his head in disbelief, the shock from three hours earlier not yet worn off. Why had Ali Quli attacked Koka? Why had he killed him?

His wife's voice cut into his thoughts. "Will she be safe?"

Ghias sighed. "I don't know, *jaan*. Her fate lies in Allah's hands."

Asmat Begam sat down by her husband and leaned her head on his shoulder. "Can you ask the Emperor to bring her here?"

Ghias put an arm around her and kissed her gently, wishing he could wipe away the worry lines from her forehead. "The Emperor is distraught at Koka's death. And Koka was killed by our son-in-law."

Why? The thought smote him again. *Why?* Never had he imagined this end when Jahangir had seen Mehrunnisa at Arjumand's betrothal.

Asmat raised tearful eyes. "Mehrunnisa was not responsible for Koka's death. She must come to us. Her life is in danger."

"I know," Ghias said. "I also know that Koka's family has sworn vengeance on Mehrunnisa and Ladli. But until the Emperor summons her to us," he spread his hands out helplessly, "we can do nothing."

Asmat buried her face in her hands and wept. Ghias watched her in silence, forcing back his own tears. What good would crying do? Ease the heartache for a few hours, perhaps, but the worry would always be there. And Mehrunnisa was at Bengal, alone except for the protection of this Haidar Malik, a man they did not know. *Allah, please, please look after my child.* As he had said to Asmat, he could do nothing, only pray for his daughter's safety.

He turned away from his wife. Another matter was troubling him. True, it paled to insignificance next to Ali Quli's death, but it was important nonetheless. He did not have the courage to ask the Emperor to provide Mehrunnisa with an imperial escort to Agra because of Ali Quli and because of this other matter. But that too would soon come to light. Then he could well have no standing in the empire. Why Allah, why did trouble come to ambush when one was already down?

IN HIS CHAMBER, Emperor Jahangir sat staring at the flickering shadows on the wall. Around him the palace slept, peaceful and serene. He was thinking about Koka. There were many memories of his foster brother, almost from the time he had memories. Koka's mother had been his wet nurse; they had both drunk her milk, both had lain against her breast sated and content. As children they had slept in the same bed, fought ferociously over the same slingshot, forgetting—as children always forget—that one was a royal prince, heir to an empire, and the other a commoner. Jahangir's own brothers, Princes Murad and Daniyal, had grown up in other apartments, and he had not seen much of them as a child.

When he was older, he had known them only as threats to his claim on the throne. But Koka: from Koka there had been no such danger, only a deep devotion. And now he was dead. The message from Bengal said he had died in great agony, calling out his Emperor's name with his last breath.

Jahangir looked down as tears blurred his vision. There was no time even to grieve for him. Kings never had time to grieve. The empire demanded his attention. A sudden wave of anger washed over him. The army should have brought Ali Quli back to him alive, so that he could have had him pulled apart by elephants. But Ali Quli was dead. And Mehrunnisa was at Bengal.

He wiped the tears from his face. Was his love for her worth so many other lives?

Even in this sorrow he could not stop thinking and worrying about her. Now she should be safe; now she must come to him. He would summon her when some time had passed. But . . . so much had changed. The manner of Ali Quli's death had changed everything. He had been killed by Koka's men, by the Emperor himself in some sense. Would Mehrunnisa think he had ordered Ali Quli's death? Would she forgive him if she thought so?

SIXTEEN

*Itimad-ud-Din, Diwan or Chancellor of Amir-ul-Umra, had a
heathen in his service named Uttam Chand, who told Dinayat
Khan, that Itimad-ud-Daulah had misappropriated 50,000
ropia. Dinayat Khan told the King whereupon Itimad-ud-
Daulah was placed in the custody of this Khan.*

— B. Narain, trans., and S. Sharma,
ed., *A Dutch Chronicle of Mughal
India*

A SLIGHT BREEZE WHISPERED THROUGH THE STILL ROOM, CATCHING
the lantern. The light flickered uncertainly, darting shadows around the
room. The man at the desk put his quill down, rose from the divan, and
went to the window. He shut the panes and leaned against the sill, resting his head on the glass.

Now the lantern spread its warm, comforting glow around the room,
lighting up the low desk and the account books on it, smudged with figures and numbers. Ghias Beg drew a deep breath and went back to his
place. Quill in hand, he started adding the rows and columns again, looking for a discrepancy, a fault.

A shadow fell across the doorway, and he stiffened, motionless but listening. Asmat Begam stood there, lines creasing her forehead above anxious eyes. After a few minutes she turned and left, the long skirts of her
ghagara swishing on the stone floor. Ghias hunched over his books again,
the numbers blurring in front of his tired eyes.

In a vase next to the desk stood a sprig of spring jasmine blossoms, lily
white and pearl pink. Their gentle aroma filled the room around him.
Mehrunnisa liked to wear these flowers in her hair, threaded into a gar-
land, Ghias thought suddenly. Then he put his head down on the desk. It

had been six months, and still there was no direct news from her, only another brief letter from Haidar Malik. She was well, he said, as was Ladli, but a price was still on their lives. It was unsafe to travel just yet from Bengal. Six months of waiting. Ghias raised his head and looked over the account books again. Six months of waiting. Now this burden, too.

A few hours later the lamp sputtered and went out, plunging the room into darkness. Outside, the sky lightened, and the night watchman called out the hour. There was something comforting in the sound of his voice; it was a normal, everyday event. Ghias listened until the sound of the watchman's tapping stick faded into the distance. In a few hours it would be day . . . for him the day of reckoning.

"INSHAH ALLAH, GHIAS Beg."

"*Inshah Allah*, Dinayat Khan."

Dinayat Khan put out a hand. "Stay a minute, old friend. I have something to tell you."

The *diwan* looked at his friend with a sinking heart. The courtier's face was grave.

"Uttam Chand came to me last night," Dinayat said quietly. "I think you know what he had to say."

Ghias nodded. He turned blindly toward the window, leaned out, and breathed in the cool morning air. Was this the end of his brilliant career as *diwan* of the empire? Things were happening too fast, without warning. Whatever had possessed him to embezzle money from the royal treasury?

He thought back to the day the money had lain so invitingly in front of him—money he had thought would be lost in the enormous accounting system of the court. One of the court contractors had sent in an estimate for an additional wing to the fort at Lahore. The royal treasury had sent the money to the *diwan*. And then, inexplicably, the costs had fallen by fifty thousand rupees. It came at a time when Ghias was especially in need; Arjumand's betrothal had exceeded his income. He had taken the money, leaving the treasurer under the impression that it had gone to the contractor.

A month ago, the contractor had sent in his bill, now filed in the royal treasury. Today was the day the annual budget was accounted for, and try as he might, Ghias had not been able to return the money to the royal treasury or fix the account books so that the discrepancy would be overlooked. Only one other person had known: Uttam Chand, his clerk. He had been present the day the contractor sent in his bill.

"How could you do it?" Dinayat Khan's voice broke into his thoughts.

Ghias turned wearily from the window. "I don't know. It was a momentary weakness."

"I will have to inform the Emperor. You know that, don't you?" Dinayat said gravely.

Shame washed over him. He was mortified that he had let the need for pomp and show get to his head. At least, Ghias thought, his father was not alive to see this. But his wife was. His children were. What he had done would reflect on all of them. Now he must take his punishment. It was only right that he do so. He could no longer preach a code to his children and not follow it himself.

"Yes." Ghias Beg looked Dinayat Khan full in the face. "It is your duty to do so."

"I'm sorry." Dinayat put a hand on Ghias's arm. "I will do my best to plead your case, Ghias. You have been kind to me, recommending me for the position of accountant in the treasury. Now I want to pay back that debt. I hope the Emperor will be forgiving."

I hope so too. Ghias bent his head and followed his friend into the *Diwan-i-am,* where the Emperor was holding court.

JAHANGIR FROWNED IN irritation as he entered the *zenana* reception hall. He was tired; the morning audience at court had been interminable. And just as he retired, Dinayat Khan had requested another audience. Why couldn't he have come forward earlier?

"What is it?" Jahangir said curtly, cutting short Dinayat Khan's salutation.

"Your Majesty, I beg forgiveness for interrupting your rest. But this matter was too delicate to bring up in open court."

"Go on." Jahangir settled back on the divan and prepared to listen. His frown deepened as Dinayat spoke. This was too much. How could Ghias thus betray his trust? First Ali Quli had killed his beloved foster brother; now another member of the family had committed a felony. And with all this, he was still sick with wanting Mehrunnisa. Yesterday he had given orders for her to travel to Agra from Bengal under an imperial escort. The time had not yet come to approach her; people would remember and talk of Ali Quli's death. Why couldn't he just forget about her? Mahabat Khan was right; she and her family were more trouble than was worth. The Emperor groaned and slid down on the cushions of his divan. He looked up to find Dinayat Khan waiting for his response.

"Clap the *diwan* in irons," Jahangir ordered his Ahadis irritably.

"Your Majesty, Mirza Ghias Beg has served you well. He has been a loyal and just administrator . . . until now. Please forgive him," Dinayat Khan said.

"No," Jahangir said. "I will not abide any more infractions from that family. Ghias Beg has broken the law and must be punished. He will be treated like any other common criminal."

"Your Majesty, please . . . ," Dinayat Khan begged. "At least, allow him to be in my custody until you can think of a punishment for him."

Jahangir glowered at Dinayat Khan. What was the use in procrastinating? Why did Dinayat care what happened to Ghias? Silence lengthened in the room as Dinayat continued to kneel before him. The Emperor took a deep breath. He would give Ghias a chance to clear himself. After all, he *had* served the empire well. And he was father to the lovely woman in Bengal who consumed his every thought. A sudden ache came over him. There was always some obstacle to gaining Mehrunnisa. Her husband had been in the way, and now her father stood before him on the charge of embezzling from the royal treasury. Jahangir sighed. Could he expect loyalty from no one?

"All right," Jahangir said finally to Dinayat Khan. "You will be in charge of him until I decide what to do. But remember," he raised a finger in warning, "if he escapes from your custody, you will pay for it with your head."

"I understand, your Majesty." Dinayat Khan bowed his way out of the Emperor's presence.

That evening, Ghias Beg was put under house arrest, and his duties were suspended temporarily. He paid back the money to the royal treasury, along with a fine of two hundred thousand rupees, and settled down to wait. Only time would erase the Emperor's doubts, and he could hope to be back soon in Jahangir's good graces.

At least the worst had passed. What more could happen?

THE YOUNG MAN turned back to look at the guards. They were out of earshot. He put a hand on the prince's elbow and said softly, "Your Highness, I have a plan."

Khusrau stopped short and stared at his jailer. "For what?"

"To relieve you of your confinement, your Highness." Nuruddin glanced behind again and gently urged Khusrau on.

The two men walked on down the garden path at Lahore. It was early in the morning, and Khusrau had stepped out as usual for his daily constitutional. Four heavily armed guards trudged sleepily behind them, struggling to keep pace with their royal prisoner.

When the imperial court had moved to Kabul for the summer, Prince Khusrau was left behind at Lahore in the custody of the Amir-ul-umra Muhammad Sharif, and a courtier named Jafar Beg. Muhammad Sharif had followed the court to Kabul, leaving Beg and his nephew Nuruddin in charge of the prince.

Khusrau glanced sideways at Nuruddin, keeping his expression stoic, but inside he trembled with anticipation. He had carefully cultivated Nuruddin's friendship, recognizing him almost immediately as an impressionable young man. Was it possible that Nuruddin would help him escape?

He took a deep breath to steady his voice and asked casually, "How can you do that? I am under heavy guard here."

"There is only one way." Nuruddin glanced back again to assure himself that the guards were out of earshot.

"The Emperor will never let me go free. If I escaped, he would surely send the imperial army after me."

"Not if he cannot, your Highness," Nuruddin said quietly.

Khusrau stared at him, perplexed. What was he talking about?

Nuruddin leaned over and lowered his voice. "The Emperor is vastly fond of hunting, your Highness. He visits the imperial hunting grounds often. What if on one of his hunts, he suddenly meets with, shall we say . . . an accident?"

Khusrau involuntarily quickened his step. An assassination! His face flushed with excitement. "How can we do that? The Emperor's personal bodyguards are fiercely loyal to him. We cannot hope to infiltrate the ranks."

Nuruddin smiled. "It has already been done, your Highness. Two of the Ahadis are willing to lay down their lives for you. They will accompany the Emperor on his hunting trip and accidentally shoot him. No suspicion will fall on you. Once the Emperor is dead, the nobles will turn to you. After all, you are the natural heir." Nuruddin paused and looked at Khusrau.

Khusrau stared back at him. To be Emperor! It was his fondest desire, and now it seemed it could come true. A thought struck him. "We will need an army to fight off my brothers."

"I have already gathered forces, your Highness," Nuruddin replied. "Begdah Turkman, Muhammad Sharif, and Itibar Khan will arrive here tonight with their armies to swear fealty to you."

Khusrau's eyebrows went up in disbelief. "The Amil-ul-umra is willing to support my cause?"

Nuruddin grinned. "Not the Grand Vizier. This Muhammad Sharif is the *diwan* Ghias Beg's oldest son. You might know, your Highness, that he and I are distant cousins. My uncle Jafar Beg is Mirza Beg's first cousin, thus the relationship."

They turned hastily as one of the guards came up. "It is time to go in, your Highness."

Khusrau nodded absently. He gave Nuruddin a quick glance.

"I shall leave you now, your Highness." Nuruddin bowed formally to the prince and walked away.

JAHANGIR WOKE TO the sound of his attendants moving around the royal tent, lighting fires in the coal braziers. He stretched his arms above his head lazily, strolled to the front flap of the tent, and peeped out. The camp was shrouded in a thick, heavy mist. He frowned and hoped that the mist would clear soon.

"Your bath awaits, your Majesty," a slave girl said behind him.

Jahangir nodded and went toward the shining copper bathtub filled with steaming water. An hour later, bathed and dressed, he looked out again.

The mist had dissipated, and the sun shone bright, promising a clear day. It was perfect for the hunt, the Emperor thought as he sat down to his breakfast—golden-brown *chappatis* roasted in *ghee*, and curried eggs cooked with cummin, onions, green chillis, and tomatoes.

"I have to see the Emperor."

Jahangir glanced up irritably from his plate. Why was he always disturbed at his meals? He turned to Hoshiyar Khan. "Go see what the noise is about. I do not wish to be disturbed."

"Yes, your Majesty." The eunuch bowed and went out. He came back almost immediately. "You Majesty, Khwaja Wais, *diwan* to Prince Khurram, requests an audience. He says that the matter is urgent and he must see you at once."

Jahangir grimaced. "It can wait. Tell him to come to me this evening, after I have returned from the hunt."

"Your Majesty, I beg permission to see you."

"Isn't that Prince Khurram?"

Hoshiyar peered out of the tent and nodded. Jahangir beckoned with his left hand.

Khurram lifted the flap and entered. He put his hand to his forehead in the *konish* and bowed from the waist. Straightening, he scuffed his foot against the thick pile of the gold and green Persian carpet and cleared his throat.

"What is it, *beta?* I am still at breakfast."

"I apologize, Bapa. But it cannot wait. Khwaja Wais wishes to speak to you. He has something important to convey." Khurram hesitated and looked at the tall eunuch, who stood hunched under the low canvas ceiling of the tent. "In private."

"Hoshiyar Khan is a trusted member of my *zenana*. You can speak in front of him."

Khurram rubbed his smooth cheek and rushed into his words. "Your Majesty, a plot to assassinate you today has been unearthed."

"What?" Jahangir roared, his food forgotten. "Who would dare to do so?"

Khurram hesitated, shifting his weight from one foot to another. He had not wished to be the bearer of bad news, but Jahangir had refused to see Khwaja Wais. And what he was about to say would not make the Emperor any happier.

He took a deep breath. "Khusrau. Two of the Ahadis are in his pay, and they were to accidentally shoot you during the hunt. Khwaja Wais found out about the plot and rushed to tell me. I thought you would wish to interrogate him yourself, so I sent him to you."

Jahangir glowered at Khurram. His anger mounted, and a red flush rose up from his neck. Khusrau—again and always Khusrau. Had he not learned a lesson on the way into Lahore? Did he still think he would wear the crown? Even death would not be enough punishment for him if this news were true. Was every father blessed with stupid sons?

"Bring Wais in here."

Khwaja Wais, who was waiting outside, came in immediately and performed the *konish*.

"How did you hear of this?"

"The prince gathered four hundred men to help him, your Majesty.

Although they all swore allegiance to him, a few were our spies. One of them came to me with the news. The attendants were to attempt an assassination today. Your life is in danger, your Majesty. Please do not go on the hunt." Khwaja Wais bowed his head.

"Have you any proof?"

Wais reached inside his *qaba* and brought forward a packet of letters. "This is the correspondence between Prince Khusrau and his eunuch, Itibar Khan. The prince has outlined the plan of action clearly. There can be no doubt of his complicity in the plot, your Majesty."

Jahangir wiped his hand on a silk towel and took the packet from Khwaja Wais. "How did you get hold of these letters?"

"I bribed the eunuch's servants."

Silence fell as the Emperor skimmed through the letters. He recognized his son's handwriting. There could be no doubt that Khusrau was actually plotting to kill him. Rage came boiling up in Jahangir. All the hatred and dislike he had so far suppressed from a sense of duty, a sense of responsibility, were set loose when he saw Khusrau's scrawl on the pages. The wretched boy wanted him dead; he was no longer content with simply wanting the crown. The letters fell from his grasp, and Jahangir involuntarily rubbed his hands on his *qaba* as though he had been contaminated. He looked up at the three men standing in front of him.

"Arrest the leaders and bring them to me," he said curtly, then, turning to Hoshiyar, "Cancel the hunt."

GHIAS BEG STOOD with his head bowed as the four men walked up to the throne. They paused before the Emperor and awkwardly performed the *konish*, their iron chains clanging loudly in the silent and crowded *Diwan-i-am*.

"Nuruddin, Itibar Khan, Muhammad Sharif, and Begdah Turkman, you are here on the charge of conspiracy to assassinate the Emperor!" the Mir Tozak's voice rang out.

Ghias drew in a sharp breath as he heard those words. He looked sternly at one of the men. Muhammad Sharif doggedly kept his head bowed, unwilling to meet his father's eyes.

How could his son betray him thus, Ghias thought, sorrow grabbing the pit of his stomach. All those years Muhammad had spent under his roof, all the guidance he had given him, had led him here to conspire against his own Emperor. All through his life Muhammad had been dis-obedient—always restless, always seeming to stretch to that one thing beyond his reach. He should have known something like this might hap-pen. When Muhammad had talked of supporting Prince Khusrau during his escape to Lahore, Ghias had hushed him and paid little heed to it. But, thought Ghias, how does one anticipate conspiracy in an assassina-tion attempt on the Emperor? Had Muhammad no shame? No sense of what was right?

Earlier that week, Ghias had visited Muhammad in prison. He had barely been able to get permission to see his son, because of his house arrest. But he was still *diwan* of the empire, and the title carried some influence. The meeting had been brief and hurried. Ghias had stood outside Muhammad's cell, peering into the gloom in search of him until he saw him hunched in one corner. He had talked to him, told Muhammad of his mother's grief, of her sorrow, even of how his deeds had blackened their family's name. Muhammad had listened in silence, almost ignoring his father until the last sentence. Then he had raised his head and asked softly, the words melting into the darkness of the cell, "And did I do any worse than you, Bapa?"

That had been the end of their encounter. Now Ghias stood watching his son, knowing he was right in some ways. He had done wrong himself; how could he expect any better of Muhammad?

"Put them to death!"

A shock went through Ghias's heart as the Emperor spoke. He had known that the punishment would be harsh. But that his son should be taken away from him forever—this he could hardly believe.

"Your Majesty—," Ghias started, forgetting court etiquette in his agi-tation. No one spoke in the Emperor's presence unless spoken to.

"What do you want?" Jahangir turned to glare at his minister.

Ghias shook his head. What could he say? What right did he have to plead leniency? First Ali Quli had murdered Koka, then he himself had been guilty of embezzlement from the royal treasury. . . . Ghias's cheeks flamed. Now his son was under arrest for an attempt on the Emperor's life. How could he ask for anything?

"Well?"

"Nothing, your Majesty," Ghias mumbled and backed away.

Jahangir turned away from him and nodded.

The Ahadis pounced on the four men and dragged them to a corner. Ghias buried his face in his sleeve as their swords flashed in the sunlight. He heard the terrible thud of steel meeting flesh. The screams of the dying men pervaded the courtyard, falling to whimpers and then silence. Justice had been served. The punishment in front of the jammed court would serve as a lesson to others contemplating any acts of treason.

Ghias Beg stood back from the other nobles, not aware of the tears on his face. His world had suddenly become dark. He would have to go home to Asmat with the news that her eldest son was dead. With anyone else he would have thought it just punishment. Attempts on the Emperor's life were not taken lightly. But Muhammad had been his son: for all his stubbornness, his pride, his disobedience, *he was his son.*

"YOU HAVE DONE well, Mahabat." Jagat Gosini handed him two embroidered bags full of gold *mohurs.*

"It was nothing, your Majesty," Mahabat protested mildly, reaching out nevertheless to grab the bags. He felt their pleasant weight in his hands.

"Things have turned out better than we could have hoped." The Empress leaned back on the stone bench and crossed her arms on her lap. "The Emperor talks no more of that woman. When he does, I remind him gently of her treacherous family—that their blood runs in her veins."

"And I do my part at court, your Majesty."

"Yes, and very well. You are a loyal servant, Mahabat."

Mahabat bent his head self-deprecatingly, allowing a small smile to crease his face. "I have another plan, your Majesty."

The Empress shot upright and gave him a penetrating glance. "What is it?"

"The Emperor is very upset with Prince Khusrau. Perhaps we should convince him that Khusrau's existence is a threat to the throne. That way there will be fewer claimants."

Jagat Gosini looked down with a small smile. "My son Khurram would be the ideal choice for the next Emperor."

"That is obvious, your Majesty. Prince Khurram has all the qualities needed for the position."

The Empress turned to Mahabat with admiration. He was truly an asset to her. If he could get rid of Khusrau, then Khurram would find it easier to ascend the throne, and she would continue to be powerful long after Jahangir's death. But the Emperor was no fool; the suggestion could not come from her. "I cannot talk to the Emperor of this matter."

Mahabat's eyes gleamed. "Then allow me to do so, your Majesty. I wish to be of service to you yet again."

Jagat Gosini gazed long and hard at Mahabat. While she was growing up, someone—she could no longer remember who—had taught her not to ask favors of people she did not like, for repaying them would cost more than a pound of flesh. The Empress did not like Mahabat, but she found him useful and admired his cunning, and the childhood lesson had been long forgotten.

So she said, "You are a good man, Mahabat. I shall not forget your loyalty."

"YOUR MAJESTY, IT is best that the prince is executed. If he remains alive he will only be a problem for you."

Jahangir looked at his two ministers and slowly shook his head. Any fatherly feeling he had had toward Khusrau was long gone. Although he often thought that putting Khusrau to death would be the best way out of this recurring dilemma, it could not be done.

"The ladies of the *zenana* will not forgive me if Khusrau is executed," he said.

"Then why not think of some other punishment, your Majesty?" Sharif said, his eyes agleam. "Perhaps the prince could be blinded? He would not be much use to his minions then."

The Emperor bent his head, tracing the engraving on his jade goblet with a finger that suddenly trembled. Here, finally, was a way out. He would get rid of the Khusrau menace once and for all; then he would be able to enjoy his reign. Somewhere deep inside him, sadness flared briefly. Man Bai, Khusrau's mother and his first wife, had left the boy in his custody. She had died because of Khusrau's rebellion. She had pleaded mercy on his behalf, but—here Jahangir's guts tightened—she had not lived to see her son plot his father's assassination.

"Yes," Jahangir said finally, all doubts erased. "Take him," he paused, "to Sultanpur, where he fought so valiantly with my army. It shall be a lesson to him. He will be blinded at Sultanpur." At last the matter had been decided. Khusrau would no longer be a problem to him.

"And, Sharif," Jahangir continued, "we shall make our way back to Agra now."

The Emperor's orders were carried out just as he had said.

Khusrau was escorted to Sultanpur in a cage set atop an imperial elephant. People came out in hordes to stare and point at the miserable prince, who had nowhere to hide from their accusing gaze. At the scene of his defeat, red-hot wires were poked into his eyes. The prince suffered for a few seconds before sinking into the relief of oblivion.

The blind Khusrau was then taken to Agra, there to await the arrival of his father's entourage. On the latter half of the journey, Khusrau lay on the floor of his cage, holding his hands to his ears to shut out the cat-calls and insults.

At least he could no longer see his tormentors.

SEVENTEEN

*Mher-ul-Nissa was a woman of haughty spirit. . . . To raise her
own reputation in the seraglio, and to support herself and slaves
with more decency, than the scanty pittance allowed her would
admit, she called forth her invention and taste in working some
admirable pieces of tapestry and embroidery, in painting silks with
exquisite delicacy, and in inventing female ornaments of every
kind.*

—Alexander Dow,
The History of Hindostan

A SOFT GENTLE MONSOON SUN SANK IN THE WESTERN HORIZON,
spreading golden rays over the city of Agra. When the sun finally disappeared over the flat lines in the west, twilight would be brief, just a few
minutes, scooping the day into the edge of the earth. Then the dark night
would come swooping down over the royal palaces, fended off by lanterns
and oil lamps, hovering in the shadows around pools of light.

There was still an hour to sunset now, and the royal palaces lay silent
and satisfied from the day's happenings. Once the lanterns were lit, the
women in the *zenana* would transform themselves into wondrous bejew-
eled butterflies, bathed in rosewater; scented with heavy, drooping jasmines; and dressed in thin, shimmering muslins, ready to please. The
monsoons had been timely this year, drunk thirstily by the dry, caked
earth, and the lawns grew lush with green. But no one was around to
enjoy the waning rays of the sun. The royal *malis*, done with their daily
chores of weeding and watering, were long gone. The ladies of the harem
used the hours at the end of the day to rest and prepare for the evening.
Even the birds had long roosted in trees in anticipation of the coming
night.

One figure worked alone in the melon patch in the *zenana* gardens. She was dressed in green—a fresh, young, melon green, melding with the colors of the vines sprawling over the ground. The vines spread huge, fleshy, triangular leaves, using them to hide their fruit. The woman knelt on gunnysacks on the soft, loamy ground to keep her *ghagara* from being soiled. Her hair was long and coiled down her back in a mass of midnight sky, blue-streaked and glittering in the setting sun. She wore no ornaments, not even earrings, but two silver bangles tinkled as she vigorously spaded the ground around the fruit. Every now and then, she would gently lift a melon and use one of its big leaves as a platter to set the melon upon and another leaf to cover it from the harsh midday sun. Someone had told her that the ripest, sweetest melons came ripened under the green light of their own leaves. She stopped to wipe the sweat on her forehead with the back of her hand, leaving the mark of the earth upon flushed cheeks.

"Mama!"

Mehrunnisa looked up from her work. Ladli stood at one corner of the garden, her eyes searching through the foliage, her mouth beginning to pout.

"Here, *beta*," Mehrunnisa called out, lifting a hand. The sun's rays glanced off her silver bangles, and Ladli suddenly saw her. She ran toward her mother, stepping over the melons with the nimbleness of a gazelle, her small feet sinking into the soil.

"Be careful," Mehrunnisa called out, but Ladli was already on her way, her face alight with smiles. She came up to Mehrunnisa and flung her arms around her, almost knocking her off her knees. Then she kissed her on the cheeks, first one, then the other.

You are dirty, Mama," Ladli said, wrinkling her little nose. She pulled away and dusted her *kameez*. "All this mud—why are you working in the garden now? Why are you not with the Dowager Empress?"

Mehrunnisa laughed as she sat back on the gunnysack. "The Empress does not need me today, so I thought I should garden for a while before the sun sets. How were your classes? Did you learn anything, or were you naughty again? The *mulla* has been complaining quite a bit about you."

"The *mulla* complains about everything, Mama," Ladli said. "He is so boring; he teaches me nothing. I am only a girl and do not need it, he says. Can I sit with you for a while?"

"Yes, *beta*," Mehrunnisa said, shaking out the dust from another gunnysack. She smiled at Ladli's words abut the *mulla*. Once, a long time ago, Mehrunnisa herself had complained to Asmat about *her* teacher, finding it cumbersome to be contained within a classroom for learning. She watched with amusement as Ladli sat carefully on the sack, pulling the edges of her *kameez* onto the square piece of cloth and away from the earth. It was hard to believe Ladli was only six years old; she was already a young lady. Mehrunnisa had often chanced on her daughter preening in front of a mirror, moving one way, then another, to see how an enameled hair clip sat on her head or how a *dupatta* draped over her shoulder. Or she would pull out Mehrunnisa's jewelry box and try out all the ornaments, laying them back carefully on the padded silk when she was done. "Mama, when will this be mine? And this? And this?" she would ask, sliding a large bangle almost to her shoulder.

Watching the bright eyes intent on her, Mehrunnisa put a muddy hand under Ladli's chin and raised her mouth for a kiss.

"Mama, you are dirty!" Ladli pulled away and dusted off her face.

Mehrunnisa shook her head, smiling at the child. At Ladli's age she was climbing trees, using a slingshot to shoot at birds, trying her best to knock the *gilli* more times than Abul. But then she had had Abul and Muhammad to play with. Ladli had no one.

She turned and plunged her hands into the rich soil, indifferent to the dirt under her nails and in the creases of her palms. Only during these times in the gardens could she escape thinking of all that had happened in the past four years. And only this intense physical activity would bring sleep to claim her at night for a few hours, and she would not wake screaming to nightmares of Ali Quli's death.

The sun dipped a little deeper in the west, and the two stayed on in the melon patch. Ladli was sitting as prim and proper as a princess on a gun-nysack. Mehrunnisa, clad in plain unadorned green like a maid, tendrils of hair escaping to cling damply to her face, her arms mud-smeared to the elbows, tended to the melons, deep in thought—though she had promised herself she would not think of the past today.

After Ali Quli's death, the Emperor had sent an imperial summons to Bengal, commanding her presence at Agra. Haidar Malik, henchman to the dead governor Qutubuddin Koka, had looked after Ladli and her dur-ing the six horrifying months in Bardwan that followed Ali Quli's death. Somehow he had kept them safe, and when the Emperor's summons had arrived, he had used the gold-and-gilt sealed order to buy pack horses and food for the journey, and freedom from harassment by Koka's relatives.

Mehrunnisa had returned to Agra still in a daze, not knowing what to expect. Her parents were at court in Kabul, but the Emperor had made plans to return to Agra soon, and they too would return with him. Until then, she needed a place to stay. A few days after her arrival, Ruqayya Sultan Begam, now a very discontented Dowager Empress, had sum-moned her back to the harem and into her service. Which was just as well, since Mehrunnisa needed a place to hide, to nurse her wounds, to think. The imperial *zenana*, with its maze of palaces, courtyards, and gar-dens and its numerous occupants, was the best place to be anonymous. As the months passed Mehrunnisa started to sew and paint when Ruqayya gave her the time. Soon she was designing and making *ghagaras* and *cholis* for the women of the harem. The money from this she kept carefully in a wooden casket. For what, she did not know yet, but it was the first time she had money of her own—not from Bapa, not from Ali Quli, not from Ruqayya.

Then the court had returned to Agra, and Mehrunnisa had waited to hear from Jahangir. There had been nothing but silence, only news of him from the *zenana* ladies. He seemed to have forgotten her.

Jahangir had since married twice, first to the granddaughter of Raja Man Singh, who was Khusrau's uncle. The relationship had become complicated. Jahangir was now married to his son's niece, and the grand-

niece of his wife, Khusrau's mother. The marriage was obviously a political one; the Emperor was making sure that Raja Man Singh would think
twice before he put his nephew on the throne and made his own granddaughter a widow.

Jahangir's other marriage came a year later, when the imperial army
conquered the kingdom of Raja Ram Chand Bundela. Bundela offered his
daughter as a wife to the Emperor in an effort to maintain good relations
with his new sovereign, so the princess came to Jahangir's *zenana* as his
latest wife.

"Shall we go in, Mama?" Ladli's gentle voice roused Mehrunnisa from
her thoughts. She realized that the sun had already set and the brief twilight was being chased away by the night. She packed her spade and sacks
into a basket, and they picked their way through the melon patch back to
their apartments.

Mehrunnisa washed her hands, fed Ladli her dinner, ate something
herself, and put her daughter to sleep. While she slept, Mehrunnisa took
a long bath in the *zenana's hammam* and came back to her apartments. As
she had almost every night for a long time, she sat down at the mirror on
the wall and lit one of the oil lamps.

Mehrunnisa touched her face slowly. Her complexion was still
unblemished. Around her eyes little lines had developed, very faint, but
visible under harsh sunlight. Even seated, she could see her figure; her
waist had retained its youthful trimness, and her hips curved out from
under it. She was as sensual and desirable as a younger woman . . . but
she was young no longer and had been widowed for four long years. She
would probably have to live her entire life here behind the walls of the
zenana and grow old like some long-forgotten concubine. But at least she
had Ladli.

Mehrunnisa looked over at her daughter. Ladli slept with the abandon
of a child, easily slipping into that life-giving unconsciousness, unaware
of all the drama that had taken place in her young life. She remembered
little of Ali Quli and asked few questions about him. But one day his
unfortunate death would come to prey upon her when she was old

enough to be married. Hopefully the events surrounding Ali Quli's demise would have been forgotten by then, or would at least have been dimmed in people's memories.

Mehrunnisa rose and went to the window. She opened it and the cool night air rushed into the stifling room. The pleasant smell of wet earth drifted to her nostrils as she leaned out, thinking again, as she almost always did, of the Emperor. Jahangir was showing himself to be a shrewd statesman, she thought. Emperor Akbar would have been proud of him. *She* was proud of what he had done for Khusrau.

A few months after the court had returned to Agra, the Emperor had finally seen his son one afternoon after the *darbar*. Jahangir felt wretched at Khusrau's miserable and disfigured face. He sent for the empire's best physicians and ordered them to try to restore sight to his son's eyes. The physicians only partially succeeded. The prince could now see quite well out of one eye; the other was blind forever. But he was nonetheless carefully guarded; even as Jahangir reinstated Khusrau to the royal favor that all his sons enjoyed, he watched the one who had wanted the crown while it still sat on his father's head. Khusrau's rebellion was not something either the Emperor or the harem ladies had forgotten. The crown would eventually belong to one prince, but only after Jahangir's death.

Furthermore, a year earlier, with the gracious permission of Jahangir, the Portuguese Jesuit fathers had converted three of Jahangir's nephews to Roman Catholicism. The ceremony was held at the Jesuit church at Agra, and the celebrations that followed were hosted by the Emperor himself at the royal palace. The three boys were sons of the late Prince Daniyal and were put in the care of the Jesuit fathers when they were brought to court. The Jesuits had pestered Jahangir to allow them to convert the children, and he had agreed, with an outward show of reluctance.

Mehrunnisa smiled into the dark night. It was a brilliant move. Once the boys had been converted they would no longer pose a threat to the throne. It would be free for Jahangir's heirs. It was unthinkable that the Mughal Emperor of India should profess any religion but Islam, and certainly that was a painless way of getting rid of any rivals his sons might have.

The Jesuits had been in India for a long time. Now there were other *firangis* also. The world was indeed opening up. The newcomers styled themselves "ambassadors" from a tiny island in Europe called England. It was said to be many miles away, and the journey by sea took at least six months. The men who came to court as representatives of King James I of England were little more than traders and merchants. They had no diplomatic skills and came to request trading rights from India.

Jahangir had ignored the merchants, treating them as he would Indian merchants—and rightly so, Mehrunnisa thought. It was highly insulting to the dignity of the Mughal empire to be approached by merchants instead of qualified noblemen from the court of England. What were the English after all but a country of fishermen and shepherds? How could such a tiny island hope to compete with the glory of the Mughal Empire? India was self-sufficient and wanted nothing. The foreigners wanted the spices, calico, and saltpeter that India had in abundance. If so, they should have taken the trouble to approach the Emperor with an appropriate ambassador.

The captain of the first English ship to anchor off India's shores, William Hawkins of the *Hector*, was an erudite man. He spoke good Turkish, the language of the courts. Mehrunnisa, in the *zenana* balcony with Ruqayya, could remember being impressed by him on the day he was presented to the Emperor. But, fluent in Turki or not, Hawkins was a mere merchant. In any case, the English had yet to prove their worth to the empire if they wished to be granted any special privileges. Right now, the Portuguese Jesuits held too strong a position at court. They had been in India for many years.

Mehrunnisa drummed her fingers on the windowsill, childhood fretfulness overwhelming her again. When she was young she had been aware that only the ladies of the imperial *zenana* could break the rules this society imposed on women. Now she was a member of that *zenana* and realized that just being here was not enough. Even here, only a handful of the women had power—those married to the Emperor, those related to him, or those who were his favorites. Oh, that she had been born a man and could take her place at court. English presence in the empire had put the Jesuits in a quandary, and if Jahangir had a skilled advisor, he would know how to set the two sides off against each other, to the advantage of the empire. But here she was, doomed to spend her life in the *zenana*, with no hope of marriage to the Emperor, no excitement of court life and political intrigues in her future.

The eastern sky lightened as Mehrunnisa turned away from the window. While she had been immersed in her thoughts, the night had passed. She crawled slowly into bed and shut her eyes tightly. She needed to sleep; in a few hours it would be time to rise and attend to her duties.

"HERE SHE IS. What took you so long?" Ruqayya demanded.

Mehrunnisa bowed to the Dowager Empress. "I beg pardon, your Majesty. I overslept."

"Again?" Ruqayya raised an eyebrow. "You really must sleep better at night, child. Now help me dress. Khurram is on his way to visit me."

For the next hour, Mehrunnisa tried her level best to please her mistress. Outfit after outfit was held up for Ruqayya's approval and discarded. No, it could not be this one; she had worn it twice. Were her ladies-in-waiting fools to think she would be seen in something she had worn twice? Why hadn't it been thrown away already? Not that one either, it was blue; today was not a blue day. As for that one—until the *zenana* jeweler brought her new rubies set with diamonds, that simply would not look good. Finally the Empress decided. The ladies-in-waiting heaved a sigh of relief and went to work. As Mehrunnisa was pinning the Empress's veil on her head, Prince Khurram entered. All the ladies bowed.

Khurram went up to the Empress and kissed her papery cheek.

"How are you, Ma?"

"Fine. And would be better if you came to visit me more often," Ruqayya said in a petulant voice.

Khurram grinned with good humor, having heard this complaint frequently, and sat down net to her. He knew how to twist his grandmother around his little finger very well and make her forget her anger. Mehrunnisa smiled as he reached over for a *burfi* from a silver dish next to the divan and fed it to her, wiping his *ghee*-smeared hands on a silk towel. The first time she had seen the young prince, Ruqayya had fed him a *burfi* with the same affection. He was unconsciously imitating her after all these years.

"*Inshah Allah*, your Highness," she said.

"*Inshah Allah*, Mehrunnisa." Khurram ran an appreciative eye over her.

"Khurram," Ruqayya laid a hand on his arm, unwilling to let his attention slip from her for even a second, "what have you done with yourself this last week?"

The prince turned to his grandmother, and Mehrunnisa looked at him. He had grown into a fine young man at nineteen years of age, and everyone was speculating that he would be the next heir to the throne. Lucky Arjumand, Mehrunnisa thought, and then realized that although her niece and Khurram were officially engaged, four years had passed since the day Jahangir had seen her at the engagement. Her family had fallen into disgrace one by one, starting with—Mehrunnisa flinched, the memory still raw—Ali Quli's murder of Koka. She wondered whether the marriage would ever take place. Her family was technically no longer in dishonor, and her father had even managed to regain the Emperor's good graces. But Jahangir seemed to have forgotten about the engagement. So also, it seemed, had Prince Khurram.

She smiled as he gave her a furtive wink without stopping his narrative. Ruqayya was lying back on the divan, her eyes closed, her hand still clutching Khurram's arm possessively.

"Will you be attending the Nauroz festivities?"

Mehrunnisa turned to the prince. "Yes, your Highness." The New Year was right around the corner.

"What about you, Ma?" Khurram asked Ruqayya.

The Dowager Empress put out a hand and fondly stroked Khurram's hair. "I will be there too, darling. Mehrunnisa will be attending to me."

"Give her some time to herself, Ma. The bazaars will be magnificent this year. I plan to spend all my time there—after paying my respects to the Emperor, of course," he added hastily.

"Don't forget to present yourself to his Majesty every day," Ruqayya warned. "He will be very upset if he doesn't see you."

"I will." Khurram nodded. "My mother said the same to me. I do know what etiquette demands, Ma. Why do both of you insist on telling me what to do?"

About halfway through, at the mention of Jagat Gosini, Ruqayya's back had begun stiffening until she held herself straight as a plank. Slipping behind the Dowager Empress, Mehrunnisa desperately tried to divert Khurram's attention, but he went on, switching the topic. "And what about Mehrunnisa? Will you allow her some time so that she can wander around the bazaar? How is she ever going to find a husband if you keep her locked up here with you?"

But the Dowager Empress stared straight ahead of her and said in carefully measured tones that echoed years of hatred and hurt, "If your mother tells you what to do, then you must certainly listen to her. Why listen to an old woman who has no say in anything around here anymore?"

With great reluctance, Ruqayya had relinquished her title as Padshah Begam to Jagat Gosini upon Akbar's death. Ever since then, the two women had met in icy silence, barely bowing to each other. Ruqayya thought the whole situation unfair, but Mehrunnisa knew how cruel Ruqayya had been to a young Jagat Gosini when she had demanded and taken her son from her. Now, at the receiving end, Ruqayya hated her situation. It galled the Dowager Empress to be pushed aside for—as she put it—a mere chit of a girl. But it was Ruqayya Khurram called "Ma." That word was a constant reminder of the past to both women—a reminder that made Ruqayya gleeful and Jagat Gosini furious.

Much as she had disliked Jahangir's wife earlier, Mehrunnisa had pitied her for losing Khurram during his formative years, just as she now pitied Ruqayya. But Mehrunnisa's dislike for Jagat Gosini had not waned. Over the past few years she had come to learn just how much the Empress had tried to keep Jahangir from marrying Mehrunnisa. In the imperial *zenana*, nothing was secret.

Mehrunnisa knew also that Jahangir never came to visit Ruqayya because of her own presence in the Dowager Empress's apartments. If she could have, Jagat Gosini would have dismissed Mehrunnisa, but Ruqayya had insisted upon her services. Jagat Gosini let the matter go, knowing better than to annoy the Dowager Empress, for she would certainly create enough of an uproar to attract even the Emperor's attention. And the last thing she wanted was Jahangir's attention focused back on Mehrunnisa.

Now Khurram went down on his knees next to his grandmother and put his cheek against hers, his arms around her plump shoulders. "Who wouldn't listen to you, darling? You know how important you are to me, don't you?"

"Really?" Ruqayya's sour mood was fast disappearing. Khurram could charm her out of her worst tantrum.

"Really," said Khurram, kissing her loudly on both cheeks. "Now tell me, what is Mehrunnisa going to do at the bazaar tomorrow?"

Ruqayya threw back her head and laughed. "Why the sudden interest in Mehrunnisa's marital status? Why don't you marry her yourself?"

"Ma," Khurram protested mildly. "You know I cannot do that. Although . . ." He turned to look at Mehrunnisa with a speculative gleam in his eyes. "She is beautiful."

Mehrunnisa stood uncomfortably under Khurram's keen gaze. This was too much. Even if Khurram wasn't aware that his fiancee was her niece, at least she was. Sometimes Ruqayya's mischievous side went too far, and she didn't know when to stop.

"Your Majesty," she complained. "It is highly improper to talk of such things. Please . . ."

"All right." Ruqayya waved a hand, bored with the little game. "Go, Khurram. I will see you at the celebrations tomorrow."

Prince Khurram bowed and left the room with a wide grin on his face.

Mehrunnisa went to the wardrobe and began folding the Empress's clothes, her cheeks still flushed with embarrassment.

"You know, Khurram is right."

Mehrunnisa turned to the Empress.

"If I let you go out more often, someone or the other will want to marry you." Ruqayya's eyes twinkled in her lined face. "You must go unveiled in the bazaar. The only men there will be from the royal family. Who knows—the Emperor may see you."

At those words, Mehrunnisa's heart seemed to stop. She turned away from Ruqayya, her eyes bright at the thought of seeing Jahangir again face to face after so many years.

Ruqayya watched her carefully, seeing the slim curve of her back, the mass of heavy hair at the nape, the slender fingers folding silk, and she remembered the Emperor's madness for Mehrunnisa. She had some power over him that no other woman in his *zenana* could match. A thought began to form in Ruqayya's active mind. Mehrunnisa's beauty must not be wasted within the imperial harem. Jahangir had once been enamored of her; perhaps—just perhaps—he still would be. A little push in the right direction . . . and she, Ruqayya, would reap the benefits of any union between the Emperor and Mehrunnisa. But more importantly—Ruqayya smiled a sly little smile—that would really upset Jagat Gosini, wouldn't it?

EIGHTEEN

The king, who was deeply in love with her, sent an order to the governor of the city of Patana (Patnah) that as soon as Sher Afgan should arrive there with a letter he must be slain. This was done, but the valorous soldier, although taken unawares, killed five persons in defending himself. . . . She was a woman of great judgement and, of a verity, worthy to be a queen.
—William Irvine, trans.,
Storia do Mogor by Niccolao Manucci

"ARE YOU READY? CAN WE GO NOW?" LADLI JUMPED UP FROM THE stool and pranced around the room, her eyes bright with excitement. "Will we see the Emperor? Why are we waiting? When can we go?"

Mehrunnisa smiled at her daughter's impatience. "Soon, *beta*. We have to wait for your Dadi."

"When is she coming? Why isn't she here?"

"She is." A chuckle came from the doorway. Asmat Begam opened her arms; Ladli flew into them and hugged her tightly.

"Let's go, Dadi." She pulled away and tugged at the skirts of Asmat's *ghagara*.

Mehrunnisa went over to her mother. Through all their trials, Asmat had held steady. She had taken Ghias Beg's fall from grace with courage; in her was an implicit belief that her husband was right, that he was always right, even when he faltered. There had to have been a reason for the embezzlement. When Mehrunnisa had met her parents upon their return to Agra, she had not known what to say to her Bapa. But Asmat had taken her aside one day and said simply, "He is your Bapa. He gave you life; he taught you what you know. In many senses you are what he made you, *beta*. If anything has gone wrong it is because he misjudged the situation. You know how open-handed your Bapa is with his money, how no one in need is turned away from our door even if we have little at home. Now go back to him. Your silence pains him deeply. It is not for a child to forgive her parent. I cannot believe your Bapa is wrong; *you* must not do so."

Now, looking at her mother, Mehrunnisa smiled at the memory of that conversation. With her Bapa, her relationship had always been open; they had talked, joked, even argued on occasion. Asmat was more silent, more thoughtful; but with her gentle hand she guided her as she had that day. So Mehrunnisa went to see Ghias in his room. He was at work on some treasury ledgers and lifted tired eyes when she entered. Mehrunnisa sat down next to him and leaned her head against his shoulder. Then they talked for many hours, sitting like that, their voices weaving new life through the shattered pieces of their relationship. And things were all right between them because her mother, always in the background, had stepped forward this one time.

"Aren't you coming, *beta?*" Asmat asked Mehrunnisa.

"Not yet, Maji. I will join you later," she replied.

Asmat nodded and ushered Ladli out of the room. A few minutes later they disappeared from the doorway, and Mehrunnisa could hear Ladli's delighted squeals as she skipped down the corridor.

She walked slowly to the balcony outside her room. Benign cotton-ball clouds strolled lazily across the blue sky, the sun playing hide-and-seek behind them. It was late in the afternoon, and the golden, slanting rays had lost their strength to burn. Mehrunnisa's gaze drifted down to the court-yard, where the Mina bazaar was in full swing. Sounds of laughter floated up to her with the delicious aroma of golden-brown *jalebis* sputtering in hot oil.

The bazaar had been set up in the courtyard adjacent to the Mina Masjid in the fort at Agra. Stalls lined the four sides of the courtyard, gaily festooned with fresh flowers and colored paper flags. The vendors sold everything: flowers, jewelry, silks, satins, even vegetables and spices.

The ladies of the imperial harem—for whom the bazaar has been specially commissioned—enjoyed themselves enormously, pretending to be normal housewives out to buy groceries for their families. The vegetables and fruits they bought at the bazaar were sent to the imperial kitchens, and the cooks prepared dishes from them for the night's meal.

Mehrunnisa looked down at the array of fresh vegetables in one of the stalls: plump tomatoes, green mangoes, cabbages, creamy cauliflowers, carrots, cucumbers, long white radishes, slim snake gourds. A eunuch stood guard as the lady of the stall chopped the carrots, cucumbers, radishes, and gourds into neat slices and arranged them in a row. When that was done, the eunuch nodded and wandered on. So much for free-dom in the *zenana*, Mehrunnisa thought. Even the vegetables were cut up so that the ladies could not misuse them.

The Emperor had a harem numbering three hundred women, which included wives and concubines. The women were lucky if their lord vis-ited them at night at least once or twice a year and if one of those visits resulted in a child, preferably a male one. Through that came power— the ultimate power in a *zenana* filled with women—of being the mother of a potential heir to the throne. Wives and concubines all vied for that privilege. Yet, many of them spent their entire lives without ever seeing the Emperor, and after they reached thirty years of age, neither the Emperor nor any other man saw them again.

The *zenana* still held a charm for Mehrunnisa despite its disadvan-tages. Through it she, a mere woman, could become rich and perhaps even bear an heir; she could become powerful in this world of men. But she was thirty-four, her mind told her sadly, and no man would find her attractive, let alone the Emperor.

A slight cough attracted her attention, and she whirled around. A eunuch stood at the doorway. "Her Majesty commands your presence," he said.

"I shall come immediately."

The eunuch nodded and left the room, slinking out as softly as he had come in. The *zenana* was always thus: prying eyes everywhere, whis-pered conversations in the air. To try and escape it was futile. The only thing to do was to live with it as best as one could—alert, vigilant, for ignoring it was also dangerous. When Asmat and Ghias returned to Agra they had tried to convince Mehrunnisa to come home to them with Ladli. She was their daughter; where else could she live? But Mehrunnisa had wanted this small bit of independence. Here she had work as the Dowager Empress's lady-in-waiting. And all the skills Asmat had taught her—to paint, to sew—came in handy in making clothes for the ladies of the *zenana*. Mehrunnisa was paid well for these skills. In all, living in the imperial harem with its rooms of glass walls still had its compensations. Nowhere else could she have found this excitement, this intrigue, this basic instinct for survival in a gilded cage.

Mehrunnisa went to her bed and picked up a veil. She pinned it on her head and stood back from the mirror to look at herself. Her white *choli* and *ghagara* were embroidered with gold thread, and around her neck and wrists she wore thick gold chains. Her armlets were of milky white pearls, and two huge pearls dangled from her ears. The outfit contrasted with her hennaed hands and feet and with her blue eyes blazing from a delicately tinted face.

A slow smile spread over her face. No woman over thirty would dare to wear white; it symbolized purity and virginity. But the reflection in the mirror proved that she could wear it well. She took a deep breath, smoothed down her *ghagara*, and went in search of Ruqayya Sultan Begam.

The Dowager Empress was holding court in one corner of the bazaar, surrounded by eunuchs, her ladies-in-waiting, and Prince Khurram.

Mehrunnisa approached Ruqayya. "Your Majesty wished to see me?"

"Yes," Ruqayya said, her round face creasing into deep smile lines. "Go to the Emperor and tell him that I request his presence here."

"To the Emperor, your Majesty?" Mehrunnisa stammered, the command taking her by surprise.

Both Ruqayya and Khurram were watching her intently, their faces mock serious. They were up to something. Some plot had been hatched, some snare set. What was it? A plan to humiliate her? Surely, Ruqayya would not do that to her. But Mehrunnisa knew that Ruqayya, much as she was fond of her, was quite capable of playing a small, cruel trick on her every now and then. She stood hesitantly at the Dowager Empress's side, one part of her mind telling her to go—that this was a brilliant opportunity; what did she have to lose?—and the other holding her back.

"Well? Are you going?" Ruqayya asked sharply.

"As you wish, your Majesty." Mehrunnisa bowed and turned away, pulling her veil over her head as she did so.

"Leave your veil off, Mehrunnisa. The Emperor will deem it a great insult if you go to him veiled. After all, there are only ladies present here."

"Yes, your Majesty." She walked away slowly. If she was to go, and unveiled, then she would not go meekly. If she had only had time to prepare for this, she would know what to say. Would he remember her? Had he thought of her all these years? No, he must have forgotten. If he had remembered, there would have been some sign, some indication. Her mind awhirl with thoughts, Mehrunnisa picked her way through the bazaar. Behind her, the ladies, who had been silent so long, burst into laughter.

Somewhere in the distance, Ruqayya cackled with glee, and Mehrunnisa heard her say, "Give me my ten *mohurs*, Khurram."

"Not yet, Ma." Khurram's voice floated to Mehrunnisa's ears. "Let us wait and see."

Ah, Mehrunnisa thought, it *was* a snare. They had bet on her. For what reason? Mehrunnisa's step faltered. Then, her chin lifted higher in the air. *Ten mohurs only?* Surely she was worth more than that. Although the Dowager Empress dripped with money, she loved to wager with anyone who would give her half an ear, and she also demanded payment adamantly when she won. Which one of them had bet on her being the victor?

"YOUR MAJESTY." A hand tugged at the Emperor's arm. "I want a ruby necklace."

Jahangir looked at the girl. She dimpled prettily at him, raising a hand to brush her hair back from her face, giving him the full benefit of her slender waist and firm breasts.

"You shall have it," he replied, putting an arm around her and pulling her close. "Where can we find a ruby necklace?"

She pointed immediately to a jewelry stall. "There, your Majesty."

The ladies of the harem parted to give them way. As they walked the Emperor ran his hand over the girl's slender back, and she giggled happily, her eyes alive with energy.

Jahangir sighed with contentment. It had been a good day so far. In the morning, he had been given gifts and presents from the courtiers, and all the nobles had lined up under the great canopy to pay their respects. After the noon meal and a short nap, he had come to the courtyard to visit the Mina bazaar.

This was the best part of the Nauroz festivities. He squired his various wives and concubines around the stalls, acting as a broker for them, haggling with the shopkeepers and flirting outrageously with all the women. It was a pleasant break from lengthy, boring state duties. And there were so many beautiful women, all eager to please.

The wives of the nobles brought their daughters to the bazaar in the hope of catching the Emperor's eye, for to be inducted into the royal harem even as a concubine was an honor. Besides, if a noble's wife herself managed to capture Jahangir's attention and became his mistress, it would mean great rewards for her and her family. So all the women turned out in their best finery. The bazaar was filled with gaily clothed ladies sparkling with jewels, the sounds of happy laughter, the tinkling of anklets, and the aroma of perfumed bodies.

They reached the stall, and the merchant's wife brought out all her wares for the Emperor's latest favorite. Jahangir watched in amusement as the girl picked out a necklace for herself, a frown of concentration on her face. He liked to see his ladies happy, and the smile of pleasure on this concubine's face told him that she would do her utmost to please him tonight. The thought sent a shiver up his spine.

He looked around for Hoshiyar Khan, who came forward and paid the shopkeeper.

"Thank you, your Majesty," the girl breathed as she put on the necklace. Her eyes shone with adoration. Jahangir grinned at her. "Let us look around now." He put his arm around the girl and looked down at her face as they strolled. Surely she must be the most beautiful woman in his *zenana*. Ah, it was good to be Emperor.

Suddenly he stopped short and drew in a sharp breath. The sun had moved behind a cloud, and in the dull afternoon light, the woman approaching him seemed to float on air as she moved, her white veil flowing to the ground like mist.

The ladies became silent and watched the Emperor curiously as Mehrunnisa came near. He stood still, waiting for her, the young girl by his side forgotten.

When she reached Jahangir, Mehrunnisa gracefully performed the *konish*. "*Inshab Allah*, your Majesty. The Dowager Empress Ruqayya Sultan Begam requests your presence."

Mehrunnisa. He was struck dumb by the sight of her. Four long years. And every day he had thought of her; every night she had come to his dreams. He had known she was in the *zenana* but had not gone to seek her. Too much had happened. Mahabat had advised caution. What would future kings say about Emperor Jahangir if he allowed a woman to captivate him thus? He had listened to his advisors, knowing they were right. Other matters had absorbed him: the campaigns, court proceedings, even marriages for political reasons. But when he saw her there, standing in front of him, all those reasons were swept away. He cleared his throat.

"Lead the way, Mehrunnisa. I shall certainly obey my mother's command," he said, standing back to let her pass. He followed slowly, taking in the slender waist, the straight back, and the graceful sway of her hips as she walked. He was suddenly overcome by the irresistible urge to caress the smooth skin of her waist and rest his hand on the curve of her spine. Age had not diminished Mehrunnisa's charms. The past four years had been restful, turning her into an even more graceful woman. She was more comfortable with herself, her skin, her body. Jahangir walked behind her, his breath catching in his chest, so painful was it to watch her and not touch.

The whole bazaar became silent. The ladies nudged each other, stopped haggling, and turned around to stare at Mehrunnisa with open curiosity. She could hear them whispering her name. They all knew of her, of course; almost half the ladies in the *zenana* were wearing some garment she had created.

When they reached Ruqayya, Mehrunnisa stood aside.

Jahangir came up to his stepmother and bowed. "Your Majesty, you did not tell me you had such a jewel in your keeping."

"You have found out now, son." Ruqayya looked at Jahangir shrewdly. "Remember, she is very precious to me."

Jahangir stared at Mehrunnisa for an eternity while the ladies around them kept silent. *And to me*, he thought. What was her charm? Why did he remember every detail of their meetings, every smile on her face, the laughter of her eyes? His heart pounded as Mehrunnisa took a deep breath and her color heightened. The first thought that rushed to his mind was the hope that she had not married again. He could not lose her. Not now, not again. She had to be his.

Aware that every eye in the bazaar was turned on them, he said to Ruqayya, choosing his words with care, "If your Majesty permits, I would like to show her around the bazaar."

A wide smile split Ruqayya's face. "Take good care of her, *beta*. Very good care."

Jahangir turned to Mehrunnisa and she nodded briefly, barely lifting her head to look at him. He wanted to put his hand out to her but held himself back. Instead he said to Ruqayya, eyes still on Mehrunnisa, "I will always obey your Majesty's command."

At the Emperor's words a buzz started and became louder as the news flew all around the bazaar. The Emperor and Mehrunnisa moved away, walking at arm's length from each other.

As they left, Khurram slipped ten gold *mohurs* into his grandmother's outstretched palm.

JAGAT GOSINI WAS looking at a turquoise and pearl necklace when her slave girl leaned over and whispered in her ear. She straightened and turned around to see where the girl was pointing. Jahangir and Mehrunnisa had stopped before a cloth shop. The lady of the stall was unrolling bolt after bolt of brightly colored satins and silks.

The Empress stood still, her face expressionless. She watched as the Emperor put his arm around Mehrunnisa's shoulders and she said something. At once, the Emperor removed his arm and laughed down at her.

Jagat Gosini turned back to the shop.

The shopkeeper looked at her. "Would your Majesty like to buy the necklace?"

"No," she replied absently.

She stood there in silence, thinking hard. Not Mehrunnisa again. Would that woman give her no peace?

"Get Hoshiyar Khan," she said to the slave girl.

A few minutes later, the tall eunuch was bowing to her.

"How did this happen, Hoshiyar?" The Empress's voice was sharp.

Hoshiyar shrugged. "Her Majesty, Ruqayya Sultan Begam, sent Mehrunnisa to the Emperor."

"Why?"

"So that he would notice her, your Majesty. I can think of no other reason. It was an obvious ploy to capture the Emperor's attention."

"Find some pretext to call the Emperor away. I want Mehrunnisa out of the *zenana* by nightfall. The Emperor is not to see her again."

Hoshiyar shrugged again. "I can do nothing, your Majesty. The Emperor will not allow me to distract him." Seeing the frown gathering on Jagat Gosini's brow, he added, "I have already tried, your Majesty. Besides, as you well know, Mehrunnisa is part of Ruqayya Sultan Begam's entourage. The Dowager Empress . . . er . . . does not take orders from anyone."

Jagat Gosini nodded and turned away with a frown. She would beat
them at their own game. Hoshiyar could not help her anymore. Neither
could Mahabat Khan. Over the past few years, just as Jagat Gosini's
influence had grown in the *zenana*, so had Mahabat Khan's at court.
Jahangir had settled back into his easy lifestyle, allowing Mahabat and
Muhammad Sharif to make most of the decisions as long as they did not
go too much against his wishes. So Mahabat had been initially kept away
from his clandestine meetings with the Empress, and as time passed their
relationship had waned. Besides, this was a *zenana* matter, one in which
Mahabat would not be of much use. His value was in other things: at the
court, outside the harem.

So this, she thought, was something she had to manage on her own.
And she would. She had known that somewhere, sometime, a meeting
between Jahangir and Mehrunnisa was inevitable. But time had been on
her side. Mehrunnisa was no longer young. Surely her charms were a
thing of the past. The Empress turned to look at them again with a triumphant smile that faded almost instantly.

Mehrunnisa was smiling up at Jahangir. In the muted light from the
sun, she glowed like a pearl among the brightly clad ladies surrounding
her. She seemed not to have aged at all. If anything, she possessed a new
maturity, her movements were more assured. And the Emperor was not
oblivious to those charms. He was leaning over her with a look of unbri-
dled lust in his eyes. A deep ache came to the pit of Jagat Gosini's stomach. Once, many years earlier, Jahangir had looked at her in that manner.
Once she too had beguiled him, rising out of the pool in her apartments
naked, water glistening on her body, secure in the hold she had over her
husband. But that was a long time ago; Jagat Gosini had aged with the
duties that were demanded of her.

Just then, Mehrunnisa's gaze flickered to Jagat Gosini, and the two
rivals stared at each other for a few seconds. Mehrunnisa raised a well-
shaped eyebrow at the Empress and then turned back to the Emperor.

The Empress stood frozen, a wave of hatred washing over her. That
woman would not come into the *zenana* if she could help it. There was a

nagging doubt about her that the Empress could not shake off. What was it Mehrunnisa had? Beauty? Charm? But at least a hundred girls in the harem were more beautiful and more charming. She had not been so uneasy about the rest of Jahangir's wives. They had all been much younger—barely out of the schoolroom, immature, more interested in beautifying themselves and preening in front of the mirror.

From the moment Jagat Gosini had stepped into the harem, she had taken charge. She spent long hours with the *mullas* and tutors, learning Turkish, Persian, history, philosophy, and poetry. Even in her youth she knew that beauty was transient; the Emperor would need a wife who was a companion, one with whom he could converse knowledgeably, one who would excite not only his passions but also his mind. And she had worked hard to achieve that position. She was chief lady of the *zenana*, with no one above her.

Jagat Gosini shook her head. What was she thinking? She had given the Emperor a fine son, one who would be the next Emperor. She had lived with Jahangir for twenty-five years. How could anyone displace her? Even if Mehrunnisa came into the harem, she would have to prove her worth by providing an heir to the throne. Unfortunately, that was all too possible; she was still young enough to bear a child. But even if she did, Jagat Gosini told herself, the Emperor would forget her after some time, as he had all his other wives. And he would return to Jagat Gosini for companionship. When the Empress turned around to face her attendants, her face had resumed its normal placid expression. Only someone who looked at her carefully would have noted the fire of battle in her eyes.

NINETEEN

A LOW, EARLY MORNING MIST CLUNG STUBBORNLY AROUND AGRA.
It swirled white and damp down the cobbled streets, over the ramparts of
the imperial fort, into the gardens, and through the red sandstone
palaces. Only a few people were awake at this hour: lamplighters dousing
and cleaning street lamps; milkmen leading their cows to doorsteps to fill
brass cans with fresh, frothing warm milk; sweepers washing down the
streets with jars of water; grocers returning from the *sabji mandi*, carts
piled high with vegetables for the day's sale.

Ghias Beg's house, set well back from the street in a broad tree-lined
avenue, lay cloaked in the mist. The house was silent as most of its occupants slept. In the stables, horses champed down on fresh hay with
rhythmic jaws. In the yard behind, hens squabbled in the dust for nonex-
istent specks of food. Only the cook and his helpers were up, the main
chula already lit, blowing white smoke through the yard.

In a room upstairs, Mehrunnisa lay asleep on a bed, a cotton *razai* half
up to her waist, head pillowed on her palm, her hair spreading around her
in a mass of ebony. A rooster crowed, suddenly aware of its duty.
Mehrunnisa's eyes opened slowly, and she stared at the wall opposite.
Where was she? The paintings were unfamiliar. The room was much
larger than the one she occupied in the imperial *zenana*. Then she real-

ized she was at her father's house. She had come back home the previous night, leaving Ruqayya and her duties.

The mist sent its cold fingers into the room through the shutters, and Mehrunnisa shivered. She pulled the *razai* up to her neck and burrowed under its comforting warmth. Too lazy to go stir the dying embers in the coal brazier, Mehrunnisa turned to the window and watched the white glow of a faltering morning sun brighten the room.

The Dowager Empress had not been happy when Mehrunnisa told her she was leaving. "For how long?" Ruqayya asked sharply.

"I don't know, your Majesty. I simply cannot stay here anymore. Now I should be with my father; it is at his house I should be," Mehrunnisa said, turning away from Ruqayya's scrutiny. So the palanquin had been ordered, and Mehrunnisa had slipped out through one of the back passages of the Empress's apartments, carrying a sleeping Ladli in her arms. Bapa and Maji had been asleep but woke when she came to the house. They asked no questions, said nothing to her, did not comment on her eyes red with weeping. Maji merely sent a maid to prepare a room for Mehrunnisa and took Ladli to their own bed.

Ghias had come to her just before she slept. "I am glad you are home, *beta*," he said, kissing her forehead.

"I hope it is not too much trouble."

"Can it be trouble to a father when his child comes home? Sleep now. Maji will take care of Ladli, and we can talk later."

In that way, a week after the meeting with the Emperor at the bazaar, Mehrunnisa had come home to her parents. She lay in bed and listened to the sounds of the house stirring. The grooms were awake, too, and she could hear a soft swish as they brushed down the horses in the stables beneath her window.

The past week had turned her whole world upside down. The day after the bazaar, attendants had streamed into Ruqayya's apartments bearing gifts. There were jewels shimmering on gold trays, bottles of wine, yards of satins and silks, and with them an invitation to meet Jahangir for the evening meal. Mehrunnisa sat stunned on her divan, looking at all the presents spread out in front of her. She sent them all back with a note. Dinner was not possible; the gifts were too much. She hoped his Majesty would understand.

A day later, Jahangir came himself, and they walked in the *zenana* gardens together. Conversation was almost hopeless. The royal *malis* were all out gardening. Almost every harem lady had chosen that time to take a walk or sit under the shade of the *chenar* trees. Eunuchs and maids passed by on myriad errands. The Emperor seemed not to notice them. For Mehrunnisa it was very difficult. Suddenly, she was the cynosure of all eyes, of whispered dialogues, of sly glances and nudges as she passed. So Jahangir and she had walked in silence. At the end, she said, "Your Majesty, perhaps it would be best if we did not meet for another week."

"I want to see you. Not just tomorrow, but always."

Mehrunnisa bent her head, then looked up at him. "I beg a little time, your Majesty. That's all."

"All right. But before you leave," Jahangir reached out for her hand and held it in his warm grasp, "know that I do remember you, Mehrunnisa. Four years ago I wanted to invoke the *Tura-i-Chingezi*. It was not a decision lightly taken. It was not a decision I forgot, not even after Ali Quli's death."

When he let her go, Mehrunnisa almost ran away, leaving him standing there. The week was up yesterday, and last night Mehrunnisa had fled to her father's home.

It had been impossible to think in the *zenana*. Before then she had been nobody, not worthy of notice. In the past week, the slaves, eunuchs, scribes, and even the cooks found the time to stop and stare at her. Ruqayya was not above this scrutiny, either. Each time she looked at Mehrunnisa, a little smirk of triumph lit her face. From every person there were expectations: that she would marry Jahangir, that when she did it would benefit them somehow. So people were nicer than they had been before, more deferential, and—to Mehrunnisa's mind—more false. She was no longer certain of what *she* wanted.

Mehrunnisa sat up in the bed and tucked the *razai* around her knees.

What was it she wanted? Jahangir? Yes. Of that there seemed to be no doubt. It was what she had wanted when she was eight, and that want had been unwavering even through the years of her marriage to Ali Quli. Now she could have him; she only had to say the word. And a life of unimaginable luxury—one she had witnessed from the fringes—would be hers. Then why did she falter?

There was already talk about her wiles in capturing the Emperor's interest and holding it for so long. She was a sorceress; she had cast a spell on him. These rumors were hurtful and mean, but they came from mouths that were otherwise filled with envy. And despite Jahangir's station in life, his calling as Emperor, Mehrunnisa did not see why his love for her could not be as strong as hers for him.

But her life would be different. She would have to learn to share Jahangir with others, to defer to more senior wives, to establish her place in the hierarchy of the *zenana*. Of the three, it was the first that gave her pause. Mehrunnisa did not want to share Jahangir's affections with anyone else—his time, perhaps, but not his thoughts. Those should be hers. She did not know how to react to this man whose laughter made her smile inside, whose presence lightened her heart. The power of her feeling for him terrified her, more now than ever before, since there were no more obstacles to their being together. But he had been her choice when she was eight, was still her choice when she was thirty-four, and would be equally important to her for the rest of her life. If she were to survive him, there would be no other man. Of this she was certain.

Mehrunnisa wove her hair around her fingers, pulling at it. She was frightened that perhaps his love would die, that in sharing himself with the others, he might find another more beguiling. She could not bear that thought. But she also knew that her happiness lay in him. It was a chance she had to take.

She would not marry Jahangir for Ruqayya, or for her Bapa, or for anyone else who might profit from it. If, after all this time, she were to marry again—when she was no longer dependent on a man for money, no longer faced the pressure to marry or to have a child—it would be because in the end, she loved him as she had loved no other man.

A wry smile crossed her face. She must be the only woman in the empire to have ever given so much thought to marrying its king.

The door of her room opened. Ghias came in carrying a cup of *chai*.

"Did you sleep well, *beta?*"

"Yes, Bapa." Mehrunnisa twisted her hair into a loose chignon. "Bapa, I must tell you why I came back. I—"

"I think I know," he said gently, offering her the cup. "Maji told me of your meeting with the Emperor at the bazaar. I know through courtiers of the gifts he sent you. Why did you send them back?"

Mehrunnisa shook her head. "I could not accept them. There is yet no standing between the Emperor and me. He came to see me the next day, Bapa. But it was so hard, there were so many people. What should I do, Bapa?"

"That you must decide, *beta*. Wait; only time will tell what must be done. I trust you to make the best decision. But think before you decide anything, Nisa. Remember, it will not do to anger the Emperor. I will say no more. Here." He took out a letter from the pocket of his *kurta*. "This came for you at daybreak."

Mehrunnisa took the letter and turned it over. The red seal on top was frozen in the shape of a crouching lion with the sun ablaze behind it. Emperor Jahangir's seal. She watched her father leave. Then, taking her *chai* to the window, she used a gold-plated letter opener to cut through the royal seal.

THE SUN STRUGGLED through the persistent mist, sending golden shafts over the royal palaces at Agra. In the distance, from the mosques around the city, came the melodious call of the muezzins for the first prayer of the day.

Jahangir rose from his divan, pulled out a prayer rug, and laid it on the ground. He knelt on the rug facing west toward Mecca, raised his hands, and followed the prayer of the muezzins. When it was over, he touched his hands to his eyes and face and sat back on his heels, his mind temporarily at peace.

Then thoughts of Mehrunnisa came rushing back unbidden, occupying his mind as they had for the past week. He had never known a woman so lovely, so charming, so quiet, so secure in her beauty. So much a woman. It had been years since their last meeting, and she had been full of life then, teasing, with a quick wit. But she had hardly spoken during their walks at the bazaar, and later at the *zenana* gardens. He had not felt it necessary for her to talk. It was enough to know that she was there, with him, by his side. He studied her intently, seeing the way her lashes curved on her cheek like a half moon, wanting to touch the pulse at her throat, desperately wishing for even a tiny smile from those blue eyes.

Jahangir rose and went to the window, looking out at the smoothly flowing Yamuna river. He leaned against the windowsill and watched the sun chase away the morning mist. Now she must have received his letter. Now she must be reading it. What would she say? Would she send him away again? He put his throbbing head against the shutter and closed his eyes.

Upon his return from the bazaar, he had summoned Mahabat Khan to ask whether she was married, and waited anxiously to hear the reply. She was not. Ali Quli had been dead for four years. She could come to him, to his *zenana*, soon. Yet, she had sent him away, almost crying. What had he done wrong? He thought back to their walk in the gardens. Everywhere their steps took them, they stumbled over someone. Jahangir did not care about the people; that was a king's life, there was rarely any time to be alone. Even now, behind him, slave girls and eunuchs straightened out the apartments. Just outside the door were ministers waiting for a morning audience. What he ate, when he slept, where he bathed—nothing was secure from an audience. And how did it matter, anyway? But did it matter to her?

He rubbed the back of his neck tiredly. All week he had thought of her almost every moment of the day, knowing she was so close by and yet he could not be with her. Then, last night, the *zenana* servants had brought news that she was leaving. He had let her go. What else could he do? No woman had ever denied him anything before. And there was no one to talk with, no one to ask. Whom did a king turn to for ideas on how to woo his love? So he wrote her a letter, faltering over the words, not want-ing to show his fear that she would say no again.

Four nights earlier, at the evening meal, Empress Jagat Gosini had uncovered a dish of lamb *pulav* garnished with raisins and sultanas. She offered him the *pulav*, saying distinctly, "Mirza Qutbuddin Koka loved sultanas. He always asked for a dish of sultanas when he was a child." Jahangir had not thought of Koka for some time, but at Jagat Gosini's words the memories of his foster brother came flooding back. He had always teased Koka that the overeating was making him fat and would take him from this world sooner than he ought to go. But it was not the overeating that had taken him away; Koka had died at Ali Quli's hands. Suddenly suspicious, Jahangir looked at his second wife. But she had turned away from him and was talking with the head server.

More recently, Jagat Gosini had invited him for a *havan*. As Jahangir sat before her altar of Hindu gods, the Empress had put a *tikka*—a red vermilion mark—on his forehead. "This *puja* is to thank Lord Krishna for keeping you safe from assassins, your Majesty. These are difficult times. Why once, even the son of the *diwan* Mirza Ghias Beg conspired against your life."

Jahangir nodded, leaving his wife's apartments deep in thought. The Empress was warning him against Mehrunnisa. Why? What did she care? She had never shown any enmity toward his other wives or concu-bines. She had been born a royal princess and knew that the marriages were important politically. *But this was no political marriage.* Was that it?

It had not mattered, though. His mind had been too full of Mehrunnisa to give much consequence to Jagat Gosini's attempts to deflect him. He had written her a letter, thinking long and hard through the night. Unusually for him, he was afraid that she would not come to his *zenana*. Could she possibly think he had ordered Ali Quli's death?

"Your Majesty."

Jahangir turned to see Hoshiyar standing next to him, a silver tray in his hands. In the center of the tray lay a small folded note. He reached for it and waited for Hoshiyar to bow his way out of the room. With a heart that suddenly raced, the Emperor opened the note. In it was one word. He put his lips to the paper; her hands had touched the same spot not long before. "Come."

MEHRUNNISA WAS WAITING for him alone in an inner courtyard in Ghias Beg's house. It was later that afternoon. The sun, which now hung low in the sky on its way to the horizon, had burned the mists away. Outside, it was still breathtakingly hot, but in the courtyard, the brick floors were cool, the verandah shadowed. A champa tree gracefully spread its arms in the center. Mehrunnisa sat on the round brick plat-form around the base, leaning against the trunk. She looked up at the tree; it had bloomed for the first time, seven years after it was planted; its flowers were cone shaped with a tight circle of creamy petals. The air in the courtyard surged with the heavy perfume of the champa, sweet and almost cloying.

She sat quietly, her hands clasped in her lap, listening for the Emperor's footsteps. Ghias Beg had insisted on having a few maids pre-sent when Jahangir came to visit. Mehrunnisa said no. She had to see Jahangir alone, without an entourage. She and her father had their first argument in years. What about the scandal, Ghias had asked. But Mehrunnisa did not listen, would not explain. Some inner voice told her to be alone with Jahangir.

An outer door slammed, and she looked up, the prayer on her lips dying away. The carved wood door to the courtyard opened, and Jahangir entered. He stopped there, framed by a bougainvillea creeper that spilled delicate maroon and white flowers over the doorway. Mehrunnisa rose, touched her fingers to her hair, and bent her head in the *konish*. "Welcome, your Majesty."

She straightened and met his gaze, overwhelmed by his presence. Every other thought evaporated from her mind.

"Thank you," Jahangir said. He stumbled over the next words. "Please . . . sit."

"I hope this will do, your Majesty." She gestured around her.

He barely looked. His eyes were hungry on her face. "It will. Sit, Mehrunnisa."

She sat down on the platform, suddenly shy. She had wanted to be alone with him; now alone, she did not know how to form words to speak what filled her. "Thank you for waiting for me, your Majesty."

"I would have waited longer if you had wished."

Then he sat next to her, took off his embroidered silk turban, and laid it by her side. "I come to you, not as a king, but as a suitor. If you will have me."

If she would have him. Her heart skittered. And she knew there was nothing else she wanted. She sat looking at him—at the hair on his head, more gray than black; at the high cheekbones that defined his Timurid ancestry; at the stubble of beard on his chin. His hair was flattened where the turban had sat on it, a ring indenting his forehead. He was changed from the slim, impetuous boy she had met in Ruqayya's gardens. He was quieter, more leisurely in his movements, now a mature man. His hands were strong, a warrior's hands more than a king's, with a dusting of white hair. Yet the years seemed to melt away between them; it was like the first love, with the same passion and the same aching, but tempered with patience.

Reaching into the inner pocket of his *qaba*, Jahangir brought out a slim book, bound in red leather, Persian characters embossed in gold on the cover. "This is for you. I did not know what to bring . . . I thought perhaps you have read Firdausi. . . ."

She took the book from him and turned the gold-tipped pages. "From the imperial library." Her voice was hushed.

"My father, Emperor Akbar—"

"I know who your father was, your Majesty." Her eyes danced with laughter.

"He had this edition in the library. I thought you would like to read it. It tells the story of Rustem, the great Persian king. Your history, Mehrunnisa."

Mehrunnisa touched the pages reverently. The Emperor's library was famous for its huge collection, its bindings, and its exquisite calligraphy. Some of the library was housed in the imperial *zenana*, some outside, but Mehrunnisa had not been able to get permission to go into it while she was in the harem. Prose and poetry in every language conceivable— Hindi, Persian, Greek, Kashmiri, Arabic—lived within the library. "It is a beautiful book, and I know the story of Rustem, the king who was cut from his mother's womb because he grew too heavy inside." She rushed on in excitement, pleased to be able to hold in her hands a book from the library. "But she survived, healed by a poultice of musk and milk and grass. He was a gift for her from Khuda, the brave son of Zal, the grand-son of Saum."

"But he killed his own son one day."

"Yes, but it was a son he did not know existed, whose birth was hid-den from him by his wife. So when they met in the battlefield, they met as strangers."

"But Sohrab asked him time and again if he was the great warrior Rustem, and Rustem denied it."

Mehrunnisa turned to the end of the epic poem by Firdausi and pointed to a page. "See—his mother laments Sohrab's death and won-ders why he did not tell Rustem that he was his son. She asks why he did not show him the bracelet that would have proved their kinship. Why he was so stubborn, why time and again he met his father in the battlefield and on the wrestling mat and did not tell him."

The Emperor smiled at her and leaned back on the champa tree. "I see you have read the poem. It is not so easy sometimes to speak of what is closest to your heart."

She looked at him. "You did, your Majesty, in the letter you sent me."

Thus they talked in Ghias Beg's inner courtyard, safe from prying eyes. The days passed in that way: slow summer days replete with love. They mostly talked, rarely touched. Every now and then Mehrunnisa would lean forward for a kiss, trembling at the touch of his lips, drawing back with exhilaration at her power over him. Once Ladli had come rushing into the courtyard, wondering where her mother was. When she had satisfied herself that Mehrunnisa was still in the house, she climbed onto Jahangir's lap and pulled at his moustache to see if it was real.

"Ladli!" Mehrunnisa said, shocked.

"Let her be," Jahangir said, laughing, turning his face this way and that from the child's hands. He finally allowed her to tug at his moustache, grimacing in mock pain.

"Oh, it *is* real," Ladli said, disappointed. "I have to go tell my Dadaji. He said it was not." She ran off, her long plait swinging behind her.

"Your Majesty, I apologize, my Bapa would not have—" Mehrunnisa stopped, her face red. The child talked too much. She cursed herself for having never before curbed Ladli's tongue.

Jahangir said, still laughing, "I know, Mehrunnisa. She probably misunderstood what Ghias Beg said. Do not scold her tonight. I remember so little of the childhood of my sons. She must be a blessing to you."

"After losing many before," Mehrunnisa whispered, more to herself than to him.

Jahangir stopped laughing and turned to her. "What? I did not know."

She wound one end of her veil around her fingers. "How could you have known? It was no secret, but I did not talk about it much. And then Ladli came, and there was no point in talking about it. But I sometimes wonder who they would have been, what they would have become, what joys and sorrows would have painted their lives."

"How many?" Jahangir asked.

Mehrunnisa bent and put her face in her hands. When she spoke her voice was muffled. "Two. Two before Ladli. None since."

Jahangir put an arm around her shoulders and bent close to her face, still shielded from him by her hands. "It would not have mattered to me. You were all I ever wanted."

He kissed her gently on the forehead, and she leaned into him, knowing that what he said was true. He had sons from other wives, but from her all he would have asked was that she love him. In return he would have given her his love. Jahangir rocked her gently in his arms, then

pulled her onto his lap. Mehrunnisa let the tears flow for those spirit children of hers, glad to be able to do so with someone at last. She had tried
not to cry in front of Maji and Bapa; it would have hurt them deeply. In
front of Ali Quli she had not been able to cry—not for this reason, anyway. When her sobs died down, Jahangir lifted her chin and held his
handkerchief to her nose.

"Blow," he commanded.

Mehrunnisa backed away. "Your Majesty—"

"Don't argue, Mehrunnisa. You argue too much. Listen to your
Emperor and blow your nose."

She did as she was told and smiled at him through her tears, at this
man who treated her with such kindness. Then she kissed him, their lips
meeting with fire, her tears smudging his face.

The next day the Emperor gave her another gift, brought in not on a
gold tray by attendants but by himself. Twelve emerald-studded bangles,
thin as wire, glittered in the sunshine.

"For you, Mehrunnisa," he had said simply, watching for her response
with anxious eyes.

She held out her hand for them, saying nothing, and he set them down
to slip them one by one over her hand, his fingers lingering on her knuckles. Six on each wrist. Mehrunnisa reached out slowly to touch his hair,
the bangles tinkling as she moved.

"Come back to the *zenana*, Mehrunnisa. I want you there. I want to
look after you, to take care of you. Come to me, my darling. Please say
you will come." He smiled and went on, "All this courting is tiring me. I
am not young anymore. I need you with me."

Mehrunnisa stood before Jahangir, her mind full. Those were the
words she had wanted to hear. She put a hand out to him and then drew
back. Nowhere was there a mention of marriage, of a wedding. Her face
flamed with shame. Perhaps Bapa had been right after all. She had
insisted on not having a chaperone during their meetings; now he was
treating her like a common woman.

She remembered, after all these years, sitting in Ruqayya's gardens that afternoon, watching as Akbar's concubines painted henna patterns over one another. They had little value in the imperial *zenana*—no titles, no respect, no real position—so they vied with one another for ways to capture the Emperor's attention. She had been thankful then that she was not one of them. And young as she was, she realized that if Salim did not come to her with a desire that blinded and deafened him to everything else in the world, she would not be able to bear it. How long she could sustain it, she did not know. But that it could be sustained she was certain. Now he came to her with the words she wanted so desperately to hear—of his need for her, of his desire—but wrapped in paper, not in silk. Tears welled inside her, and she fought them away. He would not see her cry again. Why would she cry for this man?

Choosing her words carefully, she said, "Your Majesty, it is best you leave now. I cannot—I will not—be your concubine."

Jahangir recoiled, his graying hair whiter in the sunlight, the frown lines on his forehead more pronounced, his face heavier. "Why?" It was a cry full of anguish.

Mehrunnisa stared at him helplessly. Why? He asked why? Was he stupid? Had she not made her intentions clear? She was deeply angry, because now she was a fool to have thought anything more could come of this courtship.

He took her hands, grasping them when she tried to move away. "Mehrunnisa, please, tell me why. I cannot live—" He stopped for a while, looking down at her hands, kissing one, then the other. "No, this is not about my need, although you know of that well. That I cannot live without you again, that I need to wake in the morning with you by my side. I had hoped that this was what you wanted too. I thought you had shown me that."

"I have, and it is true, your Majesty." Tears came then, fast and furious, splashing down on their joined hands. They had already, in these last two months, talked more than Ali Quli and she ever had. Of poets and poetry, of the empire and its concerns, of the *zenana*, of the Emperor's passion for hunting, of his promises to teach her. They had laughed, touching faces, leaning against each other in what seemed like absolute comfort, with no expectations from each other, no wants the other could not satisfy. And through all this, Mehrunnisa had learned more about Jahangir than she had ever known of her husband of thirteen years.

But now she could not tell him why she denied him—his simple request, as he saw it. What would she say? Make me your wife, your Majesty. And then wonder for the rest of her life if that was why he had married her.

Jahangir wiped away her tears with an end of her silk veil. His touch was gentle, as though she were a child. "Then why? Tell me; I do not understand. Other things—about the empire, the kingdoms I acquire, the battlefield, even the *zenana*—these are simple. But why are you saying no?"

She shook her head mutely.

He put her hand against his mouth and spoke into it softly, his troubled gaze resting on her face, "This much I do know. I offer you a better life than you can ever have. And now, after all this time with me, if you do not come to the imperial harem, your reputation will suffer. People will talk, Mehrunnisa. The Emperor's discarded concubine can have no standing in society. I know," he held up the other hand to silence her when she opened her mouth to protest, "that we were never . . . never that close. But no one else knows that. Even I cannot stop them from gossiping. But in the *zenana*, you will be under my protection, where no one can touch you with their malicious tongues."

She pulled away, anger flooding out at his words. "So that is why you offer me this exalted position of concubine, your Majesty? To protect me? You forget that I have looked after myself for four years now, with no help from either you or my Bapa. I will doubtless be a fallen woman, but I will not—absolutely will not—come to your *zenana* as a concubine."

Jahangir stared at her, stricken, empty of feeling, her words tearing through his heart. Then slowly, heavily, as though he had aged in the past hour, he turned and went out of the courtyard. He did not look back at her.

Mehrunnisa watched him go, wanting to call out—I will be your concubine, your Majesty—not wanting to let him go. But she could not speak for anger, for shame, for the deep hurt she felt. From him she had not expected this base offer of protection. He had not spoken of love—well, yes, he had, but casually. More insistent was the fact that he made this offer for her sake, so she could hold her head up in society. All those years when he had ignored her, everyone—Bapa, Maji, Ruqayya—had echoed his words: that without a man's guardianship she would not have any status.

Would this devastation pass? Would her strength return? As it had when she had lost two children and not known whether she would hold her child in her arms. As it had when she fought to keep her name and her reputation, when her father was labeled an embezzler, her brother was put to death because he attempted to assassinate Jahangir, her husband killed the Emperor's favorite.

She cried aloud, collapsing on the floor of the courtyard, the sobs wrenching her body. Her world was shattered. After so many years of wanting Jahangir, she was certain she would never again see this man who should have been her husband.

TWENTY

It is scarcely necessary to recall the romantic story of Nur Mahal
(better known by her later title of Nur Jahan)—her marriage to
Shir Afghan, his assassination, and her subsequent union with the
emperor, who had already been attracted to her before her first
marriage. At this period her influence over her husband was so
unbounded that she practically ruled the empire. . . .
—William Foster, ed., *The Embassy of*
Sir Thomas Roe to India

AAOONGH! THE LOUD DEEP-THROATED ROAR SWEPT THROUGH THE
imperial palaces and courtyards at Agra, jerking the royal family out of
sleep. In the *zenana*, the women clutched one another or their children,
listening as the sound echoed around the walls before dying down to a
low rumble. Then it came again. *Aaoongh!*

Emperor Jahangir sat in front of the cage where the tiger paced, watching its loose-limbed stride. It walked the forty-foot length of the cage in
unhurried, measured steps, muscles rippling under its gold and black fur.
It turned, tail whipping in the air, looked at him, and opened its mouth,
baring its teeth. *Aaoongh!*

A shiver passed through him, bringing goosebumps up his arms. The
roar seemed to rattle his bones. He sat close, just four feet from the cage;
only slim iron bars separated him and the tiger. It was the mating season,
and the tiger roared at night, every night, in quest of its companion.
Jahangir had ordered a pair of tigers captured alive because the creatures
fascinated him. Tigers had intrigued him ever since that ill-fated adven-
ture with the tiger cub long ago. The cages were built and hauled inside
the fort at Agra, on the western end near the Delhi gateway. They were
erected side by side: the tiger in one, the still unimpressed tigress in

another. Torches burned around him, lighting up the beaten mud expanse in front of the cages and the forty guards, armed with matchlocks and muskets. If either tiger escaped, it would wreak ruin in the fort. And these were known to be man-eating tigers, captured from the periphery of the forests around Agra, where for months they had terrorized neighboring villages. Once a tiger killed a man, it could never go back to killing wildlife, for humans were easy prey. They were weak, and if unarmed, they rarely fought back.

Jahangir waited in silence for another roar, waited for the tigress to respond. He sat on a wooden crate near the cage, his chin resting in the palm of one hand, meeting the tiger's passing golden gaze unflinchingly. It seemed to pay little attention to him as it paced, its nostrils quivering every now and then at his scent, the scent of a man, of food, even though it had just been fed.

He smiled to himself, a wry, mocking smile. He, Emperor of Mughal India, could command a man-eating tiger and its mate captured and caged, but he could not bring to himself the woman he loved. With Mehrunnisa, it seemed there were no rules.

For two weeks now he had lived in a kind of stupor. He went to the *jharoka* balcony and the daily *darbars* as usual, but paid little heed to what went on. Why did she refuse? Why couldn't she see that his plan would be the best solution for her?

In his brief saner moments, he wondered what his fascination was for Mehrunnisa. He tried to think about it logically, but it, she, thwarted all logic. He had wanted her longer than he had wanted the throne. It was not just that she was a beautiful woman. Beautiful women he could command at the snap of his fingers, the merest inclination of his head. He admired her fierce independence, her deep sense of self, her convictions about her actions. She scorned the rules, trod on them.

One day he had been preoccupied during his visit with Mehrunnisa. "Tell me," she had coaxed, "let me take the burden."

"The Jesuit fathers are unhappy about the English ambassador William Hawkins's presence at court," Jahangir said.

"Why?" Mehrunnisa asked. "They have come here to proselytize; Hawkins is here for a trade treaty. There can be no conflict."

"Hawkins promises security for our trading ships in the Arabian Sea."

"Ah," Mehrunnisa said, eyes gleaming. "And that encroaches on Portuguese domain, because they now protect our ships. The Jesuits grow too arrogant. As long as they are the only ones offering us protection, with no competition, the empire will be under their sway. You cannot let Hawkins go, your Majesty. Use him."

Jahangir rubbed his chin. "It is not that easy, Mehrunnisa. Muqarrab Khan writes of the ill behavior of the English soldiers in Surat, how they loot and plunder and beat up our people. And Hawkins, much as he styles himself an ambassador, is just a merchant—with dirt under his fingernails, his coarse laughter, his ill manners, and his lack of etiquette."

"Then why have you kept him by your side for so long?"

"Because he entertains me. He talks Turki fluently; I don't need an interpreter with him. Have you listened to him at court? He is like a monkey taught tricks."

Mehrunnisa agreed. "Then teach him new tricks, your Majesty." She put a hand on his arm. "Tell me, hasn't Muqarrab Khan recently converted to Catholicism?"

"I heard a rumor to that effect," Jahangir said slowly. "That he now calls himself John. Do you think he acts under the influence of the Jesuit priests?"

"It is possible that he bends the truth, your Majesty. He would not dare lie to you—not openly, in any case. If Hawkins promises safety for our ships, then you should consider his offer."

Jahangir had gone back to the royal palace that night deep in thought after his conversation with Mehrunnisa. He had already known what she had told him, already thought about it long and hard. What surprised him was that she knew, that she—merely a woman—would be interested in the affairs of the empire. It thrilled him to be able to talk with her about it. Unlike his ministers, she was a safe counsel; she had no personal agenda, no wish other than what *he* wanted. So he did what she said, what he had already mulled over in his mind, and watched with amusement as the Jesuits scrambled for better gifts and toys with which to please him.

Mehrunnisa was wrong in thinking that he had had no knowledge of her for these past four years. Jahangir had known her whereabouts and kept an eye on her. He sent an armed escort for her from Bardwan to Agra. He asked Ruqayya to look after Mehrunnisa—a request she had easily acceded to, for the dowager Empress was fond of her. Within the walls of the *zenana*, even though Mehrunnisa was employed by Ruqayya, she had been under his protection, for the harem—with its palaces, courtyards, gardens, and the various people who lived in it—was his property.

The tiger stopped and faced Jahangir. They stared at each other, man and beast, conqueror and conquered. He put out a hand to touch it and then drew back hastily. It looked benign, like a large adorable cat. It almost deceived him. The tiger bared its teeth with a hiss, then moved disdainfully away to pace again, the scent of the tigress filling the air.

Jahangir sighed and bent his head. Sleep was impossible at night. Only for a few brief hours did his body give him rest, but Mehrunnisa obsessed him in his dreams. Perhaps he should have gone to her earlier, not let her be, not wondered and feared that she would hold Ali Quili's death against him. That was his weakness, perhaps.

The tiger roared again, throwing back its massive head. *Aaoongh!* The sound set the bars of the cage clattering, and Jahangir shuddered. Then, finally, he saw the tigress lie on the floor of her cage and moan slowly and softly in response.

The Emperor rose and went back through the night to his apartments, not seeing the guards bow low to the ground as he passed. He knew he could not lose Mehrunnisa again. He had wanted the crown with an intensity that had frightened him, for any other alternative would have been unimaginable. Now he wanted Mehrunnisa even more, and he could not imagine life without her.

*   *   *

"THE EMPEROR IS coming! The Emperor is coming!" Ladli rushed into the room, waving her little arms in excitement.

Mehrunnisa looked up from her book at her daughter with a delighted smile. "Did you see the royal barge?"

"Yes," the child replied breathlessly. "Oh, Mama, what do you think he has brought for me today?"

"*Beta,* you must not ask for gifts so shamelessly. Now go and wash your face and hands. We must not appear before the Emperor like this— and remember, perform the *konish* as I taught you."

Ladli promptly performed the *konish.* "Is that right?"

"Yes," Mehrunnisa said. "Go now." She shut her book of Firdausi's poems as Ladli ran off. Then she rose and ran out into the balcony.

The afternoon sun drenched the balcony, and Mehrunnisa put up a hand to shade her eyes. She could make out the royal barge coming down the Yamuna, the Emperor's flag with the crouching lion in front of a rising sun glowing gold against red silk. She leaned weakly against the ledge, her legs suddenly giving way. Why did he come?

The last two weeks had passed slowly, miserably, every moment filled with Jahangir, with memories of their meetings. Bapa and Maji left Mehrunnisa alone for the most part. Bapa came to her once, two days after the Emperor had left in anger. In front of them, for them, she tried to look normal. It was difficult to smile, to eat, to sleep, to pretend nothing was wrong. But she had to do it. The hardest task was to pacify Ladli. Jahangir always brought her a little gift: a box of marbles, a wooden horse, a set of tiny brass pots and pans. So when he did not come, Ladli asked after him and Mehrunnisa said, "He is the Emperor, *beta,* a big man. His other duties call him away."

The barge neared, cutting silver streaks through the calm waters of the Yamuna. The Emperor stood forward, watching for her eagerly. When he saw her, he waved with all the ardor of a lover at least fifteen years younger. Mehrunnisa raised her hand; even the sight of him sent shivers down her spine. Did he come back merely to torment her?

Would there be another unpalatable offer, another overture she would have to refuse?

Mehrunnisa turned away. She had not allowed herself to think of what might have been, or what might be these past two weeks, even though the Emperor had indirectly made a gesture of goodwill the day after she had driven him away.

Jahangir had invited her father and her brother Abul Hasan to the *Diwan-i-am*. There, in front of the entire court, he had increased Ghias's *mansab* to eighteen hundred horses. Her brother was likewise honored with the title of Itiqad Khan and an increased *mansab*.

And that evening, Ghias spoke to her for the first time about the Emperor. After the disagreement about the chaperoning, Mehrunnisa and her father had talked little; she was too full of Jahangir to talk with anyone, even Bapa.

He came into the room where Mehrunnisa was helping Ladli with the Turkish alphabet. Ghias watched his daughter as if he were seeing her for the first time. He noted her graceful movements, her calming presence, and her melodious voice as she corrected Ladli's mistakes. It was easy to see why the Emperor was so enamored.

But Ghias Beg held no illusions about his Emperor. Jahangir was notoriously fickle in his love affairs. He was surprised that Jahangir's infatuation had lasted so long, and practical enough to realize that although his daughter was beautiful and looked younger than her years, the Emperor had a harem filled with much younger women, whom he could have at a moment's notice. Ghias shook his head. He adored Mehrunnisa with a father's passion for his child, but what was this hold she had over Jahangir?

At that moment she caught her father's eye. "Enough for now, Ladli. Go to your Dadi. I want to talk to your Dada."

Ladli obediently closed the book and went out of the room. Mehrunnisa folded her hands in her lap and waited for Ghias to speak.

"The Emperor has increased my *mansab*, and he has also honored Abul."

"I know." Mehrunnisa allowed a triumphant smile to flit across her face briefly. It *was* a distinction for her family, thanks to her no doubt. And Jahangir had done this after their fight. When she remembered that, her smile faded. What use were honors if he was not here?

"Mehrunnisa, you must know why the Emperor honors us thus. Is it wise to refuse him so long? There is no shame in being a royal concubine."

Mehrunnisa raised surprised eyes to him. "How do you know?"

Ghias smiled. "He is the Emperor, *beta*. Everyone knows what he does, where he goes, what he says. The news came to Maji from the imperial *zenana*. You have lived in the harem; you must be aware that little is secret. But is this wise, what you are doing? Many women would die for such favor from the Emperor."

"I know that, Bapa," Mehrunnisa said slowly. "But you do not know the Emperor as I do. Oh," she waved away his protest, "you know him as a king, an Emperor, but I know him as a man. A man in need, not of another concubine—he has plenty of those—but of a woman with a loving hand to guide him, to be with him always. Do you remember, Bapa, when the Emperor wanted to marry me seventeen years ago?"

"It was not possible then, Nisa."

"Then, I wanted to marry him too. I always have wanted that—when he was a prince, and even," she hesitated, "when he was Emperor. Why would I give it up to be a mere concubine now?"

Mehrunnisa let her words sink in as she opened Ladli's book and riffled the pages without seeing the printed words. If she was to be his wife, she would be everything to him, not just an Empress, but a lover, a friend, a *wife*.

"I did not know," Ghias said, his face tormented. "I always thought it was the prince who desired you. . . . I did not know you too . . ."

"That was why I balked at marrying Ali Quli. But it was so long ago; too many things have happened since."

Ghias sat down heavily. How could he have been blind to this? Perhaps if he had known, he might have had the courage to talk with

Emperor Akbar. His request, even if it was to be denied, would have been listened to. But Ghias knew that the man he was then, seventeen years ago, would not have asked Akbar for his daughter's happiness for fear of falling into disfavor with Akbar. He thought of himself as a deeply fallible man, one disgraced through his own doing, and one yet blessed with forgiveness from the people in his life. Jahangir had condoned his embezzling from the treasury; his children had overlooked the troubles that had beset them as a result of that one act. And Asmat—she had never doubted him. Her faith in him was more unwavering than his faith in himself. And now that he had been thus blessed, he too would repay his benefactors. The man he was today would not stand in the way of his daughter's wishes. He looked at her.

"Mehrunnisa, I have a great respect for you. You must know that; no father has been blessed by a brighter and more intelligent child." He stopped and then went on, "I will say no more of this matter. It shall be conducted as you wish."

"Bapa . . . ," she said desperately, wanting to explain and not wanting to at the same time. If she cut off all ties with Jahangir, they would all suffer. Even if the Emperor did not directly take revenge on them, the court gossips would. And everything Bapa had worked for all these years would dissolve in the actions of his willful daughter.

"No," Ghias said. "I understand, but I want you to be happy, Nisa. Nothing else matters as much. If we must leave Hindustan, we will find a home elsewhere. I did it once before; how difficult can it be to do again?"

Mehrunnisa turned away from her father, knowing that he lied but grateful that he did.

And then again the silence from the Emperor. That brief heady feeling of power was replaced all too soon by doubts. Why did he stay away? Why honor Bapa and Abul and say nothing after that? Was it a farewell present?

Mehrunnisa looked down from the balcony. The boat docked at the pier outside her father's house, and Jahangir jumped out. He entered the house, and Mehrunnisa went back into the room to wait for him.

Suddenly she was very tired. There were so many expectations from her. Her father advised caution, advised accepting the Emperor's first offer. A few days ago even Abul had said something in passing. Even the Dowager Empress had sent her a caustic note: *Did she think she was someone too special? Don't be tiresome, Mehrunnisa.* Ruqayya wanted to regain her footing in the *zenana* and thought she could do it through Mehrunnisa. Nothing would give her more pleasure than to see Jagat Gosini displaced and humiliated, and Mehrunnisa seemed to be stupidly throwing it all away.

And then a few days ago, Hoshiyar Khan had brought her a basket of green mangoes from Empress Jagat Gosini. It was an insult, like the gold bangles she had so patronizingly bestowed on Ladli. Unripe mangoes for an unfulfilled dream.

But no matter, Mehrunnisa thought. No matter what people expected, it would happen the way she wanted. Her neck drooped as her head sat suddenly heavy on her shoulders. Then she took a deep breath and straightened up.

The Emperor entered the apartment with a spring in his step, belying his forty-two years.

"*Inshah Allah,* your Majesty."

Jahangir came to her eagerly and held out his hands.

"Sun of Women," Jahangir breathed reverently as he held her hands tight. "Your name is perfect for you. But I shall bestow another title upon you, my darling."

Mehrunnisa raised her eyes to his.

"I know now that I was mistaken in offering you the position of a concubine," Jahangir said. "I am . . ." He hesitated with the word, unused to saying it. "I am sorry."

She said nothing, watching him.

"I did not know . . . did not think that it would be important. Just having you with me would have been enough." The Emperor's face flushed. "But of course it is. Without a title, you would have no standing in the *zenana.* So say you will come as my Empress. Will you? Please?" He looked at her anxiously.

At last. At last he understood, and without her telling him. This was what she had waited for; yet her heart thundered in her chest, beating out every other sound, every thought. She could barely hear the Emperor when he spoke again.

"Say that you will be my wife, Mehrunnisa."

Mehrunnisa stood still in the middle of the room, her hands clasped in Jahangir's. At the start of this courtship, she had promised herself that she would never ask to be Jahangir's wife, since to him it would mean little. The asking, that want, must come from him. Now he had finally asked. She looked at him again. In Jahangir's eyes there was nothing but a deep, abiding love. He was not merely asking her to be his wife. He was giving her his life.

"I can hardly disobey your Majesty's command." Her voice was low, so low that Jahangir had to lean over to hear her.

He sat down on the divan next to them and put out a hand to her. "Come here."

Mehrunnisa took his hand and sat down on his lap, leaning into his shoulder, her head resting near his. He rubbed her arm gently, his nostrils filling with her scent—the jasmines in her hair, the oils of camphor and aloewood she bathed in. She filled his arms, his world. He wanted to never let her go. They sat like that for a while, both safe with each other.

"I was afraid. . . ." Jahangir said abruptly.

"*You* were afraid? That I would say no?" Laughter sang through her. Was it possible to be so deliriously happy?

"I did not order Ali Quli's death, Mehrunnisa. I want you to know that. Yes, court proceedings have recorded it thus, that I gave Qutubuddin Koka the order, but—"

"I was there, your Majesty," Mehrunnisa said quietly. "I saw it happen. Ali Quli drew the first sword. I never thought—despite the rumors—that you had ordered him dead because he refused to obey your command." She drew closer to him, mischief lighting her eyes. "It is inauspicious to talk of one husband when I am to have another."

They half-lay, half-sat on the divan, close to each other, breathing the same air, their faces so close that their lips almost touched. When Jahangir hesitated, Mehrunnisa reached up and put her cool arms around his neck.

"Do you remember the kiss in the *zenana* corridor?"

"Every single instant," Jahangir said, pulling her tighter into his embrace. "What of it?"

Mehrunnisa shook her head. "Never mind; it was a long time ago." Then, as a puzzled frown drew lines on his forehead, she covered his lips with hers. A raging consuming fire flowed through them, scorching out every other thought. She could smell him, taste him, feel the smoothness of his skin as she slid her fingers through the collar of his *qaba*. She clung to Jahangir, pressing against him, wanting to never let go.

When they parted at last, inhaling harshly, Jahangir said, "I shall go and talk to your father." He covered her hand with little kisses, his breath hot on her palm. "Do you think he will grant me permission to marry you?"

She laughed at him then, her eyes full of honesty. "I think he will. He has waited for nothing else for a long time, your Majesty." She rose from his lap and put out a hand to pull him up from the divan.

As he left, Jahangir turned back for a moment. "Wait for me, Mehrunnisa?"

She laughed again in happiness. He might not remember, but she did. He had used those very words that day in the *zenana* gardens when he had asked her to wait for him. And she had not waited then.

"I will be here, your Majesty," she said softly. "I will be here when you return."

JAGAT GOSINI SAT at the window in Jahangir's apartments overlooking the river. It was after midnight, and the Emperor had not yet returned from Ghias Beg's house. Today the Emperor had left for his visit to Mehrunnisa, smiling mysteriously to himself like a child, delighted with himself, and no amount of cajoling had made him divulge his secret.

Jagat Gosini frowned as she peered out of the window. The Yamuna flowed calmly by, no barge marring the smooth flow of the river. Where was Jahangir? Why had he stayed so long? The visits to Ghias Beg's house worried her. Never before had she seen Jahangir so purposeful, so consistent in his actions. Could he really be falling in love with that woman?

An hour later, Jahangir walked into his bedroom, yawning. He stopped short when he saw his wife. "What is the matter, my dear?"

Jagat Gosini's heart sank as she saw the happy smile on his face. "My lord, I just wanted to see that you were safely in bed."

"That is very considerate of you. But I was visiting Mehrunnisa."

"I know, my lord," she said. "Why don't you have her here, at the *zenana?* That way you will not tire yourself with these nocturnal visits."

"She will soon be here." Jahangir removed his cummerbund and started unbuttoning his *qaba.*

"We all await the day, your Majesty. She will bring you happiness," Jagat Gosini said cautiously. "I will have the slaves prepare a chamber for your concubine."

Jahangir turned to her. "But she will come here as my wife, not as my concubine. I will personally give instructions to Hoshiyar Khan to make up apartments for her in the palace. I may even build her a palace. She deserves all the riches and presents I can bestow upon her."

The Empress felt the blood rush from her face, leaving her with a sick feeling. She pulled herself together with an effort. Perhaps there still was time to change the Emperor's mind. But even as she spoke she knew the attempt to be useless. Once Jahangir made up his mind, right or wrong, all his life he had not stepped back from a decision. It was like a breeze trying to move a mountain. She searched for words. In her haste she used a ploy already used, already proven futile. So great was her distress that Jagat Gosini let her carefully cultivated skills at managing the *zenana,* managing the Emperor, slip.

"Your Majesty, please do not forget whose wife she was. We all miss Qutubuddin Koka. His death was a great blow. I looked upon him as a brother. And he died at the hands of that scoundrel, Ali Quli."

Jahangir turned to the window and contemplated the clear, dark night. Again that hint, the same one she had dropped so many times these past two months. What were they up to—Mahabat, Sharif, and Jagat Gosini? Would she create trouble for Mehrunnisa? He knew Mehrunnisa could look after herself, or would learn to. He never interfered in *zenana* politics and would not do so now. But this could not go on.

"It is improper to talk to me of these matters. All the ladies in the *zenana* will make every effort to welcome her," Jahangir said in a quiet tone. "Is that understood?"

"Yes, your Majesty," Jagat Gosini replied with a heavy heart.

The Emperor turned away from his wife and spoke again. "Go now, and send Hoshiyar Khan to me. I will undress and prepare for bed."

The Empress bowed and left the room, her feet dragging on the marble floor. Mehrunnisa would come to the palace as Jahangir's wife—but not as the chief Empress, not if she could help it, Jagat Gosini thought savagely. Her back straightened as she walked down the corridor. By the time she reached her apartments, the Empress's mind was already working furiously, planning the next level of onslaught.

MEHRUNNISA LOOKED AROUND in bemusement. She was back at Ruqayya Sultan Begam's apartments in the royal palace. The Dowager Empress had insisted on hosting the wedding ceremony. As Mehrunnisa sat on the Persian carpets, eunuchs streamed into the chambers carrying large gold and silver trays, heaped with all sorts of presents.

Dozens of yards of satins, silks, and velvets in a myriad of colors appeared. Tray after tray of jewels: pearls the size of pigeons' eggs, glowing pink and white against black velvet; huge diamonds set in necklaces, earrings, bracelets, and armlets; rubies gleaming in gold buttons; deep purple garnets and amethysts set in silver goblets. Rich red wine from the foothills of the Himalayas in gold flasks set with semiprecious stones. Perfumes in tiny gold, silver, and glass bottles from all over the world. Wooden caskets inlaid with mother-of-pearl, spilling over with yards of richly colored silks.

She took a deep breath. Never in her wildest dreams had she imagined such riches. She reached out to caress a diamond necklace, her fingers sliding over the delicately cut stones.

One of the servants coughed at her elbow, and Mehrunnisa looked up. He silently proffered a scroll of paper. It was sealed with the Emperor's seal on top, denoting it to be a royal *farman*. She broke the seal and read the *farman*, her heart thudding against her ribs. Jahangir had bestowed upon her the *jagirs* of Ramsar, Dholpur, and Sikandara.

All the ladies in the royal harem were given annual incomes according to their status in the *zenana* or, more often, at the pleasure of the Emperor. The income was at times provided half in cash and half in the form of a landholding or estate, which in turn generated sufficient income to make up the whole.

Mehrunnisa stared at the *farman*. She was rich. Of the three *jagirs*, the one at Sikandara was the most precious. It was a small town across the Yamuna from Agra. Its position was strategic, for all the goods from eastern and northeastern India came through Sikandara in order to pass on to Agra. If she positioned officers at Sikandara, they would collect enormous duties on the goods passing through to Agra: cotton from Bengal; raw silk from Patna; spikenard, borax, verdigris, ginger, fennel, opium, and other drugs as well as the goods meant for local consumption such as butter, grains, and flour. Her income from Sikandara alone would exceed her father's at least three times.

She wrapped her arms around herself. So this was what it meant to be an Empress. And once she married Jahangir, she would have to worry no longer about Ladli's marriage. Offers would pour in for the Emperor's stepdaughter. Koka's death would be forgotten; Ali Quli's ignominy would be lost in conveniently short memories.

But more important than all these riches were those two sweet words, *Jahangir's wife.*

She leaned back on a velvet bolster, the imperial *farman* lying on her chest. In ten days she would be Empress.

* * *

THE DAYS FLEW by. Nobles scurried all over Agra for suitable gifts. William Hawkins, the English merchant, was by now familiar with the etiquette at court. He sent his broker out to the marketplace to choose jewels for Jahangir and Mehrunnisa, which he would present himself to the royal couple in impeccable Turki—the one advantage he had over his Portuguese counterparts.

The exclusive trade treaty with the British East India Company had not yet been ratified; the Emperor was busy with his latest love. However, there had been indications of favor, Hawkins thought, now after three tedious years spent in this uncivilized land with its faithless infidels. Lately, Jahangir seemed more interested in talking with him in court, asking about his affairs. Was he well rested? Did his servants give him trouble? Were the guavas from the imperial gardens to his liking? So Hawkins's broker went to the bazaar to look for something fancy for the Emperor, and Hawkins hoped that the gift and the contentment after the wedding would make the imperial hand more amenable to signing the treaty papers.

Hawkins was not alone in his quest. The Jesuit fathers scrambled around too, outbidding his offers, watching his every move with suspicion, tremulous and angry at this other foreign presence in *their* land. And every courtier vied for the best and most unusual present: something that would catch either Jahangir's or Mehrunnisa's eye, for that would mean honors and gifts in return from the royal couple.

THE DAY OF the wedding finally arrived.

The city of Agra was decorated with garlands of fresh marigolds and jasmines and multicolored paper flags. People thronged the streets in their best finery to celebrate their Emperor's twentieth marriage. Everyone sensed that this marriage would be unusual. For the first time in his forty-two years, Jahangir had made his own choice, motivated by a charming pair of azure eyes and a bewitching smile, not by political strategy. Rumors were rife about Mehrunnisa's beauty, so much so that people began to think of her as a goddess incarnate.

The fort at Agra wore the same festive air as the city. Attendants spent days preparing the *zenana* apartments and the fort. Royal gardeners had been hard at work trimming the hedges, mowing the lawns, and forcing flowering plants to bloom. Potted shrubs provided lush greenery indoors and outdoors. Flowers bloomed in discreetly hidden pots on top of the red sandstone ramparts, garlands festooned the pillars in the palaces, and rich, shimmering silks hung unnaturally from the trees like brilliant banners.

The servants, slave girls, and eunuchs were provided with new clothes, and the ladies of the harem vied with one another to beautify themselves. Hours were spent in perfumed baths, at massages, and at the toilette.

In Ruqayya Sultan Begam's apartments, Mehrunnisa stared dreamily at her reflection in an ornate gold-edged mirror.

"It is time to get ready."

Mehrunnisa looked at Hoshiyar Khan in the mirror. "Call the slave girls."

He nodded and went to the door. Mehrunnisa leaned back on the divan and gazed thoughtfully after him.

She had won a first victory over Jagat Gosini. Hoshiyar Khan, chief eunuch of the *zenana*, who had been with Jahangir for thirty-five years and wielded enormous power in the harem, had been taken from Jagat Gosini and appointed as personal eunuch to Mehrunnisa.

Although she had never been a member of the harem, Mehrunnisa had spent enough time within the walls of the *zenana* to know that Hoshiyar would be a powerful ally. But as long as he was in service to Jagat Gosini, Mehrunnisa would have no chance of wresting power from her. The Empress had too long been chief lady of the harem to give up her position to a relative newcomer like Mehrunnisa.

Her first step upon entering Jahangir's harem would be to gain that power, because she disliked the Empress and because she knew from

Ruqayya that in this world of women only the Padshah Begam was supreme. Discretion was key, for Jahangir hated to see his ladies fight. The moment one of them came to him with a complaint, she was banished from his presence for an indefinite time. To live in the *zenana* and not be noticed by the Emperor was sure death as far as the ladies were concerned. Their lives revolved around him; he gave them the power and could just as easily take it away.

Mehrunnisa smiled wryly. She was no fool; she knew how to play the power game in the *zenana* and was going to call all her forces to hand right from the first moment. To start with, she needed Hoshiyar. A word in Jahangir's ear had been enough for that, and although Jagat Gosini fumed inwardly, she dared not complain to her lord. Which was just as well, for if the Empress had objected, Mehrunnisa would have had to withdraw for the moment. Much as Jahangir adored her—and adore her he did—she would still have to be careful. For now, though, the smell of victory was sweet indeed.

The suggestion had come from Ruqayya in the past week. "You do not want a bumbling idiot of a man around you, Mehrunnisa. Get Hoshiyar Khan," she said.

"The Empress will not like it, your Majesty," Mehrunnisa replied automatically.

Then the two women smiled smoothly at each other. Jagat Gosini would not like it. So Mehrunnisa got Hoshiyar Khan.

The slave girls bustled into the room, carrying caskets of jewels, the wedding dress, and various bottles of perfumes and oils. Hoshiyar pranced around the room, busily directing their movements and shouting orders.

He seems perfectly at home here, Mehrunnisa thought. And why not? Although he had been at Jagat Gosini's side for twenty years, Hoshiyar was a shrewd man and saw immediately that Mehrunnisa had a hold over Jahangir that no other lady had been able to duplicate. She could trust him—but not completely. As long as she remained in authority, Hoshiyar would be her ally, but once she lost it, he would fly to her opponent. However, while she was supreme in the *zenana*, Hoshiyar would do everything in his power—even lay down his life—to serve her.

"We are ready now." Hoshiyar's voice was respectful.

Mehrunnisa rose and stood still as the slave girls took off her robe. Then the process of dressing began. An hour later, a full-length mirror was brought to her.

Mehrunnisa gazed at her reflection.

She reached out and touched her garments with unsteady hands. Hundreds of tiny ruby buttons glittered all over the mango-leaf green *ghagara* and *choli* of raw silk. She wore two huge ruby earrings, a ruby and gold necklace, ruby bracelets and rings, and ruby-studded armlets. The only other colors on her body were the deep blue of her eyes and the ebony of her hair. A slave girl placed a green silk turban on her head; a single white heron feather, another gift from the Emperor, sprang from the aigrette that was a lime-sized vermilion ruby surrounded by pearls. Below the turban, her green muslin veil, transparent as pond water, flowed down her back, almost reaching the ground.

"The Emperor awaits, your Majesty," Hoshiyar said at her shoulder.

Your Majesty! A rush of excitement flowed through her veins. In a few short minutes she would be Empress. She took a deep breath to steady herself and walked slowly out of the room to the Emperor's apartments.

The corridors and verandahs leading to the Emperor's palace were lined with slave girls and eunuchs. Mehrunnisa heard them gasp as she passed. At her approach, the two huge doors to Jahangir's rooms swung open silently to reveal only a handful of people inside. This Mehrunnisa had insisted upon. Jahangir protested at the beginning, wanting a public, more extravagant ceremony. But Mehrunnisa said no. Why? Because they would spend the rest of their lives together in front of the empire. This moment of their joining must be private, so even the ceremony was curtailed. In her heart she was already married to him, had been married to him for a long time. This ritual was only a formality.

When she entered, she saw him immediately. The Emperor came up to her, his hand stretched out, and she put her hand in his. They had not seen each other in ten days, bowing to the rituals of marriage. That had not mattered to Mehrunnisa; just knowing they would be together soon was enough. They had filled the time with letters, two or three a day. She told him of her pleasure in his gifts; he told her he would send more, anything she wanted. He sent her the keys to the imperial library; to thank him she roamed the vast rooms looking for a book to send to him. She found a Persian translation of the *Jataka* tales. He came furtively to visit that night, and they sat on either side of a silk screen, delighted like children breaking a rule, obeying the spirit of the law if not the law itself. They took turns reading from the book, growling like the lion and squeaking like the monkey in the stories. As they passed the book under the screen, their hands touched, and they kissed with the cloth between them. As she drew back, Mehrunnisa asked if Hoshiyar could be part of her personal entourage. Jahangir agreed instantly. Now their wedding was at hand.

"You look wonderful, my darling," Jahangir said, his eyes filled with love.

"Thank you, your Majesty," Mehrunnisa replied softly as she took her place next to him.

She glanced around the room. Ruqayya sat in one corner, her face inscrutable, a tiny smile touching her eyes. Ghias Beg was flushed, his expression drenched in pride. Her mother had a worried look on her face. Two nights ago she had asked Mehrunnisa if this was what she really wanted. Mehrunnisa had simply nodded, tired of giving explanations. The only other person in the room was her brother Abul. He too had come to her two nights ago, but for a different reason. Arjumand Banu Begam had been engaged to Prince Khurram for four years—a long engagement by any standards. He was hoping his sister would expedite the marriage. She looked at him and nodded reassuringly, noting the relief on his face with amusement.

Then she turned to Jahangir, her attention riveted to him, a feeling of security washing over her as his large hand covered her smaller one.

Jahangir bent over to Mehrunnisa. "In a few minutes we will be married."

Her heart leaped at the words. "Yes, your Majesty."

Mehrunnisa leaned briefly against Jahangir's shoulder, letting her forehead rest on his arm, and his hand came up to touch her face just as briefly.

The Qazi called them to attention. He raised his hands and uttered a short prayer; all present joined in. Mehrunnisa held her breath as the Qazi asked Jahangir if he would take her for his wife.

"Yes, yes," Jahangir replied impatiently. "Get on with the ceremony."

The Qazi turned to Mehrunnisa and repeated the question. She watched his mouth move with the words, but they didn't seem to register. When he repeated the question, Jahangir's grip tightened on her hand. She heard a voice, her own, replying that she would take Nuruddin Muhammad Jahangir Padshah Ghazi to be her husband.

The Qazi registered the marriage and asked the Emperor to place his royal seal on the page. They were officially man and wife. Mehrunnisa watched in a daze as her family crowded around with congratulations. In the distance she could hear the trumpets informing the city that the wedding had taken place. Suddenly everyone fell silent. Mehrunnisa shook herself out of her reverie and looked around. Jahangir had his hand up.

"I have an announcement to make." He glanced down at her. "From today, my beloved Empress shall be given the title Nur Jahan."

Mehrunnisa's heart thundered in her chest. The Emperor had already given her so much. In the outer courtyard of the palace a black stone bathtub, commissioned as part of her gifts, had engraved on its side the date in Persian: the 25th of May, 1611. And now he had given her a brilliant title: "Light of the World."

A sudden anxiety whipped through her. Before now she had been anonymous in this harem of women—one of many, a beautiful face in a handsome crowd. But now she would be watched, thought of, deferred to. This was not a simple marriage. Marrying an Emperor never was. She was married not just to Jahangir but to the empire.

But the power gave her a chance to influence events. It would not be easy; women were given no such importance. All her life Mehrunnisa had known this. Bapa, when he had talked to her of his work, of the court proceedings, had not thought of her as a woman but as an equal. Much as he loved Maji, he had very rarely talked thus with her. Would Jahangir treat her the same? Would he think her worthy?

She would have to fight for supremacy in the imperial harem, and then at court. If what the infidel William Hawkins reported was true, European queens shone in court beside their husbands. Why, there had been one English queen who ruled alone, who had come to the throne in her own right as the daughter of a king.

Mehrunnisa knew she had no such advantages. She would not be able to rule beside the Emperor, only behind him, hidden by the veil. Jahangir wanted his name to glow in posterity—and it would, for his life had been entrenched in history from the day of his birth. Mehrunnisa, perhaps few people would remember. Would someone—a hundred, three hundred, four hundred years from now—take in their mouths the name of Empress Nur Jahan?

Together, Jahangir and she would make the Mughal empire the brightest and most brilliant in the world. She wanted to do this for the man she loved so deeply, because this was what he wanted. And, Nur Jahan thought—already at ease with her new title—she wanted to be the force to reckon with behind the throne.

She wanted to be the power behind the veil.

AFTERWORD

THE TWENTIETH WIFE is a work of fiction, although it is based on reality. Mehrunnisa was thirty-four when she married Emperor Jahangir, and over the next fifteen years she ruled the empire in his name. Seventeenth-century travelers to Emperor Jahangir's court lavished attention on her in their accounts at home, for she was at the height of her powers then. None of the men actually saw her; their reports to their employers at the British and Dutch East India Companies are part fact, part legend, part gossip from the local bazaars.

They all invariably hinted at the drama surrounding her birth, a love affair with Salim before he came to the throne, and the suspicion on him regarding her husband's death. Contemporary historians usually do not agree. Yet, all the authors agree on some points: Jahangir never married again; Mehrunnisa was his twentieth—and last—wife. Although he alluded to her only briefly in his memoirs, she was the most important person in his life until 1627, when he died. Theirs was a love that formed the basis of poems, songs, and ballads in India. (Thomas Moore's *Lalla Rookh* is also based on their story.)

My interest was piqued. Who was this woman hidden behind the veil, around whom legend swirled wraithlike? Why was she so firmly placed in the Emperor's affections? Why did he give her so much power? In an age when women were said to have been rarely seen and heard, Mehrunnisa minted coins in her name, issued royal orders (*farmans*), traded with foreign countries, owned ships that plied the Arabian Sea routes, patronized the arts, and authorized the building of many imperial gardens and tombs that still exist today. In other words, she stepped beyond the bounds of convention. All this came through the man who adored her to the point of obsession.

The accounts of her were conflicting. She was generous. She was cruel and mean-spirited. She loved Jahangir passionately. She so enamored him that he could no longer think for himself. She dulled his senses with wine and opium. Yet she was the one he turned to in illness, not trusting even the royal physicians. From all these reports of Mehrunnisa, written mostly after her death and during her reign as Empress, came *The Twentieth Wife*.

It is a fictional account of her life before her marriage to Jahangir, but it is rooted in history. Salim's rebellion against Akbar, Khusrau's against him, the punishment inflicted on Khusrau's men after his flight to Lahore, the threats on the northwestern frontier of the empire by the Uzbeg king and the Shah of Persia, the Deccan wars—even Mehrunnisa's niece's betrothal to Prince Khurram—all are based on historical fact. Also true are the accounts of Ali Quli's desertion of Prince Salim at Agra after the storming of the treasury, his support for Khusrau, his slaying of Qutubuddin Khan Koka, and his death at the hands of the imperial army. As for the rest, I relied on bazaar gossip, the narratives of seventeenth-century travelers to India, the legend of Mehrunnisa, and my own imagination.

When one thinks of the six main Mughal Emperors, it is usually in these terms: Babur founded the empire; Humayun lost it, was driven out of India, and returned to reclaim it; Akbar, inheriting the throne at the age of thirteen, consolidated the empire; Jahangir added few kingdoms to the legacy his father left him, but his romantic exploits are legendary; Shah Jahan built the Taj Mahal, fixing him firmly in history; Aurangzeb, steeped in religious intolerance, was instrumental in the breakup of the empire.

There are few mentions of the women these kings married or of the power they exercised. *The Twentieth Wife* seeks to fill that gap.

One fact is indisputable. The women of Ghias Beg's family had a potent hold on their men and on Indian history. Mehrunnisa, known to posterity as Empress Nur Jahan, became powerful from the time of her marriage to Jahangir until his death in 1627. To help her rule, she formed a *junta* composed of three men: her father, Ghias Beg; her brother, Abul Hasan; and Jahangir's third son, Prince Khurram. This story is told in *Power Behind the Veil*, a yet-to-be-published sequel to *The Twentieth Wife*. A year after Mehrunnisa came to the imperial harem as Empress, Khurram married her niece (Abul's daughter and Ghias's granddaughter), Arjumand Banu Begam. She died a few years after Khurram became Emperor Shah Jahan while giving birth to his fourteenth child. In her memory, during Mehrunnisa's lifetime, he built the Taj Mahal.

Although the world in general knows of Khurram's devotion to Arjumand because of the Taj Mahal, there is no doubt that Jahangir's devotion to Mehrunnisa equaled, if not surpassed, his son's to Arjumand. He may not have left a monument for posterity, but he gave her—the love of his later years—free rein to do as she pleased. Mehrunnisa did so, and she loved him enough to respect his wishes. She is known to have ruled the empire. But she was powerful because of him, not despite him.

Indu Sundaresan
May 2001

GLOSSARY

Amrit	nectar
Bawarchi	cook
Beedi	hand-rolled cigarette
Begam	respectful term for a woman, married or unmarried
Beta	literally "son"; here a term of endearment
Burfi	sweet cut into bite-sized cakes
Chai	spiced tea
Chappatis	a type of bread
Charpoy	cot with jute-knit weave tied to a wooden frame
Choli	form-fitting blouse
Chula	stove, usually fashioned from mud and bricks
Darbar	court
Dholak	drum with a leather head, usually made of *neem* wood
Dhoti	cloth wrapped around the waist, usually worn by men
Diwan	treasurer
Diwan-i-am	hall of public audience
Diwan-i-khas	hall of private audience
Diya	lamp
Dupatta	veil or wrap
Farman	royal edict
Firangi	foreigner
Gaddi	seat or cushion
Gajra	garland of flowers, usually for the hair

Ghagara	full pleated skirt reaching to the ankles
Ghee	clarified butter
Gilli-danda	street game played with two sticks
Gulab jamun	milk sweet soaked in sugar syrup
Hakim	physician
Halwa	sweet, usually made of wheat or rice flour
Hammam	bathhouse
Howdah	covered litter, usually set atop an elephant
Hukkah	water pipe
Huzoor	sire
Jagir	district
Jalebi	sweet of deep-fried flour dipped in sugar syrup
Jharoka	balcony
Kameez	loose long-sleeved top worn over a *salwar*
Katori	bowl
Konish	form of salutation
Kotwal	officer of the policing force
Kuchi	tribe of nomads in Afghanistan
Kurma	a type of curry
Kurta	long-sleeved shirt, open at the neck
Mali	gardener
Mansab	government rank of responsibility for the number of cavalry or infantry for the imperial army
Mardana	men's quarters of the palace
Mirza	title of respect for a man
Mohur	gold coin
Mulla	Muslim priest
Nan	a type of bread
Nashakhana	public house
Nautch	dance
Paan	betel leaf
Pahr	watch of three hours; the day was divided into eight *pahrs;* and the *pahr* into eight *gharis* of twenty-four minutes each

Parda	curtain or veil
Peshwaz	fitted coat
Pulav	rice cooked with meat and/or vegetables
Punkah	fan
Qaba	a long, loose coat
Rangoli	intricate designs and patterns drawn on floors and walls with rice flour or limestone powder
Razai	cotton-filled bedcover
Rishta	alliance
Sabji mandi	wholesale market for vegetables
Safarchi	table attendant
Sahib	form of address, usually "sir"
Salwar	loose trousers gathered at the ankles
Santuk	perfume made of aloewood, civet, and rose water
Shenai	fluted trumpet
Sitar	stringed musical instrument
Tabla	drums
Talaq	divorce
Taslim	form of salutation
Tava	flat cast-iron pan
Vakil	clerk or attorney
Wazir	chief minister
Zenana	harem, women's quarters of the palace